Sitting Shiva

in the Land of Nod

Dennis Cassidy

WINSTON PRESS

Book Layout and Cover Design by Maggie Pagratis

"Moods and desires come and go, like so many restless tourists, but folios remain in place, waiting benignly to be read by succeeding centuries. Buses, taxis and metros rush us about at frantic speed; placards bawl out every grubby little change in our material lives: the library stands for what is pure and true."

From "Musings in the Library,"
Love in a Bottle by Antal Szerb

The cover of a book should have a knob on it because it's like a magic door to all the wonders of the universe from the simple to the sublime. One might say that reading is the original virtual reality.

—Howard Green

Chapter 1

dank

dank (d²ngk) *adj.* **dank·er**, **dank·est**. Disagreeably damp or humid. See Synonyms at **wet**. [Middle English, probably of Scandinavian origin.] **--dank"ly** *adv.* **--dank"ness** *n.*

"**D**ank." Daniel spoke the word under his breath with no more mouth movement than an accomplished ventriloquist so as not to alarm his fellow travelers. It was the "Word of the Day" and one of a cluster that he had torn off the calendar to accompany him on his journey. Having decided that that the unit itself, what with the plastic base and all, was just too clunky and cumbersome to bring along, he opted to expropriate only enough pages to cover the span of time he would be away. Besides, it had become almost like a piece of furniture or, more specifically, one of the carefully chosen knick knacks that served to enhance the décor of his small apartment albeit the only one that got smaller by 1/365th every day. ("kitsch" had been the "Word" the prior Tuesday and he had decided after some mild consternation that his *items* did not fall into that category, although a couple could be considered borderline)

Daniel loved words and he found this one's simple but starkly expressive character especially appealing. It sounded heavy, as if when uttered it would tumble out and proceed to fall directly to the floor like a stone to the bottom of a pond.

"Dank." He whispered the word again and imagined an amorphous cave-like place, a dark, moist and spectral place teeming with all manner of sinister bacteria, lethal toxins rendered impotent by a Dracula-like aversion to sanitizing sunlight.

Daniel would have preferred driving to his uncle Howard's funeral but his Chevy Cavalier was a fickle beast given on occasion to simply deciding that it had gone far enough. Still, he almost risked it but the prospect of being stuck somewhere in transit, wholly dependent upon the good will of some alien auto mechanic to get him back in the saddle pronto, made him think better of it. He priced planes and trains and settled finally on the luxurious comfort of a Greyhound bus and as he rolled methodically toward Alabama, he was busy trying not to think about the fact that it was at least possible that he would be asked to eulogize his beloved uncle.

There was no question that he was the right man for the job as he held his uncle in higher esteem than any person on the planet, dead or alive, real or imagined. But there was the small matter of execution, which Daniel may have actually preferred to elocution. He got heart palpitations at the thought of having to address such a gathering, and the not-so-subtle churning in his stomach made it hard to think soundly. He *could* come down with laryngitis, he thought, or maybe throw himself on the mercy of the throngs by claiming emotional duress due to the loss of his beloved uncle. The impulse to abdicate roiled him, and he began to chastise himself for his cowardice but backed off quickly. In the end, he knew that even if all that were true he would make the effort, no matter how clumsy or inarticulate it might be because he owed his uncle that much. The fact that he could sometimes gain the upper hand in this type of negotiation was made possible in no small part by his uncle Howard, but the exercise had exhausted him. A nap, he thought. A nap would clear his head and then, well then he would jot down some notes just in case. He closed his eyes, laid back as far as the seat would allow and peeked down lecherously at the Camel Lights resting quietly in his breast pocket.

Suddenly feeling nostalgic for the good old days when anyone could, and a great many did, light up a cigarette and befoul the airspace in their orbit and beyond whenever the mood struck them, he looked longingly at the mini-bathroom in the back of the bus but stayed put. He reached into the side pocket of his travel bag, pulled out a dog-eared copy of '*The Adventures of Huckleberry Finn*' and glanced briefly at the inscription on the inside cover. Written in a flowery, almost feminine hand, he had turned to it a thousand times in his life the way a Christian would find solace in their chosen passages in the bible:

You're a good kid, Daniel and it ain't no matter but what nobody says!

The sentiment, including the maladroit but endearing attempt to communicate in the parlance of Twain's Huck was to Daniel the most significant snippet of literature that he would ever be exposed to in his lifetime. And, it just so happened, he was a personal friend of the author.

Eyes closed, he recounted the first time he'd opened the book and discovered the gift that kept on giving, and he had the sensation that he was falling into a black hole, a dank black hole. Howard was no more, and a motionless Daniel suddenly felt as if he were lunging violently in a futile attempt to grab a branch or anything that might break the momentum of his downward spiral. Instead, he found himself, eyes still closed tight, reaching for the page with the prescriptive words and running his fingertips over them to confirm that they had not vanished along with his uncle.

The bus decelerating and finally coming to a complete stop shook Daniel out of his reverie, and he decided instantly that he wanted to be as far away from sleep as possible. They had pulled into Johnny R's, one of the multitudes of mini-marts that have come to dot the great American landscape lest anyone ever find themselves more than a stone's throw from the staples: a pack of cigs, a quart of milk, a soda and possibly some Cheetos. For Daniel his staple would be a very, very large coffee and a bagel with a lump of cream cheese only slightly larger than the dough it was sandwiched between.

Daniel suspected that the "R" in Johnny R's was somehow akin to the Confederacy but he had no evidence and thought that inquiring might be in bad taste. He fingered the Star of David necklace resting just below the top button of his shirt, recalled the story of little Mary Phagan and thought mostly in jest that *bad taste* may be the least of his worries.

Fortified and in no immediate danger of revisiting anything but restful slumber, Daniel began the process of trying to construct a eulogy in his head, quickly realizing that being the right man for the job did not necessarily mean that he had any idea how to do it. He had decided that the back of the five by five "Word of the Day" sheet was just the right size for a cue card when it dawned on him that if he had brought something to write with, it was likely on the lower level of the bus buried deep within the luggage. Daniel skulked back into Johnny R's and bought himself a BIC Banana and while checking out found that he had a sudden yen for fruit. He snagged a Red Delicious for the road off the shelf next to the cash register while passing on the *National Intelligencer* with the story about the alien abduction in Kentucky. As he was rung up, he couldn't help but wonder if the alien had any mechanical aptitude.

Daniel had calculated that there would be enough time for two cigarettes, but the pen faux pas had cut into his smoking time, and he lit up as he exited the store hoping to squeeze one in before the call came to reboard. He fought the impulse to think of anything else but the matter at hand but acquiesced to one diversion before forcing himself to bear down on the eulogy.

He missed Golda, sweet Golda, true blue Golda. She'd been sad to see him go which touched him deeply but this was his sacred duty. She would just have to understand, he mused as the waving hand of the driver indicated that he was ready to roll. Daniel, determined to finish what he started, drew fast and hard on the Camel Light. The volume of nicotine rampaging through his brain cells left him reeling like a drunk as he made his way back onto the bus, and he stumbled back into his seat without a clue as to what he had intended when he was firing on all cylinders. The driver gave him an errant look that Daniel sensed as much as saw, but within a few minutes he had largely regained his equilibrium, and he flashed a reassuring smile to the driver to confirm the fact.

Chapter 2

First Draft:

Just jotting those two words in that format, he hoped, would lead to bigger and better things. And sure enough without raising his pen, the words followed though Daniel was unaware of the preliminary work that had been done in his subconscious even before he started.

Many years ago, I don't recall exactly when or where or under what circumstances, I heard or read that if there's one person that actually gives a damn where you are and how you're doing, it is enough to sustain you, to keep you going no matter how bad things are and how little promise there seems to be of things breaking in your favor anytime soon.

It wasn't half bad, he thought to himself, and furthermore, it could fairly be called an accurate description of his bond with Howard. He reread what he'd written and wondered if the last sentence was a bit too suggestive of how he might characterize his current circumstances but let it stand.

Buoyed by the simple fact of having broken the logjam and gotten the thing under way, Daniel set the Banana back down on the paper to see what might leak onto it next.

I do recall thinking how sad a thing it was that someone could be that impoverished and found it more than a little bit ironic as time passed, and I found myself hanging by that thinnest of threads. Well, Howard was that thread for me, and now he's gone.

No, no, no! True, yes, but much too telling and definitely too morose, he thought as he scribbled hard to cover up the evidence. This is a funeral not an AA meeting he reminded himself as he was deciding that it had become too much about him and not enough about the subject of the proceedings. The age-old conflict regarding how much of oneself one should reveal under any circumstances had reared its ugly head and stifled his momentum. Not coincidentally, his thoughts turned to Arlene, Margaret and Harriet, the three scheming accomplices with whom Howard shared a blood connection so obscure that Daniel had never quite figured it out. He had a visceral distrust of them and was not at all surprised when Howard had told him with characteristic detachment and good humor that the ladies three had found a soft spot in their hearts for him when it became apparent that his *time* was rapidly approaching. The revelation had infuriated Daniel but he took his cue from his uncle and was shamed into seeing the lighter side, if you could call it that, of at least a couple of the seven deadly sins.

His past encounters with the three women had not been particularly pleasant although there hadn't been any outright enmity. He recalled first meeting them and feeling a squirmy reluctance to engage them with anything but extreme caution. He remembered too with a little sardonic snicker, having been unimpressed by the exaggerated affectations of the "southern belles" whose behavior suggested that they would be returning by carriage to Tara when it seemed to Daniel that the more likely destination was their double-wides. Furthermore, the fact that they were probably in dire need of a thorough scrubbing, he had tossed in for good measure!

Daniel sensed that the ladies did not look kindly upon homosexuals and imagined that they believed that Howard's misfortune was the predictable punishment for his aberrant behavior although they would likely never say it, except to each other. His mind was conjuring up an old suspicion that he was guilty by association of the crime of the unnatural union, that his affinity for Howard was based on the basest of appetites when he grunted as he reined in what he had to concede was likely projection run amok. Still, there was a certain jaded pleasure in imagining the worst, all the better to stoke the anger and recrimination. Before the vitriol was exhausted, he put the pen to paper again and let it rip albeit on a separate "cue card" knowing before he had begun that it would be discarded.

I'd like to tell everyone here, these shrill leeches, these vile, opportunistic gold diggers especially, I'd like to tell them all just how truly important he was to me and what a good and decent man he was. Smart as a whip too, although none of this gang would be particularly impressed with the kind of knowledge he held dear if for no other reason than that they're too dimwitted to understand it. I'd like to tell them all that and more but then I'd have to divulge just how destitute I really am, and I'm not one to load other people's guns for them.

Daniel had kind of chuckled to himself as he chastised the misanthropes but the divergence at the end had a "Ouija" feeling about it, as if an invisible force had shepherded the notion telepathically. Still, he did not take the divined message to be gospel. He didn't dispute it outright, mind you but there were caveats to mitigate the characterization.

The exercise irritated and frustrated him and he tore the incriminating text into thin strips both vertically and horizontally and pushed them deep into his breast pocket, the weight of his cigarettes to serve as the "concrete shoes" that would keep the evidence submerged.

Daniel looked around to see if anyone was observing his suspicious behavior and felt suddenly like an ass of the first magnitude.

He wanted a cigarette. He wanted his uncle. He missed Golda.

He forced himself to change the subject and decided to revisit his favorite dream, "The Passion of the Daniel" as he had come to think of it and it actually worked, for a while.

Finally, he turned his attention back to the eulogy as he knew he must. Feeling more decisive for reasons unknown, he opted to go with the *"one person that actually gives a damn where you are"* portion and wing it from there. How bad could it be? He thought as the beads of sweat that began to appear on his brow foreshadowed the answer.

Chapter 3

The cab, late in arriving at the terminal and hung up in heavier than usual traffic, delivered a panicked Daniel to the entrance of the funeral home where he saw people filing out the side door of what he presumed was the location of the viewing. Daniel asked the driver to wait and was annoyed that he could still hear the rhythmic clicking of the meter as he made a mad dash into the parlor and accosted the first "suit" that he encountered.

"I'm not too late, am I?" he asked, with anguish lurking in his voice.

"No, you've got a few minutes yet," the answer came in the soothing tone of a professional empathizer.

"Thank you; thank you," Daniel answered sincerely, his words given an avenue when his heart had taken leave of his throat.

"Down the hall and to the right," the man in black offered without solicitation.

Daniel nodded and began the journey, a sudden inertia tugging at his legs, making it feel as if he were knee deep in water, trudging against a swift current. He had known all along what was behind door number one but finally finding himself within a hairsbreadth of his uncle's lifeless corpse sent a chill down his spine. Steeling himself for the worst, he cut hard to the right and managed to position himself in the immediate vicinity of his uncle, albeit at the far end of the room. He had anticipated a line, a single file procession past the casket, with common courtesy if nothing else dictating the duration of the "farewell." That may well have been the case five or ten minutes ago but now, to Daniel's initial dismay, the floor, as they say, was all his.

The silence in the room amplified the din in his head, but a deep breath and a reluctant acceptance of the inevitable brought his inner space more in sync with his outer space and he was able to survey the situation if not dispassionately, at least with a tad more clarity. He was struck first by the sun beaming through the sole large window in the room, replicating its rectangular panes with a slightly skewed geometry at the foot of the casket. It reminded Daniel of the card he'd acquired and held on to for some odd reason at the only other funeral he'd attended, the glorious rays bursting through the clouds as if to create a sort of solar escalator to the heavens, the expectant deceased presumably giddy with anticipation at the prospect of having been chosen although spared might better describe it. "Safely Home" was the title of the poem on the other side of the card, and Daniel recalled imagining an animated Satan in full umpire regalia barking a gleefully sadistic "Yerrrrrrrrr Out" while the poor sap whose fortunes had just been turned upside down, literally, had an eternity of hellfire to ponder the fact that he had voted against instant replay.

The fleeting thought elicited a nervous chuckle but he quickly turned his attention to the matter at hand. The enormity of the circumstance began to sink in as did the pit of his stomach in a reprise of the emotional freefall he'd experienced on the bus. In that box across the bow was his beloved Uncle Howard. How can that be, he thought, how can he be gone? Maybe he'll rise from the dead in two or three days; maybe he'll come back to see me once more and tell me how to finish this thing. God dammit, Howard, why did you have to go? Why, the tormented thought echoed in his head. I loved you, no I love you, he corrected himself angrily, and I will always love you. I can't believe you're gone.

Daniel felt himself collapsing to his knees but to his surprise he discovered that he'd traversed the better part of the distance separating him from Howard. Pulling up short, he was overcome by the certainty that he would find not Howard nestled in the pleated padded silk but himself and he squeezed Huck Finn until he felt it would disintegrate in his hands. He slammed his eyes shut and shook his head as if to dislodge the disturbing image and took the final couple of steps to the precipice as good as blindfolded.

"Hello Uncle Howard," Daniel whispered as the silent sallow image came into focus, and the flood gates swung wide open. A disembodied hand appeared out of nowhere, startling Daniel but simply offering a handful of tissues which he took without comment. He tried with some success to mute the plaintive squeals of grief emanating from deep within him, managing finally to turn the tide by looking back at memories of the two of them hiking along the creek in rapt conversation, a whole portable and very satisfying universe shared. He was seized by a powerful desire to be back at that time and place as if it would be a salve for the deep ache of the heart, but the impulse quickly passed as the knowledge that the trail blazer would be left behind sunk in.

"Hey but we had it, didn't we, Uncle Howard," he offered, as if to somehow spare Howard's feelings, sneaking a peek over his shoulder to see if anyone was in the vicinity but the "attendant", ever the professional, had made himself scarce. The room remained deathly silent save for the occasional clicking of the meter that intruded every few minutes to Daniel's profound irritation. I don't give a fuck what it costs, he thought to himself, and he meant it.

Daniel studied Howard's face and recalled the various incarnations over the years, and it occurred to him that somehow he'd managed never to have seen a picture of Howard as a boy. He struggled to remember the final encounter a few months prior and to frame Howard's living, breathing face in his mind's eye. The hug that felt somehow like a pair of trousers three or four sizes too big, the pained smile and the wave goodbye so feeble that Daniel had hustled out of the room so as to relieve him of the effort. The final haunting image, however, had remained seared into his memory perilously close to the surface: that last look, the lingering acknowledgement as he moved from the doorway of the man whom he never could repay and the astringent truth that this was the grand finale, that their seeing eyes would never meet again. All these things and more provoked another wave of sadness but a deep and enduring gratitude as well.

"Thank you, Uncle Howard?" he started speaking slowly and deliberately. "Yeah, they're inadequate words but it's the

18

best I can do right now. I know you taught me better, and I'll work on it, I promise, but for now, it's all I've got. Just know that my heart is yours, and I am forever in your debt." He paused for a moment and allowed himself a brief smile. "Well, I guess maybe that was a little better, wasn't it!"

"I'm a lucky man for having known you, Howard, a lucky, lucky, lucky man."

Daniel reached into the casket and wrapped his warm pulsing hand around Howard's cold rigid hand and tried to swallow the grapefruit-sized lump in his throat. His lip quivered, and his lungs expanded and contracted as if a doctor had requested a series of deep breaths, and he stood like a sentinel as his body seemed to cycle through its own ritual of emotions, culminating finally in the understanding that the time had come to go.

He leaned over and kissed the forehead of his benefactor, bade him farewell and in moving toward the door, noticed that the carpet was no longer adorned with the skewed rectangles. Fitting, he thought, wondering if Howard had had a chance to "escalate" before the last train left the station.

Chapter 4

No sooner had Daniel exited the building than an extremely efficient team of well-dressed men was loading the now closed casket into the back of the hearse, slapping on the magnetic funeral signs and flags and moving into the pole position. The maneuver left Daniel feeling both appreciative and embarrassed and triggered a foggy recollection of an exasperated Mark ribbing Howard about being late to his own funeral.

Howard had eschewed a formal religious ceremony, although in deference to his friends of faith, he had allowed for a brief graveside service to be conducted by an old comrade with a take on the matter that he could live with, so to speak.

The Reverend Samuel T. Bookwell, a name that Daniel would take an instant shine to, split his duties between being the acting minister in the Unitarian Universalist Church and managing a modest caseload as a Jungian psychoanalyst. Howard had met him some number of years ago on business at the humble structure that served as his church and had been surprised to see the phrase "No Dogmas Allowed" on the marquee at the base of the steps leading into the building, not the most original phrase, he had mused, but a most original application. The congregation was to say the least, diverse and as Reverend Bookwell had explained to an intrigued Howard "The common thread that binds them together is a spiritual yen and a desire to belong" adding that "If you fit that description, brother, you're always welcome." Howard didn't go often but when he did, he always felt uplifted after the fact.

Daniel felt a little lightheaded as he made his way in search of the caravan that would make the short trek to the cemetery. He figured it was due to the emotional tumult although it did cross his mind that he might have had a contagious reaction to the chemicals that kept his uncle "fresh" and he smacked his lips a few times to confirm that there had been no Botox effect.

The weather had morphed from brisk and sunny to a kind of premature dusk that mimicked the dimly lit corridors of the funeral home and it seemed to Daniel natural and right somehow that the day should be overcast and unseasonably cool. He peered up at an ominous gray sky and shivered a bit in the heavy humid air, noticing that if you looked at just the right angle you could sometimes detect a hint of mist insidiously dampening everyone and everything. It struck Daniel suddenly that there was a word, a single solitary word that could sum up perfectly the climate in which he found himself; why the place was **dank**. You might even say it was reeking of **dankness,** he thought to himself as the word thunked on the ground. As he contemplated the irony and reaffirmed the value of the "Word of the Day", the cabbie gave a little toot on the horn and his thoughts shifted instantly to the incessant meter as he turned in the direction of the cab.

"Are you going to the funeral? Excuse me but are you going to Howard Green's funeral?" The insistent voice finally drowning out the clicking and getting Daniel's attention.

"Yes, yes I am."

"And you're going in a taxi!"

"Yes."

"Isn't that kind of expensive?" the question eliciting an ironic chuckle from Daniel.

"Yes but—"

"You can ride with my husband and me if you like."

"Well, dank you, I mean thank you," he covered quickly with a nervous laugh. "I was just thinking that there's one word—I mean, well I was thinking it was dank out..."

"It certainly is and so sudden like," she added the coup de grace to set Daniel's mind at ease.

"Hey, I really appreciate it. Let me go square up with the guy."

"It's the green Pontiac third from the left in the first row there."

"Thanks a lot, I'll be right over," he finished, already on his way to silence that meter once and for all.

Daniel winced as he paid the thirty-two dollars but felt better immediately as he calculated what the cost might have been if not for the kind strangers. He arrived in the lot just as the cars were beginning the polite jockeying for a position in line as the caravan began to assemble and Daniel imagined that under different circumstances this show of civility might have an altogether different edge to it.

"So were you a friend of Howard's?" she asked as the procession began to move intermittently. "Oh, I'm so sorry. My name is Judy and this is my husband Dennis."

"Nice to meet you, I'm Daniel, Daniel Cassat," he replied, adding the surname as if it might provide some clue that would explain his presence here. "And no," he added finally when it was apparent that it didn't. "I mean yes he was my friend but he was my uncle first." There was a lull as the couple discussed the route they would take and Daniel took the opportunity to dissect the awkward structure of his response. As the convoy found its rhythm they both ended up laughing about how they really didn't have much choice in the matter.

"My mother was his sister," Daniel added for clarification.

"I was not aware he had a sister. Oh well, I guess I really didn't know a whole lot about his personal life," she replied.

Daniel, ever protective, tried to discern if that was a 'pointed comment' but somehow sensed that it was just a statement of fact.

"We both thought very highly of him," the husband chimed in as if to dispel any erroneous assumptions.

"How did you two know him, if you don't mind my asking?"

"He attended our church every once in a while."

The answer was not at all what Daniel had expected to hear and the surprise registered clearly on his face, a detail not lost on his gracious hosts.

"Hmmm, I never knew him to be a particularly religious man," Daniel finally responded stolidly but before anyone could reply, Daniel continued, pulling one up from the depths. "There was a little white building, a sweet little place with green shutters. Is that the church you're talking about?

"Yes, did he mention it to you?" asked Judy

"Actually, Daniel, that building was torn down a number of years ago after one of our folks ended up in the basement without intending to," Dennis chimed in. "The place was thoroughly infested with termites. It's a shame. Anyway, we've been renting space from a Karate school since then. It's not as charming but the karma's still just as strong."

Daniel had never heard the word used that way and he mulled it over for a moment concluding finally that it made perfect sense.

"Forgive me for going on so, Daniel. I never even let you answer the question."

"That's okay," he replied, pausing for a moment to revisit the memory. "Yes, I mean, a long time ago when I was visiting and we took a drive, he showed it to me. I remember it now, there used to be a little announcement board at the front of the property and when we drove by it, it had something on it to the effect that the speaker for the week would be 'A Different Drummer.'"

A brief silence followed Daniel's remarks after which the couple gave each other a knowing look and burst into raucous laughter. In another time and place, Daniel would likely have found their uninhibited expression of glee contagious but this was after all a solemn occasion and Daniel was conflicted and uncertain about the proper protocol. The jocularity subsided and the two looked a little sheepish, not it turns out because of their actions but out of concern for the discord they sensed in Daniel.

"Forgive us Daniel," Dennis intervened. "But for what it's worth, your uncle used to crack up over the various messages the Reverend Bookwell posted. In fact, he spurred him on to the point where the Reverend was crafting them specifically with Howard in mind and that went on for—gosh, I don't know how long. I guess until Howard didn't show up for a couple of years. We certainly mean no disrespect."

Daniel, aghast at the attention that had been drawn to him knew only that he didn't know the rules and hence was in no position to cast aspersions. It seemed that they were celebrating Howard's life and try as he might, he could not find fault with that. If anything it seemed that maybe there was a lesson in it for him. "No, no, I understand…. it's just me," he replied after a time, a little embarrassed at having caused the scene. "This is all pretty amazing stuff and I'm glad to know whatever I can about Howard. It kind of fills him out for me."

"Good, I'm glad," Judy answered as the car came to an abrupt halt. As much as Daniel hated parting on an inconclusive note, he was relieved that he would soon be alone. They were good people, he thought, of that there was no doubt and he truly did value the other perspectives on his beloved uncle Howard but more than anything he wanted to nurture his own thoughts and feelings and for Daniel that required distance, a rare commodity in a crowd.

"It was sure nice to meet you, Daniel," the two of them said almost in unison.

"And I hope… Well, good luck to you Daniel."

"Thank you and same to you," Daniel replied, glad to be done with it.

He closed the car door and got no more than two or three steps away when Dennis called his name. "I just wanted to say, Daniel, that you were right."

Daniel gave him a confused look but said nothing.

"He wasn't very religious. As a matter of fact, he wasn't religious at all, but that was okay." "I just thought that detail might be important to you," he added after a brief pause.

Daniel hesitated for a moment before reluctantly walking over to the car window. He stood silent for a moment as if giving serious consideration to what he was about to say but "Thank you. It was," was all that came out. Daniel extended his hand and it was accepted with great enthusiasm. They exchanged smiles that seemed to say that all's well that ends well and the two men parted company.

The four hearse men of the apocalypse were about to remove the casket when Daniel showed up at the side of the back left bearer, his demeanor seeming to say, "May I cut in?" and the pallbearer for hire seeming to understand.

"Would you like to take a corner?"

"Yes, very much." Daniel made sure to get a solid grip and they were off, turning in unison and marching lockstep toward Howard's final destination.

It would be their last walk together, not the peripatetic endeavors of years past but instructive in its own way and Daniel relished the task. The casket and its contents were heavier than Daniel had imagined but this too in its own strange way was a good thing. The heavier the better, he thought, feeling positively Churchillian, the physical exertion a kind of healthy corporal mortification. The lump in Daniel's throat made a comeback as he thought that he was glad that for once *he* could shoulder the burden and carry his uncle. He blinked back a tear and looked straight ahead, taking his cue from the business-like approach of his counterparts.

The slow procession traversed the gravelly walk between those already deposed and started up a modest incline to what looked to be the final resting place on the crest of a small hill and as the terrain leveled off and Daniel could see the other side, he knew instantly why Howard had chosen this spot. A good choice, my dear man. Nay, a great one, he thought, smiling inwardly.

The pallbearers gently released the coffin and stepped away one by one until Daniel stood alone, cupping his ear to better hear the distinctive sound of rushing water coursing through a vein of its own making. He looked out upon the stream, and as if a camera flashed, the sun broke through for one brief shining moment, and fire and water gently collided, glistening like a million diamonds off the swirling current. He tracked the path of the flowing waters until it fused with the horizon before looking down to Howard's vessel and felt a mixture of pain and peace. "I will see you there, Uncle Howard. That's a promise," he said softly as he turned his gaze back to the horizon.

Chapter 5

Daniel awoke to the hissing sound of the doors parting, the engine idling and passengers disembarking. The driver, it seemed to Daniel from his limited number of excursions on their buses, fit the profile preferred by Greyhound, not too tall, barrel chest resting atop an ample gut, burly arms and a thinning gray mini-pompadour. He half expected him to declare "lights out" when he strode down the aisle collecting tickets and Daniel imagined that anyone foolish enough to have boarded without one might just "spend the night in the box." There would be no opportunity to stretch his legs or more importantly, grab a smoke as the driver made quick work of retrieving the luggage, returning to his station and maneuvering the bus back out onto the highway with its monotonous but oddly soothing cadence.

Daniel was surprised to see that all but one other passenger had departed and that the lone holdout was sitting directly behind the driver and yammering away. Since the noise was little more than a murmur to Daniel, it was hard to tell how enthusiastically the driver was receiving his guest's advances although he did seem to hear an occasional 'you bet' that suggested that he was at least tolerating the fellow. It was late, he reasoned and if nothing, else the attention, wanted or not would keep the driver alert.

Daniel yawned and flipped on the little overhead light, revealing Ian McEwan's *Atonement* face down on the floor in front of the vacant aisle seat. He retrieved the book and by force of habit flipped it open to the page he'd stopped at even though he had no intention of starting up again. No, he was in a reflective mood, a mood enhanced by the sort of converse funnel created by the overhead light. It restricted the observable universe to a few cubic feet and Daniel indulged in the sensation that he had been beamed down to this hollow of demarcated airspace for the express purpose of engaging in contemplation. He set the book aside and was reminded by the picture on the cover that he had decided some time ago that if were ever to have a daughter, he would name her *Briony*.

He had not, as he had feared, been asked to "eulogize" his uncle (a description that Daniel imagined the ladies three perverting somehow) but rather to his own amazement had volunteered. Actually, the Reverend Bookwell acting the part of facilitator, had kind of opened the floor up for discussion and invited anyone so inclined to share their thoughts regarding Howard. Daniel, seeing the mild to moderate discomfort on the faces of those who stepped forward was reminded that he was not alone and was emboldened. "He came into my life at a very difficult time and made it better. And what he did for me at seven and ten, he continued to do until the day he died and I will miss him terribly," he stated simply, having forgotten all about his partially prepared statement. Upon reflection, he decided that he had acquitted himself well even though all he had done was open his mouth and let the truth roll off his tongue.

After his brief pall bearing stint, Daniel had positioned himself safely and unobtrusively in the rear, craning his neck in search of a familiar face in the gathering ahead of him and noting that it seemed to be a particularly eclectic group. Harold and Maude were not in attendance but the rest constituted about as disparate a group as you would find in any random sampling. He had decided, mercifully, after some consideration that it was not unreasonable to have assumed that it would be a predominantly gay crowd, just a little naïve. After all, he reckoned, a man that lives a full rich life is going to move in a lot of different circles and encounter a whole lot of different people, people of all types. The funny thing about it was that in a herd, it was not at all obvious who was gay and who wasn't.

Daniel was recounting his first glimpse of Arlene, Margaret and Harriet—or Larry, Moe and Curly as he had dubbed them—when he was sidetracked by a small red laser dot that appeared toward the front of the bus and a sudden gust of cool air circulating through the seats. He recalled reports he'd caught on the news of the dangers posed by these lights, especially to airline pilots but a bus driver? Or for that matter, a bus, and one that was practically uninhabited, seemed an unlikely target for Al Qaeda but who knows maybe it hadn't been an overly ambitious sleeper cell, he reasoned as a sweet scent wafted back and violated his air space. It was the unmistakable smell of a just lit cigarette. Noxious and offensive to nonsmokers, for smokers, it was the pied piper's intoxicating aroma that triggered all the receptors in the brain starving for attention. "You dirty dog," he whispered as he unconsciously reached in his pocket. He had always taken the liberty of matching the speed of police cars that were not in hot pursuit and it seemed the same logic would apply here. The pleasant thud of nicotine entering his brain seemed to nudge open a sticky door and the pixels finally coalesced into a recognizable image.

'Ichabod Crane,' That's who he reminds me of, Daniel thought as he recalled watching the Reverend Samuel T. Bookwell move front and center to take charge of the proceedings.

"Funerals make for strange bedfellows," he had opened with to Daniel's delight, and the rest of his talk had been equal parts moving, comical and inspiring. This, Daniel thought, *was* the right man for the job. He especially liked the way he had closed the show by commenting that he had been to many funerals, some in which the mourners were a mix of the serious and the profane and some at which "good riddance" was the prevailing sentiment but that there were those special few in which the manner in which many of the lives in attendance had been touched was evident on the doleful faces huddled around their fallen friend. Daniel had expected rhetorical flourishes but he didn't find it hard to believe that this was largely true. The thought prompted a quick glance at the unctuous troika, the exception that confirmed the rule.

The gathering had begun breaking up and reassembling in camps more akin to their particular ilk even as they exchanged parting pleasantries with their "strange bedfellows" when Daniel got a notion.

Possibly because he'd been inspired by the Reverend, he had tried to convince himself that maybe he was being unfair, that maybe he should cut them some slack. After all, if he was completely honest, he had to concede that they pressed his buttons, as it were, and he was astute enough to know that that usually meant that his reaction was a blend that included the seepage from a still raw wound that he'd suffered somewhere along the line.

His magnanimity in hand, he had approached Arlene, Margaret and Harriet but quickly found himself rolling out of control down that road paved with good intentions. There had always been a borderline civility proffered Daniel in the few other circumstances that had forced these unions and he had come prepared to bury the hatchet if indeed one existed at all but he immediately sensed an escalation of antipathy. There were smiles all around, naturally, but they seemed somehow blood curdling, and he felt repelled by an undercurrent of barely disguised contempt. Daniel stumbled through a cursory exchange and hightailed it to the nearest safe haven, which was anywhere they weren't.

He made his way to the banks of the stream and by force of habit toyed briefly with blaming himself for creating the scenario but stopped abruptly because he *knew* something was up, that even if he were exaggerating, there was clearly something in the air, but for the life of him he couldn't imagine what it might be.

Chapter 6

Streetlamps, porch lights and the eerily symmetrical illumination of businesses catching their breath before the next morning's bustles were able to pierce Daniel's bubble, but the big bright moon stood out and captured his fancy. It had always seemed to Daniel a mirror image of the earth, with clearly delineated oceans and continents, the distance enabling the illusion. His curiosity hadn't moved him to investigate the matter beyond wondering one fitful night in bed how a back hoe would fare chomping a bucket full of... what? The vexing question of what to call the soil equivalent on the moon; "earth" didn't seem right somehow, and if we were to actually construct buildings on the moon, would the contractors prepare the site with "moonmovers" rather than earthmovers? The answer would not come on that night or any other night, and thus the exercise was a complete success.

Daniel shifted his attention back to the day's events and specifically to the abbreviated encounter with the wicked witches of the South. It had been disconcerting, to be sure, but he could take solace from the fact that he had weathered the emotional storm albeit with an unexpected assist. Random acts of malevolence, ones without an apparent motive had always been particularly disturbing to him because there seemed to be no rhyme or reason, reason being the operative word. But as had been the case earlier in the day, it was the soothing sound of a rich baritone that would distract him from the unspoken contentiousness, and he tried to replay the sound in his head.

"Howard said you would like this spot!" Daniel recalled the voice coming out of nowhere as he fretted by the stream. He had turned around and found himself face-to-face with a tall, thin and very regal looking gentleman. He had mocha skin framed perfectly by a salt and pepper beard and a large gold ball in his earlobe that reminded Daniel somehow of a pearl in its natural habitat.

"My name's Nate and as you might have guessed I was a friend of your Uncles."

There was something comforting about Nate's presence that Daniel couldn't put a finger on. He felt an odd inclination to whine about the indignity he had suffered but that impulse was expunged when the implication of Nate's casual comment hit home.

"I'm Daniel but I assume you ...," he had started but the idea that Uncle Howard had thought of him even as he planned for his foray into eternity touched him deeply. The notion had seemed plausible, but Nate's confirmation made it real and imbued the fact with the power to pack an emotional wallop.

Daniel covered his face with his hand, extending his fingers over any orifice from which the emotion might escape, and Nate slung an arm around his shoulder.

"Your Uncle was always thinking about you, Daniel," he added softly, the sentiment making the job of Daniel's overextended hand all but impossible. "You take your time, Daniel, and when you feel up to it, there are some folks down there you might like to say hello to," he continued, the offer sounding as much like a command as an invitation.

Daniel stepped away, employing both hands in putting the final touches on the reconfiguration of his face. "Well, it's nice to meet you, Nate," Daniel said, laughing sheepishly and swiping the last of the moisture from his eyes. "I think I'm ready!"

Chapter 7

All eyes were focused on the odd couple sauntering down the hill, and Daniel felt curiously like a debutante as he gazed down upon the assembled throng. That would be the gay contingent, he thought to himself with a smile, and he was further pleased to spot a number of yarmulkes sprinkled in, clear evidence that some of Mark's friends and family were in attendance. And smack dab in the middle of the wedge at the head of the group was a woman that seemed unduly cosmopolitan for this neck of the woods; the thought eliciting an immediate rebuke for blanketing a whole region of the country with the felonious assumption. Still, everything about her said "smart and elegant." Inviting and intimidating in the same moment, she held her gaze steady as he ascended the hill, and it would have seemed somehow disrespectful to glance in any direction but hers. They moved inexorably toward one another like the chief negotiators representing disparate factions. The extended hand of the more experienced diplomat awaiting Daniel, he took it nervously but the generosity in her smile instantly created an easy, comfortable ambiance.

"It's so nice to finally meet you Daniel," she opened graciously. "I'm Eliana, Mark's sister but my friends call me Ellie."

"Aw, geez, I loved Mark," was all he could muster, the puerile tone of the sentiment leaving him beet faced but the smiles all around him suggesting that he had struck the right chord.

The mood as he was introduced around, though initially reserved and respectful of the setting was far from morose. Amid the din of friends getting reacquainted, Daniel's general orientation was conducted in hushed but energetic exchanges, and those few oddly familiar faces he'd noted did in fact turn out to be friends of Howard and Mark that Daniel had met in what seemed like a different lifetime. Finally, the amorphous buzz reached a point that suggested it was time to move the festivities to a more appropriate venue, and the group instinctively began to move en masse toward the parking lot.

"Daniel" the voice called as he was sidling in tandem with the group. "Listen, I'm not going to be able to make the shindig," the man in the rumpled suit said apologetically.

"Well, I'm sorry to hear that," Daniel replied, searching his memory for a clue to the man's identity. The stranger plowed ahead with the conversation while Daniel couldn't get past the strong resemblance to Tom Oliphant.

Suddenly, he stopped mid-sentence, donned a quirky smile and looked straight into Daniel's face. "You don't have the faintest idea who I am, do you son? And of course, you wouldn't as we've never really been formally introduced."

The slightly nasal tone of the mystery man's voice finally clicked with Daniel. "You're Herb. You're the lawyer who called me to tell me that Howard had died."

"Righto, son." Hey, hell of a way to meet somebody, I know, but it had to be done!" he added with a pained laugh.

The connection triggered memories of the conversation he'd had with Howard; a subsistence level attorney by nature who was a throw back to the old small town doctor who was just too damn decent for his own good, was how Howard had described Herb Framer. And as Herb kept rambling on he recalled Howard shaking his head as he described the futile attempts to persuade him to gussy up his sparsely furnished waiting room and describing what little furniture there was as looking as if it had come from a "Goodwill" store or been expropriated from an old government building slated for demolition before the big ball dropped.

"Your Uncle was a good man, Daniel," Herb said, his posture suggesting that his time was up.

"Yeah, I know, Herb. Thanks for tracking me down; I'm really glad I got to spend a few minutes with you anyway."

"Me too, son. Best of luck to you," he finished as he grabbed Daniel's hand and pumped it vigorously.

"Goodbye, Herb and you too."

"Sorry again about missing the shindig," Herb's fading voice exclaimed as he ducked into a car that actually made Daniel see his own in a whole new light.

Daniel turned quickly to the parking lot and discovered three different cars idling and waiting for him to choose his ride. He waved the two lead cars on ahead, and as he slid into the back seat, he spotted the troika. The objects that had appeared larger and more ominous they had actually been were now little more than a barely discernible stain in the rear view mirror, he thought with a certain satisfaction as they pulled out of the lot and brought up the rear.

They had reconstituted the gathering at a local watering hole, capping the afternoon off with a luncheon in Howard's honor, and as the glasses were raised by all in toasting the memory of the man of the hour, Daniel felt *he'd* been called home. He had toasted his beloved uncle by repeating his remarks at the service and tossing in the *"one person that actually gives a damn where you are"* portion that he'd crafted on the way down and paying little heed to the subdued silence that followed.

As the wake in absentia built to a festive crescendo, he had marveled at the motley crew hand picked by Howard and had noted that they seemed to share certain traits, and an abiding decency figured to be at the top of that list.

Chapter 8

Good people all, Daniel thought to himself, dismissing a subtle pang in his belly, a harbinger that a storm long brewing could break at any time. He could understand the appeal these people held for Howard. There was a certain "live and let live" quality about them and he wondered if maybe it was because they themselves had not been extended that same courtesy at one time or another.

As the Greyhound rolled on, he detected the first hints of an orange sky creeping up behind a distant skyline as his vision cleared after a hearty yawn. I could take a trip down sometime to visit, he thought, suddenly irritated by his little cocoon of light.

He flashed back to the call, the fateful call from Howard when he first learned that his odds were trending strongly in the wrong direction, and Daniel suddenly recalled the sick, helpless feeling sloshing around inside him during the conversation. He remembered pacing frantically around his small apartment, his mind flailing in a thousand different directions before finally settling on a course of action; he would summon a heretofore unknown reserve of determination, and he would not falter so long as his uncle was still alive. There would be no capitulation to the demons. He would stave off his occasional collapses and remain vigilant and available so long as Howard lived and breathed.

It wasn't terribly logical, and Daniel knew it even as he concocted the fantastic notion; that somehow his steely resolve would impede or maybe even reverse the progress of the disease. He scoffed at the superstitious idea but he was unable to let go of it altogether, tucking it away in a remote nook in his mind labeled "just in case."

I have done my duty, he thought as he looked skyward. The lighting shifted, or maybe his perception shifted, and rather than the moon, he saw his own reflection and imagined that he had done his own version of Dorian Gray, the troubling image further sapping his strength. A picture of sneakers in a dryer formed in his mind, an allegory for the scrum that had gone on internally over the course of the ordeal and he wondered if the bruising was too bad.

Daniel was tired and slipping, and he knew it, and he sensed that this time, he wouldn't have the ammunition to repel the attack. Reaching up and snapping off what had begun to feel like a Klieg light, he sat still and silent in the darkness. He knew his thoughts would be tinged with varying shades of grey and that the best he could hope for was that the grey wouldn't fade completely to black as he closed his eyes and reclined as far as the seat would allow.

His mind wandered back to the restaurant, and he watched as the participants negotiated a graceful exit one after another. After the bulk of them had gone, he saw each newly empty chair come to represent a nudge in the direction of where he found himself now. And finally, as he watched the last of the group bid him farewell, he imagined a curtain dropping, and there he sat, row 11, seat 2, an audience of one.

Who're you going to visit? he chided himself sardonically. Howard's gone and his passing likely blew up your bridge to his world, he thought, surprised by the ferocity of his own cognition. He wanted to set it all aside and revisit what he knew to be a genuinely positive event when he was in a position to assess it rationally. But the bully in him knew his prey was weakened and had decided to get one more dig in before slithering away.

Daniel revisited the muted reaction to his toast. He had assumed at the time that the after affect was because they understood, maybe even shared the notion and were checking their own inventories to see if they could lay claim to this vital patronage, but in the dark of night, in the penumbra and the rhythmic silence, he considered that there might be another explanation altogether. That maybe they had seen an orphan, a *gamin* – he recalled the word with an ironic snicker as a recent "Word of the Day" intruded at this most inopportune time. Maybe they had seen an exiled child lost in the wilderness, his compass still, and maybe the sight had horrified them and for the briefest of seconds, they feared for Daniel and possibly themselves as well.

It had always seemed to Daniel an unforgivable perversion of the term given his avuncular good fortune but he would cry *uncle* now knowing that the morning would come and that sunshine or not, it would be a brighter day. And as he released himself from a waking state in the hopes that the denizens of the dark would be merciful, he acknowledged finally that the dawn would formally deliver the first of a thousand days in a world without Howard.

Chapter 9

"**M**om, I'm heading over to Flo's," Nick announced casually as if to preempt any possible objection.

"Okay, hon," she began, the first word of her sentence formally green lighting the outing and sending Nick in the direction of the door.

"Rocks again?"

"Yeah."

"Just be careful — and try not to be too hard on the clothes," she added with a futile smile.

"Okay, I will. I mean, I won't. Hey, you know what I mean!" he answered, rolling his eyes at his fumbled words.

"Yes," "See you in a while," he said already half way out the door. "

"Bye, hon." "Oh, and Nick, while you're searching, keep an eye out for a big ol' diamond for me, would you?"

"You wish," he called back to her with a snicker. "I mean, sure, Mom, be glad to." She caught the screen door mid close and smiled even as she felt that mother's twinge of worry as she watched her boy vanish into the woods.

Do you dare accompany me to this scene of almost unimaginable carnage?

Are you brave enough to venture with me where someone or possibly some horrible thing has visited a lethal destruction, leaving a cadaver strewn landscape in its wake?

You will cringe even as you try to look away. Your heart will pound and your palms will sweat, but don't scream too loud lest it's not done yet!

Nick chuckled to himself as he stepped adroitly around the obstacle course of torsos, limbs and trunks in varying states of decay. He gave a soft tug on a dangling limb impeding his progress, tearing the crusty member from its socket. He tried to mimic the over hyped voice of the scary movie guy, but his bleating attempt left him giggling uncontrollably.

He made a regular pilgrimage to this neck of the woods even though he'd discovered a much shorter and more navigable route to the river, a route devoid of the boggiest terrain and the coarse and prickly thicket that to his mother's dismay had damaged more than a few articles of clothing. But this was his first trip since viewing first "Ed Wood" and then a sampling of Mr. Wood's more notable films. He had picked up the bug from his father, a B Movie aficionado since junior high school, and the campy "carnage" that had been so commonplace in the "Wood" flicks, all of a sudden inspired Nick to wonder how the indomitable director might have reacted to such a scene. A decomposing tree felled by age and the elements, he imagined, might have been described as a mutilated carcass, its festering insides laid bare, exposing the voracious vultures of the insect world gorging themselves on their putrid and rotting feast.

Nick had enjoyed toying with the idea, but the levity ended abruptly when he caught sight of his charge; a vital healthy specimen of a tree, at least thirty feet in length, with hale and hardy branches on the north face and all wrapped in a thick supple coat of bark. It apparently neither had difficulty finding its way to suckle the nourishing teat of sunlight nor had it been deprived, as had some of its dehydrated neighbors, of the sweet nectar of moisture. In fact, it had all the earmarks of a robust specimen that could expect to live a long and vigorous life, save for one; its whole lanky expanse—all thirty plus feet of it—was stretched horizontally across the good earth, grounded and pinned WWF style by the seemingly desperate act of a disease-ridden tree in a death spiral, glomming onto a strapping young sapling hoping to forestall its dusty destiny.

He had always wondered about the circumstances, whether this was a crime scene, a tragic accident or a futile act of magnanimity. His research had turned up numerous articles extolling the virtues of dead trees, how many critical functions they served even in death, from providing sustenance and shelter for a vast array of insects, birds, mammals and reptiles to erosion control and forest regeneration, going so far as to act as sort of an incubator for emerging seedlings in the admirable role of "nurse" logs. And this specimen too may well have taken on such an exalted role in death, but he still hadn't found a satisfactory answer as to how it actually happened, much less why. His suspicion was that the healthy tree no more volunteered its services as the dead ultimately would to a struggling seedling, that it was most likely simply nature being nature in all its brutal and beautiful banality and that the dying tree did what dying things do, it clung to life; in this case by conscripting the fit tree to play the role of a latter-day Rose of Sharon.

But whatever the case, he considered the point moot. His business was with the living, and he had decided instantly that it was his responsibility to set things right or upright as it were.

"And how are we doing today?" He muttered the greeting under his breath as he began the examination.

Today was a special day as the previous elevation had resulted in the corpse releasing its stranglehold on the host tree, but unlike the surgical separation of conjoined twins, the graft had yielded of its own accord, and the cadaver had simply fallen away from the heft of its own dead weight.

"I do believe we're ready to go for six," he proclaimed with the buoyed tone of a therapist encouraged by the better than expected progress. The standard incremental elevation had been four inches but freed of the lifeless hitchhiker, Nick calculated that the base of the tree was up to the task. He knelt down and scrutinized the stress points to be doubly sure and saw nothing to dissuade him from his initial prognosis.

He scavenged the area and in a matter of moments had procured just the right combination of suitably shaped rocks to prop his vertically challenged patient up another half a foot skyward. The procedure was quick and as far as he could tell, painless, and Nick, satisfied with a job well done, bid his charge adieu with an affectionate pat on the bark and continued on his way.

The big river or "Flo's" as he had taken to calling it, had been a place of solace he'd discovered while exploring his new surroundings following his family's job induced relocation a couple of years back. It had served him well during the transition, and that same special something kept him coming back well after the need had subsided, although it was comforting to know that Flo would always know just the right words if he ever needed a boost.

His destination on this day, however, was not the river but a streamlet that ran parallel to it and his purpose was prospecting its clear shallow waters for rocks shaped like states, a hobby spurned by the inadvertent discovery of a rock shaped exactly like the state of Pennsylvania. He had yet to duplicate the precision of that match but had managed to unearth some pretty good likenesses, and even though finding any state would be gratifying, he paid particular attention to the stones that even vaguely resembled his home state of Illinois, to his way of thinking, the holy grail of stones that could well result in his retiring from the trade.

It was easy to spot the most fertile hunting grounds as they lay just north of an unnatural opening in the forest through which a blast of sun shone unobstructed, a welcome and inspiring sight that always reminded him of the time his parents had taken him to his first professional baseball game, and the monotony of the cavernous concrete concourse had been broken by the encroaching light that would shortly provide a dazzling view of the rich tapestry of green with the ant sized players in their still crisp clean uniforms effortlessly tossing the ball around the vast sward of the outfield.

As he passed the gap, he stopped as he always did and just looked. He never had thoughts per se just a sense of wonder at the swirling, churning behemoth that lumbered inexorably southward, never stopping for a second to rest, never complaining. He didn't know where it began and had only a vague sense of where it ended, and although he imagined that the information was readily available, he chose for some reason to leave it a mystery, believing somehow that even those answers would not tell the whole story.

The modest current pushing the cool water around his ankles felt good as did the mud that snuck into the bottoms of his old sneakers when he raised them to step in the direction of one promising lead after another. The false positives began adding up, and after a time, he decided that one more promising lead, whether it panned out or not, would signal the end of his quest for the day, and just to be sure that didn't take too long, he lowered the standard as to what exactly constituted a promising lead. The continued drought led him to consider lowering the bar yet again just as he caught a glimpse of something with some potential out of the corner of his eye.

"Whoa," he squealed excitedly as the contour of the stone came into focus. He dropped to his knees for a closer look and in his zeal was oblivious to the cool surging water getting perilously close to the shrink wrap zone. The stone was the spitting image of West Virginia to be sure, but his momentary elation was dashed when he lifted it up and out and it broke into two pieces.

"Shit," he exclaimed as he pressed the broken pieces together and confirmed that it was a match on a par with Pennsylvania. "So close," he exclaimed to no one. "So goddam close!" He thought frantically for a moment about how he might reunite the fragments but he knew the rules, and that was strictly prohibited so he did the only thing he could do, he threw them back. The deflation coupled with the sharp pebble that had joined the mud in filling the void in his shoe was enough, and he decided that the next great find would have to happen on another day.

Perched awkwardly on the bank, Nick tugged at his muddy sneakers until he could hang both them and his soiled feet in the water for a thorough cleansing. Shaking off the mild disappointment with a philosophical "you'll get 'em next time" shrug, (fully aware that the image of a unified and whole West Virginia would pop into his head from time to time just to taunt him), he laced up his soggy but debris - free sneakers and turned his thoughts instead to the rousing success he had enjoyed a short while ago. The graduation to the six-inch elevation and the further prospect of even greater raises in the future meant that he would have to recalculate his assumptions about just how long it would be before his charge would be standing tall and proud, but any doubts he may have had about the final outcome of the endeavor had been largely put to rest. And just as Nick was preparing to affix the feather to his cap, the sullen face of his friend popped into his head, and all of a sudden his exploits as a tree surgeon didn't seem all that impressive.

He moved mechanically toward the light and conceded that he had been avoiding thinking, worrying actually, about the plight of his "best friend for life" as he had proclaimed him to be during the emotional send - off that would deposit them on opposite banks of the river. He was more than a little irritated by his own negligence, but in fairness to himself, he allowed that he wanted to help, was more than willing to help, he just didn't have the foggiest notion as to how to go about it, and besides there were few if any feelings he hated more than helplessness. As if to illustrate his frustration, he delivered a good swift kick to a flat rock doing a third - rate imitation of Texas and was surprised to see it skip six or seven times across the stream before going under for good. Here too, he wondered about the circumstances; they had been inseparable for as long as he could remember, and what he knew of his friend's life before geography separated them provided few clues as to what could have gone so horribly wrong.

As he ambled dolefully along the path, he noticed that he could not only hear the river but he could actually feel the subtle rumblings of its prodigious power, and as if by osmosis, he felt some of that strength welling up in him. West Virginia as well as his impotence in the face of his friend's travails receded, and the strange thought occurred to him that the great river had an inexhaustible supply of this elixir, and if he could only find a way to capture it and send it to his friend, it might ease his pain just a bit.

He kind of half laughed - half scoffed at the simplistic notion but decided nonetheless to take the matter up with Flo.

Chapter 10

The three women squirming on the vinyl seating were silent as they waited for the verdict. The official pronouncement, was by their reckoning, mere moments away, and to their profound annoyance, the man who would make it was running a few minutes over.

They believed it to be a forgone conclusion based on some "inside information" they'd received via the caregiver who had been hired to assist Howard as the end approached. A personal visit from Attorney Framer to finalize the details of Howard's will had piqued the interest of the nieces and they immediately seized the opportunity to gain advance knowledge of the contents lest any serious lobbying was called for. Sheila, the Hospice Nurse, was in the room as had been hoped and in fact she had served to witness the completed document. Their clumsy attempt at "gentle" interrogation had initially unearthed some encouraging information. All three were indeed included in the will, but there was little to learn beyond that except that Daniel was also an heir and that the rest had been given to what she thought was a religious organization of unknown denomination.

The triumvirate, confident that their privacy was assured, dropped the thin veneer of civility and degenerated into their natural state, a state that by virtue of a bit of doublethink that would have made Orwell proud, remained oblivious to the practitioners.

Harriet elbowed Margaret, who in turn tapped Arlene's leg, and the attention of the latter two was directed to the door to Attorney Framer's office. Smoke had begun to waft upward from the bottom causing the three of them to giggle like a gaggle of mischievous adolescents. "If they're not careful they're gonna burn this dump down," Harriet whispered with an air of contempt.

"Wouldn't that be a great loss?" Margaret chimed in cynically, and the gaggle giggled again.

Harriet made a show of looking disgustedly at her watch and they resumed waiting nervously and impatiently.

"You don't think that hospice person said anything to Mr. Framer about us pumping her for information, do you?" Arlene said in a hushed tone while spinning her head around scanning for eavesdroppers.

"I doubt it," Margaret chimed in. "And so what if she did, we have a right to know, don't we?" she added with a hint of righteous indignation in her tone.

"Look, girls, we just wanted to be able to plan, right and all that nurse did was tell us what she saw when she witnessed the "Will". "It's not like she divulged any state secrets or anything like that. We just got ourselves a little advance notice" Harriet chuckled, confident that she had completed the circle of reason that would settle the issue once and for all, staving off the need for that special brand of guilt that only emerges when one is caught red handed.

"Still", added Arlene, not quite able to shake a quiet discomfort. "She seemed pretty upset when she left."

"Look, he's dead, alright and besides each one of us helped him, didn't we? We cleaned his house, we gave him his pills, and we fed him when he could still eat. We even cleaned up him up when he shit all over himself for Chrissakes. So don't be questioning whether we're entitled or not. Besides, what did fag boy ever do for him other than call him and visit a few times?" Harriet's exasperated sentiments won the day as the others knew without a doubt that this conversation was over.

The sound of a creaky door opening startled all of them giving them barely enough time to put their new faces on. A young man preceded Mr. Framer out the door of the inner sanctum, and a billow of smoke that quickly permeated the anteroom preceded *him*. The two men parted with a nod as Attorney Framer turned his attention to the ladies who didn't seem quite certain that the demeanor they had chosen was appropriate, but there was no time to change it now. An odd thought sped across his mind's eye, an image of a "fourth sister" most likely left at home to scrub the floors and tend to various other chores as well, but he dismissed it and turned to the duties at hand.

"So nice to see you ladies again," he opened, a sincere sparkle in his eyes that was born of the hard won acceptance of human frailty. "Won't you come in?" he offered, motioning them toward the door. The ladies proceeded with caution, as if slightly intimidated. It was by no means an imposing place and they didn't hesitate to mock him, but he was a lawyer after all, and that meant that he likely had, in some peripheral way that they couldn't grasp, some connection to the law and they were, if nothing else, law abiding citizens.

The ladies made their way to their respective seats around the old metal desk that anchored Attorney Framer's "command center" and He eyed them wistfully as they gazed around a room that appeared to have been visited by a tornado in the very recent past. "One man's chaos is another man's comfort", he opened the dialogue with a smile. They smiled back uneasily not knowing quite what to make of the remark and shifted awkwardly in their seats obviously anxious to get to the proverbial bottom line.

"I'm sure you ladies have important matters to attend to so we'll get right to the meat of the matter," he continued, wanting at least as much as they did to get this thing the hell over with and part company. He drew a document wrapped in the familiar slate blue from the drawer to his right and unfolded it in such a manner that made it seem as if he were unfurling a proclamation of great import. "Before I begin, ladies, I should ask if any of you have any questions."

There was really only one and they weren't about to ask it, so after an exchange of darting glances, they folded their hands in their laps seemingly in unison like God's little angels and stared almost straight ahead.

"Then I will proceed," he said with an air of finality. "This is The Last Will and Testament of Howard Green," and it reads as follows."

The ladies leaned forward ever so slightly as the moment of reckoning neared.

Attorney Framer continued,

"I, Howard Green, of the city of Montgomery in the County of Montgomery, Alabama, do hereby revoke all my prior Wills and Codicils and declare this to be my Will. "

A flash of panic passed over Harriet's face as she did the math and realized that the document that she had the inside information on could have been revised at least one more time before the deceased got that way. Maybe he did get wind of the fact that they cornered poor Sheila after her rounds and scrapped it all in anger only to replace it with a new version that was a tad or more less generous than the prior proclamation.

She reminded herself that they had only learned that they were included and not specifically how much they stood to gain. Still, her heart thumped a little faster and even though it wouldn't change the outcome the question fell from her lips. "Um, what was the date on that?"

"I don't know that that really matters," he answered brusquely, embarrassing her, and she quickly gathered herself and clumsily tried to resume her angelic posture. Herb didn't hesitate to break the uncomfortable silence by getting directly back to the *reading*.

"FIRST: <u>FUNERAL EXPENSES</u>

I direct the payment out of my estate of my funeral expenses with the added proviso that such expenses be kept to an absolute bare minimum with the coffin to be constructed of the wood salvaged from the tool shed that blew over in the storm of 89 if possible."

Herb recalled insisting on the inclusion of the final two words of the section knowing that the directive could not be followed. He knew that Howard loved the idea and he sensed from Howard's ready acquiescence that it was the whimsical nature of the notion that really appealed to him and that he knew it to be wildly impractical. Herb's personal assurance that he would scour the countryside for a cheap casket was all Howard needed to hear, and, truth be told, Herb relished the challenge. The two shared a hearty laugh when Herb suggested that an even better deal might be gotten if he were willing to go "used."

Attorney Framer detected subtle nods of approval from the ladies and assumed they were computing the monies that would **not** be withdrawn from the estate. He relocated his place, looked up from the document and made eye contact with each, not for any particular reason. It was part of a technique he had picked up at a public speaking course in college and even though he found the "scripted posturing" of the profession somehow distasteful, this particular ploy had stayed with him almost against his will and had become an unconscious part of his repertoire.

"SECOND: <u>PERSONAL AND HOUSEHOLD EFFECTS</u>
I give to my three nieces, Arlene Bock, Margaret Ruch and Harriet Hartzell the house and property located at 417 Magnolia Lane in Montgomery, Alabama. I further give my automobiles and all articles of personal or household use

owned by me at the time of my death to said three nieces. The aforementioned items are to be divided between them as they may agree."

Attorney Framer chuckled lightly to himself in recalling the reaction of his client when he suggested that he might want to be more specific with the allocations to avoid the kind of anger and recrimination he had seen so many times before when *things* were to be divvied up without specific instructions. Howard had simply smiled and closed his eyes slowly with a look of supreme satisfaction on his face. He continued.

"If any one of the three would not survive me by thirty days, the remaining two or one, as maybe the case, will share the contents equally under the same terms and conditions. If none of the three would survive me by thirty days, all of the aforementioned property shall be liquidated and the proceeds donated to the Montgomery Department of Social Services to be distributed to the fifty neediest families in the district with the strict proviso that the monies *not* be counted as personal assets and thus subtracted from their meager entitlements."

The three angels didn't pay much mind to the prior stipulation feeling that the odds were strongly in their favor that "those" people would never see a dime of the proceeds at the same time wondering in unison why there had been no reference to Daniel. Attorney Framer plowed ahead.

"I give to my nephew, Daniel Cassat, 100 percent of the miscellaneous contents in my Safe Deposit Box and 85 percent of the cash contents held in trust at the Fulton National Bank."

The information and its implications were not lost on the ladies three, and Herb looked up briefly to see if they could conceal the visceral reaction to the mystery box and wondered if even this little twist was the handiwork of his dearly departed friend. This time it was Margaret that couldn't hold her tongue as she reluctantly posed the question. "What exactly are the contents of the box?"

"I am not at liberty to say," he answered quickly and got right back to the conclusion.

"I hereby bequeath the other 15 percent of the cash contents held in trust at the Fulton National Bank" to "American Red Magen David For Israel."

This time Herb simply gawked as the confederates quizzical looks contorted into confounded ones as they tried to process that bit of data. Before anyone could speak, he addressed their bewilderment. "The Jewish equivalent of the Red Cross is an organization called "Magen David Adom."

"Howard was a Jew?" Arlene blurted out as the three of them harrumphed in silence.

"No, no he was not of the Jewish faith, your assertion is correct. But you might recall his friend of many years, Mark. Well, he *was* a Jew and they visited Israel together in the early nineties, and the reason Howard did not have to return home alone was because of the remarkable deeds performed by this group when a suicide bomber blew up a bus in the outskirts of Tel Aviv, and Mark was seriously wounded. The organization to whom he made the gift is the American fund raising arm." As he finished, he imagined blood rolling down the chins of the ladies as he suspected that there was more than a little tongue-biting going on.

"As for your shares of the estate, he continued, "I suggest that you retain counsel individually to effect the transfer of assets in an equitable manner. Now then, if there are no more questions, ladies, that concludes today's proceedings."

There were plenty but they would go unasked and unanswered, the ladies preferring as usual to put their own particular spin on the great events of the day.

Chapter 11

Daniel scooched back against the elephant, took a sip of coffee and perused his humble digs, the cramped space, little more than an efficiency with an afterthought bedroom and the furniture in the rest of the apartment positioned in such a way as to suggest partitions between the kitchen, dining and living room areas. 'Be it ever so humble' he thought, with a tinge of satisfaction as he scanned the results of the thorough cleaning he'd done over the last couple of days, vowing as he always did when he managed to get things "just so" (the job completed only when it passed the Briony test) that this time he would keep it that way.

The purported purpose of that exercise, besides the usual getting next to Godliness, had been to get a running start on his often planned reorganization of the interior. The thinking being that getting up close and personal with the various items populating his domain, the reconfigured layout would come to him like a vision. From this vantage point, he could survey all of it save for the cabinets on either side of the bedroom door, but the hoped for inspiration had apparently been waylaid. The purchase of an additional piece of furniture would certainly help, he mused, but then something else would have to go and he had grown rather fond each and every piece, what with their individual histories leading to this last link in the chain of custody. Besides, additional furniture meant the allocation of funds that were in perennially short supply. There's always paint or maybe a throw for the couch or chair to inject a little color into the décor, he thought, with ebbing enthusiasm for the project.

Daniel had set the volume on the radio to what he calculated to be a decibel below the ding of the microwave lest he miss his calling, and in one of life's little victories, it worked.

The jazz station playing a soothing but soulful tune reclaimed the airwaves, and as Daniel moved from the bedroom into the kitchen, the phone rang just as he was reaching to open the microwave door.

"Hello. Is this Daniel Cassat?"

"Yes, it is. What can I do for you?"

"This is attorney Herb Framer. You may remember me. We met at the funeral, although the conversation was kind of rushed"

"Yes, hello Herb. Sure I remember, how are you?"

"Fine son, I'm fine. I've got some news for you." He paused for a moment as if he wasn't sure where to start. "I'm handling your Uncle's estate and he left me some instructions that are … let's see, how do I put this. Well, Daniel, number one, your Uncle Howard wanted me to tell you how much he loves and respects you."

Daniel was struck first by the use of the present tense and then by the weight of the statement, which coming out of far left field as it had, left Daniel feeling like the wind had been knocked out of him. He drew an extra deep breath and tried to regain his equilibrium. "I'm sorry, Herb," he managed to spit out and Herb understood fully.

"It's alright, take your time, son." The paternal tone and pure decency evident in his voice lapped another wave of emotion over Daniel as he struggled to compose himself.

"Want me to call back," he added.

"No, no, I'm alright the whole thing just kind of caught me off guard."

"Well, there is one other bit of information I am duty bound to share with you, Daniel."

"And what would that be?"

Herb seemed to wait a few seconds for effect and then he sprung. "Your Uncle Howard left you some money."

"Money, shit Herb I don't want his money."

"It's $163,000 and you really don't have a choice in the matter."

The sum seemed surreal, and Daniel, the master of lowered material expectations still somehow found the whole thing offensive. "I don't care, Herb. I don't want his money."

"Don't be a damned fool, son. The man loves you and wants you to have it" "He knows you never had much and he relished the thought that he could do this for you. Don't deny the man his pleasure."

It was still unsettling the way he referred to Howard as if he were still around, but as the emotion dissipated, Daniel knew that it was right and good that he take the money. He had passed the "first impulse test" and trumped greed with a higher sentiment and so could in good conscience accept the money for the gift that it was.

"You still there, Daniel?" Herb queried as the silence had lasted a little too long.

"Yes, Herb, I'm here. What can I say but thank you for both gifts, and I'll be sure to thank Howard just in case."

"It's good, son. It's all good. Your Uncle was right about you, you're an exceptional young man."

"Well, I don't know about that," Daniel said, embarrassed by the kind words.

"Listen, you put the money *and* the love to good use, Daniel, I know you will"

"I'll do my best, and thanks again, Herb."

"Anytime, son. The pleasure was all mine. Goodbye, Daniel."

"Goodbye, Herb. Herb—" Daniel rushed his name before he had time to hang up. "There is one last thing."

"What's that, Daniel?"

"Did Howard leave anything to my mother?"

Now it was Herb who was responsible for the extended silence. "Well, I do have a couple of personal items I have to box up and send to her," he answered finally.

"She's a ward of the state, Daniel," he added reluctantly, as if this might be news to Daniel. "I think Howard figured that anything of value she would inherit would end up in their coffers."

"I guess that makes sense," Daniel replied softly. "Anyway, I appreciate all you've done for Howard, Herb. You take care of yourself."

"You do the same, son."

The line went dead, and Daniel fell back upon the couch to gather his thoughts.

"You know, Golda, the world can be a right good place," he said to the guinea pig rustling around in her cedar shavings and paying rapt attention to her benefactor. It had been a gift that Daniel didn't know quite what to do with and had come by its moniker when it drew blood from Daniel's earlobe while sitting on his shoulder. "My ear, my ear," he had cried at the sight of the crimson globule and its name was a foregone conclusion. Howard's friend, Mark had a particular fondness for the little rodent.

He replayed the "right good place "comment he had just made again and again not because it was deep or profound or even true for that matter but rather because it was so uncharacteristic for him to confer such a positive sentiment on humanity in general. "An exceptional young man indeed," he barked with a laugh tinged with irony. "As the saying goes, Golda, my dear, It's all in the eye of the beholder."

The image of Howard prostrate in that bargain basement coffin with a few too many coats of polyurethane, hands folded across his stomach and all his beloved books surrounding him like so much packing material and still, so still that it seemed like time stopped, moved at a snail's pace across his mind's eye. A tear rolled slowly down his cheek and Golda watched intently feeling the same way she always felt in moments like this, sad for her friend and maddeningly frustrated by her inability to help.

Chapter 12

Daniel had heard the horror stories of the forlorn lottery winners who had managed to squander their fortunes in almost as little time as they had acquired them, and although he suspected that good old fashioned jealousy might have been at the root of some of the cautionary tales, he did concede that it could happen and vowed to act accordingly. At least his good fortune was not splashed all over the newspapers as was the case of the lottery winners, he thought to himself as he turned into the parking lot of the bank. No wonder long lost friends and relations approaching double digits in the "removed" category start coming out of the wood work, his train of thought continued. Who needs that shit? "Come to think of it, maybe I do!" he proclaimed under his breath with a gallows laugh as he leaned in with his thigh to force the car door shut.

Having arranged for the money to be wired directly into his checking account, he headed directly for the ATM to confirm that the transaction had been completed before proceeding inside to reconfigure his accounts. The last thing he wanted was to find himself stammering about how he expected to extract thousands from an account that struggled mightily to inhabit the hundreds column. He punched in the pin number, instructed the gizmo to fork over twenty dollars in "quick cash" and stood spellbound as the machine buzzed, clicked and whirred its mechanical symphony before finally giving of its bounty. Daniel grabbed the bill, stuffed it hurriedly in his pocket and pressed the "No I don't want another transaction" button with a little extra oomph as the anticipation mounted.

As Daniel rocked back and forth and imagined himself whistling nonchalantly on the one hand and taking a sledgehammer to the machine to extract a confession on the other, it occurred to him that he had always kind of appreciated the lightness of the numbers on the receipt because the paltry remaining balance was not something he relished viewing too easily, and he applied the same logic to those customers that stood behind him on occasion awaiting their turn. This time, he found himself hoping that the toner cartridge had just been replaced and he wouldn't have been all too upset to find an overly curious customer standing in line behind him.

Finally, he caught the first glance of the rectangular slip and in his excitement, grabbed a hold of it and yanked it out, seemingly stretching it like a piece of taffy.

It read;
Date: 5/1/2003
Account # XXXXXXXX2417
Time of transaction: 11:47 AM
Remaining Balance: $163,217

He was stunned! Even though he had every reason to think it would say exactly what it did, it nevertheless was an excruciatingly novel sight to behold. He was suddenly glad that there was no one in the immediate vicinity, and in his giddiness, he shook his head in a comical almost cartoon like manner before neatly pressing the receipt between the pages of *The Grapes of Wrath* as if it were a delicate rose being enshrined for posterity in a scrapbook after a first prom.

Though stoic to the naked eye, Daniel felt buoyant on the inside as he pushed open the glass doors to the bank with the swagger of a gunslinger disdainfully parting the barroom doors. There was a definite bounce in his step, but he made a point of forcing the whole of his foot to make contact with the tile floor so as not to draw undue attention. He found himself thinking about the Viagra commercial where *all* of the fellow's coworkers sensed a change had taken place but couldn't quite put a finger on just what it was. "From limp noodle to Yankee Doodle and all because of a little white tablet, it truly is better living through chemistry," he chuckled to himself as he dutifully stood in the line of two for his turn at the teller.

"Hello, Joan," he said nonchalantly, and she smiled and asked what she could do for him. "Well, I'm planning a little trip and I need some cash."

"How much would you like?" she asked in her usual upbeat manner.

"Hmmm, let's see, oh how about fifteen thousand dollars and let me have ten thousand in twenties and five thousand in fifties. I believe that would be five hundred of the former and one hundred of the latter."

Joan looked a little flustered to begin with, and then a big old grin began to work its way across her face. "You devil," she said as she shook her finger at him in a playful manner.

Daniel maintained his composure, but his impassive demeanor seemed to provoke an even greater spasm of laughter. He was known to the tellers as the "quiet man," a tad odd but in no way offensive, everyone and no one knew him. He was always polite but had very little to say, and he was dubbed as a nickel and dimer in the parlance of the tellers, which translated to little in, little out. The incongruity of his all of a sudden demonstrating a comic side threw her into a tizzy, so much so that it caught the attention of the other tellers. Joan tried to get a handle on it but couldn't stifle the giggles that kept slipping out. She punched up Daniel's account to see how much he might really take and stopped so abruptly that it drew even more attention from her coworkers.

"Jesus H. Christ, Daniel, what'd you do win the lottery or something?" she blurted out, and the others immediately began typing furiously to see for themselves.

"It was a gift," he said with an unintended air of mystery and left it at that. "You know, I think I'll put forty thousand dollars in a thirty-six-month CD," he added casually after glancing over at the promotion board announcing the banks assorted financial instruments. "Can you help me with that?"

"Sure, Daniel, yes I can," she replied as she began to execute the transactions in a very business like manner.

As he waited, he took the time to really look around the bank, the cash cathedral, as he fancied it. He found himself instinctively looking to the ceiling but it was the absence of Zeus and Europa that informed him of why he had looked in the first place. It was another target of the ferocity dispensed by Anders in *Bullet in the Brain,* a delicious morsel of creativity penned by Tobias Wolff that Daniel had always thought had all the elements of a beautifully crafted short story. And as his vision returned to the matter at hand, he noticed the tellers' heads turning to their work and away from the curious sight of Daniel Cassat, magnate. He thought about how anonymous he'd always been and how all of a sudden he was the cause célèbre. "Is that a wad of bills in your pocket or are you just happy to see me?" He imagined the talk at break time and wondered to himself if Jesus actually had a middle name and if it really began with an "H."

Joan returned with a zippered canvas bag with the bank logo emblazoned on the side. The way Daniel nodded his approval gave the transaction the feeling of a stick up as she began shoveling the crisp rectangles with the tight red bands into the bag, carefully showing Daniel so that he could count along with her. She set it on the counter just as the Certificate of Deposit documentation was delivered for his signature and after quickly penning his John Hancock, he turned to thank Joan for the service but she spoke before he could.

"Daniel," she started slowly and deliberately, searching for just the right words, "I'm really sorry, I honestly wasn't laughing at you."

"Don't worry about it," replied. "I would have been as surprised as you. I mean let's be honest, no one ever mistook me for Bill Gates before so you can be forgiven for not doing so now. Besides, you know how things have a way of getting back where they started, kind of like water seeking its own level," he added with a touch of fatalism, the lottery losers no doubt lurking in his psyche.

It suddenly occurred to Joan that that single sentence contained more words than the sum total of all the others

Daniel had uttered in all of their previous encounters. The implication of the comment got by her, but the tone was reassuring and she smiled an embarrassed smile of appreciation.

Daniel turned and headed for the door. He passed the beefy bank manager and resident financial advisor putting the squeeze on a middle - aged couple and explaining that over the long haul, the market is the place to be and questioning them regarding their tolerance for risk. He thought to himself as he smiled sweetly on the way by, **get a fucking job!**

Chapter 13

Dunkleberger's was to Cabela's what Mini-Me was to Dr. Evil, a small scale version of the much bigger prototype, or so Daniel thought. Drawn in initially by the unusual name, it had become one of a number of haunts that he patronized periodically, traveling in a circuitous route to stagger his visits lest it appear to the sales clerks that he really had nowhere else to go.

Everything about the place suggested grand adventure: canoes and kayaks, screaming orange attire for when you wanted to be seen, and woodsy camouflage for when you didn't; a vast array of camping and hiking equipment, and an arsenal of firearms that would have made Charlton Heston proud.

It was customary for Daniel to make a token purchase, a pair of thick wool socks or a key chain with a little compass affixed to the end, a modest contribution made in the same spirit as a donation to the basket passed around at church and presumably for the same reason, as a small measure of voluntary compensation for an uplifting experience. But this day was different. This day Daniel had a purpose, and as he ambled through the aisles, he got to feeling a bit like old Huck, and he couldn't help but imagine himself sitting on a log in the pale moonlight, serenading the unseen creatures of the night with a plaintive tune on his harmonica while the wise old owl in the tree behind him hummed along.

"Can I help you with anything?" the inquiry from the appropriately ruddy faced clerk startled Daniel from his reverie. Daniel checked his list against the contents of his cart. He had the sleeping bag, the lantern, tent, Coleman stove and cooler.

"Yea, as a matter of fact you can," he replied. "I haven't come across canteens in my travels. I assume you've got them.

"Far end of aisle three, bottom shelf," he instructed in the no nonsense voice of a man accustomed to surviving on berries and bark in the wilderness. "Anything else?"

"No, thanks," Daniel replied, too embarrassed to ask if they sold harmonicas.

Daniel's big idea was not a new one. It had been on "lay away" for quite some time along with a number of others whose execution was rendered inoperable by the very same missing ingredient, money. And even though the sum that has come into my possession is not going to land me on the cover of "Fortune 500", he calculated, it can buy that most ethereal phenomenon, freedom. He felt a jolt of excitement and a measure of relief as he knelt down in aisle three to peruse the canteens, at the prospect of not having to spend a good percentage of his waking hours engaged in mindless drudgery simply to procure the basic necessities of life. It will give me some breathing room, he thought relishing the opportunity to try to get at some of the vexing problems that had plagued him for years.

Daniel acknowledged that although the sum constituted a king's ransom in his relative world of scarcity and abundance, it was nevertheless a finite number, and at some point the well would run dry. Still, he figured he couldn't help but be better equipped to have at it all over again when that time came and since he had vowed never to be so foolish as those lottery lunkheads, that could be quite some time.

In the meantime, he thought, I'm gonna make the most of Uncle Howard's parting gift, dust off that dormant impulse and do my own version of Steinbeck's *Travels with Charley*. Daniel glanced down at his mini-compass and tracked true north, which it just so happened would deposit him right smack in the middle of the checkout counter. As he navigated his way past the rods and reels and the hip boots, he decided that he would dub his journey "Travels with Golda" and even as he laughed to himself, a part of him couldn't wait to share the news with his little amigo. Unlike Steinbeck, Daniel didn't know exactly what he'd be looking for, but he had a feeling it would be kind of like that judge that couldn't define pornography; he would know it when he saw it.

Daniel had to back into the counter area as his tent was cantilevered out across the bow of the cart like a menacing spear, but he maneuvered it deftly and no injuries were sustained.

"With you in a jiffy, friend," the clerk proclaimed in a distracted voice as he tended to a matter made private by virtue of his not having turned around.

Daniel felt a twinge of irritation. Hey, if you're gonna call me friend at least look me in the face, he scolded the fellow silently. After a quick survey of his cart, Daniel was satisfied that he had procured all that he'd intended and he turned his attention to a "Prevent Defense" first aid kit next to the cash register that had caught his eye as he approached the counter.

You never know, he thought to himself as he pored over the laundry list of items jammed into the kit with the picture of the football player with the red cross on his helmet.

"Are you a hunter?" the clerk asked finally with an air of joviality as he stepped over to ring up the sale.

"No."

"A fisherman?"

"No."

"Just gonna spend some time in the great outdoors, huh."

"Daniel paused for a moment. "That, I do intend to do."

The clerk smiled with satisfaction at his powers of observation as the phrase "No shit, Sherlock" popped into Daniel's head. "Well, you enjoy yourself" he added as he completed the transaction.

Daniel grabbed half the gear and headed out knowing he had exceeded the "12-minute courtesy parking" and was only slightly concerned with the three-dollar ticket he might have earned, what with his new found wealth and all. He loaded the gear into the back of his 1989 Chevy Cavalier and headed back in for the balance. The clerk stepped ahead of him and held the door smiling.

"Vagabond," Daniel said obliquely. "Excuse me." "It just occurred to me that vagabond fits the bill as well as anything else."

The clerk looked confused and offered kind of a half smile in parting. Daniel smiled back and moved on.

Chapter 14

Daniel was of two minds as he puttered along in his terminal Chevy Cavalier. On the one hand, there was a palpable excitement fluttering through him as he headed for the "strip" to acquire a set of wheels more suited to a man of his means. And on the other, his was a heart made heavy by that very same act. It's doing would instantly render the trusty old workhorse obsolete, leaving euthanasia as the almost certain fate. "They shoot horses. Don't they?" popped into his head as he watched an ashen Red Buttons whirling like a desperate Dervish dying to grab the brass ring. Perhaps they make exceptions for the especially speedy stallion whose loins contain the seeds of future success, he mused, but this old horse would likely end up being fast tracked to the glue factory. As he sighed at the prospect of the inevitable, a last gasp flash occurred to Daniel that there might be another way, that some spunky high school kid with a knack for the metal and gears might salvage her for participation in a demolition derby, but the thought somehow sickened him as he likened it to the ignominious end suffered by Mountain Rivera.

The "strip" or the AUTO MILE as it was commonly referred to, covered pretty much all the bases when it came to filling your automotive needs. Like an international bazaar, a large number of nations hawked their wares, along this great white way, everything from the sublime to the ridiculous.

Daniel shook his head in amazement as he rolled past the flapping flags, the blinking lights and those signs—some exuded such cock-sureness that they were simply a logo set on a majestic nature scene. Most suggested that life would be infinitely better in their particular model, while some of the lower end name plates lacking that intrinsic gravitas tried the circus barker approach to luring prospective customers. "Where your satisfaction is automatic even if you're shiftless" grabbed Daniel's attention just before he locked eyes with a shiny new midnight blue Corvette that had him momentarily straddling lanes.

The notion of the carefree highway had got in Daniel's blood and good and as he neared the dealership he'd scoped out beforehand, his mind wandered back to a certain television series that had mesmerized him as a kid. "Get your kicks on route 66." He could suddenly hear the song in his head and the reaction was visceral. The show had seemed to offer unlimited possibilities for excitement and adventure, but most importantly, it had represented a ticket out. Like a giant balm, it had soothed the ache of the heart as he imagined himself buddying up with another cool customer and heading from town to town, horizon to horizon, anywhere for that matter other than the bleak and painful circumstance that was his life. When the show was over and the credits were rolling, he recalled, he would sit, still staring at the TV, oblivious to the new images, still relishing the thought of motoring on up and out to that "dee luxe adventure in the ski-hi-hi."

To this day, that sensation would reprise itself from time to time and leave him in the throes of that great yearning, but it had always been extinguished by the unavoidable acknowledgement of his limited means. To allay his disappointment, he would imagine the cool customer ending up broke and having to suffer the indignity of another shitty job for little money and less respect, lonely and depressed in a strange town. But thanks to Uncle Howard, things had changed. If I bag the cool part and temper the expectation of grand adventure, he thought as the excitement pushed the sad thoughts of his Cavalier to the background, there's nothing to stop me from expanding my horizons and who knows what could happen. He had, however, grudgingly eschewed the Corvette for something a little more practical. Maybe I'll make it my mission to prove that you **can** be cool in a Volvo.

"Buy a Volvo. They're boxy but they're good," or something to that effect was the way the mock commercial went in a movie some years ago about turning the advertising industry on its head. Well, no more, Daniel thought to himself as he pulled into the Volvo dealership. Someone apparently decided that Volvos could be pretty damn snazzy looking too. Brains *and* beauty, great concept! Daniel exited the Cavalier trying to stifle his enthusiasm and get his game face on in preparation for what he imagined could be protracted negotiations. Always a window shopper of necessity, he relished no longer having to console himself with the thought that he had "good taste" even if he lacked the means to close the deal. As the moments dragged on and nary a salesman made his way over to offer assistance, Daniel wondered if something about himself didn't scream exactly that. Finally, they could ignore him no longer.

"Can I help you?" The dapper Dan had sidled up as if it was his duty to give a few moments of his precious time to the needy.

"Well, maybe you can," Daniel answered guardedly. "I'd like some information on the XC70." Now, Daniel was not a tiger, nor was he apt to be a terribly effective haggler, but he knew that knowledge was power, and he had taken the time to ascertain not only the dealer cost of the automobile in question but what he should expect to pay for the car outfitted every which way from Tuesday with the various optional appendages.

"What exactly would you like to know?" the dapper one said with a slightly condescending air.

Daniel glanced furtively at his crib sheet, drew a deep breath and pounced. "For starters, why is it exactly that option packages 000142, B9XX, 000446, 000399, MC295, 000322 and 000319 all require TMP006?"

He had thoroughly scanned the packages in the literature and been struck by the fact that the majority of them seemed inextricably linked to the mysterious TMP006. He had figured it had to be at the very least the master chip, the brain from which all manner of information was imparted down the neural pathways to coordinate literally thousands of functions simultaneously. Reading on, he'd been dumfounded to learn that TMP006 was of all things a power glass moon roof.

"Frankly, I can't make sense of the connection," he added, never mentioning the word "moon roof" in a tacit challenge of the salesman's familiarity with the product line. Daniel had thrown down the gauntlet and was anxiously awaiting the response. He suspected that he had taken the salesman to school, that the poor chap's memory - banks would register insufficient funds and that he would be tongue tied at best.

"It doesn't make much sense does it?" he answered with disarming honesty. And he followed that revelation with yet another morsel of unabashed transparency. "They do these things in an obvious attempt to steer you toward the value added extras because that's where the real margins are, and schmucks like me have to try to pass it off with a straight face by concocting some tortured logic to explain it. Well I just can't do it. Look, I'm as much a company guy as anyone and I do believe that these are great cars but I hate to insult people and compromise my credibility in one fell swoop."

Daniel hesitated for a millisecond, thinking that this too was part of the shtick, the honest approach, the "I'm really on your side" approach but he passed on the cynical speculation and took to lashing himself for having created this scenario before he even entered the showroom. As he was wont to do, he marveled once again at the powers of projection and doubted that there had been any condescension at all or any reason for the extra time it seemed to take to approach him other than that everyone was busy.

"Yeah, well I appreciate your frankness," Daniel finally replied trying to mask the turmoil swirling around inside him. "By the way, my name is Daniel and yours is?"

"Joe, Joe Haney."

"Well Joe, as you might have guessed, I have more than a passing interest in the car," Daniel said, still feeling kind of sheepish.

"I got that impression," Joe replied with a bit of a grin."

"It's a "Custer" decision," Daniel said distractedly as he turned his gaze to the object of his desire.

"Little Big Man," Joe added without further explanation and the two shared a moment.

Daniel felt suddenly uncomfortable and found it odd that his mind wandered back to his prior conversation with Golda. "The world can be a right good place." The two hunkered down to some serious planning and specked the vehicle that satisfied all of Daniel's desires, capping off the creature comforts and the various high tech conveniences with Daniel's "must haves," a Global Positioning System and a Lo-Jack type car retrieval chip. When the matter of the trade - in was raised, Joe took one look at the Cavalier and got a pained look on his face. Daniel expected the offer to be little more than condolences, but Joe simply said, "It will be whatever the book says but don't expect much," prompting no argument from Daniel. After determining that there was indeed a car that fit the bill to be had on the lot, Joe headed back to his cubicle to work up a final tally, telling Daniel as he left that he would do the best he could for him. Daniel for his part believed him, which was no small feat, and was comforted by the realization.

Joe returned in short order with the paperwork awaiting Daniel's blessing and signature. Insofar as Daniel could tell, Joe had been true to his word regarding both the new and the old, and following a handshake to seal the deal and affixing his signature to a seemingly endless succession documents, Daniel pulled out his tattered plastic checkbook and proceeded to write a check for more money than he had ever even had in his life prior to the inheritance. Joe accepted it graciously without question, further strengthening the bond between them, and the two agreed to rendezvous in forty-five minutes down at "detailing" for the official unveiling. He took the check and the paperwork for processing back to his manager, whom having caught sight of Daniel promptly chose to forego the usual electronic means of check verification and put in a call directly to the bank.

Daniel went to spend a solemn last hour with the Cavalier, removing what was necessary and saying his goodbyes. He was grateful for the opportunity to tell his old compadre how important their relationship had been to him, and he was ever so patient and gentle as he emptied the glove compartment and tugged on the cushions in search of loose change and whatever other valuable paraphernalia he might turn up. Finally, he drove over to the point of delivery to unload the recently acquired camping gear and set it out next to where his new wheels would be rolled out. He grabbed a Phillips-head screwdriver and slowly removed the license plate. It happened very quickly and there seemed to have been very little pain. That's the way to go, Daniel thought to himself, followed by, we should all be so lucky, followed by, I'm fucking nuts!

Before long, out it came, still sporting beads of water from its cleansing that seemed to languish in the sunlight before reluctantly falling prey to gravity. Daniel was mesmerized in spite of himself and had a vision of a salty bead of sweat sliding slowly down the very tan back of a bikini clad beauty on an exotic beach. "It's all good, son," and for a few brief shining moments, it actually was.

Daniel circled the car ceremoniously a number of times before kneeling down to install the license plate. Joe, who was accustomed to making congratulatory pronouncements at this point in the process, sensed that that wasn't called for here. He gave Daniel his orientation in a very deliberate manner and offered his hand one last time to conclude the encounter. Daniel took it with gusto, looked Joe square in the eye and said simply, "Thank you." Joe watched as Daniel backed up to aim his new wheels in the general direction of destiny. As he pulled out, Joe was puzzled as he noticed the vanity plate tucked into the back bumper. It read "**BOURGLAY**."

Chapter 15

"Slow down, Golda. "Christ, you're gonna get indigestion!" he commented sharply as Golda snacked furiously on a piece of lettuce in her cage. She gave him a kind of "What you talkin' bout, Willis?" look and resumed the assault.

Daniel went back to punching numbers into the calculator, looking up occasionally at the boxes, suitcases and travel bags situated near the door. He was seized by a sudden spate of fondness for his humble abode but would have none of it.

"Hey, you gonna look after the place for me while I'm gone? he asked Golda, who paid him little mind. Finally, as if the anticipation was killing her, he blurted out, "I'm just kidding, of course you can go. We're a team, me and you, and where I go, you go." Just to be sure, he leaned down over the glass cage and followed up, "Got it? Good, now don't you forget it." Daniel sat back down, pulled up the paper that had been spit out the back of the calculator and perused it like an old time stock ticker. Apparently satisfied with the figures, he transferred them to a check and headed downstairs to set things straight with his landlady. She arrived at the door after a single knock as if she had anticipated the visit.

"Well, praise Jesus, hello, Daniel," she said with genuine enthusiasm. "Won't you come in?"

Daniel entered her musty domicile with his usual preemptive phrase, "Well, I've only got a few minutes," knowing that getting in was a hell of a lot easier than getting out. He did like Arletta. She was the only person he knew who spent more time alone than he did and he'd never heard a word of complaint from her. Besides, she would argue that she was never alone because Jesus was always with her. "I've got something I need to tell you, Arletta. I'm going away for a while," he said abruptly, instantly wishing he had kind if eased into it.

The news seemed to catch her off guard but she quickly bore through a collage of emotions and gathered her equilibrium.

"But we just renewed your lease last month."

He sensed that he had indeed surprised her, but he knew that her comment about the lease had nothing at all to do with money matters. Financial concerns had never been any kind of an issue with her; his, hers or anyone else's for that matter. To her way of thinking, if you had your health and of course your faith, you were in possession of great wealth, end of story. In spite of his rather Spartan lifestyle, it never would have occurred to her to question whether or not he had the means to undertake such a venture.

"And where might you be going, Daniel?" she added finally.

"Well, there are some people I want to see and I just felt like it was time to seize the moment and go do it." Technically, that was true. There were any number of people he would like to see, Benjamin Franklin and Bridget Bardot for instance, and his parsing words enabled him to tell the truth while not having to admit that he didn't have the faintest fucking idea where he was going or whom he might see along the way. He'd always tried not to lie to Arletta. She had gotten the notion early on that he was in her camp, so to speak, and he could never bring himself to tell her that it wasn't quite accurate. Whenever she ascribed the hand of God to any event, he nodded in agreement because, he argued, he couldn't disprove it anyway. And if he happened to pick up a biblical reference from any source, he always managed to work it into their conversations because he loved to see the fire in her eyes when he did even though he felt a bit like a fraud after having done it.

"I don't know how long I'll be gone so I've written you a check for eleven months' rent so that neither one of us has to think about it until next year."

"I do thank you, Daniel but it's really not necessary. You know I trust you."

I know you do, Arletta, and I appreciate that very much, but I don't want to have to worry about it, and this is the easiest way."

"Well, you be careful on your...," and without finishing the thought, she turned suddenly and walked across the room to a closet by the stairs. With a lift, a tug and a jiggle, she pried the barely closed door free and pulled it toward her slowly as if she expected an avalanche to come crashing down upon her. Not sure what to do, Daniel further committed himself and took a few steps into the room. He noticed the picture on the mantle that had grabbed his attention the first day he ever set foot in the place to inquire about the apartment. It was a young Arletta, but not a staid and proper version as he would have expected, but the vision of a surprisingly beautiful young woman all glammed up and striking an almost provocative pose with a kind of an alluring come hither look. Noticing that he had noticed, she had said simply, "That was another lifetime," and left it at that. The wrenching sound of a swollen, old cockeyed door being forced into a space built for a thinner plumb and square version distracted Daniel, and he was about to come to her aid when she managed with the help of a well placed shoulder to get it closed.

"You take this with you. It will ease my mind," she said earnestly as she handed him a small statue of Saint Christopher.

"Why, thank you very much, Arletta. I will cherish it and think of you each time I look at it."

She lowered her head in accepting his gratitude, and he felt a deep wave of affection for her. Daniel felt a small lump welling up in his throat, and that was his cue.

"Thanks again, Arletta and I wish you nothing but good things," he offered in lieu of stating outright that he wished that there had been more people like her around when he was young and vulnerable and in the midst of people that could smell fear better than any dog.

"I guess all I can say is goodbye and good luck, Daniel."

He seized the opportunity and quickly replied, "How about, vaya con Dios?" His last image of Arletta was with a taut jaw and a roaring fire in her eyes almost saluting him as he bid her farewell.

Chapter 16

"Hi, Irene, it's Daniel. Is Art around?" Daniel queried with the little hitch in his throat that turned up most times he mentioned his boss's name.

"He's upstairs in 'couches' showing a young couple around. Anything I can help you with?"

"Well I need to talk to him. Do you know what he's got going the rest of the afternoon?"

"I don't think so but just a minute, let me snoop around his desk a bit," she answered with a chuckle as she stepped away from the phone. "Daniel, I don't see anything on or around his calendar but I can get him for you if you'd like."

Daniel nixed that idea in a millisecond. The last thing he wanted was twenty questions about why it was so damn important to see him right away. "You know what, Irene. Just tell him that I'll be over in twenty to thirty minutes unless he calls or has you call to tell me he's got something else he has to be doing at that time."

"Will do!"

"Thanks, Irene."

"My pleasure. You behave now," she replied, concluding the conversation with her pet phrase and as always sounding like she'd like nothing better than to do anything but.

Art and Daniel had always had a symbiotic relationship. Daniel needed work and Art needed at least one steady and reliable delivery guy who underestimated his value and was thus unlikely to use the leverage that he seemed completely unaware of to press for more money or better benefits. Their interactions were generally cordial but there was always that underlying potential for conflict should Daniel realize how good a hand he actually had.

Daniel tapped some of the nervous energy surging through him and leapt up onto the loading dock with the grace of a hurdler before making his way into the bowels of the building where Art's office was located. It was nicely furnished, if a bit eclectic and upon closer inspection, one could see that each piece had a pretty serious flaw that would have made it tough to move even at heavily discounted prices.

"So what's up?" Art asked with an air of forced casualness while leaning back precariously in his chair.

"Well, Art, I'm here to give you my notice," Daniel answered not fully aware of the fact that he held all the cards now. "I'll give you the full two weeks if you need it but I'd like to leave as soon as possible."

"You're leaving, where the hell are you going?" Art asked angrily, knowing that Daniel held all the cards now and regretting the tone he had taken for that reason. "Look, if it's more money you want, it's not in the cards," Art added with his best poker face on knowing full well that if Daniel forced the issue, he'd acquiesce.

"It's not money. I don't need the money," Daniel replied, already having decided that if the issue came up, it would be strictly name, rank and serial number.

"Oh you don't need the money, huh. Tell me something Daniel, how's that Cavalier running, and when was the last time you bought yourself a new pair of shoes?" Art spewed with malice knowing that his ace in the hole had been neutralized somehow and pissed that he had no idea how.

Daniels blood came to a slow boil as he realized that the whole equation and for that matter their whole relationship had degenerated into *this*, Art's hissy fit because he might be inconvenienced for a time. Daniel doesn't do anger well. For him it's like a door into Dante's Inferno and it's a place that he is loathe to go but he does have his honor and in spite of his fear that he'll squeal like a stuck pig, he forced himself to speak his piece. "You know Art", he started, disregarding his sweaty palms and the uncontrollable trembling of his upper lip. "I came here to do right by you. It just so happens I don't need this fucking job, and I could have simply blown you off and never shown up again. I don't know that you've been overly generous with me or even fair for Christ's sakes but you gave me a job and for that I am grateful, so I felt like it was my duty," he finished with a strong voice in spite of the atrial fibrillation.

Art was taken aback by a side of Daniel he'd never seen before and he knew there was no fighting the inevitable. "Shit, Daniel, I'm sorry for the tone I took. You've been a good employee, reliable as hell, and that's been a luxury I'm not accustomed to having. Things have been tough. The economy is in the toilet, and sales are down. Truth be told, I was going to lay off the new kid this week. I guess I won't have to now," he ended with a smile that Daniel didn't bother to reciprocate.

Some of the tension had gone out of the air, but the truth had been laid bare and Daniel couldn't muster up much sympathy for the man. "So, you're set then and you won't need me anymore."

"I guess you could say that," Art responded flatly. "You've got three or four days pay coming. You want me to send it to you?" he added.

Daniel felt like saying "Fuck you, send it right up your ass," but something wholly different popped out. "I want you to put it in Curt's pay and tell him it's a performance bonus. With a little bit of effort on your part, you might have better luck with your employees," Daniel said, finally understanding that he had nothing to lose."

Art kind of looked away instinctively as if eye contact might have reignited the enmity.

"I'll be going then," Daniel said abruptly.

"Good luck to you." Art said halfheartedly.

"Yeah, you too," Daniel replied equaling Art's enthusiasm and out the door he went. Whenever Daniel got riled emotionally, he had a strong urge to be alone, to sort through the inner chaos that ensued, and he was headed in just that direction when he ran into Curt, sucking down a cigarette on the loading dock. Shit, he thought to himself, here we go again.

"Hello, Curt," Daniel said trying to sound calm even though he was still pretty charged up.

"Hey, Braniac, how the hell are ya?" Curt replied in his own inimitable style.

"I don't have much time so I'll get right to it. I resigned today. I'm going away for a while."

"No shit, where ya going?"

Daniel hesitated for a moment while he concocted this particular version of his intentions. "I've got a sick uncle in Alabama that needs some help managing his business until he recovers."

"Will you be coming back?" Curt asked as if he really cared.

"Well, not if I can help it," Daniel answered, allowing himself a little laugh.

"Hmmm, oh well, anyway good luck to you." He paused for a second. "So I guess Jimmy will be sticking around after all."

"Looks that way," Daniel replied, a little surprised that Art had tipped his hand. "I think he'll do alright. You show him the way, Curt." Daniel snatched one last panoramic view of the premises that he'd spent countless numbers of hours in and around. "Well, you hang in there, Curt," he offered with finality, anxious to close this chapter.

Daniel started to exit stage left and turned his trunk toward the parking lot to signal that he was heading out when Curt stuck out his hand. Daniel took it and was more than a little bit surprised when Curt held on for longer than the proscribed amount of time for a relationship of this nature.

"Daniel, I knew you wouldn't stick around. I always thought you were too smart for this kind of work and even though I probably never really acted like it, I enjoyed the hell out of working with you." Curt said, clearly embarrassed by the show of affection, but he was on a roll and not done yet. "I mean, you're different and all, but I respected that you weren't like the other knuckleheads that have passed through here."

Daniel, too, was embarrassed and even more surprised by this turn of events and found himself at a loss for words. The silence hung thick, and Daniel figured it was his turn so he started his mouth moving hoping that what came out wasn't too asinine.

"Uh, gees, thanks Curt. I've enjoyed it as well, I mean, we ran a pretty tight ship and we had some laughs." Fuck it, Daniel cursed to himself. He hated few things more than the sound of his own stammering. Usually it was anger that tied his tongue but now and then this kind of thing snuck up on him, but he got his bearings and looked Curt in the eye. "Curt, those were kind if unexpected words and I want to thank you sincerely for having the courage to share them with me. I think people let too many opportunities go by to convey those kinds of things and they usually regret it. Well, we won't have to now, will we." Daniel had found his sweet spot, the one that you can locate only by not trying to, it would pass quickly enough but it was always good while it lasted.

"See, what'd I tell you, you are one smart bastard," Curt exclaimed, reverting to the hyper mode that Daniel was more accustomed to, but the deed had been done and they were both the better for it.

"Goodbye, Curt, take good care of yourself."

"Yeah, Daniel, you do the same."

Daniel completed the pirouette he had started some number of minutes ago, and with one last wave, headed for the parking lot.

The smooth hum of the XC70 caught Art's attention, and he watched and wondered as Daniel segued on out of his lot—and life.

Chapter 17

There's something about the smell of early evening, he thought to himself as he scaled the exterior steps for what seemed like the thousandth time. It would be two more trips up and down toting his assorted baggage to the car before he would connect the dots and realize that it wasn't simply the sweet air he was enjoying but the scents of new life emanating from the trees and shrubs coming out of hibernation and preparing to further encroach on the stairway. Arletta's handiwork, he mused, and a reflection of her love for all living things. Daniel himself had trimmed the foliage back last fall just as he had mowed her lawn and brought her paper in from the road and deposited it on her stoop, never saying a word when she raved about the service provided by the papergirl.

The more errands he recalled performing for her, the more concerned he became about how well she'd be able to manage without him. He stopped on the seventh step to fret on the matter and began to suspect that that the scared little boy in him was likely looking for an out, an excuse to nix the whole crazy idea and stick to the safe and familiar, the tried and true. Aw hell, she'll be fine. He scoffed as he resumed his descent. She's a strong and resourceful woman. I wouldn't be a bit surprised if she didn't have Jesus himself mowing her lawn, he opined with a laugh as he heaved the psychic yoke over the rail.

Daniel beamed with an air of satisfaction as the best laid plan had in fact turned out pretty much the way he had drawn it up. The phalanx of the eclectic grouping of packing containers had been organized in such a way as to leave a space big enough for him to stretch out comfortably with the back seat folded down. He tucked the last couple of items into the few remaining nooks and crannies and was pleased to find that there was a slot that appeared to have been custom fitted for his last entry, the "Prevent Defense" first aid kit. There was something compelling about that strange little picture of the football player with the red cross on his helmet he thought to himself as he headed back up to the apartment to go over the details one last time.

"Did you ever notice that no matter how well you plan, there's always that certain something that gets left behind?" Daniel asked Golda who was otherwise engaged at the time. He looked over at her as if he had expected a response and continued anyway. "Well, I've made a list and I'm checking it twice, and you watch, little lady, when we get, oh say, twenty five miles out of town—I do believe the rule is twenty five—all of a sudden that errant item magically pops into your head." Still not a whisper from Golda.

Daniel kept looking around to make sure that he had covered all the bases. The place was as clean as a whistle and the only items that he hadn't packed were the clothes he would wear, the towel he would dry off with after his morning shower and the toiletries he would need for his last hygiene session to gussy up for the brave new world. He finally had to accept the fact that he had been as thorough as he could possibly be and that at this point it was in the hands of fate, which left him with nothing on which to spend the nervous energy that was bubbling up inside him.

He grabbed a caffeine free soda from the fridge, picked up Golda's cage and made his way over to the love seat. He gently set Golda down, flopped and flipped on the TV and began surfing through the channels. As was his custom, he climbed the rungs of programming, and if nothing caught his fancy, he ended up at his default selection, the History Channel. The featured presentation that particular night was "The History of Sex." Ordinarily, it would have been a topic of great interest to Daniel, but on this night, it was just a painful reminder of one more thing that was sorely lacking in his life. "Okay, we got it, people like fucking, always have and always will," he groaned having to concede that he was "people" too. He tried scrolling again in descending order but still got no satisfaction. "What do you say we hit the hay, Golda?" Daniel asked, not really that tired but anxious to move in the direction of morning. He picked up Golda's cage, turned the soothing jazz station on low and headed for the bedroom, making a mental note to have a little talk with the paper girl before he skipped town.

He lay still and found himself thinking about Christmas as a kid, how in spite of the turmoil, it still held the promise of something new and shiny and how he used to go to bed well before he had to for the very same reason he had done it on this night.

Navigating his memory banks in an attempt to forget that he was *trying* to get to sleep was always a perilous endeavor.

95

Invariably he would end up in a place that he would just as soon not have gone, and the odds didn't favor him because *that* side of the ledger had a great many more entries than the other. And if by chance he ended up in one of the "dead zones" as he had come to refer to them, he would make a conscious effort to "switch the channel" to more pleasant recollections. Failing that, he would revert to a technique that he had developed as a teen and had been employing ever since, that of reconstructing in his mind the process by which of any one of a number of the more prominent structures in the world had been built. It was always well beyond his capabilities but that was all the better.

He had started with the great Pyramid of Giza, and over time had tackled the Light House of Alexandria, the Hanging Gardens of Babylon and the Pantheon among others. He was always careful to employ only the technologies that were available at the time and of late had become enamored with skyscrapers and on this night he chose the Empire State Building as the object of his affection. Having decided what would constitute sufficient depth for the foundation to carry a building of that size and scale, he had moved onto the logistical problems posed by the removal of all the excavated earth and stone that would have to be trucked off site. Before he had even settled on the most efficient means of extricating the mass of material from a hole of that magnitude, it occurred to him that he hadn't given any consideration to the water, sewer and power lines that would undoubtedly be fed into the bowels of the behemoth somewhere below ground level. It was the introduction of this vexing set of tasks that put his lights out for good and he slid into a hardscrabble sleep.

It was the one recurring dream that he had, the one that distinguished itself from the jumble of chaotic images that floated through his mind much more often than he was able to recollect. And it always started the same way, walking down a road somewhere in the flatlands of mid-America. The road is the color of the beach but the particles that sparkle in the sun are not sand but pebbles. There are ripe cornfields ready for harvest on either side of the road, and the same thought occurs to him each time he notices the occasional stalks that rise well above the masses surrounding them, Ayn Rand.

He is dressed completely in denim, dark dungarees and a shirt the color of prison issue. Denim, the way it was originally intended, durable, flexible and infinitely adaptable, well before it evolved into a fashion craze. He crosses the Steven's Creek Bridge as is indicated on the cornerstone, stopping midway to toss a small stick into the docile current below and watching it with great fascination until it sails completely out of view. The sun is strong but not oppressive as he continues down the road finally reaching an intersection that seems to appear out of nowhere. He turns right without hesitation and soon finds himself at the gate of the same white pickets staffing the rest of the fence. There is no mystery. He has fully anticipated the destination thus far and it feels good and natural. He is home! And always at this juncture in the dream, his perception is altered slightly. The world appears to his eye as if he is looking through gauze. He has no idea why the shift occurs. Maybe it's just the way a dream is supposed to look, and it takes him a while to figure out that he is actually dreaming.

He heads up the flagstone walk and veers around the side of the old clapboard house to the apple orchard that's nestled between the corn crib and the modest abode. He sits down on the edge of the picnic table and looks out over yet another example of the bounty provided by God's green earth, a vast sea of soybeans swaying almost imperceptibly in the gentle breeze. He pulls out the standard red neckerchief and wipes the salty sweat from his brow. As if on cue, a pretty little girl of five or six delivers a tall glass of iced tea accompanied by a hug. She scurries over and droops her body through the tire swing dangling from the thickest branch of an ancient walnut tree and smiles beatifically at him. He looks over to the porch that extends out from the back of the house and sees a woman, in his mind a beautiful through and through woman and she waves and smiles almost as big as the little girl. He takes a hearty gulp of the tea and through the portion of the glass that's been cleared of the beverage, he can make out the image of a man standing in the living room window. The stranger is tall, balding, and craggy faced and dressed in all black like a preacher or an undertaker. He's got a strap over his shoulder that supports the banjo he's strumming, but Daniel can barely hear it. He moves cautiously toward the window, and the closer he gets, the clearer the sound becomes. The man smiles so big that he seems to be mocking the love beams that had been directed at Daniel just a few minutes prior, and then he starts to sing:

There's a big old hole
in the middle of my soul
and I don't know how to fill it.

There's a pain so deep

I just can't sleep
And I don't know how to kill it.

There's a cracked old mug
filled with my blood
and I fear I'm gonna spill it

In truth, Daniel had largely reconstructed the verses from the snippets — hole, soul, pain so deep, my blood, spill it etc. — that he'd gleaned from his multiple viewings, and with time and repetition he'd convinced himself of their accuracy or that they were at the very least "close enough for government work" as his boss had a habit of saying.

Between each stanza, the stranger smiles that mocking smile and after the third, Daniel rams his fist through the window and grabs a hold of — nothing. He withdraws his crimson arm, which is leaking like a sieve. He turns quickly to check on his fair ladies, but they are nowhere to be seen. There is only the tire swing ticking like an overwrought pendulum surrounded by a great emptiness. The sky, only a few minutes prior bathing the expanse in glorious sunshine, turns gray and foreboding with mean spirited winds on the prowl and dusty swirling currents in search of someone or something to spend their wrath on.

Daniel awoke with such a start that the commotion shook Golda from her stupor. His t-shirt, drenched with sweat, was discarded with such ferocity that it might have been a nest of wasps all simultaneously drilling into his flesh. As Golda watched out for the "incoming" that sailed just over her cage, Daniel sat up on the side of his bed, rubbing his eyes to remove any vestiges of sleep, rose and headed into the kitchen. He had a powerful yen for some iced-tea but settled for the few remaining dribbles of orange juice he was able to squeeze from the carton. He grabbed the pack of Camel Lights from the pocket of the shirt draped over the bedroom door and risked his eyebrows, lighting the thing on the flickering flame of the gas stove. There were rumblings within, and the first deep drag helped to take the edge off. He noticed the music that had been playing all the while as everything was finally slowing down. The alarm had been silenced, and he drew hard on the cigarette and watched as the white cylinder a few inches from his eye got poker hot, creating a red wave that rolled in, leaving only a dull gray ash in its wake.

He looked inward and saw the vastness of space juxtaposed with a scared and lonely little man, sitting by himself in a kitchenette in the middle of the night illuminated as much by a nightlight as the moonlight, and a great sadness overtook him. He heard Golda rustling around in the bedroom and seized on the distraction to defer the ache for a moment. "Of course, you can come out here. What, did you think I'd leave you all by yourself in there while I'm out here having all this fun?" he said in a la – de - da manner that irritated him as soon as he'd heard it. He retrieved his partner and set her on the counter ledge that served as a table and decided that this was a circumstance that warranted a suspension of the "two hours between cigarettes" rule. The two sat in silence for a time, but Golda had a way of getting Daniel to open up, and she waited patiently for the opening salvo.

He looked over at the attentive face of his one true friend and felt a mixture of pity for himself and affection for his little amigo. He reached into the cage, and with great tenderness picked her up and stroked her fur. The emotional fever had run its course, and the aftermath always left him pensive. It's strange how leaving tends to push things toward the heart of the matter, he thought to himself, reflecting on the events of the last few days. Everyone has their routines, a comfortable predictability and yet there's often a kind of "Last Picture Show" quality to it all. His stream of consciousness had found a theme and Daniel continued to mine it. When someone breaks out, it seems to evoke a primal longing in people that you can sense as they bid you farewell, like some kind of wanderlust gene or something has been nudged from its slumber. He recalled Steinbeck in *Travels with Charley*, noting that of all the people that he encountered on his journey, there were precious few that didn't want to be somewhere else. He thought about how things get felt and said that wouldn't if you were going to see that person the next day and the day after that and how it's a little bit awkward when you run in to that party again before you finally make your exit because that wasn't part of the bargain.

And then Daniel thought about Arletta who wanted for nothing and who possessed, at least it seemed she did, that elusive quality that he experienced only accidentally and for reasons that he could never quite grasp: clarity. It occurred to him that it's a dicey business thinking that you can pigeonhole anyone regardless of whether you ascribe the highest or the lowest of motives and character traits because people are much more complicated than that and because single acts or even series of similar acts are just that and there is often much more to the story. Still, he thought, there's little not to admire about

Arletta. She is, quite simply, a good and decent person if ever there was one. She seems perfectly content, never gripes or complains, she's always pleasant and seems to genuinely care about the well-being of other people which translated meant him. The truth is that her heartfelt and genuine concern for him had so choked him up that he was barely able to get his breath as he made his way out of there.

He remembered a quote he had read once that went something like "Every great work of art begins with a lump in the throat" and he thought what the guy was saying was that when something grabs you, I mean, *really* gets a hold of something deep inside of you, your sense of self is obliterated, and you are melded into the vastness of all things, and it's such an alien but profound experience that you want to record it, to try to somehow articulate in some fashion, any fashion. It could be marking on the wall of a cave, painting a picture or writing a poem or a hundred other things.

"No, Golda," he said, realizing that he'd left her out of the loop, "it's not the Arletta's of the world that plague me, more like the Arts, and I'm not referring to the *fine arts*." Daniel's mood turned surly for a brief moment with the mention of his former boss's name. "Here's a guy who's a taker, a "greed is good" guy whose relationships are governed by one simple equation, how can this person benefit me? he continued, shaking his head in disgust. "I'd attribute some of it to the fact that he's trying to make a go of a business, but it's more than that. Everybody has to make a living everywhere, and that tends to make lots of folks a little overprotective of their turf, like the hunters and gatherers of old that didn't take kindly to others poaching in their territories. And yea, a lot of people walk out their front doors in the morning with the same mentality and seem willing to do things to other people that they would never think of doing under any other circumstances." He looked over and noticed that he had put Golda to sleep, and he smiled and grabbed another smoke. Fuck it he thought as he headed over to the love seat to stretch out and really enjoy this one guilt free.

Maybe I'm naïve but I just don't believe it has to be that way, he thought, and for a case in point, the image of Joe from the Volvo dealership popped into his head. Joe had the one thing everybody needs, Daniel argued to himself, that intervening variable that whispers to them on occasion that there are limits and that even in circumstances that would seem to proscribe against it, there's something to be said for acting honorably. He puffed away satisfied that his logic was sound and felt that delicious fatigue that signaled the end of the struggle overcome him. He snuffed the butt and decided that he was plenty comfortable right where he was. And as Daniel faded to black, he was confident in the rightness of his cause, and he decided that the pangs of homesickness that had been creeping up on him were just an overreaction to the unexpected warmth he'd experienced over the last few days getting the best of him. It had all achieved the irrevocable status of a Custer decision. He would go, and furthermore whatever else he might find along the way, he would keep an eye out for the one thing that dare not speak its name, love.

Chapter 18

Daniel couldn't quite put a finger on why he felt compelled to leave the place in immaculate condition. He just did and he wasn't going to fight the impulse. As he scrubbed the sink, he had a fleeting thought of a mother reminding a daughter to wear clean underwear in case she was in an automobile accident and wondered if there might be a correlation, but he completed the project before arriving at any conclusions. He set the scrubby perpendicular to the faucet, just the way he liked it, undid his imaginary apron and stepped back to admire his work. The apartment was clean alright, so sparkling clean that even the most fastidious would have to have a mean streak to lodge a complaint. He was pleased with the way he had organized it as well, imagining in a fit of fancy that it was arranged in such a way that it could have been an exhibit in a museum. Not that there are "museum quality" pieces on display he noted in the spirit of full disclosure. Rather, it seemed to resemble a setting that might be unearthed in an archeological dig a thousand years hence, cordoned off and illustrating the lifestyle of its twenty first century inhabitant. "Relax, dude," he admonished himself. "The place looks good, but come on!"

Daniel looked around his humble quarters one last time to make sure that nothing had been left behind and concluded that everything that would be going was in the car except for Golda, who seemed to get that this was unlike any other morning they'd shared as she anxiously awaited her benefactor's next move. He worried a bit for her. After all, it was her place as much as his, a space shared through good times and tough times, in sickness and in health. Nor had she traveled much, but she seemed to Daniel resilient, and he believed that she would adapt quickly and that whatever unease she suffered now was a purely temporary situation and that once she felt the wind in her hair why... or something to that effect. She'd be fine! Hell she may take it better than me, he thought with a chuckle as he moved toward expulsion from the womb.

"Let's do it, kiddo," Daniel said, as he approached the cat crate that he had adapted for the trip. "Yeah, you've got lots of room in there," he added, still trying to emphasize the positive and ease her worried little mind. He did a quick "room to room," double checked the light switches, found to his immense satisfaction that the radio had been turned down not off, rectified that oversight and finally managed to position himself in the general vicinity of the door. He stepped gingerly down the stairs so as not to jostle Golda, made his way to the passenger door and inserted Golda's domicile through the open window and onto the front seat that he had loaded in such a way as to elevate the crate, giving her a panoramic view of the road ahead. Daniel took a deep breath as if to sample the local fare one last time and gave the neighborhood a thorough once over to imprint the image indelibly in his mind, but the rush of possibility was kicking in and he halted the sentimental exercise abruptly. The last bit of unfinished business was to *hide* his spare key to the apartment in the faux gray rock by the rhododendron at the base of the steps, and he did it swiftly, ignoring his doubts about the efficacy of this very low-tech security apparatus.

He turned and headed straight for the car and marveled again as he got in and shut the door at how well made the thing seemed to be before reminding himself of the clunkers he had to compare it to. He buckled himself and his precious cargo in securely, reached to adjust the rear view mirror and was not surprised to find it perfectly positioned. "How the hell do they do that?" he said, laughing and headed out to fuel up both himself and the car before taking that proverbial first step on the journey that would far exceed one thousand miles.

The name of the restaurant was the All States Inn, and from the looks of the place, it may well have been there when the term "all" meant thirteen, but it had a certain charm and Daniel had spent enough hours there sipping coffee and reading books and newspapers that it could be fairly described as his number one haunt. Besides the obvious "aesthetic" appeal of the place, there was another draw that kept him coming back for more. Her name was Chelsea, a pretty blonde self-described "military brat" who was born in the area but bred down south, Kentucky to be exact. Uncle Sam had ordered her and the family back to the New England area just about the time she had finally stopped referring to automobiles as "cahs," and only an entrenched few were still making fun of the odd moniker that had been hung on her.

On his way in to the restaurant, Daniel unconsciously tapped the Video Poker Machine with the digital winnings that weren't recognized as legal tender in any locale that he was aware of. He had pumped more than a few of his hard earned quarters in there, but it tended to be on those rare occasions when Chelsea was not on duty. That would not be the case today as Monday was the one day that she always worked the day shift, and it worked out well because it just so happened that Monday was the one day that Daniel liked to have breakfast out before work. His one concern was that her boyfriend, who should have been named Biff but was tagged with the unlikely name of Lester, might be out of work again and thus passing his idle time wheedling the good folks at All States out of a coke and a burger.

Daniel thought of Lester as your classic endomorph, thick and muscular and prone to thinking that his gregarious smiles were always returned in kind and dismissive of the dolts who were fool enough to fall for his exaggerated affections. The kind of guy that made you feel that you were forever on the verge of a nugee, which on the surface seemed like your usual puerile roughhousing, but Daniel suspected that he really just wanted to get his paws on you to let you know that he could snap your neck like a dry twig if he chose to. Daniel surveyed the spinning counter seats, shifted his glance to cover the booths as well as the more "formal" dining area and was pleased to find that the coast was apparently clear.

"Well, look what the cat dragged in," Chelsea trumpeted as she always did to signal his arrival.

Daniel enjoyed the playful if redundant nature of it and always smiled to himself about the double-entendre that he doubted very seriously was intended. "Hello, Chelsea," he replied with a little more oomph than usual. He made his way to the end booth, *his* end booth, which he always took when available and for which he waited when it wasn't, and she smiled as she passed nearby to let him know that she'd be there just as soon as she'd handled the orders in progress.

Chelsea liked Daniel, and when Chelsea liked someone she was not averse to showing it. She thought him "different," a little more refined than most of the guys she knew, smart without being pedantic—he had once used the word pedantic with her and when he told her what it meant she just laughed and said she couldn't imagine someone using the word without sounding pedantic—decent and sensitive and just a tad mysterious. She didn't really understand him but tended in general to remain neutral to positive toward things and people that she didn't quite get and for a guy that grew up in an environment in which all mysteries were dispatched with extreme prejudice, this was a most appealing quality. To Daniel's great dismay, there did not appear to be a sexual component to be found anywhere in the equation, which is why, he imagined, she could be so demonstrative with her affections. He was like a "girlfriend" to her and though not altogether happy with the arrangement, there was enough good stuff in it that the decision had been made some time ago never to jeopardize it by exposing the prodigious need that was incarcerated in various locations in his body. And of course, there was Lester.

Daniel liked Chelsea for a number of reasons, but mostly because she was everything he wasn't. Her world was largely black and white but with enough wiggle room to allow for human foible, and even then, she was a forgiving soul; whereas his world was comprised of so many shades of gray that a good many of them had never been identified. He could conjure up a similar humanity, but it was a rigorous and circuitous exercise that meant cycling through a whole host of lesser impulses before it could be arrived at. She seemed solid and unfazed and in control of her direction, and he always felt willowy, easily distracted and tentative. The fact that she was a fine specimen of a woman figured in there somewhere as well.

Daniel perused the menu even though in his million odd visits to the place for breakfast, he had never wavered from his beloved western omelet with a little extra Swiss for cohesion, whole-wheat toast and charbroiled home fries. Daniel tried to maintain a demeanor that suggested that this was a day like any other even though the "news" was like found money burning a hole in his pocket.

He sensed a presence approaching and redoubled his efforts to act "natural." He turned too casually and found himself looking up at Rose, the affable hostess who had been a fixture in the place for as long as anyone could remember and who apparently subscribed to the notion that you could subtract a decade from your age for every half inch of make up you plastered on your face. She was beaming down at him with arms crossed and a very knowing look on her face. She knows, he thought. How the hell can she know and more importantly, did she tell? Of course she told.

"Hello Rose, well I guess..."

"Whose car are you driving?" she interrupted him with what felt like an interrogation.

"What? Oh yeah, the car. Well that's mine Rose, I just bought it the other day," he answered relieved, that his secret was safe.

"Well, I must say, Daniel, we're moving up in the world," she added with an approving nod.

Not comfortable with the whole station in life thing, he shifted the emphasis. "I tell you, Rose, there's enough stuff to worry about in life that it's nice to have that one little corner that you can pretty much bank on."

Daniel listened politely while Rose droned on about the first *new* car she and her husband had gotten many years back while he snuck a quick peek out of the far corner of his eye in search of Chelsea. It turned out that she had been at the table just to the left of them, and he caught sight of her passing by, paying particular attention to her well-turned calves as she weaved through the maze of tables and sighing to himself as he watched her bring home the bacon to an elderly couple at the other end of the booths.

"Well, I don't really know much about cars, but it seems to me I've heard good things about that old slant six somewhere before," he tossed in absentmindedly to placate Rose and disguise his distractedness, but she was relentless, and he thought he'd better handle the engagement at hand. "Now, Rose, I can't imagine that you're too impressed. I mean I've seen that big fancy Lincoln Continental you drive," he interjected, trying to slow her momentum and polishing the apple a bit at the same time. And she did seem slightly embarrassed by the observation.

"My husband bought that for me. Claims it was some kind of business expense."

"He runs a heavy equipment company, doesn't he, backhoes and bulldozers and the like?" he added, looking for a way to wind this down but before she could answer, Chelsea popped up. "I'll bet you five hundred dollars that I can predict what you're going to order," she joked upon arrival.

"You're on," Daniel replied without hesitation.

"You want a piece of that action, Rose?" she asked concerned that Rose was feeling excluded.

"No, no, I've got customers to tend to, no time for gambling now. Besides it's illegal, isn't it?" she added with a chuckle. Rose excused herself smiling graciously as she left the two "kids" alone.

Chelsea's beautiful, Daniel thought to himself. Yep, hair all bunched up in a bun, orthopedic shoes, mandatory "All States" uniform, a run in her left stocking, and she's still a sight to behold, he continued to marvel.

"Well, what's it gonna be, Buster?" she asked, feigning impatience and breaking his spell.

"So you're telling me that you're willing to gamble five hundred dollars on the hunch that I'm so anal retentive—another concept he had explained to her some time ago to her immense enjoyment—that I can't, just this once step completely out of character and order, say, French toast or oatmeal or maybe just a couple of eggs over easy," he said playfully.

"That's right," she answered with a big, intoxicating smile. "So what *will* it be today, good sir?"

The salutation further enraptured him, and by this time, he had forgotten completely about the big news. He paused, rubbed his chin, stared intently at the menu and said finally, "I think I'll have—no scratch that. Maybe I'll make it—no, no, hmmm, I haven't had that for a while. Okay I've got it, I'm going to have a western omelet with a little extra Swiss for cohesion, whole-wheat toast and charbroiled home fries." He raised his eyes from the menu and bore directly into hers. He could almost hear her mental gears grinding as if she was rechecking the numbers on a lottery ticket to see if they truly did match.

"No way," she finally blurted out as she ripped the menu out of his hand. "Well, I reckon you owe me five hundred big ones, pardner," she said as she extended her upturned palm with a kind of a pay up or else look on her face as she burst out laughing.

"Will you take an IOU?" Daniel asked with mock earnestness.

"Yeah, I suppose I can trust you," she replied with a little less jocularity as she noticed that some of her other customers were beckoning. "Hey, I've gotta go, Daniel. They need me."

"No—yeah, I mean, go. You've got duties and responsibilities, go," he answered, trying to find his most persuasive "hey, no problem" voice. Chelsea smiled sweetly and headed for table four.

"Graceful extrication" was the key in Daniel's mind, and although it had never come naturally to him, with dedication and persistence, he had come remarkably close to perfecting the art. People sense need. They smell it and they recoil. It may be unconscious; it may not, but the trick in Daniel's world was to sense its presence in himself and take the necessary action to mask it at all costs.

His meal was ready in relatively short order, but the place was filling up and as Chelsea delivered the goods, she only had time to make a veiled threat about what happens to guys that don't pay their debts before table four needed her again.

Daniel glanced surreptitiously at her chatting with her customers, who like most that entered the premises seemed to know and love her. Her regulars, he thought. "I'll bet I'm her only irregular," he mumbled beneath his breath. He saw that a lock of hair had broken free from the net that bound it and that was all it took. The little giant was awakened, and he found himself imagining her performing her duties naked save for the orthopedic shoes, as the rest of her locks, emboldened by the success of the first, threw off the yoke as well and cascaded down her back, all in slow motion naturally, just like in the TV commercials. And as she turned around to give him a playful wink, her lovely tresses flowed just ahead of her movement and covered the better part of her breasts. He got a hold of himself and retreated lest anyone notice the trance he had fallen into, shuddering suddenly as if a demon had been exorcized and went back to tending to an appetite that *could* be satisfied. "They need me," she had said, Well, that makes two of us, he thought with a bittersweet resignation.

The pleasant buzz Daniel was riding from the playful exchange was still stirring, but it was little more than a warm ember, and he had fanned it as much as he could. The surge of anticipation that had shot through him as he was leaving his apartment had dissipated, and he got to thinking about the big adventure again in an attempt to rekindle his enthusiasm. Chelsea was, however, a tough act to follow, but he knew full well as he had always known that as desirous as he might be, there was no future to be found here. He could come back here two or three times a week for the next ten years and it would always be the same. Mr. Anomaly at your service, the peculiar guy who's always got his face in a book and uses words most average folks have never heard of. He thought about the profound appreciation he had for her, never having made anything of the fact that for such a supposedly smart guy, he didn't tend to get the most intellectually challenging jobs. The simple truth was that none of the negative things he'd projected onto her had ever occurred to her. He was always playing defense against someone on his own team. Yes, she is special, he thought, and I'm damn glad to have known her but it's time to move on.

Rose delivered the check along with the offer of a coffee refill, and he took both, the latter because he needed to buy time until he could steal a few minutes to say goodbye to Chelsea. He thought about telling Rose but was concerned as before that she would get to Chelsea before he did.

"Thanks, Rose," he said looking past her and toward the register, gauging Chelsea's proximity to it. After a few false starts, the timing of the orchestrated rendezvous struck and he acted. Daniel sauntered toward the register and caught Chelsea's attention by waving the check. She picked up the cue, and it worked just like the coach had drawn it up.

"You here to wipe the slate clean?" she asked with a wistful laugh as she punched in the figures.

"You know, I might need a little more time," he answered playing along. "I kind a been down on my luck lately, but I'm good for it, honest I am," he added with an impish smile and they both laughed. He wanted to follow up with a bit more witty repartee but was struck dumb. For whatever reason, he was finding it impossible to deliver the intended message.

She sensed the lull and as usual, intervened to move things forward. "So how was everything, good sir?"

He blushed, suspecting immediately that she had picked up on the visceral reaction he had to the same words a short time ago and felt painfully transparent. Hey, this is Chelsea, he reminded himself, concluding finally that it was perfectly natural for her to do a little something for his pleasure if she could. Still, he was in the throes of some terribly unsettling feeling, and he suddenly wanted to scream at the top of his lungs. But rather than a blood curdling cry, the words rolled out simply and softly.

"Chelsea, I'm going away," he offered vaguely, unintentionally leaving only his cryptic intonation to lead her to his full meaning.

"Going away where, Daniel, and for how long?"

"I don't know the answer to either one of those questions," he replied. "Look, I'm not trying to be mysterious or anything of that nature. I really do not know."

She looked concerned as if she suspected there was something horribly wrong that he was not telling her. "Come with me," she commanded, taking him by the arm and leading him out the doors to the foyer. He accompanied her without so much as a whimper, feeling a profound affection and the terror of uncharted emotional territory in the same moment. "Now, you tell me what's going on Daniel," she said with such force that he was taken aback.

It suddenly dawned on him that this was his swan song, his opportunity to close this chapter with the honesty and forthrightness that it deserved. He cared deeply for her and unrequited or not, he wanted this to be authentic, authentic for the sake of posterity, even if it meant being carried out on his shield. The route was circuitous as usual but it had produced the desired effect. He was calm and focused, and his words were the whole truth and nothing but the truth.

"Chelsea, I like you very much. In fact it's more than that. I can't say exactly how much more because I honestly don't know but the snippets of time we've shared over the last number of years have much more often than not been the highlight of my week. I suppose that sounds kind of pathetic but it's the truth." He had a rhythm going and felt fearless, liberated even, and he proceeded wholly unconcerned as to how she might react. "I'm not sick or dying or anything like that, and I do very much appreciate your concern, I really do. I am, however, rotting here, and I desperately need a change of scenery. I inherited some money, which is the only reason I can afford to be so impetuous. I am most assuredly not laboring under the illusion that the grass is going to be greener, but it will be different and maybe better suited to someone with my, well, let's just say, proclivities. I just don't know." He paused for a moment, taking a big gulp of oxygen and allowing himself a glance at Chelsea, who seemed to be in the middle of assimilating all that had been said. He felt like he should be embarrassed, and normally he'd have been well beyond such a state, but he held his composure and moved to practice her art of filling the void. "I don't know how to communicate this without sounding moribund or even maudlin," and with that she whacked him on the arm without looking up even as she continued to rifle through her emotions and he got it and felt a great warmth overtake him.

"Anyway, what I'm trying to say is that I'm a pretty damaged guy, and just the day to day stuff is often very difficult for me. I have ideas, lots of them, in fact, as to why that is and what I can do about it, but it's hard stuff to fix, and believe me I've been at it long enough to say that with a certain amount of authority. But, hey, that's my lot, and I'll keep hacking away at it and it will be alright." He ended his dissertation on an optimistic note but was getting to be a little bit concerned that she still hadn't said anything, her head still down, seemingly staring at the carpet. "Just out of curiosity, exactly how many of those little arrows are there in each section of that carpet?" he said with a laugh, trying to move things in some kind of direction.

At first, nothing, but before Daniel's concern could graduate to alarm he detected a hint of motion. Chelsea tilted her head up by degrees so slowly that he instinctively placed his hand under her chin, his fingers landing almost in such a manner that he could have been checking for a pulse. The question of whether the action was a bit too forward became instantly moot by what he saw next. The sight of tears sliding down both cheeks made his knees buckle. "Christ, Chelsea, what's the matter?" he asked, bewildered by this latest turn of events.

She grabbed his arm and squeezed with such force that he wanted to wince at the very least but somehow managed not to. She wiped her tears with her sleeve and broke her silence. "I don't know exactly, Daniel," she said, sniffling a bit before continuing. "All that stuff you just said about yourself, I knew all that, maybe not the gory details, but I knew that at some point in your life you had been wounded and seriously, but you never let on. You never moped or complained and I respected — I should say, respect you so much for it."

Daniel was rendered speechless as he scrambled to make sense out of these revelations.

Chelsea paused for a brief moment and started again. "I heard you talking to Rose about your new car, which she told me about before you even set foot in the place, by the way," she interjected with a muted laugh. "And I think what you said to her about having that one little corner that you could pretty much bank on, well, in some way I can't explain, you were that for me, and now, now you won't be there anymore."

"Sweet Jesus," Daniel exclaimed, his head spinning a mile a minute with possibilities that he refused to consider. "I had no idea, Chelsea and I really don't know what to say."

"I wonder about you sometimes late at night when I'm all alone in my bed," she said unabashedly.

And with that Daniel had to put a hand on the Video Poker Machine to stay up right.

"What you do," she continued. "What you think about, what you want out of life. You know as sappy as it sounds, whenever I hear the name of that movie *A Beautiful Mind*, I think of you."

Daniel was overcome. He felt like a lightning bolt was snaking through his body, culminating in a prodigious jolt to his forehead that had him reeling in a spasm of ecstasy like the lost souls he'd seen on TV ingesting the Holy Spirit in the wee hours of the morning. He discarded the inhibitions and encircled her with his arms, drawing her tight against his chest, and they swayed gently in silence. The past dissolved and the future would as always, wait its turn. There was only this moment, this magic moment, and if he never had another like this, he thought to himself, he would always 'have Paris.' He beat back again the beckoning temptation to want to parlay this moment into some imagined happy ending and just held her. He didn't know how this would end, and he didn't care. He would leave that in her hands, and she would oblige.

She hugged him hard and ran her fingers up and down his back before she slowly drew back just far enough to cup his face in her hands and stare deep into his eyes. "I will miss you, Daniel Cassat," she said softly, and with those words, she pulled his face toward hers and kissed him long and tender with a slow smoldering passion that engulfed him. "Goodbye, Daniel," she said as she ran her finger down his arm, across his hand and over his fingers until she reached the very tip of his index finger. She pressed hers against his as if to initiate that final cosmic transference, like God's exchange with man on the ceiling of the Sistine Chapel, smiled one last smile, turned and disappeared into the restaurant.

Daniel stood up straight. He felt fortified and famished at the same time. Fleeting images of the two of them motoring across the highways and byways of North America, talking, laughing, reveling at the wonder of it all swept across his mind's eye, but it was done and he knew it and furthermore he could not have been happier about it. He turned to head out to his car and found that his gait was a little shaky. He grabbed the rail to steady himself and by the time he hit the macadam he was fine. He was glad all of a sudden that he had written what he did on the napkin at his table inside as he pressed the button to unlock his chariot feeling a bit like an Okie for his unending fascination with his new toy. "Hello, Golda," he said genuinely happy to see his faithful companion. "You know, Golda, sometimes the world can be a right good place," and he burst into tears.

Chelsea moved toward Daniel's table with a touch of melancholy. She allowed herself a smile when she saw the dishes stacked neatly, so clean that they might have been used to set the table again right then and as she lifted the stack, she noticed the napkin with his distinctive scribble on it. She picked it up slowly and found ten crisp fifty dollar bills underneath it.

"I *always* pay my debts," the note started., "Alas, my knees are safe!!!! In truth, Chelsea, this meager stipend is a pittance compared to what you've given me. I will always be in your debt and I will *never* forget you. Love always, Daniel."

Chelsea slipped the napkin and the bills carefully into her uniform pocket and headed for table four.

Chapter 19

Daniel sat sobbing quietly, keys in hand, stuck in neutral in his wondermobile and perplexed by the sadness that overwhelmed him. The countdown had been initiated but there had been a major malfunction at T minus 1 second, and the launch had been delayed until the mechanical breakdown could be analyzed and rectified. This was supposed to have been the easy part. He had imagined this moment a thousand times, the final systems check, ignition and blast off, but now that the moment was upon him, he was paralyzed. His mind was muddled and lurching blindly in search of an explanation, but he couldn't quite get a handle on his sudden malaise. There was no doubt that the unexpected turn of events with Chelsea was a factor, but he wasn't ready to sort through that conundrum yet, figuring that it was safer for all concerned if he didn't revisit that event in depth until he was well out of town. Daniel seized on the realization that by having handicapped his mental faculties by keeping maybe the most significant part of the equation out of bounds, he was unlikely to resolve anything by sitting here in a funk.

Suddenly, freed of the burden of settling the matter at hand, he opted to put his trust in the all-purpose antidote, motion. Movement, Daniel reasoned, was the antithesis of paralysis, kind of a rolling and popping the clutch technique that just might shock the system into volition, and sure enough its employment here set his heart to pumping just a little bit harder and triggered the release of the juices that were the stuff of life.

"Ergo, it's time to go," he said, finishing his stream of consciousness with a verbal affirmation. Having stepped out of himself, the world around him began to come back into focus, and as the haze lifted, his mood followed grudgingly behind it. And as always, his trusty sidekick sat silently in the ready, awaiting his next move. "This is it, Golda. We're off to see the wizard," he said, with all the enthusiasm he could muster, and with that he inserted the key into the ignition and turned, relishing the smooth murmur that bespoke power *and* finesse. He reached instinctively to adjust the rear view mirror and managed a small laugh as it was once again perfectly positioned recalling finally that this particular event was made wondrous by the fact that the mirror in the Cavalier changed position with each little bump in the road. In it he could see the queue at the register, with Rose diligently ringing them up, and as he grabbed the shift lever, an apparition drifted in and out of view. "Goodbye, sweet Chelsea," he said with a residual pang of desire.

Daniel was about to head for the highway when he realized he had forgotten one very important detail. He felt the lump in his jacket pocket and reached for the little icon that would carry him safely across even the most treacherous stream. Lacking a metal surface to anchor him to, he wedged Saint Christopher between the glove compartment and the console, and true to his word, he thought of Arletta. "Vaya con Dios," he said to Golda and they were off.

Chapter 20

During the planning stages, Daniel had given serious consideration to a couple of side trips to track down a few of the small number of people that had mattered in his life, but looking back was for Daniel much like looking down from a razor-thin ledge on a very tall building. The more he thought it through, the more his enthusiasm waned. "Were," was the operative word. They *were* important at a point in time, but that time was long over, he ruminated. Still, the yen persisted, and so he compromised. If he happened to find himself within close proximity of one or more of those folks, he thought, he would make a decision at the time. He liked his odds.

In the end, the whole of Daniel's itinerary was designed to achieve a single objective: to cover enough real estate to make a clean break from the wide swath that he had become intimately familiar with during the course of his travels "Furnishing Your Castle for Less" as the ditty for his former employer, Royal Furniture, proclaimed. He figured Providence, about two hours due east, to be the perfect place to heave the map and start freelancing. He departed Dennis, traveling the back roads for a brief spell to East Dennis, cut a hard right onto Route 138 on his way to picking up US-6 West just North of South Dennis. It wasn't the most direct route he could have chosen, but it had a certain symmetry that appealed to Daniel, and besides time was something he had plenty of.

"Route 6, well, maybe we can get our "kick" anyway. Say Golda," he said as they arrived at the stretch that would mitigate the need to do much sign watching for a while. Come Providence and there would be no need to worry about missed connections and errant intersections, and Daniel viewed this welcome reprieve as a kind of dress rehearsal.

He settled in to the monotony allowed by not having any more to worry about than staying in his own lane as the never-ending series of yellow rectangles appeared and were immediately dispatched. It got him to thinking about Steinbeck's observation in *Travels with Charley* regarding the prodigious efficiency of the interstate highway system. How he understood its value but nevertheless bemoaned the utter sterility of it and how he believed it possible to travel the length and breadth of the country without really seeing anything, prodding Daniel to look around as far as he was able and to conclude that the man had a point, but somehow it didn't seem to matter a whole lot to Daniel at that particular moment. Fatigue was setting in although all the heavy lifting he'd been doing was in his mind. He didn't want to think just now. He was always thinking and as he thought about not thinking, an article he'd come across recently—describing the original "eureka" moment when Archimedes, giddy with excitement over having solved the riddle of how to compute the proportion of gold in King Hiero's crown—popped into his mind. The solution had had to do with density, buoyancy and the displacement of water, and a determined Daniel pored over it numerous times, but it wouldn't click. To make matters worse it was the dumbed down version and although his pride was piqued then and now, he wasn't taking the bait. In time, he thought to himself, scoffing at subjecting himself to further humiliation. Rather, he turned his attention momentarily to wondering what the antonym for eureka was in Greek.

"Music," Daniel thought turning the page, music to soothe the soul of the savage beast and to that end he opted for number three on the CD carousel. "Side one", as it was known in its previous vinyl incarnation, was a solo piano recital lasting twenty-seven minutes, unrehearsed and hand-crafted by maestro Keith Jarrett in Koln, Germany.

There were no words and more importantly, no ideas, concepts or expressions of love, heartache, anger or despair, to trigger Daniel's natural fecundity. Oh, all those things were in there, but it was a different language, a visceral language, and though hardly fluent in it, it was on occasion a welcome departure from his native tongue. He would ride the piece like a musical magic carpet, ascending slowly and cautiously into the stratosphere, dipping, soaring, racing and crawling before spinning into a chaotic turbulence and reaching a crescendo that felt like riding a bucking bronco before finally being tossed gently into a placid current and carried out to sea. With the last note, in spite of the music or maybe because of it, the gnawing feeling that had been waiting patiently took its cue and paraded onto center stage. Images of people, places and things from the most recent life he'd left behind floated through his head, and the more he saw the less buoyant he became. Eventually, the obvious became apparent, even to him. Daniel was in mourning.

The life he had known in that place in time was ending, and even though that life was far from rich and fulfilling, desolate was the word that often came to his mind, it was still *his life*, with it rituals and familiar routines and faces. There was some good stuff, he thought, but not enough to dissuade him from embarking on his mission, and although the sudden recollection of Chelsea's soft sweet lips on his gave him pause, he quickly righted himself and stayed on message.

There was a part of Daniel that actually welcomed the "mourning" process and did not want to try to circumvent it. It had the rare power to hold him in the moment and slow down the frenetic pace of mental activity. And, he believed, it was his body's way of saying that the experience had meant something, and he was quick to seize on any evidence that he was not *that* unlike "normal" people. That no physical barrier existed that would preclude him from ever returning to the area simply was not anything he could lend credence to. Without really having thought it through, he believed it highly improbable that anything of the sort could ever occur.

As for Chelsea, he couldn't help but take note of the fact that he was making a concerted effort not to rehash the events of the day. It was as if she were a vintage bottle of wine that needed just the right occasion to be broken into and he decided then and there that he would, if he could, postpone his "due diligence" of the matter until later that night when he was settled into whatever accommodations he found himself in and sated by whatever fine cuisine he chose to partake of. That way, his thinking went, he could look forward to the company of a lovely lady on his first night on the road, and the full stomach would enable him to focus on one appetite at a time.

That certain scents, sights, sounds and sensations would seep from his memory banks between now and the appointed time was a foregone conclusion, but he was confident that he could keep the dam from bursting as deferring gratification was one of his greatest strengths.

The mental meandering was abruptly terminated when out of the corner of his eye, he caught a passing glimpse of a sign for Route -25/Route-28 S to Providence /Boston/Falmouth. He managed to maneuver across a couple of lanes with an assist from another motorist, doffed his imaginary cap to him and rolled up the ramp. He breathed a sigh of relief at not having gone astray this close to the time that it would no longer be possible to do so and imagined that the last destination listed was founded by people with less than a stellar sense of direction who had expected to find themselves in Boston but missed a trail and ended up in the middle of nowhere. "Fuck it. I'm staying here," Daniel said out loud in his deepest baritone as he envisioned the leader of the pack throwing in the towel and articulating the sentiment of the group as a whole as great leaders of men are wont to do. And the scribe, no doubt one of the more genteel in the group, nominated the articulated rendering of the spirit of the moment as an apt name for their new world. Hence, Falmouth was incorporated and as can happen with surnames over the course of generations, the spelling was slightly modified but its true meaning has stood the test of time.

Daniel allowed himself a little chuckle even as he wondered if he were afflicted with some Tourette-like syndrome of the mind that created involuntary forays into bizarre ideation. But duty called, and his attention was quickly diverted back to navigation. Daniel caught I-95 W and decided to stop along this stretch for a bite, as he wanted clear sailing without interruption post Providence.

He came upon a spot about fifteen miles shy of I-95 S and pulled in next to the small picnic area. "Gee, thanks, Gov." Daniel said as he read the sign suggesting that the current governor played a significant role in the creation of this little oasis even though it was likely constructed a number of administrations ago. Daniel had a mind to go upscale and have himself a sit-down lunch with a glossy menu that could be read horizontally but opted for fast food as he had already left Golda alone in the car for longer than usual earlier in the day. He scanned the big board behind the counter to peruse the "victuals." The word rung a bell, and he remembered springing it on Chelsea a year or so ago in what had become their little ritual.

He had always acted nonchalant as he tossed out the "word of the day" in a casual conversational tone. It had started early on when she was telling Daniel about one of the new girls whose continued employment was in question because of a general uncertainty about everything she was asked to do. Chelsea tried to put a finger on the problem, describing her at various times as timid, reserved, having no self - confidence etc, when Daniel replied earnestly that "he could see how this kind of setting could pose problems for the diffident." Now, Chelsea was nobody's fool but neither was she terribly well read and she was not familiar with the word, and for some odd reason she lit up and just had to know immediately if not sooner exactly what it meant. Daniel was more than happy to oblige and from then on made it a point to keep a list of the more arcane words he came across so as to dazzle her in the future. Chalk one up for Skinner, he thought to himself as he approached the counter and ordered a Whopper with the lettuce on the side.

Daniel and Golda ate in silence under one of the mini-pavilions that had been constructed to shield the public from the elements. Between watching people stretching and making mad dashes for the rest rooms, Daniel glanced at his traveling companion and wondered what she was making of all this. She seemed unfazed as she munched on her lettuce, and he was satisfied that she was adjusting just fine. "Just you and me in the middle of everywhere, little buddy," he mumbled. "And you might as well enjoy the ride because we're gonna be on it for a while." Daniel looked out at the interstate with the cars and trucks whizzing by, seemingly paying little heed to the posted speed limits and thought again about Steinbeck. He would, he decided, dig out *Travels with Charley* when he settled on and into a place to hang his hat for the night. He seemed to think he had a reasonably good idea which box the book ended up in. He wasn't looking for inspiration or even direction, rather camaraderie, some sort of connection with someone else who had felt the need to spread his wings and explore, to challenge assumptions and left home and hearth to scratch the itch.

There were, he acknowledged, a great many more differences than similarities between the two willful nomads. Steinbeck was highly accomplished and lauded internationally. Daniel had achieved nothing of merit and only a few people locally even knew he existed. Steinbeck was wealthy. Daniel was traveling on his Uncle's dime. Steinbeck seemed fortified by and took a keen interest in his fellow human beings, seeking out encounters with them to get their take on the scheme of things. Daniel seemed allergic to members of his own species and could only tolerate exposure to them for brief periods of time. Steinbeck had a loving wife and a vast circle of friends tracking his movements and breathlessly awaiting his return. Daniel had scant few romantic memories and even fewer friends and no intention whatsoever of returning to his point of departure, but those minor differences aside, Daniel suspected that this impulse they shared had a very similar etiology. "Hey, you consider me a dear friend, don't you, Golda," he said, disembarking his train of thought with a verbal utterance as he often did.

Daniel felt that signal welling up in him that directed him to lament the paucity of his existence but was able to get his footing and shook it off, feeling suddenly anxious to get back on the road. He sensed that nothing would feel truly "official" until he had passed Providence, and he gathered up his refuse and his dear friend and headed for the car. He just shook his head as he spotted the little tiny windshield wipers that lay idle by the headlights as the duo got in and buckled up.

The last leg of the first leg of the trip went quickly and it was all he could do to spot each successive sign, never having bothered to activate the GPS, his aversion to mastering the mechanics of the latest technological marvels outweighing for now his desire to marvel at their mysterious capabilities. Besides, you could hardly call it "winging it" if you're employing satellites to get you where you want to go—presuming, of course, that you had a destination in mind to begin with!

The marker appeared, hailing his entry into Providence. It further informed him that the city had been established in 1636 and offered him a hearty welcome to boot. He recalled with an ironic satisfaction that it was founded by a guy named Williams as a haven for religious dissenters. "This is it, Kiddo," he exclaimed with a new burst of excitement. He flung the map to the way back of the car with gusto and put his palm up to share an imaginary high five with Golda. He was right. There *was* a whole different feeling about the journey ahead now that he was in unfamiliar territory. Providence had indeed been a divine choice to kick off the trip.

Daniel found himself driving along a causeway overlooking a large body of water that he assumed was Narragansett Bay and decided the occasion called for a ceremonial smoke, at the very least. He found a small rest stop with coin operated binoculars and pulled in next to a car taking up one of only three spaces in the lot. He felt a certain sense of peace that he tried desperately not to analyze as he positioned himself on a rock with a view, his companion perched next to him in her cage. The air was crisp, and the sun more than compensated for the hint of chill. The new growth was showing green as the foliage had been given the all clear signal. "You know, Golda, sometimes the world can be a right good place," he said as the two peered out over the water.

Daniel took a final drag on his cigarette and extinguished it with great caution, carrying the butt over to a receptacle and depositing it on his way back to the car. He was about to place Golda in the shotgun seat when the "binoculars" caught his eye. "What the hell?" he said, digging in his pocket for a quarter. He set Golda on a stone ledge next to the viewfinder and deposited the quarter in the slot. "Talk about your cheap thrills," he exclaimed, mesmerized by the sun twinkling like a million stars on the rippling water. He swung the apparatus to the left and caught sight of a bevy of boats of all shapes and sizes, rocking gently in their moorings, and a ways beyond that a grouping of some of the most magnificent houses he had ever seen. He steered back to the right and stopped on what looked to be marshlands with a small variety of birds doing whatever birds do in that setting. Some looked stoic, some nervous, some were preening and a good number of them were engaged in the never-ending quest for a bite to eat. Daniel strained to focus on the face of a big old fat bird that looked imperturbable when out of the blue, the whole lot of them bolted in every direction.

Within seconds, a figure emerged from the tall grass. Daniel had stepped back from the mechanical eyes but could make out that it was a woman, a dark haired woman. His interest piqued, he buried his face back in the contraption for a better look. "Jesus Christ," he mumbled as she came into focus. It was, in fact, a dark haired woman with a long chestnut mane, to be specific, and to Daniel's surprise, dressed not in jeans and a sweatshirt as one would imagine in this circumstance but in what appeared to be business attire. She was barefoot and barelegged, for that matter, with a tan skirt that would nearly qualify as a mini. She wore a fluffy, pale yellow blouse under a navy blue blazer and was festooned with jewelry in all the usual places that would intercept the sun and flash sort of a Morse code every few seconds—Dot- dot, dash- dash, dot- dot- dot—and the more rugged the terrain, the greater the number of reflections bouncing back at Daniel. ** *-- *- -* - -*-- --- **- "What's that?" Daniel mumbled in Golda's general direction as he watched for another signal. -* --- *-- I believe she said, "I want you... now," he said laughing at his little flight of fancy. He looked over at Golda whose expression suggested that she had gotten an entirely different message.

Daniel turned for another gander and just as he got her perfectly focused, her eyes had locked onto his big glass ones. He felt suddenly like an intruder that had somehow violated her space, but she smiled a goofy smile and cranked up a big wave. He kind of half waved back and quickly sought another object of interest to spend his remaining time on, but the shutter closed with an unexpectedly loud thud, and all he could see was gray. He felt odd, like he'd been exposed and that always wreaked havoc on his equilibrium. Daniel wanted to bolt, to jump into his car *Dukes of Hazard* style but instead, he moved slowly and deliberately, employing his "ain't no biggie" gait.

She sauntered up the path with an air of relaxed confidence and turned for one more, big gaze at the bay before plopping down on a bench by her car. They exchanged polite hellos and close up, he could see that she was maybe thirty- five, moderately pretty, not a knockout, but attractive and impeccably dressed. She certainly did seem friendly enough, he thought. Daniel had put Golda back in her spot and decided that checking the air pressure in his tires would be a wise move with him about to embark on the grand odyssey and all.

"I like your car," wafted out of nowhere and Daniel dutifully rose up from bended knee to respond.

"Thanks," he answered casually. Not sure what to say, he reprised the line he'd used with Rose back at the All States Inn." "Well, I tell you, there's enough stuff to worry about in life, it's nice to have that one little corner that you can pretty much bank on." A bit inane but at least it was in the ballpark, he thought to himself.

"Well, yeah, that makes sense," she said with a smile, and he instantly believed that she was one of those fortunate few that had more than their fair share of things they could bank on.

"Do you come here often?" just sort of fell out of his mouth, and the time-tested and failed cliché sounded so unctuous to his own ear that he burst out laughing. "Jesus Christ, can I rewind that?" he asked, still struggling to get the giggles under control.

His laughter had lightened the mood and she caught the bug as well. "Well, actually, I do. It's one of my favorite places, and I sneak down here between appointments whenever I get the chance." After a brief silence that Daniel didn't fill, she continued. "I work in my father's real estate office and I spend most of my time showing homes."

Daniel had largely regained his composure, glad to have gotten making an ass of himself over with early. "Like those over there," he asked, pointing to the palatial homes dotting the landscape to the far left, still imposing even without benefit of magnification.

"Sometimes," she replied. "Only, when I show those, I drive the Mercedes. It's kind of expected, you know."

"Well, yes, that makes sense," he said, parroting her previous response. "So, the Buick over there, that would be for a middle-class type neighborhood."

"How perceptive," came the response that he wasn't quite sure how to read. "How about you?" she asked, while leaning

134

over and brushing the dusty residue of the hike off her feet. "I've never seen you here before."

Her posture exposed a valley born of cleavage, and Daniel wished that he'd been wearing shades.

"Well it's my first and last time," he answered trying to maintain a field of vision that included the valley but enough else that he had an alibi. "I'm just passing through on my way to Pennsylvania to visit a friend from college. She raised her head and smiled.

"Christ, she smiles a lot," he thought as he bent down to check the tires on the other side of the car. He saw her looking at her watch as he genuflected by the rear tire and hoped that this encounter was just about over.

"Well, you have yourself a good trip," she said distractedly.

He looked up to thank her for the well wishes and gulped as he saw her drawing her hosiery up toward her thigh. He felt like Benjamin to her Mrs. Robinson but was pretty sure that nothing of the sort was going on. He tried to keep his focus on the pressure gauge, but a sidelong glance at her snapping on the garter gave him pause. He finished his task and saw her approaching his car. She appeared to be a full six inches taller than she had been just a few minutes ago

"By the way, my name is Mandy."

"I'm Daniel," he answered a little sheepishly.

"Well, Daniel, it's been nice chatting with you."

"Likewise," was all he could muster. "And good luck with the sale," he added as he got behind the wheel.

"Thanks, bye." She was about to reach for her door handle when she noticed Golda in her spot and shrieked with just a little too much glee. "Oh, who's your little friend?" she asked leaning down to get a closer look.

Daniel looked over to see up close and personal the sheer magnitude of her breasts. From this vantage point it was very difficult not to conclude that this display was intended for his consumption. "What the fuck do you *really* want," he felt like saying as a bolt of anger surged through him, but he could only manage to communicate that his 'friend' was a guinea pig and that her name was Golda.

"Aww, she's so cute," Mandy said in that voice women use when they're around something safe and cuddly.

Daniel now strongly sensed that there was some ulterior motive in her prolonging the encounter and tried to construe a method to graciously put the thing to rest. "Well, on behalf of Golda, I thank you and now we've..."

"You never did tell me what you do for a living, Daniel," she interrupted, making him feel like a job applicant sweating through a second interview, and he froze like a computer trying to process one too many commands. Finally, he found his tongue, but he had not been privy to the decision-making machinery that determined what would come out of his mouth next. "I'm a vagabond," he said, with absolutely no intention of explaining further."

Mandy's demeanor changed instantly and she drew away from the window just a bit. "Oh my, will you look at the time? Gotta run. See you," and with that she was off, to Daniel's great relief.

One hell of a send-off, he thought to himself as fired up the wondermobile. You'd have thought I said gigolo. He looked over at his trusted friend and was not the least bit surprised to be getting "the look," that, tsk, tsk, there you go again, what the hell am I gonna do with you, look. Shamed, he killed the engine and kind of mock banged his head against the steering wheel. He imagined Golda chiding him: "Did it ever occur to you that maybe she was simply a nice girl that was attempting to be decent and civil and engage in a little friendly conversation? And what, I'm not cute and charming enough to elicit a little squeal of glee? Give me *some* credit will ya!"

Daniel kind of smiled to himself at Golda's imagined protestation, but he was in fact a little perplexed by his own actions, by what exactly had piqued his ire and what caused him to want to get as far away from her as quickly as humanly possible. Was it simply that this was his big moment, and he didn't want any interlopers with suspect motives? Maybe, but the display exceeded even his normal aversion to others of his species. Fuck it, it's done, he thought, disgusted with his relentless ruminating. The simple truth is that I'll never see her again so even if I was a bit of a cad, there's no going back now. Even as he balked, he knew that it wasn't over, that he would, no doubt, revisit the events of the last twenty minutes and try to put them in some kind of perspective but for now all the impurities had been unceremoniously burned away, and all that he was left with was the image of one of the finer pairs of bosoms he had ever laid eyes on. "Christ, I have got to get laid," he lamented as he pulled back out onto the highway.

Chapter 21

Daniel measured his personal growth in ways that may not have made a whole lot of sense to some but were perfectly logical to him. A downward trend in the severity of the penalties he imposed on himself was one of his major benchmarks as was the shortening "turn-around" time of his *episodes*. The "Mandy" incident, for instance, warranted only a small number of lashes, and he allowed for character witnesses to speak on his behalf before that sentence was handed down. He also allowed for the "provocation factor" and considered it a mitigating circumstance. This was a vast improvement over the not-too-distant past when the entire onus was on him and the punishments were swift and harsh and recovery time was measured in days not hours.

There were still "grand mal" episodes on occasion in which he felt like nothing had ever changed, but even these had become more infrequent with each passing year. Time and experience had also taught him that virtually everyone was flawed, that everyone's armor could and likely had been pierced at some point in their lives. Furthermore, he was able to benefit from these insights a reasonably good percentage of the time.

Daniel cracked open all the windows and let the warm moist air circulate through the vehicle. He had severed the big umbilical cord and was finally doing what he had set out to do when he hatched this scheme, floating horizontally across the landscape unencumbered by any obligation of any kind. "You have just entered the *Twilight Zone*, he said aloud in his best Rod Serling impression. He thought of Huck Finn floating down the Mississippi and recalled long hours, as a kid, pretending that he was on such a journey. Hiking down to a local stream was the closest thing he could find to a river, and he remembered approaching the smooth flowing water and feeling as if he were at a train station. Each drop of water of the trillions upon trillions that constituted the river was headed where he wanted to go, and now he was on that train.

The human imagination is a mighty powerful thing, but it's much more art than science, and as the miles slid by and the initial elation began to ebb, Daniel had to acknowledge and grapple with this fundamental truth, but on this day he felt up to the task. It occurred to him that he could choose to perceive his current status any number of ways, and each would have equal validity, and each would be equally meaningless. He popped *Buddhism Plain and Simple* into the cassette player for the same reason he always did, to listen to lessons that he knew he was not prepared to implement in the hopes that the seed would be planted on some deeper level and jump up and surprise him at a later date when he least expected it and most needed it. So solid was he feeling that he was able to simply accept the fact that there would be plenty of time to construct the grand rationale for not only this journey but for the whole of his existence. His profound inadequacies in the more mundane arena of human relations would have to be looked at somewhere along the line, but for the moment, he aspired to no more than taking his place next to the trillions of other things in the universe that flowed to the beat of their own drummers without intent.

Chapter 22

The miles slid by, and Daniel alternately gawked at the landscape, searched the radio to sample the local fare and did his best to avoid signs and highway markers lest he get a sense of where he was and end up following some unconscious impulse to a chosen destination. He would stop at areas that caught his fancy and grab a smoke. He didn't have the heart to soil the wondermobile with the noxious fumes and chemical agents that marked their territory like an ambitious dog. Besides, there were Golda's little lungs to think of. He rode through small towns still anchored by "main streets" with visible evidence of erosion, suburban enclaves and the best and worst of modest cities and found himself on a hilly rural stretch with geometric fields starting to sprout and quaint farmhouses with their barns and sheds nearby. Some were clearly more prosperous than others, as was evidenced by the size and quality of the homes and outbuildings, especially a towering silo that he imagined was the closest thing these parts would ever come to a skyscraper. He crossed paths with an occasional motorist, but even that was becoming more infrequent. A quick glance at the gas gauge put his mind at ease, but the sun looked tired, and

Daniel thought maybe it was time to start keeping an eye out for a place to bed down for the night.

"How're you doing, girl?" He asked his mini-amiga and was satisfied that she was holding up just fine. The road was bending more and more, and he found himself in that odd predicament wherein it was difficult to tell if you were going uphill or down, and as soon as he convinced himself of one, the other began to make its case. He soon reached the bottom (or was it the top) and ended up on a smooth, straight run that left no doubt as to its inclinations. He could see twin peaks in the offing and it looked as if he would squeeze right between them.

"And lo, though I walk through the valley of the shadow of death, I shall not want — well maybe just a little," he said aloud with a chuckle in the direction of Golda. "You're gonna think I'm nuts, little girl, but I really do think that Mandy had other ideas, if you get my drift." He glanced over at his little friend and noted a distinct "when will you ever learn" look on her face. The peek that he'd been privy to of Mandy's "twin peaks" had resurfaced and set Daniel to thinking. "Yeah, maybe not but, but — it's not completely out of the realm of possibility. Aw, what do you know? You're a girl too, is this one of those sisterhood things?"

Now, Daniel was by no means ambivalent about sex. It was or at least it could be, he felt, one of the highest forms of human expression, like the rhapsody produced by the flawless execution of a world class symphony orchestra. He would not deny that it was easily debased and had a potential to unleash all manner of exploitation, degradation, violence, skullduggery, lying, conniving and general disingenuousness rivaled only by politics and religion. But approached properly with the right attitude and for the right reasons, he liked it just as much as the next fellow.

He had heard the statistic claiming that men think of sex every four and a half seconds, or something like that, but figured that if true it must somehow be related to the well-being of the organism much like a chain saw needs a steady dose of oiling lest it overheat and seize up. Still, Daniel secretly railed against being lumped in the general category of "men," having heard the term used too often in such a way as to a constitute prima facie evidence of a whole host of contemptible characteristics, and although he would concede that there was no shortage of "strutting cocks" to bolster the argument, he knew that there were plenty of exceptions to the rule and all other quirks and pathologies notwithstanding, he considered himself to be exhibit A.

Daniel had been in transit before and, although it was a trip with a destination and an approximate arrival date, he'd found himself in strange towns in close proximity to women that were either in transit themselves or sensed that he was just passing through and hence wouldn't be available to testify. He had concluded that men and women in this type of a vacuum, bereft of the normal inhibitors were likely to temporarily remove the governors on their desires and could and sometimes would act on impulses normally accorded no more than "pure fantasy" status.

He remembered his trip to Massachusetts and an incident that took place at a diner he'd stopped in for a bite along the way. He'd had a strong sense that the woman sitting a couple of booths in front of him was eying him and trying to convey that interest without being too obvious. She was attractive, and he was horny but wholly unaccustomed to such attention. Consequently, rather than pursuing the matter, he dismissed the prospect out of hand for the same two reasons. He recalled looking up from his newspaper and locking eyes with her for a millisecond before she looked away. He looked up periodically after that, and each time she seemed to have just looked back down at whatever she was reading but dangled a hint of a smile to keep him off balance. The more convinced Daniel became of her signals the more he tightened up. He had long believed the distance between "apple of her eye" and "lecherous stalker" was very short indeed and subject to one of the more fickle forces in the universe in matters such as these, a woman's prerogative.

He sat frozen, and after a while, the offer that had he imagined had been tendered was yanked from the table. Five cups of coffee and two local newspapers later, he was still bemoaning the lost opportunity. He got philosophical for a bit, turning his usual logic on its head and trying to convince himself that she was **not** interested in him before reverting to longing for another shot at the brass ring. The whole, *nobody's kidding anybody here kind of sex thing,* or R. D. Laing sex as he had subsequently labeled it, suddenly became extraordinarily intriguing. Still, he felt that it was unlikely to rear its lovely head again anytime soon, and he may well have forgotten all about it if it hadn't been for the events of the next evening in a truck stop/diner/motel on Route I 95 in Delaware.

She was three tables away, reading and, best of all, smoking. Shorter than the first and dressed much more casually, she had long black hair and a hint of olive in her complexion, although it could just as easily have been the lighting, and he figured her to be Greek or Jewish or maybe Italian. The signals weren't quite as strong, but he was "well oiled" after the previous day's debacle and he convinced himself they were sufficient to act on. Daniel, not ordinarily a bold sort, rose and kind of pushed himself in the direction of her table, unlit cigarette running interference lest she have other ideas about his motives and after bumming a light, found the courage to ask if he could join her.

Her "yes" lacked enthusiasm but a green light is a green light, he thought to himself. The fact that he would exit the plaza north and she south was established pretty early on, and Daniel took that to be a good omen. He learned that she was a nursing student on her way to an internship in some big hospital in the Baltimore area, but there didn't appear to be the kind of spark he had hoped for, and the conversation was small and shrinking, and he began to have serious doubts about the whole endeavor. Mentioning the fact that he had already rented a room for the night and her immediately sharing that she intended to do the same seemed to get things humming a bit. When she began whining about the cost of the room and the meager state of her finances, Daniel perked up even more. Her suggestion that maybe they could split expenses seemed to seal the deal and made Daniel tingle in some very special places.

He was secretly plying himself with "you da man" hosannas when she started laying down the ground rules and the more she talked, the further his testicles receded into some warm and safe place in the areas most often frequented by urologists. "This is strictly intended to save each of us some money and absolutely not an invitation for some type of sexual encounter," was the opening salvo in a litany of do's and don'ts that would codify the parameters for the evening's festivities or lack thereof. Daniel half expected an attorney to pop in, cup her ear for privacy and whisper sage counsel so as to ensure that she said neither too much nor too little. There would be no alcohol. They would sleep in separate beds and lights would be out by 11:00 as she needed to be on the road early, and in an act of great magnanimity, she would allow the control of the remote to be rotated every hour until lights out.

Daniel's dismay had peaked. It was clear that there would be no naked romping and frolicking engaged in on this night, and even the thought of "the pleasure of her company" seemed a bit distasteful. He longed to be back in the sanctuary of his own booth where he still had control of his destiny but frankly (literally) didn't have the balls to call the whole thing off. She surprised him further by reverting back to the relatively normal girl she had appeared to be prior to establishing that he would not become a male succubus or anything thing else of a remotely amorous nature. Gone was the severe demeanor of unquestioned authority as she casually asked him what he planned to do in Massachusetts. He struggled to switch gears and adjust to the new ambiance and fumbled to answer the query in as normal a fashion as possible. The conversation continued in a polite vein, and Daniel resigned himself to the arrangement. After all, he figured, there was the matter of saving a few precious dollars, and that was always a good thing.

After a last cup of coffee, they headed to their respective cars to retrieve their bags and rendezvous in 211. As expected, it was an uneventful evening spent mostly watching TV and reading. Daniel was glad to have his face buried in the local newspaper and curiously, discovered that he was intensely interested in the goings on at the meeting of the Zoning Hearing Board in Basil County. At around 9:30, Karen headed to the bathroom to do whatever things women need to do before retiring, and Daniel decided that now was as good a time as any to hit the hay. He had been assigned the bed by the door, and as he drew back the blankets and sheets a panic overtook him. He always slept in his underwear, but the thought of dropping trough engendered more than a little anxiety as the thought of Mrs. Hyde's returning gave him goose bumps. He did not want to sleep in his pants and was in no mood to negotiate when a compromise occurred to him, shorts. That was simple enough. Put on some shorts, hit the hay, up and out early, absolutely no breakfast until a town or two down the road and the whole bizarre thing would be over.

He thought about changing while she did her business but just knew that as soon as he got the pants off, the door would open so he sat silently on the bed waiting his turn in the bathroom. He glanced over at the article that described the contentious dispute over the size of the water detention pond that would be required by the new department store that was to take over the building that had been a grocery store for thirty-five years until the big regional chain muscled in and knocked out the family owned store, and he actually got kind of caught up in thinking about the pros and cons of a scenario that seemed to be playing itself out more and more in those days.

As he pondered the value of local ownership and community relationships relative to lower prices and the concomitant lower wages and a membership in the community that would never exceed its worth as a marketing ploy, he was grabbed by the back of the head, seemingly with great force, and thrust forward. He had the sensation that he had been torn asunder by a tsunami and was tumbling wildly and uncontrollably. By the time he got his bearings, he realized that the only moisture he'd encountered were the damp sweet drippings from Karen's vagina. She was humping his face with the fervor of a frenzied canine with a leg fetish. He assumed that she intended for him to "eat her pussy" but he wasn't "biting" so to speak and the end result was that she was fucking his nose. He tried to pull back but could only manage to roll his eyes toward the heavens. He expected to see Karen's contorted face but a hefty midriff bulge that had been cleverly concealed by the tarp like top she'd been wearing, obstructed his view. He was sucking air in through his mouth as his nose was otherwise engaged, when he heard the first of a number of weird sounds bellowed staccato style from an orifice that he would become all too familiar with before the evening was done. He yanked his head back again but once more it was to no avail as she had a vice-like grip, and she wasn't about to release it.

Daniel had serious reservations about the direction the evening had taken but could not immediately come up with a good enough reason to fully disengage himself. His revulsion was trumped by his depravation and although unsure of exactly what his role was, he adlibbed by stiffening his tongue and lapping with all his might and each time it stroked her, she jumped, yelped and shuddered and looked like Mr. T being lifted of the canvas by one of Rocky Balboa's explosive left hooks to the body. As abruptly as his head had been yanked forward, he was propelled on to his back, watching the button to his pants flying toward the ceiling and those very same pants heading toward his ankles and off at breakneck speed. She gobbled up his cock with such ferocity that he feared that it might no longer be attached to his body and sucked with the force of an industrial vacuum cleaner as her gold crucifix bobbed up and down, slapping him rhythmically on the balls. And still somehow, bizarre muffled noises continued to emanate from some deep dark place within her.

Daniel's head was spinning a million miles a second. Be careful what you wish for, was one of the items that flew past as he considered his predicament. The vision of the reluctant starlets in the old Hollywood films that resisted the amorous assaults with great aplomb before yielding to the latent passion that had been unleashed, made an appearance as well. Don't. Stop. Don't. Stop. Don't stop! I'll go, Captain, the odd thought popped up and he decided that having come this far he might as well forge ahead and become a full partner in this venture.

He looked first at what he could see of her tits as they caressed his thighs and then tried to focus on the phalanx of flesh as if he were watching a porn flick to enhance the mood. Unfortunately, the pressure on his cock was so great that he hadn't the slightest idea if he had an erection or not. She rose up suddenly and the room seemed ablaze, a blue smoke like that which wafts from dry ice framing her demonic image.

"You're mine, motherfucker" he imagined he heard the she-devil scream with mocking contempt but decided that he had conjured up that bit of melodrama to match the decor. She was breathing heavily, panting actually as she tugged hard on nipples that were capped by the largest areolas he had ever seen. He was relieved to see that the penis was intact so far as he could tell though it didn't seem to know whether it was excited or mortified and kind of hung at half-mast unsure of which direction to go next. The answer came swiftly and definitively when she rammed her middle finger up Daniel's rectum and the reluctant warrior stood ramrod straight and ready for battle.

Karen flipped quickly, landing on all fours, and Daniel instantly surmised that he could enter from any number of angles. He opted for right down the old pike and thrust his throbbing member in with as much force as he could muster. He knocked her forward a foot or so, and she emitted such a piercing shriek that he thought he might have harmed her. That notion was quickly dispelled as she rocked a couple of times for momentum and thrust powerfully in reverse, grabbing a chunk of his butt cheek with her right hand and trying to drive him in deeper yet.

Daniel had shed all illusions. This was not at all what he had in mind, this was freaky, angry, psycho sex and a certain part of him felt now like he wanted to hurt her, to punish her for luring him onto the conveyor belt to perdition.

"Gimme all you got and more, Mr. fucker," she commanded and this time there was no mistaking who said it yet somehow it inflamed him further.

150

"Take it, you crazy cocksucker," came his subtle (and aptly descriptive!) reply and she squealed with delight. And with each prodigious thrust, she screamed louder and louder and louder. Such noises, he couldn't imagine coming from a member of his own species. She further enhanced his audio pleasure by pounding on the wall between each bellow, and in a minute's time, the neighbors above and below and on either side were pounding back. And the more they pounded, the louder she screamed, and the harder she pounded.

Daniel felt he had gone completely insane, imagining that at any moment the door would be broken down, and the two miscreants would be dragged away, like a modern day Adam and Eve, naked and ashamed to a cacophony of hoots and jeers from the irate neighbors whose peace had been disturbed. He wanted out but was convinced that there was no exit prior to her getting her pound of flesh so he pumped harder and faster to hasten the process along.

"Come, come now, you fucker, come on hot wad, blow a load in me," she pleaded and demanded at the same time.

Daniel grabbed her haunches and pushed so hard he feared he might be sucked into the black hole never to be seen again.

"Now, hot wad. Now"

And always the accommodating one, he blew. The explosion was such that he felt like a fireman trying desperately to hold on to the big hose with thousands of pounds of pressure coursing through it. His mojo fully spent, he felt woozy and unsteady. He reached for something to steady himself and came away with a long braided lock of hair that prevented him from pitching over backwards. As his eyes dropped back into the normal positions in their sockets, he noticed something oddly different about the room. It was quiet and stranger yet, Karen was still, catatonic like still. Was it simply a post orgasm torpor? he wondered. He had no recollection of her coming, although he had to concede that with all the gyrating and yowling it would have been hard to pinpoint the exact moment it happened and then too, he *had* spent an indeterminable amount of time oblivious to all but shock wave sensations and the corresponding psychedelic imagery that had commandeered his mental airwaves. He tugged on the braid to swing her face around to where he could see it and not only was there no expression, but her eyes seemed to be rolling back up into her head.

Daniel felt a sense of panic overcoming him. Is she dead? he thought to himself as he reached forward to her neck in search of a pulse. He was reasonably certain that he detected a faint throb, but a nagging doubt persisted. Maybe she's an epileptic, or shit maybe I fucked her into seizuredom! the frightful but fanciful notion gave him pause, sparking a sense of satisfaction on some perverse level in spite of the gravity of the situation. He wanted to shake her but was afraid of making things worse.

"Jesus Christ, Karen, are you alright?" A hint of sluggish stirring brought a sigh of relief that she had at least survived the ordeal. Finally, she started to move slowly and deliberately but still with little evidence of respiration, dropping first to her elbows and then buckling her knees as she gently let the rest of her body come to rest on its side the way a horse does before it rolls.

"I'm fine, Daniel, just tired. It must be getting close to 11:00," she replied dulcetly, her voice barely a whisper.

Right on schedule, he thought, certain that his balls had turned into pumpkins before the appointed time. He was irritated by the seeming "normal" tone of her voice but grateful that the crisis had apparently passed. Daniel collapsed on the bed next to her. He was exhausted and troubled by an unsettling feeling, a sort of nauseating buzz that permeated the whole of his being. He spent the next half hour staring blindly at the ceiling before finally garnering sufficient strength to slither down the side of the bed and make his way to his assigned spot. He grabbed his shorts mid-bed and pulled them on as a precaution even as he stared into the soggy heart of darkness that he had inhabited a short while prior.

Daniel always did his best thinking when he was able to put some time and distance between himself and whatever vexed him, but this he couldn't manage to set this aside for future consideration. He had been escorted to a place he'd never been and he was reasonably certain he never wanted to go there again, and it was that kernel of doubt that distressed him most. Sex, no matter the setting or circumstance, had always had an element of tenderness, of consideration for the partner's needs and satisfaction. He had never wanted to hurt someone before, and maybe that was the key. Because of the way he had been mauled, he had always tried desperately not to inflict pain on others and maybe he simply didn't like what he had become during the act.

He glanced over at Karen from time to time as she slept the sleep of angels. There didn't seem to be a definitive answer in the cards on this night. Yes, he had been duped, but he could have stopped it and he knew it, and yes, if the roles had been reversed, he could be looking at five to ten right now, but it was what it was. Why the pretense was the question that he kept circling back to. Why the elaborate ruse? He considered the possibility that there was malevolence involved but couldn't bring himself to believe that. He thought maybe she was crazy or damaged, but that was too easy as that can be said of 99 percent of us and there are serious questions about that other 1 percent.

For whatever reason, Daniel finally concluded, she needed to do it that way. That he might ever comprehend just what that reason might have been seemed a remote possibility at best without further investigation, and he damned sure wasn't going there, he thought with a shudder. "Don't ask, don't tell," he half mumbled to himself as he finally headed to the bathroom (appropriately clad, naturally) to take his turn doing the things men do to get ready for bed. The pre-sleep leak exposed the ring of lipstick adorning his withered member, and he ran the water warm to moisten a washcloth to remove it. The vivid recollection of Karen's oral vice-grip explained all too clearly why no amount of scrubbing would erase the hopefully temporary tattoo. He glanced at the mirror, saw shame and skulked back to bed, dismissing the fleeting notion of grabbing his stuff, making a break for the car and hightailing it out of town.

He suspected that in time better answers would come and most likely they would have a lot more to do with him than with her, but for now, he thought it's done and as far as he could tell, everyone was safe if not exactly sound and with that he went to work on the vexing problem of properly constructing and submerging the caissons that would make possible the construction of the Brooklyn Bridge.

Chapter 23

Daniel "came to" with a jolt and clutched the wheel hard as it seemed that he hadn't even glanced at the road during the whole of his mental detour. His grip extra firm and his hands properly aligned at ten and two, the sudden vitriol he had felt toward Mandy made a little more sense, and he felt a little foolish for having been so suspicious of her motives. He still wouldn't concede that there wasn't "something" in the air but "so fucking what if there was," he bitched to himself. Years after the fact it still made him a little nauseous to think of the encounter with Karen. She had a habit of paying Daniel a visit at the most inopportune times, and he hated her for the legacy that transcended their brief détente. He recalled how difficult it had been to shake the aftermath and how long it took him to make sense of the lingering angst. The physical act itself had never been the source of his discontent nor was it even his desire to satisfy what he considered to be normal, natural and healthy impulses. Rather, it was the sense that "drive" had trumped all else, running roughshod over resistance that was feeble at best and allowing him to participate in an egregious fraud, a big lie. He had compromised himself and handed control of his very being to a less than perfect stranger, and that, for Daniel, was the cardinal sin.

He looked over at his little friend and imagined her little paws over her eyes, waiting for him to resume paying complete attention to the road, but in fact, she was completely unconcerned with what he paid attention to. The fatigue he'd acknowledged prior to his reverie hadn't lifted, and the suddenly greater urgency to locate food and shelter shifted him out of ruminating mode and into one that focused on his more immediate needs. He was in no frame of mind to be particular and decided that the first place he spotted, so long as it met both needs either on site or within walking distance, would be the one he would patronize.

It seemed that he had lowered the standards in the nick of time as he saw the Dew Drop Inn up on the left and imagined the owner petitioning the courts to copyright the name and being laughed all the way out of town. Daniel finally managed to locate a parking place that wasn't plagued by potholes and pulled in with great caution. He thought it a bit ironic that being flush with cash for the first time in his life, he would end up in the most humble of digs. He could save a few bucks *without* subletting half the room, he thought to himself with a sardonic chuckle as he let himself into the office.

He was not surprised to see the keys dangling from their little tin-ringed fobs, with the numbers handwritten on the paper portion, draped on small brass nails on a crudely painted board behind the counter. As he wondered if the brass was an attempt to add a touch of elegance to an otherwise dismal arrangement, a fellow of about forty stepped through the hanging beads and ambled up to the counter.

"How do?" The fellow greeted Daniel with a drawl that had no geography attached to it.

For reasons Daniel couldn't explain, the salutation seemed warm, sincere, natural and inviting, setting him almost at ease and drowning out any concerns generated by his "unusual" appearance.

Kenny was the man's name, and he definitely had a stereotypical look, kind of a hippie cross bred with a biker look, with semi-long dirty blonde hair parted in the middle, and a tattoo of a mermaid with the name *Wanda* just below it on one arm, and a ship being tossed perilously from wave to wave on the other.

"How can I help you?" he followed up as Daniel had failed to respond in any fashion.

"Oh, yeah, shit, I'm sorry. I need a room for the night. Is there any room at the inn?" Daniel said facetiously as he looked at the "key board" with only a couple of empty spaces.

"Hmmm, well let's see," Kenny replied with a kind of mock seriousness as he peered over imaginary spectacles at the very same key rack. He turned with a big toothy smile to Daniel and said, "You're in luck. We just had a cancellation."

"I don't suppose it was a suite," Daniel said, feeling comfortable enough to laugh out loud.

Kenny just grinned and swung the book around for Daniel to sign just like they do in the movies. "Twenty-nine bucks a night including tax and you get the pick of the litter."

"What do you recommend?"

"Well, they're all pretty much alike but 129 down there is the closest to the hot tub which stays hot twenty-four seven by the way."

"That sounds fine," Daniel replied even though he'd never been in a hot tub and didn't figure to start any new practices tonight. He peeled off a ten and a twenty and held his hand up to indicate that he would not accept the change. "By the way, how's the food at the diner across the street?"

" 's good as any. Serviceable, you might say," Kenny said as he handed him the key. "You won't rave but you'll feel like you got your money's worth."

"Well, I'm famished. I think I'll head over," Daniel said thinking that "starving" would have done just as well.

"Well, you enjoy, and if there's anything you need, just come on in here and ring that little bell right there by the "Kenneth & Wanda Blazer, Proprietors" sign, and either me or Wanda will pop right out."

"Thanks, I will," Daniel said as he headed out the door. He moved the car down by his room, straddling two parking spaces in order to keep all four wheels somewhat level, promised Golda he wouldn't be long and crossed the deserted highway.

The Grille as it was called was exactly as advertised, not too big on the ambiance thing but clean, quiet and very lightly populated, which translated into top-flight service. After a New York Strip steak that had likely never been anywhere near the state much less the "Big Apple", Daniel tipped generously as had become his custom, (refusing to let the little voice that mockingly called him "Mr. Big Spender" deter him), and made a beeline for his room, retrieving Golda on the way.

The lock could have used a little WD-40 but with a little jiggling he managed to enter. The room smelled kind of musty, but it appeared to be reasonably clean and it seemed that

Kenny or maybe Wanda had popped in while he had been eating and given him fresh sheets. The drapes looked to have been in place for a time, and the furniture was moving rapidly toward antique status, but the room had obviously been painted in the not too distant past, and the overall effect was quite pleasant if you disregarded the linoleum that bore a striking resemblance to the hide of a hippopotamus.

Daniel noticed with some interest that the old console television had a cable connection protruding out the back that snaked half way around the room at the foot of the baseboard before turning a sharp ninety and vanishing into the wall. He pulled on the "power" toggle and heard a crackling sound as a beam of light appeared at the center of the screen and began growing tentacles in a number of directions before filling out and evolving into some semblance of a color picture. "Let's play hardball," the box barked, and Daniel, encouraged by his initial success began surfing, quickly learning that of the one hundred and twenty or so advertised channels on the little promo card on top of the set, he'd be lucky to have access to a tenth of them. He looked on the bright side and figured he could distract himself just as well with twelve channels as he could with a hundred and twenty and opted for some 'softball', scrolling back to the episode of the *Dick Van Dyke Show* he had passed a few channels back. A little snack for his little lady, a Diet Pepsi with no caffeine that he'd picked up at the Grille, a couple of well-fluffed pillows, a dose of light fare to stand in for the running commentary in his head, and hey, who could ask for more? Daniel kicked off his sneakers, fired up a Camel Light and was glad that this amorphous mass of a universe had belched out a character like Dick Van Dyke.

The episode ended exactly the way it had the six or seven other times he'd seen it over the course of his life, but the pleasure he derived from it didn't diminish with each rebroadcast. The TV went to commercial, and Daniel stepped out into the surprisingly cool night air to get his shaving kit and his equivalent of carry-on luggage that contained a change of clothes and a few other essentials. He opened the bureau drawer and systematically laid out the fresh clothes in the order that he would don them the next day. It was a ritual that even Daniel found peculiar, but it bugged the hell out of him the one and only time he tried to take a more random approach so he chose not to fight or worry about it, for that matter.

The blare of bugles heralded the start of the news, and Daniel resumed his position on the bed to see just what was going on in this neck of the woods. The show had been on for five or six minutes when Daniel realized he hadn't heard a single word the newscaster had said. It was a local broadcast, and naturally one would not expect the production values of a national newscast or the polish of say a Peter Jennings, but this gal, in mimicking the actions and postures prescribed by her trade, had so exaggerated the head movements that she reminded Daniel of the bobble-head dolls that had been popular many years ago and had found new life of late as promotional items at major league sports venues across the country.

"A head talker! The woman is a head talker," he blurted out, unaware of the origins or the significance of the remark. And then he remembered the "Low Talker" and the "Close Talker" episodes of *Seinfeld* and wondered why the comedian had never done a show on this particular malady. As Daniel

160

imagined the zany cast reacting to the "bobble head" and what kind of story line they would wrap around it, the overly jaunty anchor faded to a commercial and an upbeat, young fellow strode and talked his way through a mammoth showroom, showcasing the latest offerings from a certain automobile manufacturer. It was as if the confident and borderline aggressive gait was intended to add gravitas to his words, and Daniel could almost sense the cameraman backing up as his space was invaded again with each successive step. And Larry David and company could have followed up that particular episode with the not-so-subtle swagger of the "walking talker", he thought with a hint of self-satisfaction, convinced that the two odd talkers had unlimited comic possibilities.

Daniel crawled across the bed to reach for the dial and peruse other offerings but was stopped midstream by a commercial for the Franklin Diner. The breakfast combos looked scrumptious. The tuna melts and burgers seemed to burst with flavor. The pretty-in-pink prime rib oozed its luscious brown juices, making his mouth water, and the homemade apple pie along with the other delectable desserts had him hoping this place wasn't too, too far away. But the most appetizing item was featured at the end. Willow, the waitress, with a smile at least as sweet as the pecan pie, invited each and every member of the viewing audience to "come on down and sample the exquisite cuisine" and proffered her personal guarantee that "the service would be every bit as good as the food." Daniel forgot about his hyper stimulated taste buds and punched the off button with such force that the old console was set back on its heels.

"Chelsea," he exclaimed as he sat motionless at the foot of the bed. The events of earlier in the day came rushing back so vividly that he instinctively cradled his head in his hands lest the continued onslaught overwhelm him completely. Whatever else he had envisioned or even hoped for, there was no way he could have anticipated what had actually happened. She had dynamited the vault deep within Daniel that had held all urges and desires that can drive a man crazy in the same way the sun can surly blind you if you're foolish enough to stare directly into it. He was struck by the lunatic notion of picking up the phone and calling her, but he knew the moment had come and gone, and he didn't want to taint it by bumbling through an awkward call that could ultimately achieve nothing but humiliation. Maybe she's lying in bed this very minute wondering where I am and what I'm doing, he thought, and that was all the more reason to let sleeping dogs lie. He reminded himself that his success with her was at least in part due to the fact that he knew and respected certain boundaries. He had never put himself in a position in which she had to say no even though he knew that if it were to have happened, the anguish would have been all his, and she would have found something tender and positive about it and gone on like nothing had changed. It suddenly occurred to him that the remote possibility that she would not have had to say no was the much more terrifying proposition, and for whatever reason, that line of thinking sent his blood pressure plummeting twenty points and the frenzied domain that was his psyche started to simmer down.

He looked back at his readily available maiden and reached over for a cigarette. An extra deep drag and Daniel had started down the path toward regaining his equilibrium. The seemingly unbearable ache was ebbing and giving way to a quiet appreciation of what had transpired. Fuck the peripherals, he thought to himself. She's an amazing woman and she thought that I was a "pretty swell guy," and all in all, it's hard to find fault with that equation. A bit simplistic, of course, but he didn't have the strength to hang on any longer, and the fact that he knew full well that he was nowhere near ready for that "happy ending" emotionally further solidified his chosen position.

"A truly amazing woman," he said softly to no one, and it saddened him that they would not share the more modest rituals any longer much less the brief foray into passion and possibility. But sense and sensibility had carried the day, and he was where he was supposed to be as no doubt was she. Daniel sighed deeply, and in one continuous motion, he stubbed out his cigarette in the ashtray on the bedside stand and pitched forward on the bed, his "stubbing" arm draped over his face. He rolled slowly over onto his back, eyes to the ceiling and with great care and deliberation replayed the events that had already achieved a place of the highest prominence in his limited inventory of moments to savor.

He winced all over again as he remembered how she took a hold of his arm and led him to the foyer. He felt the tug at his gut as he discovered the tears rolling down her cheeks, he felt his knees buckle as she confided that she sometimes wondered about him in her bed late at night and he felt the warm glow overtake the whole of his body as her lips gently found his. "Jesus," he said aloud, "Who knew? Who knows any fucking thing?"

He rose, thinking it incredibly ironic that he was as far off the mark with Chelsea as he had been with Karen some years ago, albeit in very different ways. Daniel concluded that he was barely literate at best when it came to reading people and decided that it was just as well and Mandy's smiling face popped into his head as if to underscore the point.

The emotional havoc left Daniel feeling spent but oddly restless at the same time. The aptly named boob tube had no appeal to him, and he thought about going out to the car to get *Travels with Charley* to read for a bit before retiring but was distracted by muffled voices coming from behind the unit. He peered out the frosted bathroom window and could make out the shapes of Ken and Wanda in a dimly lighted area in and around the hot tub. He suddenly felt a most unusual sensation, a longing for human contact unaccompanied by the shrill wailing of alarms that usually stifled the impulse. Daniel decided he'd better move before the system detected the rash notion and extinguished it and scrounged up a pair of shorts from his travel bag. Clad for the occasion, he grabbed a towel, folded his Camel Lights inside it and made his way out the door and just short of the corner of the building.

"Everybody decent?" he called out to his prospective hosts.

"We're good," came the answer from a female voice, presumably Wanda's. "Yea, and we're not nekkid either," followed the affirmative, and Daniel felt safe in rounding the corner.

Wanda was standing by the side of the tub, toweling off. She was thin as a rail with knees that protruded further than her breasts and her hair drawn tightly in a bun. "You could be naked and I wouldn't even know it," she said with a cackle as she squinted just to be able to see her glasses to wipe the fog from them. "There, now I can see you. You must be Daniel. It's hard to keep the names of all the guests straight," she said with a mischievous smile and the three laughed heartily. "Well, it's nice to meet you, Daniel but I'm afraid I was just on my way in. You won't take offense now. Will you?"

"No, no not at all," said Daniel "It's nice to meet you too."

"See you in a while, darlin'," came the voice from what looked like the disembodied head of Kenny.

"Night, Hon and don't keep Daniel here up all hours. You and I have to be in Canterville at eight tomorrow morning. Night, Daniel," she said as she turned toward the office which doubled as their home.

Daniel inched over by the hot tub but wasn't sure about the entry protocol. "There's a step around the back here if you're unsure of your footing," Kenny said, pointing to the spot. "Yeah, climb on in here fella and we'll engage in a little persiflage."

Daniel froze momentarily until his mind located the word and its meaning. "That does mean what I think it means," Daniel said with an air of exaggerated concern, which Kenny seemed to find very amusing.

"Yeah, hey, what's a little light banter between strangers? I picked that up in the "Word of the Day" in the *Sentinel* this morning and odds are I'll have forgotten it by tomorrow. Hell, when I read it, I thought it meant some kind of high-tech handbag that would be invisible to snatchers," he added with an infectious laugh.

Daniel recalled the feeling he had when he first encountered Kenny, an instant comfort level that was an extremely rare event, but it was being reinforced at that very moment. He used one of the two steps and felt his way to one of the built-in seats and sank ever so slowly down into the bubbling cauldron. "Jesus, that's nice," he said as the warm turbulence soothed his whole body and set him even more at ease. "You know, I always check out those "Word of the Day" things too," Daniel said, failing to add the part about Chelsea and thinking about the kick she would no doubt have gotten from the "high-tech handbag" comment.

"Well, I guess we have something in common," Kenny added with a smile.

"Yeah, I guess we do. You know I've never been in one of these things before. I never knew what I was missing."

Kenny just nodded knowingly and the silence that followed was surprisingly comfortable. Daniel didn't even bother to come up with an alibi for the inevitable question of where he was headed. The day's last light had faded quickly, and the two of them stared up at the vastness of space with the moon at half-mast and the countless number of stars peeking through the blackness.

Finally, Daniel spoke. "So how did you get in to the motel business?"

"You got a few hours, do you?" Kenny asked with a laugh.

"You're the one with the early morning appointment. Me, I got nothing but time. I'm all ears."

Daniel's comment about "time" seemed to pique Kenny's interest, but he ignored it and went ahead with the story.

"Well, I was managing a marina in a little town called Bay Point in Maine, not too far from Lewiston and a bit north of Portland. And I had headed to the boardwalk to get a bite to eat. I stopped at a place called Sal's Pizza. Sal was one of those old country guys that had brought the secret recipe along and made each pizza personally, not like 99 percent of the other joints down there where they train kids for an hour or so and turn the operation over to them. Sorry for digressing, all I'm saying here is that this stuff was the real deal, not that he needs the plug. Anyway, I stopped at Sal's, and there was a new girl working the register and we just clicked. We dated for a few months before she figured it was time for me to meet her Dad, whom it just so happens was the owner of this fine establishment."

"Would it bother you if I smoked?" Daniel interrupted. "I'm sorry to—"

"You go right ahead, but I feel compelled to tell you that those things aren't good for you," Kenny replied.

Daniel was a little surprised at the response and ordinarily would have taken umbrage at the preachiness of such a comment, but he figured he meant well and let it pass. He reached over and pulled the cigs from the towel, lit up and gave Kenny his undivided attention.

"As I was saying," Kenny continues, "we left early on a Saturday morning to arrive in time for lunch and when we pulled in, the place was eerily silent. I mean, I sensed that something was amiss, and I had never been there before. Maybe I was picking it up from Wanda because she got real quiet and intense, and she didn't say a word. In any case, she just opened the car door and walked directly into the office. I tagged a few steps behind, not sure what the hell was going on. I could see that she had stopped dead in her tracks, and as I opened the door to join her, I saw her Dad on the floor of the bedroom. It looked like he had died right in the middle of putting his pants on and had just tumbled to the floor in a heap. Wanda's respirations got real slow, and she walked very deliberately over to the body as if she knew there was no chance of helping him. She turned back and looked directly at me, and I moved toward her and sort of reached out, expecting that she would just collapse in my arms, but she didn't falter. You know what she did, Daniel?"

Daniel was spellbound by the narrative and had not expected a question, but he didn't miss a beat in responding. "I can only imagine," he said and left it to Kenny to fill in the blanks.

"She caressed my face, turned, bent down and with the strength of two men rolled his body over to get a look at him. Tears were streaming down her face, but she was smiling so sweetly, it was like a rainstorm with the sun shining bright. I felt like a helpless fool, so I just stood there waiting for instructions. He had been face down for a good while, and his nose and everything was smashed flat. The tears kept flowing through the beaming smile as she massaged his face and tried to get it to look like she remembered it. She nodded to me, and we hoisted him up on the bed—and let me tell you, he was heavy—but she didn't grunt or grimace or anything. I guess everything had kind of let loose when he died because everything was soiled, if you know what I mean."

Kenny stopped for a moment and looked as if he was amazed all over again by Wanda's actions. He smiled to himself and continued. "She stripped off the dirty stuff, walked into the bathroom and got a warm moist, towel. It killed me that she made sure it was just the right temperature, like you'd shake the formula for the baby onto your wrist to make sure it was not too hot or cold. She cleaned him up immaculately and dressed him to the nines, still harboring that strange combination of pain and pleasure, and by the time she was done, he looked like he was taking a nap before attending the big event that he'd gotten all gussied up for. Then and only then did she call the county coroner to pronounce him and the funeral home to remove the body for, get this, cremation."

Kenny paused for a moment and continued. "You know, before that day, I kind of thought I loved her. I don't mean to minimize it, but it was just that standard feel good kind of love that you tend to want to stick with for a while, but this catapulted it to a whole new realm, a realm of great depth as well as breadth, if that makes any sense. After the incident, I had absolutely no doubt that this was the woman I wanted to marry, if she would have me.

"That's quite a story," Daniel found himself saying with great sincerity even as he recalled the numerous times he'd spit out the same sentence in response to the countless homilies he'd suffered through by blowhards who were legends in their own minds.

"Yeah well, anyway, we were married within a month and we've been living happily ever after since, right here at the Dew Drop Inn.

"And there's enough traffic to make a go of it?" Daniel asked hoping that he hadn't overstepped the boundaries.

"Barely, but yes. It's strange, but we have regulars if you can believe that, mostly around the hunting seasons, but they come for various other reasons as well. I guess Wanda's Dad was the kind of guy people are drawn to for a number of reasons, and even though there are a lot of "nicer" places in the area, a good number of folks keep coming back. Hopefully, we can continue to build a clientele of our own, but you know, it's not one of those things where you get all kissy assy. I think it's more like Wanda's Dad used to tell her; people respond well to *real*. The fact that her Dad had a bit of life insurance helped as we've been upgrading all the mechanical systems, and we'll eventually get around to shingles, macadam, carpets, furniture, fixtures etc., your so-called capital improvements as the accountant refers to them."

Kenny looked at his watch, and Daniel figured he was about to call the game on account of darkness. "Jesus, I've been jabbering on for days, what say I let you get a word in edgewise for a change."

"I'm not much of a talker," Daniel replied. "Especially when it's on cue," he added with a laugh.

"Well, don't feel obligated," Kenny said and Daniel felt a rush of gratitude and loosened up. "I *am* pretty tight lipped as a rule, but every now and then under certain conditions I get to going on like a thirteen-year old girl." He failed to add that it was an instinctive trust in someone's basic decency that greased his vocal cords, feeling that that was a little too personal to put out there at that point.

Kenny half expected a demonstration of this prolixity, but Daniel just clasped his hands behind his head, leaned back and looked up at the night sky. "Are you familiar with 2001?" Daniel asked suddenly.

"If you mean the space movie, yeah, I've seen it." Kenny answered.

"Did you know that according to Arthur C. Clarke, the crew of whatever "Apollo" spacecraft was up there in '68 actually discussed radioing back to earth that they had come upon a large black monolith?"

"No shit, like the one in the movie, huh. Jesus, that's rich," Kenny replied, laughing harder the longer he thought about it. "I never took those guys to be wiseacres, but hey, you never know about people, do you?"

"Amen to that brother," Daniel replied as some of his more notable missteps flashed through his mind.

"Hold the fort," Kenny said as he emerged from the bubbling water and hopped over the side.

Daniel pondered the "star farmers" and lit up another Camel Light while Kenny put an appropriate distance between them before taking a leak. The water temperature Kenny had just come from heightened the chill in the cool night air considerably, and it had Kenny doing a bit of a jig as he did his business and created a sense of urgency in getting back from whence he came. "Oh yeah," Kenny exulted as the hot soothing waters engulfed him. "You ought to step out for a moment. It'll remind you just how damn good this thing really feels," Kenny suggested enthusiastically.

Daniel pulled himself up, parked on the rim of the tub and decided he'd gone far enough. He watched the goose bumps abruptly arise and kind of marveled at the fact that instant relief was but a few feet down. He chose to artificially prolong the "suffering" and dipped himself back in a few inches at a time. He continued to peruse night sky and began to think it a bit odd that Kenny hadn't asked a single question of him—how he happened on the place, where he was headed, where he had come from—the usual stuff. It occurred to him that it might be part of some kind of Innkeepers code not to pry lest you create an uneasy circumstance. The ironic thing was that he actually felt like talking about it.

Out of the blue a question came but it was not one that Daniel had anticipated. "You got a light?"

Daniel was more than a bit surprised. "I got the impression you weren't a smoker."

"Well, I'm kind of a social smoker, which means I smoke very little. Besides, they *are* bad for you, but so is a lot of other shit, and it was supposed to have been a joke anyway." Daniel just smiled as he handed him the lighter.

"I must have blown the inflection," Kenny said with a sheepish grin as he lit up. It didn't take Daniel long to figure out that this was a very special cigarette as the piquant aroma wafted his way. A hand was extended across the bow all the way from the sixties. Daniel gratefully accepted the doobie and wasted no time inflating his lungs with the magical medicament. "The "buzz" was instantaneous, and Daniel further decelerated. "You know, if we took a Valium right now, we might go back in time," Daniel said with kind of a snort laugh. "It's been quite a long time, by the way," he added.

"I was pretty sure you weren't a Fed," Kenny said as he toked again and passed it over. They worked it down to a nub, and Daniel deferred the last toke. With no roach clip handy, Kenny set it on the side of the tub and siphoned the remaining smoke into his nostrils while Daniel watched with fascination. The both of them simultaneously adopted that earnest look that comes over an imbiber while the shift from one state of consciousness to another is completed. Comfortable in their new surroundings, they resumed the night's festivities without missing a beat.

"Speaking of movies, did you happen to catch *About Schmidt*?" Kenny asked.

"Jack Nicholson, Yeah," Daniel answered as he taxed his brain trying to recall more detail.

"Dear Ndugu," came from the direction of Kenny, but the Nicholson impression was so dead on that Daniel half expected to see the man himself hop over the side of the hot tub and join the party. Jack continued. "I'm as big a fan of the female form as the next son of a bitch, but gawd amighty, don't let that woman get in here with me. At the very least, cover her hefty ass up a little, would ya?"

When all the parts crystallized, Daniel was struck so hard with a laugh that it paralyzed him momentarily before it made its way out of his throat. Kenny just chuckled at the sight of Daniel's spasms. "Wanda scolded the hell out of me when I did that bit for her. Said it was disrespectful and I guess she was probably right." He paused for a moment as if crafting a defense. "She laughed too but insisted it was the Nicholson voice that got her. Ah, who knows?" he added, not wanting to further prosecute the case, knowing she had the upper hand.

Daniel finally managed to stop sputtering and had a yen for a smoke. He pulled one from the pack for himself and offered one to Kenny. "No thanks, I don't smoke," he said with dead seriousness and after a moment's hesitation, the two of them cracked up. They puffed away in complete silence. It was one of the things Daniel loved best about a good high. Laughter, like everything else was more intense, and the skewed perspective presented a much broader range of comic possibilities, but rhythm and momentum didn't count for much in this realm. You could segue from unbridled hilarity to meditative reverie in the blink of an eye, and it made perfectly good sense at the time.

The moon loomed large, larger than it had been, it seemed, and got Daniel to thinking about the episode of Dick Van Dyke he had seen a while ago. "You know, when you're making a list of capital improvements, you might want to add newer cable ready TVs or converter boxes at the very least," Daniel chided.

"Not a bad thought," Kenny replied. "But I feel compelled to tell you that too much television is not good for you," he added with a wry smirk and predictable laughter followed. "Nothing in the "dirty dozen" appealed to you huh?" Kenny asked.

"No, I managed fine. I caught the end of an old episode of the Dick Van Dyke Show, which I've always loved, and ironically, it was the one where he and Buddy were freaked out by this "oity oit" kind of sound that they thought was from aliens that had invaded the planet. You know what struck me most about 2001 was that there were no conquests per se. The unnamed things, the alien beings didn't seem malevolent at all. The fact that they scoured the universe in an attempt to foster the evolution of intelligence, or "mind" as Clarke put it, was an absolute stroke of genius. And "Moon Watcher" was one of the first beneficiaries. Now, what they chose to do with that intelligence, well, that's another matter, but the alien beings — for lack of a better term — had patience greater than Job himself, and it seems to me that it's a good thing to remember when we get to thinking that the world will always be all fucked up. Well, it probably will, but shit takes time. You know, I had the thought at the time of the big millennium celebration that the one good thing you could say about the twentieth century was that during that period of time, it became uncool to simply take over another country because you could. That not the case at all in the beginning of the century—although this recent fiasco with Iraq has set me to wondering"

Daniel's disjointed dissertation came to a screeching halt. He wasn't always the first to know when his enthusiasm took on a manic tone, but he caught on pretty quickly. "Jesus, I'm sorry, man. I think that stuff kicked in fully and bumped me in to overdrive. I hate to ramble on like a lunatic free-associating," Daniel said with enough wherewithal to be deeply embarrassed.

Kenny studied him for a long moment. "I'd say, you're more like a fourteen-year-old girl," he said with a good natured laugh as he grabbed Daniel's shoulder and gave it an affectionate squeeze.

Daniel liked this guy, and that was all there was to it. The shame that he'd heaped upon himself waned quickly, and he was overcome by an appreciation that he had no idea how to express, so he simply smiled and vowed to better manage the tempo.

"You know, I happened to catch a PBS presentation—I think it was "Hallmark Hall of Fame" although I'm not sure. Anyway, Dick Van Dyke and Mary Tyler Moore were reunited for the first time since the series was canceled in the sixties," Kenny added to further ease Daniel's mind by picking up as if nothing unusual had happened.

This guy's got a bit of Chelsea in him, Daniel thought to himself before responding. "You know I heard about that, but unfortunately, I missed it," Daniel chimed in, having pretty much forgotten his imagined faux pas. "It was a little bit weird in that they played a couple of elderly curmudgeons in a retirement home of some sort, and they were not very likable people, especially him."

"Hmm," Daniel intoned still making a conscious effort to keep it brief.

"Even stranger, Kenny continued, was that they both had incredibly foul mouths. God dammit, shit, son of a bitch, and on and on. They were really letting it fly."

"No way," Daniel replied. "You're not shitting me are you?"

"No, I'm dead serious. When he said, "fuck" I was surprised, but when she, sweet Mary, dropped the F bomb, I just about fell out of my chair."

"No way," Daniel replied again, still finding it hard to believe. Daniel chuckled a bit, pondering the incongruity of it all before introducing the next morsel of profundity into the evening's chronicle. "Did you happen to see the episode where Mary Tyler Moore got her big toe stuck in the faucet of the bath tub?"

"Yeah, boy did they know what they were doing or what?" Kenny answered. "I mean they couldn't even show a double bed because of what it implied, and Carl Reiner, that brilliant bastard, managed to get a good percentage of the American male population fantasizing about Mary nude behind that bathroom door."

Daniel's eyes kind of glazed over as if he was engaged in that very exercise at that very moment. "You know," Daniel started as if coming out of a trance. "If she had dropped the F bomb in that episode, I bet half the men in America would have creamed in their jeans."

This time it was Kenny who choked on his laughter before finally expelling it with a heave of his chest. "Jesus, I haven't heard that term in twenty-five years," he said still quivering.

The laughter slowly subsided and it was Kenny's turn to zone out. Daniel took his cue and explored the odd clarity that the altered state had engendered. He found himself staring at the tattoos on either of Kenny's arms and although the mermaid made sense, he couldn't help but wonder about the significance of the ship being bandied about in the choppy seas.

Kenny sensed his curiosity and flexed his bicep just enough to make it appear as if "Wanda" was shaking her booty. "She says she hates it, but she laughs like hell whenever I do it," Kenny commented as if the whole matter had been under discussion.

Daniel seized the opportunity and asked about the ship.

"You know something, Daniel, most people ask questions that they really have no interest in getting an answer to. And you keep asking questions that could be answered in a couple of sentences but that really go a whole lot deeper than that. And I'm happy to oblige because you seem genuinely interested."

Daniel was a bit flattered and completely baffled as to how to respond." "I don't know what to say except that the truth is most people bore my ass off, but I've always blamed myself for that. How 'bout I just say you're a fascinating fellow and we'll leave it at that." Daniel laughed nervously as that old vulnerable feeling welled up in him.

"Hey, I'll take it," Kenny said good-naturedly before launching his spiel. "Well, I already told you how we met, and as you may have figured, it was the combination of the sentiment and the sea that resulted in the mermaid, that and the fact that Wanda always wanted to be one. I got it just before we got married and sprung it on her on our honeymoon night. It was probably the best night we ever had together." Kenny paused for a moment and took a good hard look at Daniel. "You still awake over there?" he asked with a chuckle.

"Yeah, yes, go on."

Kenny was fishing for a little more encouragement than he got, but that would have to do. "About a year later, we had maybe the worst night of our lives. Things were tough here. Shit had been building up for a while, and nobody was giving an inch. It sounds ridiculous now, but then that's almost always the case, isn't it? We both seemed to be looking for something to get at each other's throats about, and her superstitions were ideally suited to the task. In fairness, I should add that they were her beliefs. I just didn't happen to see it that way. Now as a rule, I do not—I repeat, do not meddle with people's beliefs unless they're flogging me with them, so I have to concede in retrospect that I saw a big red button and just couldn't help myself."

"What kind of beliefs, or whatever you want to call them, were you two arguing about?" Daniel said trying to usher him to the point.

"She's kind of a romantic sort, and she's got a lot of different ones, but the bone of contention was this business of there being that "special one" out there for everyone if only you can find them. And if things don't work out, well, you obviously did not find Mr. or Mrs. Right, and you have at it again and again if necessary until you get it right, kind of like reincarnation. It never occurred to her that some people are on a life- long quest to find someone to kick them in the teeth because deep down, that's what they feel they deserve. That whole idea was the one that got things humming. I scoffed, and she felt like my cynicism was a veiled reference to our relationship. I suppose I did have a bit of an edge, but all I was trying to say was that it ain't that simple. That it's much more random, that human beings make choices for a whole host of reasons and that once made, there are mechanisms by which we work to sustain and reaffirm those choices because — well, I guess because we feel like it's worth the trouble. She thought it all sounded less like love and more like an epic struggle and I said what the hell's the difference? She was steadfast in arguing that we are all two halves in search of a whole. She repeated it for emphasis "two halves in search of a whole" Now what I should have said was, "Hey babe, it's just semantics." I mean we're here because we want to be, we've chosen to be, etc. But what I said just before she threw the lamp at me was that she was half right so long as she dropped the "w" in the last word."

It took Daniel a minute but he got it. "Ouch!" was all he could muster through a laugh at the sheer genius of the comment at the same time he was imagining a wounded and angry Wanda.

"If you go in the office and move the key board you can still see the hole in the wall, and as you might have figured that was the only "hole" I saw for a while. That's on my list of capital improvements by the way," he added with a laugh.

"What about the tattoo?" Daniel asked anxious to get to the point.

"Oh yeah, the tattoo. Well I flew out of the place, drove like a lunatic back to the shore where we'd met for some god dammed reason, headed straight for the tattoo place and told the guy I wanted a symbolic representation of the perfect storm, and this is what I got."

"You obviously patched things up."

"Hey, I love her man. What can I say besides she's worth the trouble?"

The whole "love" thing put the first serious dent in Daniel's armor, and in spite of his best efforts, he felt himself sinking. He tried to keep a stiff upper lip but his deflation gave off a certain aura, and he sensed that Kenny had picked up on it, which made him want to conceal it all the more.

Kenny did in fact get the feeling that there had been a sudden sea change and was unsure of how to proceed. "Hey, you okay," he asked.

"Yeah, I'm just tired. Been a long day."

"You want to call it a night?"

"Maybe we should," Daniel replied with little conviction. The two of them kind of looked at one another, waiting for the other to take the lead.

"Did you ever see the show, *To Tell the Truth?*" Kenny asked.

"No, it doesn't ring a bell," Daniel replied flatly.

"Well, it wouldn't make much sense then." Kenny figured that someone needed to make the first move and since Daniel seemed bolted to the hot tub, he started to rise.

"I'm a fraud." Daniel said.

Kenny turned quickly. "What's that you say?" Kenny asked, uncertain that he'd heard him correctly and eager to clarify what he imagined had to have been misconstrued.

"Let me amend that, I *feel* like a fraud."

"Jesus, I thought you said something to that effect. What the hell do you mean?"

"I didn't mean to be so melodramatic, I needed to throw that out there to ensure that I would have to explain myself. Things were winding down, and I had some stuff I wanted to say but was reluctant to."

Kenny contemplated that for a moment before speaking. "Daniel, we're like bartenders in this business. You can share whatever you choose and know that it will be held in the strictest confidence, but we make it a point not to pry."

"You know, I kind of suspected that," Daniel replied. "Anyway, when we were about to wrap things up, I kind of panicked. I've enjoyed our time together and I have you to thank for it," Daniel said, seeming to have found his voice through the churning emotion.

"Well, hey my pleasure, I try to be a reasonably good host," Kenny replied not quite sure where this was going

"It's more than that, Kenny. It's who and how you are that enabled me to relax and enjoy the evening. Shit, how do I say this? I don't function too well in most circumstances; more to the point, I don't do well with people in general. But you set me at ease from the moment we met, and that's no small feat."

"So, how does the *fraud* thing come into play?"

"Just an old habit of kicking myself when I'm down. Your story about your tattoos and the ups and downs of your relationship with Wanda made me kind of melancholy, I suppose, because I've had so little of that kind of thing in my life. Then I got to feeling that I couldn't have been who I was tonight without your participation, hence I'm a fraud and now I'm feeling like you must think I'm a complete head case."

"No, Daniel, no I don't think that at all. The truth is that I don't feel like I know anything at all about you and didn't feel it was my place to ask. I mean, shit, it's like you fell out of the sky like *My Favorite Martian*. For what it's worth though, I will tell you this was an unusual evening for me as well. We do seem to be on a similar wavelength, and that doesn't happen that often or that quickly, and it made for a good time."

Daniel felt like he was blushing and took to heart the kind words. "Ordinarily, the anonymity would be just the way I like it," He said. "It's not that I want to be mysterious; I just prefer not to be known because, well, because it's easier, I suppose. My forays into the "social world" usually end up being painful reminders of how inept I am at it, but it's more than that, and this is where it gets a little complicated. On those rare occasions in which I felt accepted or involved, I felt like I was going to suffocate, kind of like that old Peggy Lee song, "Is that all there is?" and I was never sure if it was me or them or what the hell was going on."

Kenny looked hard at Daniel and paused for a long moment before speaking. "So you're saying that like everybody else on the planet, all you really want is to love and be loved. "

"As much as I hate to admit it, I guess it really is as simple as that. Simple in theory, that is, but, of course, the execution is another matter."

"You know, I did watch you pull in, which tells me you weren't beamed down from a saucer, so why don't you tell me where you come from and where you're going. I've been wondering all night but didn't want to go against the "Innkeepers Creed."

Daniel allowed himself a laugh, in part in response to Kenny's comment and in part because he had no idea what the hell he was going to say. "Shit, where do I begin? On the heels of Rimbaud." The phrase followed as automatically as Pavlov's dog's saliva when he rang the bell.

Kenny raised an eyebrow and Daniel proceeded. "I read that on the liner notes of a Bob Dylan album, and ever since when I hear the "Where do I begin" in any form it's the first thing that pops into my head.

"Well, now we're getting to the heart of the matter," Kenny replied unctuously.

Daniel took a deep breath as if it were time to finally tell the story, and he was drawing a blank. "I can tell you where I came from because I left Dennis, Massachusetts about eight this morning, but I have no idea where I'm going. As a matter of fact, I have no idea where the hell we are right now, and it's all by design." Daniel glanced over at Kenny expecting to see a nonplussed expression, but the innkeeper was focused and attentive and waiting for Daniel to continue.

"I came in to some money recently. A modest sum by some standards but a veritable fortune to me. Anyway, I bought the one thing I've always wanted." Daniel paused as if trying to find just the right word and Kenny grew impatient.

"Speak up, man. Tell me where the gold is buried before you croak on me for Chrissakes!"

Daniel couldn't help but laugh but the point was taken. "Freedom, space, time, I guess."

Kenny gave him an oddly quizzical look, and Daniel continued.

"A block of time in this life that I don't have to start each day figuring out how I'm going to procure my next meal or enough money to continue to enjoy a roof over my head and a hot shower when I need one. It's kind of like in anthropology when primitive man finally had a little leisure time on his hands because of a particularly good hunt or a crop that would tide him over for a while, and he had the time and the capacity to reflect on it all and maybe try to make some sense of things."

"So it's like a spiritual quest."

"Well that sounds kind of lofty, but I suppose, in a very broad sense, it's not an altogether unfair characterization. I mean, there's no pilgrimage to Mecca, because I don't know where or what my version of such a place would be. Let's just say I'm trying to figure things out, mostly why I have such a hard time with the basics and why I don't really seem to fit in anywhere."

Kenny fell silent and looked to the stars for a long moment. His demeanor suggested that he got it and, furthermore, that his basic sense of decency was stymied by his unwillingness to toss out some glib and patronizing answer.

"Life is damn hard sometimes," he said finally, "short and brutish, as some political philosopher used to say, but it *is* worth the trouble, if you know what I mean, because now and then good shit like tonight happens. I suppose you've had your troubles and been damaged along the way, otherwise you wouldn't have the perceptions you do but I sense good things in you, Daniel, and all I can tell you is to keep on keeping on and things will be alright."

"Well, thanks for that, and thanks for everything, you've assured an *auspicious* start to my journey, if I may speak with a 'word of the day'."

"There's no need. The feeling is mutual," Kenny answered without hesitation. "I assume you'll be hitting the road first thing in the morning."

"Yeah, that's the plan," Daniel replied.

"Well, don't feel like you've got to rush off."

"Thanks, but it's best."

"Well, just know that you're welcome back here anytime. What's the guy say? I'll leave the light on for you," Kenny said with a chuckle.

"That means a lot to me," Daniel answered earnestly. "It's comforting to know there's a safe harbor out there if I need one." They both looked toward the dotted navy sky in silence for a time, not quite sure what to say next.

"I have half a mind to drive down to Sal's right now," Kenny suddenly blurted out, and Daniel nodded his head as he laughed. "And ten years ago I would have done just that," he added quietly. "Well anyway—goodnight, Daniel, and best of luck to you."

"Thanks, thanks a lot. At some point I suppose I'll make my way back through here, wherever the hell we are, and I'll be looking for that light."

"Count on it, friend,"

Daniel felt deeply humbled and appreciative, shook Kenny's hand and headed back toward his room. After a few steps, he sensed a voice trailing after him. "Don't piss it away this *time*, I mean, it may seem now like you've got forever, but you don't. Think urgent, friend but don't be kicking yourself all the time thinking you're behind schedule."

"It's a promise," he replied as he turned the corner.

Daniel, knowing that his bed awaited, allowed the full weight of his exhaustion to descend upon him. He said a quick goodnight to Golda and eschewed the construction projects awaiting him and filled his mind with imaginings of Chelsea's soft sweet body next to his.

"A decent fellow," Kenny thought to himself "Shame what he puts himself through." But he had seen this particular malady before, the thin film, like scum building up on a stagnant pond and casting a pall over the clear waters beneath it. Not an easy thing to shake I imagine, he mused finally, before turning his attention to the little nightly ritual of turning off the unnecessary lights and locking up.

Kenny tiptoed in the darkness and lay down gently next to his sleeping beauty. Historically, a bold and adventurous type, he thought for a moment about Daniel's current state of being, footloose and fancy free with a world of possibility beckoning, and he too felt the gravitational pull of the highway. But as he cuddled extra close to the lion tamer, he knew with only a healthy scintilla of doubt that he was right where he belonged. Wanda was, after all, worth the trouble!

Chapter 24

Daniel slept heavier than usual that night. It wasn't quite the sleep of angels, but the demon herd had been thinned considerably. He'd added a couple of notches to the plus side of the equation, and his body chemistry was responding accordingly. After a shower, a shave and some attention to Golda, he turned the old TV back on, hoping to catch directions to the Franklin Diner, convincing himself that it was Willow's *personal guarantee* and not Willow herself that was the draw. After wading through commercials for used cars and wood burning stoves, he decided the Grille would suit him just fine.

He stepped outside to a day glorious with sunshine, and for the first time since his arrival he could really see his surroundings. There was nothing new or shiny about any of it, but all of it had a certain character. The place was well maintained, but more importantly well made to begin with, not a lot of flair but more than your standard form following function. Daniel felt good, he wouldn't acknowledge it openly but he knew it and tried to keep a lid on it. That coupled with the fact that the simple act of approaching a diner always gave him a boost and there was a definite bounce in his step as he made his way across the street.

Daniel decided to keep it simple and forego his usual "western omelet ensemble" and order the basic eggs, home fries, toast and choice of meat. The number of patrons only slightly exceeded the previous evening's number, assuring quick service again. Daniel thought it ironic that it wasn't until he literally had nothing but time on his hands that the world had finally found its groove and become monstrously efficient,though he suspected there would still be stubborn pockets of resistance here and there. As he chowed down, he was surprised to find that he was being serenaded by a lively classical piece seemingly emanating from the kitchen. The "real" newspaper wouldn't be available until ten or so, he'd been told, so he perused a weekly publication comprised largely of ads for local businesses grudgingly sharing space with a couple of rehashed local interest stories.

"Will there be anything else?" the waitress with pen poised asked politely.

"I'll need some lettuce to go, if that's possible."

"Sure, no problem," she replied though the arched eyebrow hinted at the oddness of the request. A quick trip to the kitchen and back produced a Styrofoam container stuffed with green. "No charge for the lettuce, by the way," she said with a wry smile.

"I have a guinea pig. It's a long story."

"No need. I can take that up for you if you like."

"Sure, thanks." Daniel peeled off a ten spot that included a tip approaching the cost of his meal and handed it to her.

"I'll bring your change."

"No need!" he said, returning the smile.

"Well thanks, stranger. You just made my day."

Daniel nursed what was left of his coffee and gazed across the street at the Dew Drop Inn, trying to imagine how different a place it would be when Kenny had completed the 'capital improvements.' Not too terribly, he mused, but then that wasn't the appeal. As he headed for the door, he heard the clacking of footsteps hustling up behind him, and he patted his pockets figuring that he must have left something at the booth. Instead, the waitress handed him a small card with the name of the place and decorated with the image of a rustic grist mill, even though there was nothing of the sort in the vicinity, at least as far as he had observed.

"Your tenth meal is free," she said, still catching her breath. Daniel accepted the card and noticed that there were three holes punched out over the numbers running across the bottom of the card. "Is there a three for one special going on today or something?"

"No, but you ate here last evening."

"Okay that's two." "And well, I threw in an extra because you've been generous with us!" she said with a pleasant smile.

"I guess you would call that karma," he replied in lieu of a thank you, and her expression convinced Daniel that no explanation was necessary.

During the brief silence that ensued, he considered telling her that he was just passing through, that it would be difficult racking up the magic number to earn the freebie even with the head start she'd been so kind as to give him, but he sensed somehow that she knew all that already. "Well, goodbye and hey, you never know, a little bit of extra incentive can go a long way!"

"We hope to see you again," she said in that hostess's perfunctory tone that may or may not be tinged with sincerity, but Daniel was in a buying mood and returned the sentiment.

Chapter 25

"You know, Golda, sometimes the world can be a right good place," Daniel proclaimed, and she apparently concurred, although she was too busy with the green stuff to respond. "Why one might go so far as to say 'doubleplusgood' he added distractedly as he scanned the room for stragglers.

While she ate, Daniel carried the last of his gear to the car. I'm just waiting on you, Golda girl, he thought to himself as he lit a cigarette and took one last look around. He would have liked to have had a chance to say goodbye to Kenny and Wanda, but it was just as well. He considered tacking a note to the office door but passed on the idea. No need for graceful extrication he thought to himself, just a heartfelt thanks for providing a soft landing on a very emotional day.

"Okay, Golda girl, I think you've had enough for a while. What say we hit the road?" he chided her, but she paid him no mind and kept right on munching as he carried her to the car.

Daniel looked back at the office door without a note as he rolled to the edge of the highway and bid a silent farewell to his hosts. He didn't catch sight of the black dog lurking by the far end of the building, but it saw him. He still had little idea of his whereabouts besides the general region beyond which common sense told him he could not have traversed. He pulled the Grille card from his shirt pocket and tucked it neatly in the back of the glove compartment lest he should ever need to locate this place again. Daniel did a final systems check, shared an imaginary thumbs up with Golda and lurched once again into oblivion.

Chapter 26

The first five or six days were a blur, though not altogether without merit. Daniel had rather imagined that a good portion of the trip would be spent much like a dog with his head jutting out the car window, eyes squinted and ears flapping in the manufactured wind, reading the passing landscape by simply snorting a myriad of passing scents. And since his departure from the Dew Drop Inn, that's pretty much the way it had gone. He had loped along, eaten what and when he felt like it, from three dollars and fifty cent cheeseburgers in quaint diners to sixty dollar steaks in places he had to secure a tie to gain entry. He had dawdled in places that caught his fancy from idyllic riversides to towns right out of a Norman Rockwell painting to glistening cities with their dramatic architectural offerings and their squalid and dilapidated underpinnings. He had laid up in hotels ranging from one star to five, with the kind of amenities he'd only been exposed to on reruns of *Lifestyles of the Rich and Famous* with the ultimate wanna-be, Robin something or other, sipping champagne as he gave the great unwashed a glimpse of the big time.

Rolling across the highways and byways of America, Daniel had spent large chunks of time toying with concepts and ideas. It struck him, for instance, that the "live for the moment" ideology that he was engaged in and that was scorned by many as being self-absorbed, narcissistic and suggestive of some sort of arrested development, borrowed liberally from the same language used by those preaching enlightenment. And how those doing the preaching, while eschewing material things, never seemed to want for much, as the procurement of worldly goods was left in the hands of God or fate or whatever, but in truth were usually very well provided for in some fashion by their devotees, the implication being that they could have it because *they* didn't need it. "Kiss your own feet, asshole, and while you're at it, shove that big toe right up your ass," Daniel had bellowed with a laugh at thought's completion.

Over the many miles, Daniel debated in classic "chicken and egg" fashion whether *purpose* was derived from *meaning* or vice versa, and after some strenuous mental machinations threw in the towel and concluded that it could go either way. Down the road a ways, in a masterstroke, he postulated that a touch of paranoia did indeed have the potential to boost one's intelligence if for no other reason than the fact that one would be forced to look at matters from a number of different perspectives due to having to consider the myriad ways one might be attacked. His enthusiasm for the finding waned just a tad when he ruefully conceded that this phenomenon just might have some bearing on his own intellectual prowess.

Besides Daniel's desultory sightseeing and cognition, he had covered long monotonous stretches of road that he navigated both literally and figuratively on cruise control. "Flat lining" he had come to calling it, but even those interludes, he reasoned, were not spent in vain as he believed that nothing was ever static, and even though he couldn't say exactly what was going on inside of him, there must have been some kind of healing, ailing or agitating taking place.

"He not busy being born is busy dying," Bob Dylan had wailed on the radio before the overpass intercepted the signal and drowned out the rest of the song, and Daniel convinced himself that he fell into the former column. But a subtle almost imperceptible shift began to occur on or about the fifth day. The first clue was that he found himself rationalizing and justifying his conduct on the journey. It was as if the bell had rung, signaling that recess was over, but he wasn't done playing yet, and he wanted to bargain for more time. The second was that he began to see hints of doubt and fear in many of the faces he encountered and after the trend was well enough established, simple deduction told him that the odds were high that it resided not in them but him.

From its inception the trip had no agenda, no theme beyond motion and time to catch his breath and indulge in the twin luxuries of reflection and contemplation but Daniel knew well that there was one other consideration. And the gnawing sensation rumbling around his innards was his body's way of reminding him that he had "issues" that had accompanied him on the trip and lest he address them, they would tag along like a hitchhiker that was going "his way" and ultimately be found sitting on his doorstep at journey's end and it all would have gone "for a good time and a song" as James Taylor crooned. He fought it valiantly for a time before he clearly interpreted the emotional hieroglyphics, finally conceding that rightly or wrongly without the yin and yang of a cycle of toil and rest, the "rest" part of the equation would diminish in value. He shuddered as the message was fully realized and vowed not to let that happen. He would, he decided, moderate his hedonism and dedicate a certain amount of time and energy to trying to divine just how he might go about instituting some constructive and lasting change in his life. Kenny's seemingly oxymoronic exhortation counseling him to "think urgent, friend but don't be kicking yourself all the time thinking you're behind schedule" all of a sudden made a great deal of sense.

Chapter 27

Having coughed up an insight and committed himself to a course of action of some sort constituted, Daniel felt, work in a way, hence he argued he was entitled to a little R&R. "It's good to be king," he said out loud with a devilish little laugh. "You see, Golda, when you're the king, you not only get to call the shots, you get to make the rules and set the standards. So after an official inquiry and no small measure of circumspection, I, King Daniel, have decided that I am indeed entitled to a few more days of leisure." He looked over at his little friend, and she looked right back at him. "Yes, I know I'm procrastinating but cut me some slack. This thing is front and center now and dredging it up from the depths of my psyche was no small feat." He looked at her again, and her expression had not changed. "And hey, little friend, if anybody ought to know a thing or two about "small feet," it's you," he added as he looked over at her once more. This time her expression *had* changed. She looked like she actually got the humor in his very small joke, and the thought of that made Daniel laugh like hell at the same time that it set him to thinking. Of course, he didn't believe she actually got the joke, but it did bring to mind R.D. Laing, and for some reason, probably because it suddenly seemed to apply to guinea pigs as well as people, he decided to share his recollections with Golda.

"You know, I read a book some years ago, are you listening?" he asked looking over at her. "Well, it doesn't really matter. Anyway, this guy had theories about the ultimate inability of people to know one another, and early in the book, he demonstrated it with this little exercise that has always stuck in my mind. *I see you and you see me. I experience you and you experience me.* "You got that so far?" he asked as he confirmed in his own mind that this held true in this particular situation. *I see your behavior and you see my behavior. But I do not and never have and never will see your experience of me and vice-versa. I cannot experience your experience of me and you cannot experience my experience of you.* "The point of it all, I suppose, is to substantiate in some way the fact that there are inherent limits to the extent to which we can truly connect with other human beings or in this case, other beings. I mean I do experience you as experiencing me and vice–versa. We can infer, speculate and attempt to try to understand one another, but it can only go so far."

"You know, Golda, the blank stare I'm getting from you right now is pretty much the reaction I got from everybody I ever shared that with. I mean, I always found shit like that fascinating, but then I guess, I'm weird," he finished with a self-deprecating laugh. "I'll tell you what, Golda, one of these days I'm gonna find a woman that says, "That's kind of cool. Let's see if we can buck the odds and approximate our experiences of each other, and then, then, little friend, I'll know I'll have found Miss Right..." Hmmm, maybe that Wanda *was* on to something," he reversed the order, and finished his monologue with a thought.

Daniel noticed the gas gauge getting low, and he had a yen for a Pepsi and a Snickers and as luck would have it, he spotted a Plus Mart about a hundred yards ahead on the right.

There are days when the world, or at least the small slice of it one inhabits at any given time, is so rife with negative ions that it seems to set all the inner workings in just the right order, and one can't help but bask in the glory of it all. Daniel leaned against the wondermobile as he sated his prize with it's particular elixir, soaked up the sunshine and enjoyed the dawdling wind planting angel kisses on his cheeks. He suddenly felt like he had the eyesight of an eagle and marveled at each individual blade of grass in a clump that had poked their heads through an oil-stained patch of macadam twenty feet away. "L'echaim," he said reverently in the direction of the blades that had reached for the sky in spite of monumental odds.

The jolt of the pump tripping off startled Daniel out of his reverie, and he looked around to get his bearings. He took one more big gulp of ambrosia and tapped on the glass to let Golda know he'd be right back. Random images, each special in its own way, of the many of the beautiful scenes that had become lodged in his psyche over the years swirled around in his head as he ambled in to pay for the gas and procure his bounty. He shared a hearty "Good day," with the disinterested kid behind the counter and refused to feel trite for doing so. As he reached for his change, he felt a subtle yet somehow ominous rumble that reverberated through the store and stopped everyone in their tracks.

All eyes were averted to the east, as the incoming sound seemed to emanate from that direction. Finally, the tip of a monster truck crept into their collective field of vision and most breathed a sigh of relief. It continued on past the front of the building, and through the big plate glass windows, Daniel caught a glimpse of a woman with her head down riding shotgun and what appeared to be a young scruffy-looking girl jammed into the small space between the seat and the back window of the cab. The thunderous roar of the idling truck was enhanced by the low growl of the heavy bass of a song drowning out the other instruments futile attempts at being heard.

Daniel completed his transaction and moved reluctantly in the direction of the door. His pulse had quickened, and his palms were clammy and whatever danger he sensed was confirmed as he pushed open the door and saw the woman's head recoil violently as the beast behind the wheel shook his clenched fist in her face. He wasn't sure if the man had assaulted her or just threatened to.

Daniel froze in his tracks, immobilized by the contradictory impulses racing through his body. He imagined himself yanking the brute from the truck and rescuing the damsel in distress at almost the same time that he envisioned the berserker crushing his fragile skull with a crow bar that he kept at the ready under the seat. He conceded with a rush of self-hatred that it was a *personal* matter and that he ought not get involved while he considered calling 911 from a pay phone safely down the road. As he torturously pondered his next move, the wrenching sound of metal scraping metal forced his attention toward the truck that he would have to get past to reach the relative safety of the wondermobile. "Don't just stand here, you dumb fuck," he scolded himself under his breath. The frightening brute's one scarred leather boot and then the other hit the pavement before the wrenching sound was repeated. He spit out a few more choice words to his prey in the truck and turned toward the building and Daniel.

Daniel tried desperately to appear calm and cool and even managed to kick-start his motion by putting one foot in front of the other. He looked away to the extent that he could, considering the daunting prospect of having to cross paths with the maniac. It was too late to "cross the street" to avoid a confrontation, and in spite of the arc that Daniel tried to follow to allow for a little more distance between himself and his potential combatant, there seemed to be a magnetic force drawing him ever closer to danger. They approached each other without a word, although Daniel's formidable powers of projection were in high gear, and he imagined an angry jaw jutting in his face menacing him, excoriating him in a gush of hot vile breath. "Fuck you if you don't like it loud" "Keep your fucking nose out of my business or I'll break it for ya."

At the moment their paths intersected, Daniel focused his gaze directly on the letters of his license plate, "BOURGLAY" and on some subterranean level, Daniel understood what might have driven Jules to the extreme measures that he'd taken. He read it an interminable amount of times in the milliseconds that passed, but still he sensed the glare of the brute all over him, looking for anything to interpret as hostile intent. Daniel's body was a chemical explosion of the highest magnitude. He could feel and smell this man's anger. It seemed to emanate from him in as real a physical sense as sweat.

Finally, after what seemed like hours, things began to settle down. Each step that carried him another yard from danger diminished the odds that the episode would end in Armageddon. As he passed the truck, he smelled the same pungent aroma of anger and wondered if the beast had marked his territory with his scent. He tried not to look at the truck or its inhabitants as he walked by it but he couldn't help noticing the scruffy little girl staring at him. Ordinarily, he would have smiled or waved, but under these circumstances, he thought it best not to have any kind of contact with this troubled gang. He glanced again against his will, and her pleading eyes remained riveted on him. "Shit," he muttered under his breath as he forced himself to acknowledge her. He felt bad for her and the woman and wished there was something he could do to offer some solace in what he imagined was a horrific existence.

Just as he was about to smile and doff his imaginary cap to the girl, he noticed that the woman had spoken to her, shifting her attention. He took the opportunity to extricate himself from the scene and made it at last to the door of the wondermobile. His heart was still pumping hard as he looked in at Golda. He opened the car door, breathed a great sigh of relief and slid in. He fired it up and was further comforted by the soothing hum of the engine.

As Daniel backed out, he was unable to stop himself from one last look over at the truck and specifically at the woman's face. He fully expected to see a black eye or a bloody lip, but from what he could see, there was no evidence of physical abuse. She looked beaten down for sure, but as far as he could tell, not beaten up. Daniel sensed a profound sadness and helplessness in the woman, and his heart went out to her even though he knew there was nothing he could do for her. He saw her head turning slightly, and rather than look away, he thought that at the very least he could give her a smile, let her know in some small way that not everyone was intent on hurting her. She locked her sunken, bloodshot eyes on Daniel but the vacuous stare sent a chill up Daniel's spine. All the more reason to acknowledge her in a positive way, he thought, as he pushed past the horror. In spite of the chaos rifling through his psyche, he steeled himself, doffed his imaginary cap and smiled the most beatific smile he could muster. "What the fuck are you looking at," blew out of her contorted mouth, as hot and angry as molten lava. Daniel shrunk back, managed to get his attention focused on the basics of operating an automobile and skulked out of the parking lot.

Chapter 28

The tag team of fear and anger had surged forth in an apocalyptic frenzy and stoked one another exponentially until they both imploded, and the circuit tripped. The overall impact of the incident was immediate and severe, trumping the good things that had come Daniel's way of late, sending them into remission and leaving Daniel in the equivalent of an emotional coma. He could walk and drive and eat and smoke, in other words, the autonomic nervous system of mundane activity was functional, but there was no spark, just a vapid droning.

Golda sensed that all was not right with Daniel's world, but regrettably there was little she could do about it. For the next two or three days, he flat-lined on the road and off. There was mental activity, but it may as well have been unconscious. Food was consumed and expelled, but there was no experience of taste. The amount of caffeine he took in would have had him wired for days prior to the incident, but it was barely enough to keep him awake now. His sleep, normally punctuated by multiple repositionings, was as deep and dark as the dead. In the morning, he lay sprawled across the bed, head hanging over the mattress, staring at the floor. At some point in the late morning or early afternoon, he dragged himself into the shower, planted his feet and let the hot water cascade over him for so long that the boiler in the bowels of the building had a hard time keeping up, and even that did little to cleanse the toxins from his body. He exited the shower, flopped back on the bed dripping wet and naked and took to staring at the floor all over again.

Even in his stupor, he never forgot about Golda. She didn't get the normal amount of attention and affection, but Daniel refused to allow his wasted state to interfere with her basic needs. He tended to her mechanically, but he did it and didn't bother pummeling himself further for not having more to offer. Daniel dredged up a hazy recollection of one of his blackest hours in which the fleeting thought of suicide had crept in only to be dismissed immediately because he feared that by the time anybody found him, Golda may be dead as well.

In a strange sort of way that he didn't appreciate at the time, there was a perverse healthiness in his self-absorption. Odd as it may be, Daniel was doing what he needed to do in putting his needs first, and although it was currently beyond his comprehension, Daniel *was* a believer in process. He felt that the body, for reasons he imagined were somehow tied to the evolution of the species, possessed an inner mechanism that strove constantly for equilibrium. That it had natural states and rhythms and would find the other side if left to its own devices and that you could on occasion, he believed, accelerate this process but not without the body's express written consent.

By the third night, the worst had passed and though still bordering on catatonic, the black cloud that was his psyche was moving north. There was nothing even remotely resembling clarity in his thinking, but he could kind of follow a utilitarian train of thought, and there was some logic to his movements. He took Golda out of her cage and stroked her silently, trying to atone for his indifference. He called room service, and although he was confident that her vital vitamin C intake had been covered by her pellets, they had never looked very tasty, so he made it a point to order her an orange and a side dish of broccoli. He put an ice cube in her water dish and gently set her back in her abode to partake of the feast. He watched her chow down with glee and kind of half smiled for the first time since the big bang.

Daniel turned on the TV and actually heard every third or fourth word. In flipping through the channels, he arrived at the "Optional Offerings" that naturally came with a price tag. He watched the two-minute teaser that showed enough to leave absolutely no doubt what the smarmy looking couple was about to engage in. It must have been an effective marketing tool because Daniel, not normally given to impulse buying, didn't hesitate to press the button that initiated the action almost as quickly as it electronically added the nine-dollar charge to his tab. Then lo and behold, he had a thought, a coherent thought that suggested his synapses were firing or at least sputtering which gave him an ever-so-subtle boost by virtue of simply having had it.

He recalled a piece he'd read about the amount of revenue generated by porn in otherwise respectable establishments, boosting the bottom lines, so to speak, of some national corporate stalwarts, many of whom contributed mightily no doubt to the "family values" crowd come election time. "And what the fuck does running on "family values" mean anyway?" He scowled to himself, actually making a mental note of the positive development expressed by his irritated cynicism. "What's the flip side, 'anti-family values'? And who the hell…, "Ah fuck it, he thought. "I'd better pay attention lest I let the plot escape me," he kind of chortled to himself.

Daniel began to give the "movie" his undivided attention, and the diversion was good. Even better were the tingling sensations emanating from his groin area. Just as a starving man would likely be unconcerned with the source of a morsel of sustenance, Daniel didn't bother to question the source of his inspiration, for in his current state of impoverishment, desire was much more than a mere boner. It was the driving force that assured the perpetuation of the species, and in its most fundamental sense, desire equated to want—as in I want to eat, to participate, to question, to love, to make love, to grow and ultimately to live. And "want" meant having to be proactive, to procure, which is what would eventually lead Daniel once again to move between life's many variations on the theme of getting from point A to point B.

And so he took matters into his own hands, literally. He finished with a shudder and noticed immediately how much less appealing the copulating couple was, and although frugal as a general rule, he punched the off button on the remote and canceled about eight dollars' worth of the evening's entertainment. He lay silently on the bed in a room the color of despair and wondered why the salt from his tears didn't sting his eyes before they journeyed down his cheeks.

Chapter 29

Daniel could not be considered fully back on track, but it was fair to say that he was at least on the right track. He had assumed before his slumber that he would wake up to a world at least as bleak as the one he'd taken leave of the night before, but to his pleasant surprise he awoke at a reasonable time and felt immediately that the lead levels in his blood had dropped considerably. He flipped on the TV and caught the *Imus in the Morning* radio show's simulcast on MSNBC and managed a stifled laugh as Imus aimed his acerbic barbs at some overblown Hollywood ego while a fellow named Bernie likened the I Man's western style wardrobe to that of Dale Evans.

He found himself in essentially the same position he had been in the two previous mornings since the drubbing, sprawled across the bed with his chin hanging over the edge of the mattress, but this time it was by choice. The first bit of data that crystallized into what could be called an insight was that this examination would go to the heart of the "issues" that he had vowed to address after "a few more days of leisure." He understood again that it took being in the throes of an incident of this type to drive home the enormity of what he was up against. He ventured back to the crime scene and began the forensic analysis.

Daniel suspected that as usual, he'd been the producer and the director of at least part of the action that had taken place at the Plus Mart, but the question was how much. Had there really been any danger at all? Well, yes and no, he decided. The image of his father sprung into his mind as he correlated the palpable hostility he encountered from the "beast" with the man that his father became when the firewater got the best of him. The threat back then had been constant and real as was evidenced by the assaults on Daniel's person that he could never fully anticipate. He recalled occasions when he cringed in fear, which seemed to reach some errant spark of humanity in the old man, and he would scoff and storm out. At other times, the same reaction on Daniel's part was seen as a provocation, an indictment that further fueled his father's rage, and he rained blows on Daniel with great ferocity.

There was never any discussion of the incidents after the fact and certainly no apologies. Initially, Daniel felt that he had some kind of barometer as to the "terror level" in that it almost always happened when there was drinking going on, and on those occasions, he would make himself as scarce as the circumstances allowed. But with time and terror and enough incidents that fell out of the predictable high-alert periods, it finally became necessary to assume that the danger was omnipresent. Daniel, some time ago, had pegged that as the precise moment that the world became a truly fearsome place.

But this was old news, he thought to himself, as was his propensity to project the worst of his fears onto any and everything that remotely resembled his original tormentor.

Daniel had been around any number of "similar" types and had his hackles raised a bit, creating varying amounts of emotional discombobulation but over time had gotten to the point where he was pretty much able to distinguish between real and imagined danger. The bigger question was why and how the years of "improvement" could be wiped out, at least temporarily, in a matter of minutes.

Daniel was frustrated with his inability to pinpoint the exact reason he had come apart at the seams and fearfully entertained the notion that his imagined "improvement" was mostly a mirage. "Shit," he said to no one as he reached for a cigarette. Fear and loathing in anytown, USA, he thought as he drew hard on the Camel Light. He walked around in circles as he smoked and was glad to feel the sensation of hunger. He headed for the shower and decided that today he would go the whole nine yards, shampoo, shave, maybe even some smell goods. "Fake it til you make it," he barked aloud in the direction of Golda and imagined that she winked her understanding.

The static electricity was in fact stimulating, and Daniel recalled that he did his best thinking in the shower. He quickly dismissed the veracity of the notion that the years of "work" had been for naught. After all, he reasoned, this would have been a weeks-long saga some years ago, and although painful, he felt like his recovery was moving along reasonably well, and just the fact that he was already in a position to predict with some confidence that within a week he'd be back to normal, or at least his version of it, eased his mind that much more. "Always was and always will be" was the phrase that he'd picked up from a Christian prayer somewhere along the way, and in his darkest days, it would always come back to haunt him as an indicator of where he'd been and what he could expect from the future, and that recollection seemed to clinch the argument that he had in fact made progress.

Daniel suddenly flashed back to the image of the woman's head whipsawing in the truck and seized on a partial explanation for his overreaction. It wasn't just a hypothetical or simply projection, he reasoned. He had witnessed the fact of violence, and that had raised the stakes considerably. Yeah, there's something to that, he thought with enough satisfaction that he put the whole matter aside and grabbed for the little bar of soap. As the steaming hot water flowed over him, and he scrubbed the funk from his person, he caught a glimpse of himself in the foggy mirror. The steamy haze was just blurry enough so that all he could see was a hint of flesh, and to his amazement he fancied that Chelsea had appeared in an angelic visitation.

He watched as she approached, delicately opened the glass door and stepped lightly over the elevated threshold. "I'll make a deal with you, good sir, I'll wash your back if you'll return the favor." He stood directly under the showerhead so that the only way to get his breath was to gulp air in through his mouth and imagined that she went first. He did return the favor and held the image as long as he could, but his mental sabbatical ran short, and he found himself back where he started. "Damn," he proclaimed. "She was such a sweetheart."

The longing tried to get a foothold but he nipped it in the bud. He didn't want to canonize her or start entertaining the illusion that "if only" all would be well. In an odd way, this approach safeguarded her legacy. Like a rock star who had died too young, she could be forever frozen in time as the paradigm, the template, the benchmark. The one who showed him how things could be, how human beings could consider one another.

Most of the learning he'd done prior to Chelsea had a heavy emphasis on how not to be. She personified "the benefit of the doubt," he thought and although on the face of it, it didn't sound like an achievement of great magnitude, Daniel knew how rare a gift it was.

Chapter 30

The "trauma" had receded significantly and Daniel felt like treating himself with a hearty breakfast of a western omelet with a little extra Swiss for cohesion, whole-wheat toast and charbroiled home fries. He stared outside at a lusciously sunny day and thought it ironic that as he emerged to rejoin the living, he was welcomed by such a warm embrace. As he perused the local paper and moved some of the "undercooked" home fries under the well-done portion to ensure just the right texture overall, he found himself thinking about his uncle. The remembrance of loss was quickly supplanted by more pleasant recollections. He let the paper go limp as he roamed the mental countryside, recounting all the reasons Howard had become so important to him. In the pain and chaos of his youth, the one bright spot was the periodic visit from his Uncle Howard.

Young Daniel could not have articulated the appeal of his uncle nor did he bother to contrast the acceptance he relished with the tenuous link he felt to his immediate family. He just knew that this man would never hurt him and seemed to take a sincere interest in even the most mundane details of his life. A faint churning began in Daniel's stomach as an uncharted avenue of memory seemed to be pushing its way to the forefront of his consciousness like a drowning man thrusting desperately toward the surface of the water.

It seemed that most of the time when Howard visited, he did it when Daniel's father was away hunting or fishing or just away for reasons that as he explained "were nobody's fucking business." Howard was Daniel's mother's older brother, and Daniel's father seemed to barely tolerate him. This particular visit was doubly special because it was the first time Howard had been up since Daniel had been down to Alabama to spend a few days with Howard and Mark, a trip born of Daniel's parents' escalating problems that would require that all seconds depart the ring before the serious fisticuffs began. The hope was that this last ditch attempt to recapture the "magic" would serve to strengthen a very important bond and indeed it did, the one between Daniel and his beloved uncle.

Howard and Daniel had hiked through the woods and along the creek, and Daniel remembered the conversation vividly because they had been talking about Mark Twain's *Huckleberry Finn* which Daniel had been reading for school. When asked about his impressions of the book, Daniel had gone on and on about the raft and all that it represented to him, excitement, freedom, adventure and the like. He had gotten so caught up in the telling of it that he became a bit embarrassed and timidly asked his uncle what he most liked about the book. "Well, it's been an awfully long time since I read it, but there was one passage in particular that really got a hold of me," he started, as Daniel managed to divide his attention between the rapture he envisioned rolling down the mighty Mississippi and Howard's response.

"What was it?" Daniel asked dutifully.

"There's a point at which Huck is faced with a real moral dilemma. He ran headlong into everything he'd ever been taught, and if he'd listened to his conscience, he'd have turned ol' Jim in and gone about his business. Now to you and me, it might seem like he did the obvious thing but you have to remember the time and the circumstances."

Daniel got a warm feeling from his inclusion in the realm of upright and reasonable people and was further drawn in to the story.

"He'd been taught that slaves like Jim were not, how would you say it, well, not quite full-fledged people and that the proper course of action would have been to turn Jim over to his rightful owner. Beyond that, he believed that he'd pay a heavy price for not doing exactly that."

By now, Daniel had forgotten all about his great adventures and was totally focused on every word Howard spoke, and when he paused for a moment, Daniel was quick to get him started again.

"Go on," he admonished Howard, sounding a little more forceful than he had intended.

"Yes, well, anyway, Huck not only believed he'd be scorned and ridiculed and shunned, but more than that he *believed* that the very dispensation of his soul was at stake. He battled back and forth in his mind as to what constituted the right thing to do and went so far as to pen a note to the woman that owned Jim that would seal his friend's fate."

Daniel struggled to recall that particular portion of the book, but all he saw was the raft and the river.

"All right then, I'll go to hell!" burst from Howard's mouth, catching Daniel completely off guard. Had he pissed his uncle off, he fretted. Was he not sufficiently attentive? That was the kind of thing his father would hurl at him from out of the blue, he thought, but wait, he said *he'd* go to hell, he didn't tell me to go.

As Daniel's head spun, Howard seemed to realize the havoc he'd wreaked and set immediately to fixing it. "No, no, no, Daniel," he started with a half laugh. "That's what Huck said when he finally settled the matter in his mind. Jesus, I'm sorry son. I sure didn't mean to startle you."

Daniel got his bearings but had kind of lost his stride. "I'm not sure I understand, Howard," he said trying to buy a little time to get up to speed.

"Well, Daniel, Huck truly believed that the penalty he'd pay for the decision he made was to be condemned to burn in the fires of hell for all of eternity, but he loved Jim and knew him to be a good and decent human being in spite of everything he'd ever been told about 'those people.'"

"When you put it that way, I guess it was kind of a heroic act," Daniel said as he absorbed the enormity of it all.

"Well put, son. That was exactly my point."

Daniel flagged the waitress to refill his coffee and thought it somewhat incongruous that such a pleasant memory could cause the subtle apprehension that he had felt, but as he turned his attention back to the narrative, it all began to make sense.

It had always been Daniel's intention to come clean with Howard regarding his father's drinking and abusive behavior, and each successive visit was preceded by an almost ritualistic preparation to finally spill the beans. He wasn't sure what he had hoped to achieve. He just felt like he *had* to share it with someone, and his uncle seemed like the logical choice. There *was* shame and fear, for that matter, and the concern that he might stir something up that he would "hopefully" live to regret. But the strength with which the impulse to confide in Howard grew as the visits neared reversed itself upon his arrival, and the momentum shifted back to sweeping it yet again to its rightful place under the carpet.

Daniel argued to himself that it was somehow disloyal to air the family's dirty laundry, and then, of course, there was always the hope that the situation would right itself. Then, boy, would he feel bad for having blown so minor a matter so far out of proportion and this in spite of the fact that by the time each visit rolled around, the laundry list of charges included a few more dirty items. Perhaps, it was simply that he wanted to separate the two universes lest one somehow despoil the other.

Finally, Daniel imagined that his mother must have given Howard some indication of the extent of the problem, conveniently forgetting that irrespective of all her sterling qualities, she of all people was the master of the white-wash, the ultimate apologist for all but the most heinous behavior, and even in those instances, someone who could pull a caveat out of a hat with the same dexterity as the magician would his bunny. With Daniel's recent Alabama adventure came the certainty that his uncle was in on the secret. Still, there no way to know how much had been divulged, enough to provide the rationale for the trip, he suspected and not a morsel more, and perhaps because he sensed that everything was coming apart at the seams, Daniel vowed that this time would be different.

There had been a number of opportunities along the path as they hiked but Daniel kept telling himself that the timing wasn't right, that he didn't want to intrude just then on the kind of moment that he cherished, and by the time Howard and Daniel had completed their analysis of the finer points of *Huckleberry Finn*, they were within a hundred yards of the house, and on this occasion, time and not his will failed him. They approached the gate to the back yard, and Daniel sensed that he'd lost yet another golden opportunity.

"You go on upstairs and get cleaned up for dinner, Daniel," his mother instructed him. "It'll be about fifteen minutes."

The marshy areas they'd hiked through had left his shoes, socks and the bottom of his pants a soggy mess, and as he sat down on the bed to peel them off, he heard the crackle of the gravel in the driveway and his heart sank. It was his father returning without warning from who knows where, effectively ending the visit with his beloved Uncle Howard. Howard would still be there, but the whole dynamic would certainly change as the movements of the universe would be dictated by his father. Daniel would have to be largely unnoticed and careful not to show too much affection for his uncle. His father would get chummy, but it was an aggressive show with no depth of feeling, and everybody but his father knew it was a fraud.

Howard was good about it all even though he'd have been well within his rights not to subject himself to the charade, but Daniel took it as another sign of what an upstanding guy his uncle was that he would suffer through that just to spend some time with his sister and his nephew. Of course, it also explained why the visits tended to be coordinated with his father's absence. "Son of a bitch," Daniel cursed this twist of fate under his breath as he hurled his sock against the wall. He clenched his fists and drooped his shoulders in a simultaneous act of defiance and acquiescence. He would go downstairs, though he dare not pout or give any indication of his displeasure.

As he tugged on his clean jeans, the faint buzz of conversation seeping up from the kitchen exploded into a barrage of invectives that seemed to rattle the windows. It wasn't just his father's voice but a cacophony of angry sniping that could well produce collateral damage all the way upstairs. Daniel froze with fear and cursed his father. He knew that he had to have crossed some powerful line in the sand for all hell to have broken loose in the way that it had. His mother was not assertive as a rule, but on this night, she was scratching and clawing with the best of them. Daniel wanted to cover his ears as much as he wanted to sneak down a few stairs to get a better listen. Hot, hurtful words ricocheted around as if in the eye of a tornado. "Fag, pervert, last straw, sick crazy bastard." And to Daniel's great dismay, he heard the door slam, and Howard's voice was eliminated from the din. He ran to the window to yell to his uncle, but by the time he yanked up the pane, Howard was half way down the driveway. All the while the incendiary barbs were still being tossed downstairs.

Daniel stepped lightly across the floor and sat on his bed feeling crushed, helpless and confused. He began imagining him and his uncle on a beautiful sun- soaked day, floating down the mighty Mississippi, but he couldn't hold the thought as the shrapnel flew all around him. "might do to the boy..., paranoid runt minded asshole. You're the pervert." The errant phrases snaked their way up into Daniel's room, and it would be a good number of years before he would have any idea what the hell it all meant.

A crashing sound many decibels higher than even the elevated shrieks stunned Daniel as did the utter silence that followed. He heard the door slam again and his father's truck straining to accommodate the amount of gasoline his foot had commanded as the gravel flew every which way. The stillness downstairs was deafening, and Daniel imagined all kinds of horrible things. Finally, when he couldn't stand it any longer, he inched toward the hall and peeked down the stairs. Still nothing. He knew his father was gone, and that left the fate of his mother to be discovered. He tiptoed down the stairs, stuck his head around the corner and saw his mother from the back, running water in the small utility room off the kitchen. She was breathing and able to stand, which eased his mind somewhat. "Mom," he said in a small barely audible voice. "What happened, where's Uncle Howard?" he said, immediately regretting that he hadn't asked how she was first. He moved cautiously toward her, stopping three or four feet shy of where she stood. She didn't flinch or acknowledge his presence in any way. Daniel sensed that she had been hurt and badly, and his general ambivalence toward her melted away. He tried again. "Mom, are you all right? Is there anything I can —" Her sudden movement startled him, and he recoiled slightly as she turned slowly to face him. Her upper lip was so swollen that it seemed to cover her left nostril, and her blouse was covered in blood. Daniel felt the tears gushing down his face, and he instinctively leaned toward her.

"Haven't you caused enough fucking trouble already?" she spit out of her gargoyle lip, her words dripping with venom. And with that she kind of puffed, and her front tooth hurtled toward his feet. It clacked on the tile and left a crimson dot on his clean sock. A series of strategically placed charges blew, and Daniel imploded. He turned silently, boarded the raft and pushed off from the shore.

Chapter 31

The waitress offered another refill and Daniel distractedly nodded in the affirmative. The whole episode, from the terror/projection conflation to the subsequent collapse, seemed to make a lot more sense to Daniel from a cause and effect standpoint. But there was no great epiphany, no opening of the skies of insight that would produce dramatic and lasting change. Still, it was positive movement, another piece of a very complicated puzzle and every little bit helped, he reasoned. He opted for one last Camel Light before he hit the road and asked the waitress for one last refill and a check.

The day was as luscious as when he'd entered the restaurant, as pretty, he recalled, as it had been before the unfortunate encounter had taken the wind out of his sails a number of days ago. "Let's try this again," he said aloud with a mini-burst of optimism.

Daniel had a touch of that odd feeling one has when the cast is removed from a leg after the fracture has healed, and the therapists tentatively begin to reintroduce it to the normal range of functions. He moved a little slower than usual and felt that this was not altogether a bad thing. He decided to ride unscripted again for a time and just let things develop as they may, feeling that even though he hadn't chosen the arduous detour of late, he had certainly participated, and that had to count for something. His little amiga seemed relieved that Daniel was more like his old self and demonstrated her extra gratitude for the goodies he delivered with a gracious little curtsey.

"May I never become jaded to that sensation," he said as the smooth hum of the wondermobile filled his ears.

Daniel had managed to remain largely ignorant of his whereabouts, though he generally had a pretty good idea what state he was in if for no other reason than the big "Welcome" and "You all come back now, ya hear" signs they erected at all the borders. After embarking on the journey from his native Massachusetts, he had done time in Rhode Island, Connecticut and New York. He had managed a brief stint in Pennsylvania before ending up back in New York and after an up-and-down exercise in latitude, found himself back in Pennsylvania, albeit quite a bit further west. It was there that a sign made nearly illegible by graffiti led him on a pilgrimage of sorts to the most well-known design by his all-time favorite architect, the venerable Frank Lloyd Wright.

Daniel spent a pleasant afternoon examining "Fallingwater" with an earnest group of devotees and marveled right along with them at the brilliance of the conception. As the tour guide described the importance of the use of the cantilever, one of the disciples elicited a few laughs and a few groans by commenting that "After "Fallingwater"it was no longer just a bad impression of an Italian guy explaining why he had to stay with his girl." And when the guide quoted Wright as having said that "the architecture of freedom and democracy needed something basically better than the box," a wan young woman wondered aloud if he had coined the term "thinking outside the box," and you could tell by her demeanor that she had already convinced herself that he had. Daniel considered a small stab at humor himself but held his tongue for fear of offending by suggesting that it was actually the official slogan of the abstinence movement.

He made his way to Lake Erie in Ohio and spent a pleasant afternoon on the waterfront visiting the Rock and Roll Hall of Fame, the second coming of the Cleveland Browns stadium and a science museum that featured an IMAX theatre with a movie about the "rain forest" that was a sight to behold. The rest of the great state of Ohio would be remembered as something akin to Dante's *Inferno* through no fault of its own, and Daniel took it to be a good omen that his fortunes were changing as he read the big "Howdy Do?" sign that ushered him into the "Hoosier State." Changing states was just what the doctor ordered, he thought, as he motored on in. Besides, he thought, how could you go wrong in a place where "The Welcome Mat's Always Out."

Daniel found himself on Route 265, and when it came time, he chose to forego the "scenic route" for a spell and opted for the mindlessness that Route 64 would allow. He had reached the point where he could think without straining his back, and although he considered the investigation closed, thoughts of his mother, Julie, were begging questions. There *had been* tender moments, he argued in his mind, in spite of the way things turned out. He had always held that special consideration be accorded her because she bore the brunt of the worst of his father, but much like the judges of a boxing match can be swayed by a flurry in the last thirty seconds of a round, Daniel had to push past the complete collapse and look beneath the rubble for some signs of life, some indication that at some point there had been some good stuff in there somewhere. If he'd had a rough go of it, it was fair to assume that she'd suffered abuse and humiliation well beyond what he had observed. He got a lump in his throat as he overturned granite blocks of resistance and witnessed a woman not yet mutilated beyond recognition by a prodigious and sustained assault on her person. He watched her laugh, smile and even pull him toward her for a hug. He saw her take his side during some of the earlier disputes, going so far as accusing his father of "just looking for somebody to take it out on." He watched further as her will was weakened bit by bit like a rock shrinking after eons of water have rushed over and around it. There came a point beyond which she couldn't shield him, couldn't intervene to soften the blows lest she pay an unthinkable price. She became a stranger to Daniel, and somewhere along the way, he had concluded that she had capitulated all that she held dear. He suspected that it correlated with her inability to protect her child, and that it was the subsequent self-hatred that had "flipped" her.

It was impossible to know all the reasons why she stuck around, why she didn't grab her boy and make a run for it, but she didn't and he didn't fault her for it. Daniel believed she had tried. Ultimately, she failed, but god dammit, she had tried, and to Daniel's way of thinking, that was enough. "Damn him," he said aloud without the fatalism or the hunger for vengeance that would ordinarily have tinged the utterance. "Damn him to hell."

Chapter 32

"Carefree" seventeen miles. As soon as Daniel saw the sign, the decision was made. "Hey you can't beat that, say Golda. This may be what we were looking for all along!" He would stop for lunch and to stretch his legs in the hopefully aptly named town of Carefree, Indiana. "Course, I suppose it could be the sugarless gum capital of the world as well," he added as an afterthought. He rolled down the off-ramp and the quaint town he found himself in reinforced his (Steinbeck's) notion of the sterile but utilitarian nature of the interstate. It served me well, he thought as some hidden impulse drew him off the path that led to the eateries and further into a neighborhood of modest but attractive homes. It had likely been barren at its inception some number of years ago, but the shrubs and trees that had been planted over the years had matured nicely and grown into their destined roles.

Daniel was mesmerized and had slowed to a crawl as he made his way up and down the avenues. He had the nagging sense that he shouldn't be here, that this was not a realm in which he was welcome, and further, that if he were caught, there would be hell to pay. He felt oddly like a community icon stepping out of his prescribed role, both electrified and terrified as he cruised the seedy back streets in search of drugs or a woman or even a man, for that matter.

Daniel did his best to shake off the yoke of his dark cognitions and rolled on. There was little actual activity, but Daniel imagined all kinds of goings-on—kids playing, neighbors talking, families sitting down to eat and more. It may not have been a real world, but he believed that his notions could not have been too far off the mark, and contrasted with Daniel's "foster" world, it could not have been more inviting.

A particularly sweet house caught his eye, and he imagined himself pulling into the driveway after work. He picked up the paper, petted the dog, and as he turned toward the front door, he saw Chelsea standing there, looking to all the world like Donna Reed, just waiting to plant a big wet one on him as he entered the house. She would, of course, *really* care how his day had gone and would listen attentively to every word he said. You again, he thought to himself as he acknowledged Chelsea's continuing hold on his psyche. As the illusion ebbed, he started paying more attention to his actual surroundings and realized that he had driven to the midpoint of an extremely complicated maze.

"Damn," he scoffed as the spell was lifted, and he felt more than a little foolish for having found himself in this predicament. He didn't want to think about it or its implications, rather, he focused on his hunger, his raison d'être for having exited the interstate, and he stopped the car in the middle of the road to sort out which way he would go from there. He looked to the cul de sac on the right and at the four way stop just ahead and narrowed it down to three possibilities, having brilliantly ruled out the cul de sac.

"Are you lost, mister?" came a little lispy voice, and Daniel turned abruptly to see a small boy toting what liked looked like an old army issue knapsack and holding some kind of a ball.

Having concluded that this "presence" was not an addendum to the original illusion, Daniel answered. "That I am, son; that I am. Say, would you happen to know which direction will take me back to the highway?" The boy looked a little confused and Daniel quickly clarified. "You know, the big road with two lanes in either direction that people go real fast on."

"I know what a highway is, geez," the boy said with barely disguised irritation.

"Yeah, hey, I should have figured, sorry."

"Just go straight, the boy started, apparently having forgiven the 'insult.' "You don't need to turn anymore, just go straight and you'll end up there by default," he said with a little extra emphasis on the last word as if to demonstrate conclusively that he was a pretty smart fellow.

"By default, you say, well, that sounds easy enough. Hey, thanks a lot, I really appreciate it." Daniel engaged the transmission, and as he pulled away he saw a large man bounding toward the small boy. He assumed it was his father, and he assumed that he was concerned that this stranger that popped up out of nowhere was having a conversation with his little boy. He thought about stopping to reassure the old man that he meant no harm but opted to leave that task for the little boy. That boy was, after all, an exceptionally bright fellow.

Chapter 33

Daniel made it back to the highway by default and was soon sitting down to lunch at the Red Maple Diner. On his way in, he had picked up a brochure about campgrounds in the general vicinity from one of those little racks promoting the local attractions. I need a change, he thought to himself as he envisioned setting up camp by a placid lake surrounded by a postcard perfect nature scene. Daniel could feel the warmth of the campfire countering the hint of brisk, lingering in the air as it heated the water for his morning cup of joe. He could hear the popping of the eggs as they morphed from runny liquid into delectable bite sized chunks of goodness marinating in the bacon grease still as hot as molten lava. And, oh, the aroma of bacon frying in the great outdoors, it so inspired him that he imagined it beckoning hungry patrons from the first time that primitive man put fire to animal flesh, on through the millenniums and forward to the campers and adventurers of today. The full weight, it seemed, had been officially lifted and Daniel actually felt a little giddy.

"Well, aren't we in a good mood today," the waitress said with a smile after catching the big shit-eating grin on Daniels face.

He was caught a bit off guard, but he quickly recovered.

"You know something, one of these days, I'm going to marry a waitress, and at least a couple of times a week, I'm going to have her come to the table in our little dining room and ask me what I would like, and I'm going to tell her, 'Darlin' I want you, and whatever delectables you want to add to the order will just be icing on the cake."

Betsy actually blushed as if the proposal had been made to her. "Why, that's awfully nice," she replied, still glowing just a bit.

Daniel took notice and was pleased that he didn't even have to consider whether he'd spoken out of line.

"So then, what *would* you like? Betsy asked, stepping out of the pleasant interlude, and back to the business at hand.

"Well, I was thinking bacon and eggs until I remembered an engagement I'm to attend tomorrow that, I believe, will be serving just that."

As he pondered his options, Betsy chimed in. "The waffles here are exceptional, and I'm not just saying that cause I work here."

"That sounds very good, actually. Waffles it will be."

Daniel made quick work of the waffles, left sweet Betsy a generous tip and hustled back to the wondermobile, buoyed by a rekindled sense of adventure. "Did you bring your trunks?" he asked Golda as they rolled out of the parking lot, and to his great surprise, she had.

Chapter 34

Daniel didn't bother himself with the great philosophical questions regarding modes of transit and headed directly for Route 64, and after what seemed like little more than a hop, skip and a jump, was cruising past St. Croix on Route 37 and well on his way to one of the Hoosier National Forest's finer offerings, the campsites at Celina Lake. The closer he got, the more remote the area felt from civilization as he knew it. At least, that's what he told himself. For all Daniel knew, Emerald City itself could have been just around the corner. Finally, the road narrowed to one dirt lane and even the simple lack of macadam gave him a bit of a rush. He breathed deeply, absorbing an intoxicating mixture of wood, sap, bark, leaves, needles and cones, sautéed in the self same components shed in years past, decomposing and enriching the earth.

The park "Office" was little more than a lean-to shed, and in Daniel's mind that made perfectly good sense as did the laconic attendant that seemed reluctant to give any more information than was absolutely necessary. Daniel would not need nor want, for that matter an electrical hookup. His preference would be a location as close to the lake and as far away as possible from everything and everybody else. "You asked for it, you got it," drawled the attendant. Daniel half expected "Toyota" to follow but instead he simply added, "Site Z 9."

Daniel took the "Camp Rules" from the man and walked out of the office wondering if he and the gentleman both shared the same idea as to what constituted isolation. As Daniel made his way farther into the grounds, it seemed that his wish had been granted as he had to hike some barely discernable trails to reach his destination and that was after driving for what seemed like miles. Daniel would gladly make that trek the three or four times it took to get all the provisions to the site. The tent, he thought, should be the first order of business, and he promptly hooked the propane up to the Coleman stove. He wanted to add one last element to the sweet aroma surrounding him, and he figured a little coffee percolating would be just the thing.

The quiet man did good, he thought as he scanned the extraordinary place he'd ended up. His encampment was better than advertised, a sanctuary twenty or so feet above the bank of the lake but easily accessible via a natural stairway of rock and dirt held fast by thick tree roots protruding out of the earth. The lake itself was much larger than he'd imagined, and the view was nothing less than magnificent. The heavily wooded areas on either side of him framed that view and likely filtered out objects that would have served as reminders that civilization was indeed likely to be found just around the corner.

"Work to be done," he pronounced abruptly as he headed back to the car for the fourth and final load. "You're gonna love this place, little girl, trust me," he added with certainty as he carried Golda's mini-bivouac and the bag of spikes to secure the tent back to the campsite. "What'd I tell ya, huh? Unbelievable, don't you think?" "Enjoy the view, Golda. I'm gonna put up some shelter." And having given Golda her instructions, he went to work.

To Daniel's pleasant surprise, the tent went up with very little difficulty in spite of it being quite a bit bigger than he remembered. If he stooped a bit, he could actually maneuver inside the thing in an upright position. The scent that he'd been anticipating had wafted into the area he was working shortly after he'd gotten started, and he just about dropped everything but decided that protocol should be followed and that the reward would come soon enough.

"Not a bad pad, say Golda," he said with an air of satisfaction. He dug the Cremora out of the satchel, tore open a couple of domino packets, stirred and voila, he was in business. He picked up his little friend, and together they headed for the lake. Just below the halfway point, they came upon a long rectangular rock jutting out over the lake. It looked as well engineered as the cantilevered protrusions that were so prominent at Fallingwater and in fact had employed the same structural principles so Daniel had no qualms about its soundness.

He set Golda's cage down gently and was mesmerized for the second time that day, albeit for much different reasons. He walked to the end of the granite diving board and imagined himself jackknifing toward the calm waters of Celina Lake with such grace and precision as to hardly cause a ripple as he pierced its very tranquility. He carried Golda on down to lake's edge, smoothed a spot for the two of them, lit up a cig and beheld.

Chapter 35

The quiet man had reluctantly revealed the general direction of the one general store in the area where any ambitious adventurer might be properly outfitted and supplied. Daniel felt a little odd about leaving the campsite unattended while he made the trip but with no real choice in the matter, decided to put his full trust and confidence in the basic honesty of the good people of Indiana. "Stanton's Supplies" had a certain charm, to be sure but about halfway through the store, Daniel concluded that he was apt to find most anything that didn't smack of homogeneity charming by default. As he completed the thought, Daniel realized that he would never hear that word again as long as he lived without thinking about the kid. No "golden arches" here, he thought, but unfortunately, as he would soon learn, not a whole lot of anything else either.

"Excuse me," queried Daniel of the corpulent fellow behind the counter. "I can't seem to locate the milk or the bacon or even the bread. Could you help me?"

"I ate it all," the man said with such seriousness that Daniel was almost inclined to believe him. Finally, he cracked a big smile. "Your timing could not have been worse, fellow. We get deliveries twice a week, Tuesday and Friday mornings, and seeing as it's late afternoon on a Monday, we're plum out of most things. If you can get through to tomorrow morning, there'll be damn near anything you want."

Daniel liked the guy and the place and wanted very much to contribute to this little corner of the local economy, but the die was cast, and the morning menu was going to include bacon and eggs, come hell or high water.

"Is there any place around here I can get the stuff today?" Daniel asked guiltily. "I mean just to tide me over till tomorrow," he added as if it were necessary to take the sting out of the treasonous question.

After a mock reaction with hand over heart in the manner of a jilted lover, he smiled that big smile again and answered. "Down the road a mile, take a left onto Pheasant Run Road. You'll find a big shopping center that will have whatever you need. Hell, you can pick up a pizza, stop for a haircut, get new glasses in an hour or catch a movie if you like."

"You know, you're absolutely killing my adventurer fantasy," Daniel replied with a smile of his own. "Anyway, Thanks and I *will* see you tomorrow."

"I'll be looking for you."

Chapter 36

The "pizza" thing had set Daniel to salivating immediately although he wasn't really aware of it until he was back on the road. He still wanted to rough it and prepare his own meal in the great outdoors, so he opted for a slice to tide him over. As advertised, he was no sooner putting on his seat belt than he was clicking it off in front of Tony's Pizza. Maybe he and Sal came over on the boat together, he thought, recalling Kenny's description of the finest pizza in the land. The pretty young blonde girl that took his order pretty much convinced him that it wasn't the case. Daniel popped a quarter into the Ms. Pac Man machine while his slice was heating up and was glad to hear the little jingle start right up as the "Quaters Only" sign on the side of the game had him wondering if there wasn't some special token by that name needed to initiate the action.

The pizza was good, not Sal's good he imagined but tasty nonetheless. He was in a solitary mood and thus glad that the serve yourself arrangement mitigated the need for any interaction.

Sated, Daniel headed for the Food Lion satisfied that the hefty slice he'd eaten would discourage the oddball impulse buying that he is prone to when his stomach is growling, and then he remembered that he was going to keep it light anyway so he could return to Stanton's the next day. Being a man of his word, Daniel bought the smallest quantities of each item allowed by law. He was encouraged to see that they actually sold eggs in half cartons. "Six of one half dozen of the other," he sang to himself as he moved through the dairy section.

He picked up a quart of milk and stopped at the deli-counter to order just enough cheese and bacon to cover the next day's breakfast and lunch. He had slated Swiss cheeseburgers with a slathering of Thousand Island dressing for the evening meal with potato salad and a nice crisp kosher dill pickle on the side. He picked up snacks, soda, a head of lettuce for Golda and a good sized bag of ice to keep everything fresh and traced his steps back to the front of the store to check out.

The express lane was clogged up by the usual idiot that couldn't count, or more likely faked mild retardation for the sake of a few minutes advantage so Daniel shifted to lane three, which happened to be completely empty anyway. As the short muscular fellow rang him up, Daniel was deciding that only a real fire would do, with all due respect to the Coleman stove, and was already stacking the twigs and wood just so in his mind.

"Thirty-three dollars and two cents, sir."

"What's that?"

"The total is thirty-three dollars and two cents."

"Yes, fine," Daniel replied absentmindedly as he dug in his pocket. His habit of keeping three pennies with whatever other change he was carrying proved once again to have been a very savvy financial move as he was able to give the fellow exact change. Trust, he thought as he steamrolled his metal cart headlong toward the automatic doors, which were about 99percent glass, and sure enough without so much as an "open sesame," the doors parted, and he was on his way.

Chapter 37

As Daniel approached the wondermobile, he looked in the direction that he imagined his campsite to be and saw only the thicket of trees that shielded the lake and its surroundings from view. His gaze was drawn above the green of the treetops by a dazzling lavender sky. He locked on to it as he neared the car and was stupefied. In these moments of rapture, he always found himself wondering if he was "seeing" in the Buddhist sense and then realizing that if he had been, that reflecting on the possibility had also negated it. Undeterred, he redoubled his efforts to banish the distractions and set his gaze upon the glorious sight once again. He held steady as he reached down and punched the button that would release the hatch door. He lifted it with one hand, still focused and was almost yanked from the moment by the kudos he was bestowing upon himself for "seeing" while doing. He took the bag in both hands and leaned in a bit to set it in the back of the car, and still he managed to stay in the moment. He released gently and ...

The sound of the bag hitting the macadam was little more than a dull thud, but it seemed as if a thunderclap had exploded mere inches from his ear, violently jarring Daniel from his reverie. In the maelstrom that followed, Daniel caught sight of a shard of glass that had burst through the side of the brown paper bag. He turned quickly to track its path of flight and was horrified to see the jagged shard hurtling with malevolent intent straight toward an unsuspecting woman who was herself toting two large bags of groceries. It all happened so fast that Daniel quickly concluded that he couldn't actually have seen the weapon in mid-flight, any more than he could track a speeding bullet. But the pain on her face and the thigh high laceration where it had torn through her skirt left little doubt as to the accuracy of the direction and trajectory he had imagined. And in the chaos, he marveled at how the bags she was carrying, on the verge of suffering the same fate as his, were intercepted by the same hands that had momentarily loosened their grip upon impact. He gathered himself and focused. Daniel needed to act and post haste. He squelched the self-doubt and fear as best he could and steeled himself for the task ahead.

"Shit," he cursed under his breath as he hustled over to the woman. "Jesus, I'm so sorry."

"It's alright. I'm okay, really," she said more for his sake than her own. They both looked down to see the small crimson dot on her muslin skirt, and she suddenly looked a little shaky. It quickly became apparent that the dot was only the tip of the iceberg, as a stream that had already sprung tiny tributaries broke the plane of the hem and snaked its way into her shoes.

"Give me the bags," Daniel commanded as his mind raced like a surgeon in a MASH unit. He set them next to the wondermobile, and a big whiff of pickle juice left no doubt as to the origin of the weapon. "Here, come and sit down on the back of the car," Daniel insisted as he hovered around her all the way to the car lest she should falter.

"It really doesn't hurt," she protested weakly, but she obeyed and seemed glad that he seemed to know what he was doing.

Without hesitating, Daniel delicately lifted her skirt to the location of the wound just above the knee. The culprit, what he could see of it was no more than an inch and a half long and maybe a half an inch wide. It was embedded in the flesh but it was impossible to tell how deep. He looked the woman straight in the eye and told her with his best bedside manner what the next step in the procedure would involve. "I'm going to pull this out now, slowly and carefully, and then we're going to set to work on stopping the bleeding."

She nodded her assent, and Daniel tried to get a hold of the glass in such a way that the both of them didn't end up hemorrhaging simultaneously. "Just relax," he said calmly as he tugged gently and lifted it up and out. He held it up for her to see but was immediately pressed back into service when the expanded canal allowed for a much heavier flow of blood. In spite of his professional demeanor, Daniel really wasn't sure what to do, just that he was in charge of this operating room and he had to come up with something. His synapses in overdrive, he instinctively tried the little Dutch boy and the dyke procedure to little avail as the crimson tide did the old end around and then it came to him like a vision: direct pressure and elevation, direct pressure and elevation, direct pressure and elevation. His mind miraculously coughed up the critical moments from Mrs. Kernan's first aid class in eleventh grade and armed with this no doubt life saving knowledge, his confidence soared and he jumped right back into the fray.

"It's bleeding... profusely." He had started to say "bad" but decided that "profusely" sounded much more medical. "We've got to slow the blood flow to the wound if we're going to get this thing under control," he added, as if the various other surgeons assigned to the case were all in agreement. "We need to elevate the wound to achieve that. Are you comfortable with that?"

The authorization would have to be verbal as there just wasn't time to prepare the necessary documents. "Well, yes, I guess if that's what you have to do," she replied, with understandable trepidation.

Daniel took hold of her calf and raised it up so that her knee was at the highest point, positioning the laceration just above it on a downward pitch, and at that most inopportune instant, Daniel the doctor became Daniel the man. The sight of the exquisite shape of her calf—blood and all, in his hand no less—the silky smoothness of her thigh and finally the soft bulge of her pubic hair defining the contours of her most private realm through her panties, overwhelmed him and stunned him into a reverent silence.

She saw his reaction, and he saw that she had seen it. He felt foolish and ashamed and compounded the original boner by lowering the leg to its former position much more quickly than he had raised it.

"What are you doing," she cried forcefully.

"I'm sorry, I didn't mean to—"

"No, you were right. I think it will work."

242

"Really, I mean, it should work. It's standard procedure," Daniel stated clumsily, still feeling a little sheepish.

"Take my leg," she commanded as forcefully as he had a few minutes prior. And as he repeated the procedure, she carefully gathered her muslin skirt around the "sensitive" areas that had been the cause of so much consternation. Daniel applied the pressure part of the equation a little more deftly this time, and in short order the gush of blood leaking from the wound became little more than an intermittent trickle.

Daniel noticed the "Prevent Defense" kit tucked neatly in the back of the car. "Here, pinch the skin together like I'm doing and I'll grab the first aid kit." As he reached for the kit, a third instruction from Mrs. Kernan's first aid class popped into his head: "pressure points, brachial artery for arms, femoral for legs." The realization that the location of the operative artery was way up *there*, right next to *that* led to the quick conclusion that that particular technique would only be employed if it was a matter of life and death.

"It's a hell of a thing to plan ahead and then forget all about those best laid plans," Daniel said as he dug into the contents of the kit. Gauze pads, butterfly Band-Aids, alcohol wipes and some antibiotic ointment jumped out at him as useful. "I really am sorry," he repeated as he struggled to separate the corner flaps sealing the alcohol wipes.

"Things happen," she said, with a tone of pleasant fatalism, silently enjoying the fact that someone was fussing over her. "I know you didn't mean any harm,"

"You're right, of course, but I still feel like an ass," he replied as he swabbed the laceration with the wipe. "Does that sting?" he asked without looking up.

"Just a little. It's okay, you're doing fine." Her calm and reassuring tone settled Daniel's nerves, and he took advantage of the remaining moisture in the alcohol wipe to remove some of the parched maroon riverbed where the blood had flowed. He dabbed gently down the front of her leg with the same loving care as that of someone removing the tarnish from silverware that had been in the family for countless generations. In spite of the intimate nature of his actions and especially in light of his previous reaction, he was strictly business and wholly focused on the task at hand.

She saw that and felt a curious warmth toward the unusual stranger. "My name is Ruby, by the way," she offered as an olive branch and he was quick to accept.

"Mine's Daniel, and I can only hope that you don't forever associate that name with disaster," he replied with a self-deprecating chuckle. There was silence as he applied the ointment and a first and then a second butterfly Band-Aid to her wound. He followed up by folding the gauze for thickness and fastening it with a big adhesive bandage that further digging in the "Prevent Defense" arsenal had turned up. "That looks pretty good," Daniel said, his satisfaction mitigated by the realization that he had scarred the woman for life. "Jesus, I **am** sorry," he repeated as the thought sunk in.

"There's nothing else I can say." Ruby's silence suggested that there was nothing she could add to the equation either.

"You're almost certainly going to need to get that stitched up. Is there a hospital anywhere around here?" A grand notion popped into Daniels head, and he blurted it out before she could respond. "I can pay the bill. Whatever it is, I'll take care of it."

"I don't know. We'll see," she replied as she noticed the bandage showing hints of crimson. "But, yes, it's about six miles north of here." Ruby answered reluctantly, knowing it was the logical next step but not altogether comfortable with the prospect of motoring away with an almost complete stranger.

"I will take you there," he stated simply, never even considering that the offer could be construed as anything more than the logical next step in this saga. "It's the least I can do," he added finally sensing her reluctance.

She hesitated for a moment before she answered. "Well, stranger, we've come this far together. I certainly can't drive in this condition, and besides, I'd be ashamed to tie up an ambulance and a crew to ferry me the six miles to the hospital for this." Ruby looked over at her car and figured she'd work something out later as Daniel walked around the side of his car and opened the passenger door.

"Now, now little girl, you'll be back in your spot before you know it," he assured Golda absentmindedly as he lifted her up over the seat and perched her cage in a secure position atop some blankets. There was a brief moment of panic on Ruby's part upon hearing Daniel's voice. The thought that her worst fears had been realized shot across her psyche and she actually considered running for her life.

"Weet, weet, weet, weet." Golda chimed in, giving the first indication that there might be some kind of logical explanation for Daniel's strange comments to no one.

"That was Golda, by the way," Daniel said as he rounded the corner to assist his patient into the "gurneymobile."

"Thank God," she said as the adrenaline rush subsided.

"I don't understand," Daniel said, truly mystified.

Ruby laughed inwardly but didn't bother to explain. She slung her arm around Daniel's shoulder and with his help kind of hopped around to her seat, trying all the while to keep the knee elevated. Ruby winced noticeably as he lowered her into the car. She tried to hide the pain but the gritted teeth and eyes slammed shut gave her away.

Seeing her pain made Daniel want to start with the apologies all over again, but he stifled himself and went back to work. As Daniel closed the passenger door, he caught a glimpse of the bandage that was getting redder by the minute. He rushed to the back of the car and put her bags in and considered leaving his lying there when it occurred to him that stuffing the contents into a plastic trash bag would protect the car from stains and them from inhaling pickle fumes all the way to the hospital. Daniel tried not to look overly concerned as he slid into his seat and fumbled to get the key in the ignition.

"Take a left out of the parking lot," Ruby instructed, anxious to get this show on the road. "Then, you're going to go straight for about three miles at which point, you'll be making a right."

An awkward silence ensued and Daniel strained for something to say to lighten the mood that didn't sound ridiculous or forced. He looked over at Ruby, but her eyes were fixed on the road ahead, and she seemed to be lost in thought.

"I have to work tonight," she said with an air of regret as she clicked her fingernails and tried not to think about the leg.

"You have to work *tonight!*" Daniel echoed her comment, decrying the injustice of it all. "What do you do, if you don't mind my asking?"

"I work in a restaurant that's about a half mile past the hospital as a matter of fact."

"No way," Daniel exclaimed a little too ardently.

"Way," she shot back quickly and proceeded to burst out laughing. "I'm sorry," she said. "My son went through a phase in which he watched that *Wayne's World* movie by the two guys from *Saturday Night Live* over and over again and you couldn't escape it."

The outburst did the trick. The taut air had dissipated, and Daniel allowed himself to relax a bit. He didn't even bother to comment on the small pool of blood that had seeped onto the "fine Corinthian leather" seats in the wondermobile.

"Actually, I'm the manager at one of the few really nice places in the area. It's called the 'Rotunda' if you can believe that."

Daniel smiled as he imagined all the comedic possibilities.

"We're getting pretty close to the intersection where you'll be making a right."

"Just say the word," Daniel replied. "You know, you are a hell of a sport, Ruby," he said kind of shaking his head. "I mean, you couldn't put a guy that slashed your leg anymore at ease if you tried."

Ruby smiled and kind of tossed her head in a very endearing manner. "By the Mobil Station up ahead, that's where you're gonna make a right."

Daniel executed the directive and thought about asking if a doctor's note might suffice to get her excused from work but figured he'd done enough talking for a while. He kind of glanced over to check the status of the wound and was surprised to see Ruby seemingly studying his face. He quickly redirected his gaze front and center, but he could still sense her eyes on him. Daniel tightened up a bit and just focused on the task at hand. He knew they were only a few miles at most from the hospital but it seemed like they had covered that and more. He wanted to speak again but was preoccupied with whether or not she was still looking his way. He had to concede it had only been speculation since he actually caught her in the act at what seemed like an hour ago but he could not bring himself to put the theory to the test.

"So who are you, Daniel and whatever brings you to this part of Indiana?" The wording of the question struck him as odd. She didn't ask what he did or where he was going, rather, who was he and why was he here. Daniel knew he had to say something so he figured he'd just start flapping his gums and hope that what fell out wasn't too alarming.

"Me, well, I'm a vagabond and I'm just passing through." He had spoken the truth but he knew it wouldn't suffice. To Daniel's surprise, she seemed to find his answer intriguing, laughing lightly and shaking her head.

"That's a start but there's gotta be more to it than that," she followed up, and he did his best to oblige.

"Okay then, I'm a secret agent doing very important undercover work for the government," he joked lamely, stalling for time to craft a more fitting answer. "Actually Ruby, I'm on kind of a sabbatical. I worked in the furniture industry for a number of years, but I wasn't satisfied, and I thought I'd take some time off to travel and kind of think things through.

You know, get a better sense of what I really wanted to do before rejoining the other productive members of society. On my way I thought I'd take the opportunity to visit some relatives in Nebraska that are getting pretty well up there in age. I figured I'd better get to it lest I end up regretting missed opportunities if you know what I mean."

It all sounded pretty good, and, in fact, it could be argued to be largely factual. He did have some ancient relatives in Nebraska, and he had vowed early on that if he found himself in their general vicinity, he would make it a point to stop and say hello. Daniel was comfortable with the answer, and so it seemed was Ruby. Whatever follow-up questions she may have had were mercifully put on hold as Daniel spotted the hospital looming large a little ways up ahead on the left.

"The Emergency Room entrance is the second left, I believe, Daniel."

He turned in, pulled the car under the overhang and instructed Ruby to sit tight while he rounded up a wheelchair. "Okay up we go," he said as he hoisted her up and pivoted her into the wheelchair. Daniel bent down to lift her right foot on the pad and was unable to stop himself from stealing a glance at the loveliness of it all. Daniel managed to swing the other support in an upright position and lock it in place to enable Ruby to keep the wound elevated.

"Thank you, Daniel," she said simply.

"Hey, it's my pleasure," he was quick to reply wondering if that sounded as ridiculous to her as it did to him. He wheeled her in through the automatic doors and followed the signs to "Registration." As Ruby dug in her purse for her insurance cards, Daniel looked ahead to the four or five cubicles where they would check in and was surprised to see the woman at the far end craning her neck to get a better look, apparently at him. He felt immediately self-conscious and a bit perturbed as well.

"I can help you here, Ma'am," a voice from the nearest cubicle informed them and he made a sharp right taking himself out of the staring woman's line of sight.

"Ruby, Ruby." The sound emanated from the direction of the gawker's cubicle.

"Shit," Ruby uttered under her breath. The woman popped around the corner, and true to form gawked at the both of them.

"Hello, Jeanne," Ruby addressed her with all the sweetness she could muster.

"What in God's name happened to you?"

"I got a bit of a cut on my leg and this kind stranger was good enough to patch me up and bring me down here for treatment."

"Well, I guess you've probably earned yourself a badge," Jeanne said as she shifted her gaze to Daniel, holding it a little longer than he was comfortable with.

"What am I, a fucking Boy Scout?" Daniel railed to himself. "I was happy to help," was what finally came out.

"My car's still down at the Food Lion, and I've got to be at work at six," Ruby jumped in, deflecting the conversation away from Daniel.

"Would you like me to call your husband?" Jeanne asked pointedly, and Daniel suspected it was more than an idle threat.

"Well you could, Jeanne, but he's away on business," Ruby replied, knowing that it would kick Jeanne's cognitions into overdrive.

A similarly cynical Daniel could see the gears spinning in Jeanne's head. "How convenient," he imagined her thinking, Dana Carvey's "Church Lady" getting credit for the voiceover.

"Oh," she said but Ruby took the initiative. "You could call my neighbor, Virginia, if you wouldn't mind. She should be free, and she's a good egg."

Daniel could have and would have offered to stick around and take Ruby home but was getting the distinct impression that it was not in the cards. With that off the table, Daniel was beginning to feel a bit like a third wheel. He didn't want to just up and announce that he was leaving, and he was hoping for a private word with Ruby before he left. Fortunately for all concerned, duty called, and Jeanne had to go back to work.

"Thanks, Jeanne," a relieved Ruby offered after giving her the phone number of her friend, Virginia. After a grace period of approximately eight seconds, the barrage of questions started, and Ruby did her best to keep up with the hyper efficient clerk.

"Excuse me for one second, please," Daniel interjected. "Ruby, I'm going to—"

"Stay, won't you, Daniel, at least for a little while, anyway," Ruby said with a tenderness and an urgency that caught Daniel off guard.

"Sure, I mean yeah, I'd be glad to. I'm going to locate a men's room and find a soda machine," he added, failing to disclose that those had been his plans all along.

"Through the double doors on your left, halfway down the hall, you'll see both the items you're looking for, sir" came the directions from the clerk who spoke in a staccato fashion without ever taking her eyes off the computer.

Daniel headed off to take care of his business. He didn't know what, if anything this latest turn of events meant but he assumed that Ruby wanted a moment to say a proper goodbye just as he did. It wasn't like they'd shared a foxhole in the heat of battle exactly, but he did, to his great dismay, leave a lasting impression on her, and even though it would be beyond redundant, he wanted to apologize one last time if even if she would have none of it.

Ruby caught sight of Daniel as he returned from his rounds, and he grabbed a seat and a magazine and flipped through it casually, knowing he would not be tested on the contents.

"We're getting close," Ruby informed him, and he just smiled and went back to not reading the magazine. He glanced up every couple of minutes and soon saw her closing her purse and exchanging a few last words with the clerk. He started to move toward her but saw her roll backwards, pivot and make a beeline for him. "I could not, for the life of me, remember the last time I got a tetanus shot," she started with a chuckle.

"You know, I would have been happy to pay for this, Ruby," he said.

"It's alright, Daniel. It's nice to get something for those monster premiums we pay each month, and isn't that what they're for anyway?"

"I guess so," he replied, finally accepting that the small compensatory act of chivalry was not going to happen. They fell silent for a moment, and it seemed to bother Daniel a whole lot more than Ruby.

"That Jeanne, she a friend of yours?" he asked.

"Oh, you could say that. She's a bit of an odd duck. She's known around town for her dalliances, if you know what I mean."

And Daniel suspected that he did, but with his track record, he considered asking for clarification but thought better of it and just nodded his head knowingly.

"And you know how people are," Ruby continued. She thinks because she does it that everyone else does as well."

"Mostly to rationalize her own behavior, I suspect" Daniel contributed, feeling the comment was broad enough to be safe.

"You can bet with her imagination, she's conjured up visions of you and I engaging in all kinds of illicit acts."

"No shit, her too," he thought to himself but "Wow" was all that came out.

"I'm sorry, Daniel, I shouldn't have said that," she added quickly, sensing that she had stepped over some imaginary line of provocation.

"It's okay. Hey, I assume it's true, or you wouldn't have said it."

"Yes, it is but I don't know you well enough to make a comment like that."

"It's alright. Please forget it, no harm done," he replied, relishing the role of the mature understanding one.

"There is something about you, Daniel, that seems to want to make a person open up and spill their guts. Now don't you worry, I don't intend to do that, but it's the thing that struck me about you from the beginning." Ruby had spoken in an honest and straightforward fashion, and Daniel very much appreciated it and while he wasn't quite sure what it meant, he suspected that for reasons unknown, she was a woman in search of a shoulder and he seemed a safe bet.

"I'll have to think about that one, Ruby." And there could be no doubt that he would. In his position as high priest and this being their last encounter, Daniel felt emboldened and decided to say what he'd been thinking the whole time. "Don't take this the wrong way, Ruby, but I couldn't help but notice that you have beautiful legs, and the thought that I scarred one of them forever, well it will always haunt me." It sounded melodramatic and very much like an invitation for reassurance, but he was dead serious and it showed. The "beautiful legs" part caused a rush of blood in some unknown internal place but she quickly regrouped and addressed the issue at hand.

"Stop it, now, stop it. It's done and it can't be undone," she scolded him, grabbing his wrist and positioning her face directly in front of his for emphasis.

"Okay, okay, I got ya," he said with a laugh, but he knew and she knew that it would be some time before he could see it that way.

"Mrs. Ruby Weber," a nearby voice barked out, and the two of them, still face to face and his wrist in her grip, jerked their heads in the direction of the sound. They saw the doctor approaching them, but they also saw the big shit-eating grin splashed across Jeanne's face in her cubicle.

"Shit," said Ruby.

"Oh, well," said Daniel and they both looked to the doctor who indicated that he was ready to take Ruby back.

"You know, Ruby, I really should be going now," Daniel said softly as he put out his hand.

She took hold of it and responded. "It's been … well, it's been a most interesting afternoon." She reflected on her comment for a moment before wrapping things up. "Oh and Daniel, when I happen to look down and see my little scar, I'll think of you fondly," she said with a smile, and that brought one to Daniel's face as well.

They exchanged goodbyes, and Daniel turned toward the automatic doors already cataloging this in the "memorable moments" section of his psyche.

"One last thing, Daniel."

He turned quickly in response to Ruby's voice. "Yes."

"Surf and Turf is on special at the Rotunda tonight."

"Thanks for the tip."

"Goodbye, Daniel," came the final comment.

"Goodbye, Ruby."

Oh, and Goodbye, Jeanne," Daniel trumpeted in her direction, smiling inwardly at giving her just a little bit more to chew on.

Chapter 38

As his return trip carried him past the Food Lion, it occurred to Daniel that he had two too many bags of groceries in the back of the car. He could, he thought, drop them off at Ruby's car, but the realization that he wasn't completely sure which one was hers and that it may be locked anyway nixed that idea. He was not about to turn around and deliver them to the hospital. He did not want to add further fuel to Jeanne's fire, and since this was anything but a finders-keepers situation, the only honorable thing to do would be to journey to the Rotunda and see that they were reunited with their rightful owner.

"I'm perplexed, little girl," Daniel said to his companion, who was once again riding shotgun. Golda knew the "look" all too well, but she was cognizant of the fact that Daniel was coming off a bender of biblical proportions, and she didn't want to upset the apple cart, so she just smiled and kept her thoughts to herself.

It was Ruby's casual "invitation" that left him with an unsettling feeling. Maybe if he hadn't known that her husband was out of town or that Jeanne already suspected that Ruby was doing a little double dipping, it might have acted as a governor on the more outlandish speculation. "What *do* women want, Golda?" Daniel asked facetiously of his companion. "I didn't think you had an answer," he added with a smile.

As he navigated his way back to his temporary digs, Daniel vividly recalled the chaotic scene in the parking lot of the Food Lion. He cringed at the thought of where his brief foray into enlightenment had taken him and concluded that any future attempts at "seeing" should probably take place in a stationary position and that he definitely should not be carrying anything even then. He envisioned the shard piercing the bag and hurtling with the precision of a smart bomb toward its inevitable target. As he drove past the "Office" he was smitten again with the natural scents that had so pleasured his olfactory senses, but rather than indulge, he quickly rolled up the window and returned to the scene of the crime. He saw the pain on Ruby's face, and he saw the crimson dot that sullied her crisp muslin skirt. He was temporarily derailed by the similarity that crimson dot bore to the one on his sock the day he lost his mother but forced himself not to dawdle there. He finally allowed himself a hearty pat on the back as he reviewed his short-lived medical career and then he saw her calf and parts beyond, and he felt his hunger full force.

He gripped the steering wheel tightly and accentuated the tension that was building throughout his body. His eyes seemed to glaze over momentarily, and the tug of war in his psyche raged. He tightened and released all the muscles in his body and finally, there was an apparent victor, the heightened state of yearning having been vanquished. "It's not the right brain-left brain thing that bothers me, little girl, it's the north brain-south brain thing," he said calmly, seemingly having settled the matter. "This is how it's going to be!" "Hey, are you listening?"

And in fact she hadn't been paying much attention.

"That's better. As I was saying, this is how it's going to be. Now I know this wasn't on the agenda but the situation arose and as you well know, sometimes shit happens. I was sort of invited to come for dinner at the place she works, and I'm not going to assume anything beyond that maybe she knows I'm far away from home, and she thought it might be nice to see a friendly and familiar face in a strange land."

Golda tried to mask her cynicism but it wasn't easy, and Daniel sensed it. "Remember, little buddy, we're in the Hoosier State and you know what that means—"The Welcome Mat's Always Out—Not just sometimes but *always* and I for one am going to take them at their word. I'm going to put on a decent shirt and pants, and I'm going to go and have a nice dinner and see how Ruby's holding up after the big ordeal. End of story," he said. Daniel had thrown down the gauntlet at the feet of his own worst tendencies, and as had been the case with numerous similar declarations in the past, he now had to wait to see if he could back it up.

He pulled into the campsite and was reminded of just how good his original game plan had been. There was a feeling of sanctuary, a sense of shelter from the storm and Daniel's mood picked up. In his heart of hearts, he knew that Jules Bourglay was no role model, but there was a definite affinity, and at moments like this, he doffed his imaginary cap to the lonesome traveler and imagined them sharing a cup of coffee around the campfire and commiserating about the hows and whys of life.

258

Daniel picked up Golda's abode, grabbed his cigarettes and headed directly for the cantilever. Dusk was settling in, and Daniel reveled in the same scene born anew with altogether different lighting. He drew deeply and tried not to think at all. "I was doing pretty well in that department. I could fairly argue that I was the "master of my domain", really I was, Golda," he said suddenly with a wistful tone, half wishing he hadn't ended up in such close proximity to the agent provocateur. "But, hey, C'est la vie, right, little girl," he said with a chuckle, and furthermore he meant it.

Chapter 39

Daniel headed toward the hospital and assumed that a 'half mile past it' meant on the same road. He felt a twinge of nervousness and reminded himself that this was not a *date* with only partial success.

The number of cars in the parking lot suggested that the Rotunda was indeed the hottest ticket in town. He saw the valet and turned the other way in search of a parking space that he would proceed to on his own, thank you very much!

"Now, Golda, you didn't think I was going to leave you in the hands of a complete stranger, did you?" She appreciated the gesture but suspected that what he didn't say was that he could not imagine anyone else piloting the wondermobile.

The place most definitely had an old-world feel to it with *Doric* columns, frescoes to rival those found in the Sistine Chapel—in scope if not in quality—magnificent hand woven tapestries and elegant marble floors.

Daniel had chosen blue jeans, boat shoes, a khaki button down shirt with double pockets and his "Imperial Circles" tie that had been adapted from a carpet that Frank Lloyd Wright had created for the Imperial Hotel in Tokyo. He was shooting for casual chic, and in spite of the phalanx of suits and sport coats, Daniel was satisfied that he didn't look too terribly out of place. He passed the blackboard, listing the evenings "specials" and as advertised, Surf and Turf was at the top of the list.

"Do you have a reservation, sir?" the question preceded his arrival at the podium to state his business.

"No, no, I don't," he answered. He considered dropping Ruby's name but chose to abide by the old discretion/valor adage.

"Will someone be joining you, sir?"

Well, I'd like to think that at some point in my life, I'll get hooked up with a soulmate and live happily ever after but on this particular evening, I'm alone, he thought. "No, just me," he finally replied.

"It will be twenty minutes to a half an hour."

"That's fine," Daniel answered flatly.

"The Vesuvius Lounge is on your right, or you can sit at the bar until your table is ready."

"Thanks."

"Name, sir."

"What's that?"

"I'll need your name to notify you."

"Cassat, Daniel Cassat."

"Thank you, sir."

Daniel opted for the bar, as it was the only place in the restaurant that he could smoke. He pulled his dog-eared copy of *Black Dogs* from his back pocket and waited his turn. There still had not been any sign of Ruby, and Daniel began to wonder if the cut was worse than it appeared and complications made it impossible for her to work or if maybe it wasn't that bad after all, but she was able to get someone to cover for her. He disregarded the tinge of disappointment and decided that in any case he was here, and he was going to see it through. He looked up from the book periodically, hoping she'd show, but nothing.

The twenty minutes passed, then the half an hour and still no table and still no sign of Ruby. The dull pain of disappointment was now clamoring to be heard and Daniel was having a much more difficult time keeping it at bay. She never *did* say she'd be here, it occurred to him as his thoughts took a decidedly negative turn. Maybe she's just a shameless promoter for her employer, he imagined, although even he had to agree that that was probably an unduly harsh assessment. If she's not here, it's gotta be related to the laceration I inflicted on her and if she'd had a way to contact me she would have, he argued, wrenching the momentum from the dark side in an act of sheer will. And just as the two sides arose from their stools for Round 2, the swinging doors that had spewed forth a parade of waiters and waitresses, opened wide and out came Ruby.

Daniel figured her to be anywhere from thirty-two to thirty-six. He pegged her at about five foot three or an inch away from "eyes of blue" with that kind of hybrid blonde/brown hair that probably has a name but not one that he was familiar with. She was not "busty" nor was she unduly small in that department, probably just big enough that a good push-up bra could foster a respectable amount of cleavage. She was nicely built, which was to say that she was of average dimensions but solid, one might even say muscular, and Daniel could personally attest to that at least so far as the lower forty-eight was concerned. And she was pretty. She wouldn't knock your socks off, but she could certainly turn your head, he thought. It sounded like a cliché, but something about her eyes actually sparkled, but the feature that really grabbed Daniel's eye was her mouth. It somehow reminded him of Betty Boop even though she didn't look anything like her. He decided that it wasn't just the mouth but the surrounding areas as well, the cheeks and the chin, that he found so terribly appealing.

Daniel detected a slight limp as she moved from table to table greeting, joking with and generally flattering the patrons but no real obvious evidence of the wound she had suffered. He watched and marveled as she floated around the dining room, seemingly making each diner feel like nothing less than a high roller. Her dress was a rich hunter green drawn tight around her waist with a light taupe belt that matched her shoes, and she wore a scarf that included her primary colors with a few more thrown to accentuate the whole outfit. The only word that came to Daniel's mind regarding her attire was "smart," formal enough but not over the top.

"Cassat, Daniel Cassat," a young man doing the bidding of the maitre d' called out. The Cassat part didn't elicit a response, but when the name Daniel was called, Ruby's head whirled around in his direction. Their eyes met and a hint of a smile crossed her lips as she nodded her acknowledgement. As Daniel was ushered to his table, the corner man for the dark side threw in the towel and a sense of relief overtook him. He had no idea what came next other than steak and lobster and did his best not to think about it.

The ice water, coffee and a small Lambrusco had been delivered, and Daniel figured he'd spend a little time with June and Bernard until either Ruby or his dinner showed up.

The sound of her voice drew nearer and as Daniel snuck a glance over his shoulder, it struck him how often he found himself measuring distances not in feet, yards or miles but rather in the width of tables in restaurants.

"How is everything so far, sir?" she asked in her most solicitous hostess voice, and the role she was playing made her seem like a complete stranger.

"Everything's fine, Ruby. How are you?" Daniel asked, playing the patron and wondering at what point the charade would stop.

She seemed anxious and looked nervously around the room, and just when it seemed that she was taking her road show to the next table, she turned quickly, leaned close to Daniel and gave his arm a squeeze. "I'm so glad you came, Daniel," she whispered before stepping back and plastering that ceramic smile back on her face. The tone was intimate and conspiratorial, and Daniel felt a warm buzz all over.

"Me too, Ruby," he replied. He wanted to respond further, but the feline hanging from his tongue prevented it.

A couple more furtive glances seemed to relax Ruby, and she moved to within a distance that straddled that fine line between appropriate and too close for comfort. "It only took four stitches and once it was all cleaned up, it didn't look so bad."

"Good, good, glad to hear it," he replied, studiously avoiding another apology. "How does it feel?"

"It's throbbing like crazy," she answered with a laugh.

"Jesus, I am sorry," the apology was autonomic and hence beyond his control.

"Don't think about it. It's the most excitement I've had in months, " she said smiling broadly. "Besides, it's nothing a few hundred Motrin can't handle."

Daniel shook his head, smiled and raised his glass. "To one hell of a sport," he proclaimed with dramatic flair. "And to tell you the truth, it's the most excitement I've had in a while as well. Of course, I guess that's easy for me to say."

Ruby fell silent and looked hard at Daniel as a million private thoughts crossed her mind. "I've got to get back to work," she said suddenly, and she kind of got that nervous look about her again.

"Sure, you go. I mean we are at your place of employment," he said of necessity. "Stop again, if you get the chance," he dared to add with his own conspiratorial tone.

"I will." Ruby moved around the table and as she squeezed between Daniel's and the adjacent table, she took hold of a lock of his hair and gave it an affectionate little tug, and even as the lock lay down, the hackles just below jumped to attention of their own accord.

It may seem a small and relatively insignificant gesture to some, but to Daniel it would serve as a key piece of evidence in the deliberation that would inevitably follow, and follow it did. It seemed beyond refute that there was a certain "chemistry" between them, but Daniel had been "refuted" so many times in the past that he was loathe to jump to any conclusions with great certainty. He had been perfectly well prepared to walk out of the emergency room, ruing the dastardly deed of the errant shard but satisfied that he had done all he could do and grateful for her grace under pressure, with a special word of thanks for the brief, if unintended, glimpse at the contours of a woman.

During the salad and right on through the main course, he argued in his mind that had she not tempted him with the "special," he would likely be sitting around the campfire with the one woman he'd always been able to count on, enjoying nature's bounty. The prosecution argued, however, that the resolution of the extra bags of groceries and his own temerity would likely have planted his silly ass in the exact same spot it inhabited at that very moment, and as much as he hated to admit it, the point was well taken. Daniel finally concluded, in no small measure because of the "tug", that there was an undeniable something going on between them, and that was enough for the time being. What it was or where it might lead was another question altogether and one that he was willing to allow to develop naturally or maybe with some slight intervention.

"Would you like to see our dessert menu?" the waiter asked, startling Daniel from his contemplations.

"No, I don't think so," he answered distractedly. "I'm plenty full as it is."

"Will there be anything else, then?"

"How about another Lambrusco and a check."

The waiter nodded, and Daniel, knowing that his time was drawing near, scanned the room in search of Ruby and in doing, so noticed that there were any number of other areas in the building that could have her occupied. He recalled having seen a sign welcoming some group or other for their annual convention and one related to a reunion of some sort, on his way in. He nursed the wine and tried to look at his book, but a temporary case of dyslexia overcame him. To Daniel's great irritation, the waiter approached the table again.

"Will there be anything else, then?" he asked with a tone that suggested that the queue waiting for tables had stretched around the block.

"No, I guess not," Daniel replied as he reluctantly handed over his credit card.

"I'll be right back then, sir." And he no sooner walked away than he was back at the table awaiting a signature to complete the process.

"Callin' it your job don't make it right, boss," he heard Cool Hand Luke saying in his head. Daniel calculated a fair but not overly generous tip, flapped the bill shut and sat tight for another forty-five seconds just to piss the waiter off.

Daniel had no intention of leaving the Rotunda until he'd had a chance to say a proper goodbye to Ruby, and even though he had to vacate the table prematurely, the sudden urge to urinate proved just the right ruse to enable him to wander the premises in search of her.

He saw the restroom signs to the left of the bar and proceeded in the exact opposite direction, striking pay dirt down the first hallway he investigated. He could see Ruby engaged in her role, ushering some of the older members to a buffet in what appeared to be a banquet to thank local retirees for their contributions as volunteers at Mercy Memorial Hospital. So nice of them to honor the passing of Roy Orbison that way, he thought as he strode into the room as if on official business.

"Daniel," she called when she saw him approaching. "I'm sorry, I haven't been able to—I mean I've been very busy," she continued vacillating between herself and her role and adjusting her demeanor accordingly.

"I understand," he said, reading the landscape to determine what could and could not be said. The couple of biddies she was escorting smiled at Daniel but made it clear that this interruption would only be tolerated for so long. As the two of them spoke as best they could with their eyes, Daniel looked down at *Black Dogs* and saw a solution in the makeshift bookmark he'd employed.

"The gentleman from the 'Vacation Bureau' asked me to give this to you. He said he doesn't really *need* it back but if it's convenient, you could drop it off," he said with a sly grin as he handed her the brochure about the "Campsites at Lake Celina" with **Z9** boldly written in the upper right hand corner.

"Why thank you, Daniel," Ruby replied after a moment's hesitation. "I'll do my best to get it back to him."

"Good, thanks, well, take care, Ruby."

"You do the same, Daniel," she replied in a manner almost as stilted as his had been but the eyes had it, and as Daniel had hoped and expected, the Bunsen burner had a nice steady jet blue flame streaming from it.

Chapter 40

Daniel snagged a couple of toothpicks from the podium and nodded to the maitre d' on his way out of the Rotunda. A capitol idea coming here, Daniel thought to himself as he made his way across the parking lot. "It was a rather pleasant evening, if I do say so myself," he informed Golda, not that she needed to be told as a look of smug satisfaction was written all over his face.

The warm, moist air circulating through the wondermobile was Daniel's favorite, and he rolled the two front windows all the way down to maximize the experience. The drive back to Celina Lake was precise and efficient as Daniel had gotten to be an old hand at this neck of the woods, and he was navigating his way to **Z9** in short order. Daniel pulled in, jumped out of the car, made his way to the campsite and arranged Golda comfortably on the sleeping bag in the tent, turning on the lantern to supplement the moonlight. He took the leak that had served its strategic purpose without consummation, donned his jeans and a light hooded sweatshirt and immediately set to work gathering kindling for a fire. He stacked it for circulation, ringed it with stones, accelerated the ignition process with lighter fluid and before long was listening to the sweet sound of coffee percolating with his trusty amiga by his side.

"You know what I'm thinking, don't you Golda. I'm not even gonna say it," he said with a laugh. Daniel was counting his chickens save for those that had not yet been hatched. It was fair to say that he had strong hopes that the saga had another chapter or two to go, but he felt a strange serenity about what had already happened. "It's in the hands of the jury now, little buddy, and we have no choice but to honor the verdict, whatever it may be." Daniel sipped his coffee, tended his fire and gazed at the heavens as he drew on his camel light. "There's nothing but now," he thought to himself, knowing full well that there was nothing original about the thought but the execution, well, that was another matter altogether. Golda seemed to know just what he was thinking, and she was astute enough not to interfere on those rare occasions in which Daniel kind of fell into himself and didn't try to jump right back out. Eventually, of course, he did, mostly because he realized that he'd completely forgotten about Golda's dinner. "Jesus, I'm sorry, Golda. Why didn't you say something?" he said as he scrambled to the tent to rustle something up.

Having addressed Golda's hunger as well as her thirst, Daniel proceeded to feed the fire, gathering enough kindling to keep up with its appetite for a while. As he resumed his repose, it occurred to Daniel, always struggling with simply letting events play out, that much more often than not, when he did battle with desire, the object was hypothetical. Just exactly what he had in mind if Ruby should happen to show up he hadn't fully formulated, and that of course was no accident. That she was married caused a minor disturbance in some quadrant of his brain, and he did his best to convince himself that it was largely her issue but, just the fact that it arose at all exposed the obvious, that a part of him was hoping that the encounter, if there was one, would include some activities that would likely be contrary to her vows.

"What's taking the jury so fucking long?" he barked to the darkness. The cogitating was agitating him, and he longed for the fleeting serenity of a few minutes prior. He wondered if maybe they hadn't requested clarification on some of the finer points of law from the judge, maybe a more detailed explanation of exactly what constituted reasonable doubt. He wished he'd had another shot at a closing argument, but in the end, he knew that there was nothing to do but wait.

Chapter 41

The tan denim cut-off jeans and the t-shirt with the dreadlocked smiley face saying "no problem, Mon" lay crumpled on the back seat of Ruby's car, revealing a certain premeditation regarding a possible encounter later that evening. "Careful Mrs. Haslach," Ruby whispered as she adroitly guided a woman at least fifty years her elder down the couple of steps from the dais that had just been the scene of her greatest triumph. She had been the recipient of the Above and Beyond award for thirty years of uninterrupted service at Mercy Memorial. And just like the Best Picture Oscar, that most prestigious honor was always reserved for last. She had welled up as the crowd erupted in applause, and the floodgates had sprung wide open when they rose for the one and only standing ovation she would ever receive in her eighty odd years on the planet.

Ruby had become a little teary eyed herself as Melba described how she'd personally driven her husband, Henry to the hospital as a precaution when he complained of a little tightness in his chest and how he was admitted for observation and how finally she'd been the one to find him stiff as a board upon entering his room the next morning, his last desperate gasp for breath having been taken a couple of hours prior to her arrival. The doctors and nurses were beside themselves with grief and could not do enough to try to ease the sudden and profound burden Melba had to bear. It apparently never occurred to Melba that maybe someone could have done something, and to be sure that line of inquiry was never raised by anyone on the staff of Mercy Memorial. Not surprisingly, it was unanimous amongst all those that comforted her that it was surely "God's will." But Ruby didn't have the benefit of some of the more troubling details and saw only her tragic dedication, her thirty years of selfless devotion.

As Melba had told of how Mercy Memorial had become her second home on that fateful day thirty long years ago, Ruby's thoughts had turned to the unusual stranger that had stepped onto the stage of her life in an even more unusual way. She was both troubled and excited by some of the things she had felt earlier that day. She could forgive herself the vanity; the sensations stirred inadvertently. What troubled her was that she knew from the time that Daniel stepped out of the hospital that some how, some way, she was going to see him again later that night. The foregone conclusion didn't prevent her from the battle royal that would rage within her psyche, the justifications and the rationalizations regarding the proper role of a wife and mother. It was knowingly trying the case in a moot court that stung her to the core and gave her fits of self-contempt as she made her half hearted closing argument. She rallied with one last desperate ploy to stop the proceedings by recalling how Charles Manson had recruited his girls during a chance encounter, with little more than the demonic power of his personality. Was she as weak and vulnerable as those

Manson had preyed upon and ultimately ordered to murder in his name?

The thought that Daniel could be a mesmerizing madman with bad intentions made her shudder. She saw the headlines in the local paper heralding the discovery of her nude and bloated body being reeled in by some unsuspecting fisherman on Celina Lake but the scare tactics were ultimately unconvincing. She treated the prospect of danger in much the same way she allayed her fear of flying, mathematically, and the numbers were overwhelmingly on her side.

Honoring Melba's service concluded the scheduled program for Mercy Memorial Hospital, and the closing remarks had already begun by the time Ruby got Melba back to her seat.

"Thank You, dear and so pretty," Melba gushed still apparently in the throes of a serotonin rush.

Ruby just smiled politely and asked if there was anything else she could for Melba or her friends before she moved on to other duties.

Assured that they would all be fine, Ruby made her way to the various other venues she was responsible for and tried not to think about later. Although not completely at peace with the decision, she accepted the fact that unless something wholly unexpected happened by the time she was ready to leave, a side trip to Z9 was next on her itinerary. And since the Governor never called, that's exactly what happened.

Chapter 42

The fire dying down and a disquieting feeling heating up, Daniel proceeded to do what he generally did when a situation called for action. He thought.

DABDA was the acronym he'd created as a mental prod to elicit the 5 stages of emotion outlined by Elisabeth Kubler-Ross in *On Death and Dying*. Denial, anger, bargaining, depression and finally acceptance occurred generally, but not always necessarily in that order, in response to the impending confirmation of human mortality. Daniel had always found comfort in predictable process. It made life seem somehow, at least in part, like a rational endeavor. Any doubts he may have had about the certitude of her scheme dissolved when he applied the process to the first time his little heart had been shattered as a man child of thirteen.

Boom, boom, boom, boom, boom, one after the other and in the exact sequence Ross had laid out in the book. Of course, Daniel did not die, even if it seemed that he was going to, but something died for sure, and the pain of that loss taught him that it was not only family that could hurt you in unimaginable ways but a whole planet full of people.

"It was beauty killed the beast," he heard Carl Denim profess solemnly as King Kong lay in a heap at the foot of the Empire State Building, and Daniel understood. He decided that it was indeed the prospect of the pain of disappointment that had triggered this particular train of thought, and he chided himself for the melodrama he'd been engaged in. "How the hell can you lose something you never had?" he asked aloud as if the answer were blowing in the wind. But he knew that this was about a lot more than what may or may not happen with Ruby, and he wished again that he'd never laid eyes on her.

"Fuck it, he griped, Fuuuuck it! And what, you want I should bargain?" he asked of no one in his best Yiddish accent. Bargaining, the third step in the sequence had always been particularly troubling for Daniel as it drove home the point that there was really no one to whom he could direct his entreaty. He couldn't turn to Jesus, and Buddha basically told him that it was superstitious exercise in futility, and that left him back where he always seemed to end up, with only himself and his own meager resources. "Hey, we do our best, say Golda?"

Daniel gazed up at the crescent moon—stark white and shimmering against the blue-black sky with the puffy white clouds idling by, hiding and then showing off the stars that sparkled like diamonds—and felt like Moon Watcher. The incomprehensible expanse enveloped his mind and drew his attentions from all the nooks and crannies that doubt and worry, fret and obsess.

"No, if she shows, great. And if she doesn't, well, I'm not going to assume that this time I misread the signals. No, little buddy, this time, I'm going to continue to believe I got it right and that she felt—for her own reasons and they were probably very good ones—that she best not put herself in a potentially compromising position. Pretty mature, wouldn't you agree, Golda?" he looked to his little friend, and she was glad to see that he had arrived at some kind of resolution.

Daniel decided a final smoke on the cantilever would be a nice way to wrap up the day, and he picked up his trusty sidekick and headed down the path. A small flashlight lit the way, and in short order the two compadres were perched on the overhang, watching the moonlight dancing on the gentle ripples below, courtesy of a light evening breeze. A flash in the sky caught Daniel off guard, and he quickly turned his gaze upward. Can't be lightning, can it, he thought to himself and as he wondered, it happened again. He imagined a shooting star, but the flash became a beam, and the sound of tires rolling tentatively over twigs and stones confirmed it. "No shit!" Ruby was, as they say, in the house!

Chapter 43

Daniel rose slowly and with Golda in tow, headed back up the path, his heart beating just a little faster than usual. Both Daniel and Ruby had been victims of circumstance or buffered by their roles in prior encounters, but their presence now was wholly by choice, and that added a whole new dimension of prospect and peril. This and a billion other matters swirled around Daniel's head, and in his excitement and his haste, he failed to light the path with his trusty little flashlight and nearly pitched face first into the dirt when he caught an errant rock imitating a flower craning its neck for a sliver of sunshine. In spite of the near calamity, it still didn't occur to him to flick on the light. Fortunately, the moon supplemented by the neon glow of the smoldering embers provided just enough illumination to allow for safe passage. The North Star that had beckoned him no longer shone, and only the gasps and pings of a car engine no longer combusting confirmed that Ruby was in the vicinity.

He set Golda down near the remnants of the fire, turned on the flashlight and started off in what he figured to be the direction of the noise. As he picked up the pace to stay within earshot of the ebbing tics and hisses, it dawned on Daniel that it wasn't necessarily Ruby that he would encounter up the path.

All but the back end of the wondermobile was obscured by Daniel's inadvertent camouflage parking job but it looked to be his car, and Ruby was satisfied that she was in the right place, although the license plate struck her as odd. She turned and grabbed the shorts and t-shirt like so much evidence from the back seat and stuffed them into her handbag, having decided that she'd keep her options open and introduce them at a later time if the situation warranted. The ominous darkness that fell upon her by degrees as the interior light faded fully to black, sent a chill down her spine, and a part of her thought hard and seriously about just how good an idea this really was. She staved off the doubt but quickly opened the door to trigger that same light. The hazy illumination of her immediate environment was enough to take the edge off, and the sudden appearance of a straw-like ray of light bouncing off branches and shrubs bolstered her sense of relief. She thought about calling out his name but froze at the thought that there was no guarantee that it was actually Daniel making his way toward her car. She had seen a crude sign a short ways back indicating that this was in fact Z9, but she had only given it a cursory glance as she passed it and rather than walking the fifteen feet to confirm it, she pulled the car door within a quarter inch of shut. The light stayed on, but the process of closing and locking the door could be completed in a nanosecond if necessary.

The hint of light peeking through the shrubs and branches confirmed that Daniel was on the right track, and by the time it had been extinguished, he had managed to get a bead on the back of the car, which with the aid of a visual cue, he felt relatively certain, he recognized from the parking lot of the Food Lion.

The straw light had been moving inexorably in the direction of the car, and at the point at which Ruby heard twigs cracking underfoot she had yanked the door shut in a panic and locked it. The fluttering beam made a disjointed approach settling finally on the ground outside her window. She fumbled for the key, and once it was in her grasp, she cocked it and was prepared to fire should the situation warrant drastic action.

"Cool, partner, cool as a cucumber, that's you," Daniel mumbled, trying to appear calm as he neared the car, but it was no longer apprehension that stirred him up but the excitement of knowing that she came, and, moreover, that she came to see him. He was slightly confused by the lack of movement and let the beam climb slowly up the door of the car until it penetrated the window.

The laser beam struck dead center in her left eye, and as she turned away, she lost hold of the key, sending her anxiety into orbit. The story must have been true, she imagined in the foggy frenzy of fear. Apparently, the psycho killer with the hook for a hand never *had* been caught and had taken up residence in the densely wooded areas of Hoosier National Forest.

"Ruby." Daniel's familiar voice penetrated the glass and punctured the cartoon balloon with the crazy ideation.

Ruby shook her head, gulped down a couple of deep breaths and stepped gracefully out of the car. A latent surge of relief pushed her toward Daniel, and she suddenly discovered herself with her arms around his shoulders, planting a kiss on his cheek. Embarrassed by the impetuous display, she tried to cover up by going European and planting a kiss on his other cheek before she stood back. If Daniel was suspicious, he didn't let on.

"Jesus, Ruby, I'm glad to see you too," he said, a bit flushed. And lest she think he was the kind of fellow that would take advantage of her unexpected vulnerability, he added another dash for good measure. "That's about the warmest greeting I've ever gotten!"

Ruby sensed that the jig was up and tried to rewind the action and start anew.

"Hello, Daniel." Ruby reverted to her solicitous hostess voice out of a lingering nervousness, and it sounded so discordant that she immediately discarded it. "I mean, hi, Daniel," she added with a kind of "aw to hell with it" laugh.

"Hello, Ruby. I'm glad you could make it." They looked at each other from a respectable distance as if a somber patriarch were casting a critical eye on the two of them, and both were grateful for the cover the minimal lighting provided.

"Would you like some coffee?" Daniel wondered to himself just what the hell the world would do without beverages to grease the skids of awkward transitions.

"Sure, I'd love some," she answered, taking pains to hit a timbre an octave below hostess mode.

"It's gonna take a few minutes to get the fire up to speed." Daniel followed suit, doing his best to engineer an inflection intended to convey a routine conversational tone.

Daniel led the way, and as the path opened up to the clearing that was Z9, he had the sense that he was welcoming her into his apartment, his private domain, and he feared that somehow everything would not be in order even if he couldn't fathom just what "being in order" under these circumstances might look like.

"Would you mind grabbing a couple of blankets out of the tent?" he asked, sensing immediately that the request was rife with innuendo and quickly trying to set the record straight. "We can lean them against the big log by the fire there. It will be much more comfortable. It will—"

"No need to explain, Daniel. I'll get them." Ruby's tone was reminiscent of the one she'd used to settle his frazzled nerves while he was playing doctor and it had the same effect this time.

"There's a lantern just inside the tent on the right and the blankets are next to the sleeping bag."

"Got it."

As Daniel poked and prodded the fire to life, adding a little kindling to the rejuvenated flame and a dash of lighter fluid for good measure, he saw the tent suddenly bathed in amber light. Her silhouette moved gracefully toward the back of the tent, and he watched her every sinewy movement, knowing that he was invisible to her. He flashed back to the intimate glimpse he'd been privy to earlier in the day, fleshed out the whole picture literally and figuratively and imagined *that* silhouette in various positions in various places within the tent.

"Lord, have mercy!" he said to himself as he turned away, chuckling at the memory of the Irish maiden's prayer it triggered "Dear Lord, please have Murphy upon me".

Ruby set her handbag to the side as she bent down to pick up the blankets and the constricting weight of her garb got her to thinking about whether *this* was the right time to "slip into something more comfortable" but she nixed the idea as an odd shyness came over her, and she opted to get no more informal than removing her heels for the time being.

"It seems that the cicada symphony is in town," Ruby pronounced as she emerged from the tent.

"Yeah, geez, I hadn't noticed. Well, actually I had and then it just kind of became part of the general ambiance out here," Daniel replied, reflecting briefly on the phenomenon. The two of them rendezvoused by the fire, carefully stepping around the elephant and fussing with blanket placement, acutely aware of the importance of distance. Eye contact was kept at a minimum as if looking too directly could shake the lumbering giant from its languor. Daniel played it safe and chose a twin rather than a double arrangement that left six inches or so between the blankets. A little closer than Mary and Dick's set up but not dangerously so.

The fire now fully revitalized, Daniel set to arranging the percolator on the makeshift grille, and as had been the case in the car earlier in the day, he felt Ruby's unwavering gaze. He found it a little disconcerting, if not unwanted, but he met it briefly and flashed a self-conscious smile. He repositioned himself on the blanket, and the two of them sat quietly with only the snapping and crackling of the fire disturbing the silent night.

"Stay, won't you, Daniel, at least for a little while, anyway," Ruby heard herself imploring Daniel when faced with the prospect of his departure from the hospital. She had surprised herself with the appeal as much, she imagined, as she had surprised him. She recalled thinking of her whole being as having an itch that somehow his presence scratched. The relief was divine, and she wanted or maybe needed just a few more minutes of it. It was a safe, if somewhat ambiguous way, to characterize their brief assignation, and it served her well for a time.

Ruby had been acting on sensation since the incident. The debate, though driven by guilt had not got beyond the simple but treacherous act of meeting a man other than her husband. It had not strayed from the venial to the mortal. Throughout the whole of her deliberations, she had not allowed the words to form that would describe the stark reality of where it could ultimately lead. To give it form, a clear line of thought, a sentence with nouns and verbs and adjectives to enhance and empower the things she might act on would likely have shut down the whole operation. And even now as she studied his face, she studiously avoided the fact that it was attached to limbs and a torso and an as yet unidentified appendage, all of which if put to their highest and best use, could expand the parameter of that "relief" exponentially.

Daniel, unencumbered as it were, for his part had watched numerous versions of the sexual possibilities played out in his mind's eye not because he believed that anything of the sort was actually going to happen but because the mind, pointed as it had been in a particular direction, tended to follow that path to its logical conclusion. Daniel was not troubled by this phenomenon nor did he perceive it to be anything but normal and natural. It could on occasion be a bit of a distraction if he let it, but for now, he parked his graphic illusions of ecstasy safely in the far lot where they were not likely to be dented or scratched and enjoyed the simple pleasure of her company.

Chapter 44

"What does "Bourglay" mean?" Ruby asked, finally breaking the silence. Daniel laughed a little ironic laugh. The conversation could have taken any number of turns, and instead, she chose one that would of necessity open a window to Daniel's soul.

"Oh, you mean my license plate." He started, trying to buy a little time to figure out how he could phrase an answer that would satisfy her without making him seem equally disturbed.

"Yes, I mean, is it a person, place or thing?"

"It's a person, actually, most likely a Frenchman who for years walked a circuitous route through New York and Connecticut of three hundred and sixty-five miles every thirty-four days in the latter half of the nineteenth century." Daniel sensed that he had the stilted repetitious diction of a tour guide, but he was trying to maintain a certain distance between himself and the object under discussion.

"And he did this why?" Ruby asked with a tone of bemused incredulity.

"Well, it's kind of sketchy, but the story goes that he fell in love with a woman that was—how would you say this?—that was above his station. Anyway her father was opposed to the union, but he agreed to bring him into the family business to give him a chance to prove that he was worthy."

"Well, that was certainly big of him!" Ruby interjected, her words imbued with a certain disconnected angry rumbling that even she didn't detect.

Undeterred, Daniel proceeded with the tale. "Apparently, he did a bang-up job for a time, and the future looked promising, but at some point through a series of bad decisions, he managed to destroy the business, his job and naturally and most importantly, the woman that he loved—or so the story goes anyway." Daniel had managed to shed the stilted repetition, but he'd replaced it with a kind of la-de-da sing song tone that was wholly incongruous with the subject matter. He drew a breath, gathered himself and tried to inject a solemn, but not too solemn, tenor to the narrative.

"How did he end up here," Ruby asked in a voice that suggested to Daniel that in spite of his seesawing modulations, the incomprehensible desolation of this man's life was seeping through.

"Nobody really knows. Nor do they know how it came to pass that he embarked on sort of a journey without end. Apparently, he just appeared one day in a town called Harwinton and was probably looked upon as just another of the many hobo vagrant types that floated on and off the landscape never to be seen again. But he *was* seen again and with amazing regularity."

"How did he survive?" Ruby interjected, a maternal instinct evident in her voice. "I mean what did he do for food"

Daniel paused for a moment before answering as the last page of *The Grapes of Wrath* crossed his mind. "I guess he survived on a combination of his own cunning and resourcefulness and probably to a greater extent the kindness of strangers." Daniel could see the dreaded look of pity and concern on her face and a hint of puzzlement as to why someone would identify so strongly with such a tragic figure, though he conceded that he was reading an awful lot into her emotional reactions.

"It all sounds very sad," she said. "But I'm confused as to what purpose the wandering served."

"The suspicion was that it was an attempt at atonement, that he had chosen to pay his debt by sentencing himself to a way of life that constituted a most severe kind of penance."

"God, Daniel, that's a horrible story. Couldn't he have started over somewhere, I mean he didn't kill anybody or anything, did he?" she asked in a pained voice. Daniel didn't answer her query because there was no answer.

"It's a compelling story, and that's what attracted me to it. And as to why I would adorn a vanity plate with the name of such a character, I'm not really sure," he added in a preemptive response to the question that he was sure was coming. "I ordered it shortly after reading about him, and over time, I got to thinking about him more and more. I like to believe that the possibility of redemption always exists, and I think maybe all of us, or maybe I should say, some of us, have a little bit of the "Leatherman" as he was known, in us." This was as close as Daniel intended to come to conceding his own emotional impoverishment, and he moved to wrap up this portion of the evening's entertainment. "Who knows, maybe he was suffering for all our sins," Daniel said, ending his dissertation with a daring bit of blasphemy and waiting anxiously for her reply.

"You are a most unusual character, Daniel," she commented softly, still mulling over the curious information while Daniel chose to interpret "unusual" in a positive way. The "beverage segue" came in handy for the second time in a brief span as the percolator's silence signaled coffee time, and Daniel seized the opportunity to steer the evening in a new direction. As he arose to do the honors, he caught a glimpse of Golda and gave her a wink. He knew what she was thinking, erudite *and* humble! And although he was satisfied that he had acquitted himself well, he wasn't sure he'd go quite that far.

Chapter 45

Daniel had gathered the cups and the condiments, and as he joined Ruby fireside, he sensed that she was still contemplating the tortured odyssey of the Leather man.

The story does kind of set you to thinking, doesn't it? he asked as he considered how he might finally close this chapter. He thought about asking her about her life but figured that minefield was best navigated on her initiative. Instead it was she who instigated the shift by asking about the nature and duration of *his* journey.

"So let me get this straight," Ruby said abruptly. You just decided one day to up and leave and go on a kind of extended vacation to what, think about life?"

"Well, yes, in a nutshell, I guess that pretty much covers it. Ever since I was a kid, I always wanted to just up and go, travel without a particular itinerary, or a very loosely defined one anyway, and when the opportunity arose, I just took it."

Daniel could tell she was intrigued by the notion and he wasn't surprised. It almost always looked terribly appealing from the other side. Plus, he was kind of enjoying the renegade tag she seemed to have pinned on him.

"That seems pretty ballsy, Daniel," she said earnestly.

Daniel got a kick out her choice of words but passed on the suggestive responses and gave her a straight answer. "Well, I guess you could say that. It does seem that the few people that I've told are more than a little intrigued by the idea, but I always figured that most people's lives have their share of problems and frustrations and consequently the thought of 'setting out on the City Ring Road, the infinite stars towering above them' serves as kind of a relief valve, a temporary respite from the daily grind."

"Yes, but you actually did it!" she said forcefully as if she refused to allow him to minimize his effort.

Daniel flashed back to Cool Hand Luke's prison mates refusing to believe that his had been anything but a grand adventure when he was redeposited back in their midst, the hound dog's prodigious sense of smell having returned him to the fold.

"I'm sure a lot of people, even if given the chance, wouldn't go through with it," Ruby continued to further drive home the point.

Daniel began to feel a bit of a fraud and as much as he appreciated the romantic characterization, he felt in good conscience that he needed to temper her enthusiasm. "You know, Ruby, did it ever occur to you that maybe there just wasn't very much to keep me where I was and that maybe that was due to my own shortcomings?" He stopped short of offering specifics, hoping that she would get the point without benefit of the gory details.

"Well, I assumed that you weren't—involved, I guess would be the word I'm looking for, but I just figured you chose not to be for whatever reason. You're not *involved*, are you, Daniel?"

Chelsea strode past Daniel's mind's eye and threw him a mischievous smile.

"By involved, I assume you mean with a woman and no, I'm not, or a man for that matter," he added with a mischievous smile of his own, and he was buoyed by Ruby's laughter. It began to occur to Daniel that most if not all conversational paths seemed to lead to the vicinity of the paucity of his emotional life, and he chose then and there not to try to cover it up. He would not emphasize it, to be sure, but neither would he paint a false portrait. Fortunately, at least at this juncture, she seemed unwilling or unable to imagine anything of the sort.

Ruby once again seemed to be studying Daniel's face, only this time he was sitting right in front of her, facing her. He imagined that she was sizing him up, trying to get a bead on just what was up with this mysterious stranger, and he felt naked.

In point of fact, she was indeed studying his face, specifically his lips, and she was imagining how they would feel softly touching hers. In that instant, she seemed to recall every corny love scene she'd ever borne witness to in a thousand movies and TV shows where the star struck lovers gave in to the impulse, cocking their heads to the perfect angle, looking deeply and solemnly into each other's eyes and finally; contact, softly pecking at first, and when the sky didn't fall, exploding into a torrent of passion. Ruby imagined running her tongue from right to left across his lips, first caressing the bottom and then nibbling and gnawing at the top before—

"What's on your mind, Ruby," he asked jolting her out of her lustful meandering.

She looked embarrassed as if she had been caught with a mitt in the cookie jar. She paused for a brief moment and then she laughed lightly and grabbed a hold of his arm in much the same way she had in the hospital. "I'm sorry. I just kind of spaced out there for a moment," she answered, the image dispatched but a hint of guilty pleasure lingering. "Where's the City Ring Road"? she asked as she released him and herself from the obligation to elaborate.

"Boy, you are a curious sort, Miss Ruby Weber," he replied not sure why he had tossed her surname into the mix.

She smiley coyly and the buzz was suddenly palpable. Now it was Daniel's turn to want to lunge across the chasm and press his lips onto hers, but instead he lay back, gazed up at the stars and gulped a little cool air in before answering. "Well, actually, I was paraphrasing a passage from a short story I read recently by an author named Ian McEwan that just kind of stuck with me." Daniel adopted a pensive look before continuing. "Well, I shouldn't really say it just stuck with me because I read back over it about thirty times which is what I tend to do when I come across a particularly well turned phrase. I won't bore you with the details, but it's about a guy whose diminished role in his lover's life sets him to fantasizing about busting out and regaining a sense of himself. There was more, and if you're interested I'll try to remember it." Daniel chose to solicit her encouragement so as not to let his loquaciousness run afoul of good interpersonal etiquette.

"Go," she responded without hesitation and he was happy to oblige.

To lope carefree towards the orange dawn and on into the next day and again into the following night, crossing rivers and penetrating woods, to search for and find a new love, a new post, a new function, a new life. A new life!

Even as he recounted the passage, the power of it was revealed to Daniel anew, and to his enormous satisfaction Ruby seemed similarly spellbound. A reverent silence followed while the two of them digested the full measure of the words, each in their own way.

There seemed to be fire in Ruby's eyes as if the deacon had hit just the right chord and the imbibition of the Holy Spirit had welled up inside of her and unleashed a new sense of purpose and resolve, and when she finally spoke, a bit of that fire tinged her words. "Did he break out, did he strike a blow for freedom and regain his dignity?"

Daniel paused a long while, caught a fleeting glimpse of Arletta while he marveled at Ruby's enthusiasm, and then he answered. "Well, no, actually, I guess he wasn't ballsy enough."

The answer, so incongruous with her expectation and demeanor, seemed to stun Ruby for a second, but when she made the adjustment, she burst into irony soaked laughter with Daniel not far behind.

Chapter 46

When the laughter subsided, their eyes met and locked. In that split second there seemed a silent acknowledgement that in that place, in that moment a good thing was going on and that they daresn't question why or how it came to pass or how long it might last. In little more than the blink of an eye, they had managed to achieve that rare kind of intimacy that has a momentum that is close to impossible to derail. A momentum in which potential discord is quickly steered away from or nuanced adjustments are made to the troublesome content with the aid of conversion tables created for that very purpose.

Daniel reached forward to stoke the flame a bit and toss a few sticks onto the fire. The quiet was comfortable, and they gazed at the flickering firelight. Daniel reached for a Camel Light and even offered one to Ruby, who gracefully declined though quickly added that Daniel should feel free. After a time he spoke.

"I started out the day somewhere in Ohio with no idea at the time that I'd end up lakeside by a toasty fire. Nor could I have imagined that along the way I'd have disfigured a woman and for that dastardly dee more d, been rewarded by her elegant presence at Chez' Daniel's," he said with a nervous laugh.

"You never know, do you!" she replied, smiling a sweet ironic smile as she drew her knees to her chin.

"How's the leg feeling?"

Ruby looked down at the limb that had kicked off this odyssey and was reminded that it was still throbbing just a bit.

"I think it's sore more from the stitching process than the actual wound. Once the doctor had numbed it, all pretense of the "kid glove" approach went out the window, and it felt like he was in the Cub Scouts making a wallet or something."

Daniel felt a bit of relief at having cohort in crime and one that had moved ahead of him in culpability.

"You know, Ruby, being that I was the first medical man on the case, I'd kind of like to see how it turned out," he said with a mock serious tone.

The request seemed to catch her off guard but she recovered quickly. "Boy, what a fellow won't do to get a glimpse of a little leg," she answered with a wry smile, suggesting a mischievous flirtation but with a modicum of reserve.

"Hey, this is strictly in the interest of science," he responded playfully, and the two purred with good humor.

When Ruby didn't make a move to raise the hem of her dress, Daniel finally asked if he might proceed.

"May I?"

Ruby nodded her silent assent.

He reached cautiously and took hold of her dress and immediately felt her tense up. "You know, Ruby, I don't have to do this if it makes you uncomfortable."

"No, you go ahead. Don't pay any attention to me," she replied seemingly irritated with herself.

Daniel gripped the hem delicately between the thumb and forefinger and raised it slowly so as not to end up in regions not designated on his pass. "Not too much unlike what I did," he commented with satisfaction as he studied the bandage the doctor had applied. "Can I lift a side up?"

She repeated her previous action, and Daniel lifted the edge of the tape with his fingernail and ever so tenderly drew the bandage back until the stitches were visible. It did look worse than he'd remembered it with a sort of jaundice yellow mingling with the purple blue bruises, and he felt a flash of anger toward the doctor. "Jesus, he was a bit of a butcher, wasn't he?"

And before she could answer, he tossed the script and surprised the both of them by leaning over and gently planting four kisses just outside of each corner of the rectangular bandage. It was a bold, if not rash move, an unintended accelerant completely out of character for Daniel, but it put the evening much more in sync with the undeclared rhythms of their respective bodies.

Ruby cradled his head as she drew it toward hers but stopped abruptly and pressed it against her bosom and squeezed it tight. Her heart was thumping violently in Daniel's ear, and he was enraptured by the texture and the sweet scent of everything to do with a woman. He inhaled deeply as he draped his arms around her waist and fell almost prostrate against her. He listened to her life force pounding rapidly but rhythmically and found a strange serenity in its percussion. At some point he began to lift his head to move his mouth in the direction of hers, but each exertion seemed to tighten her grip.

"Ruby, what's the matter? Is everything okay?" he asked animatedly. Without so much as a word, she set him aside, stood up and walked to the tent. The lighting of the lantern recreated the amber silhouette and Daniel could do little more than sit and watch.

In the day-to-day lives of even "good girls" there are those occasional encounters or perceptions that evoke sensations that are generally experienced in a vague, mostly detached way, hypothetical emotions that may give rise to impure thoughts, but they are safe and private and no harm can come to anyone because of their very nature. But this was different; this sensation had struck like a thunderbolt and would not easily be dismissed. It seemed to multiply within Ruby like an errant virus, replicating itself every few seconds and spreading throughout the organism. And now the hypothetical was teetering on the brink of a whole other realm, a realm with actions and consequences, a realm that she dreaded, once entered, she would not be able to step back from.

Ruby positioned herself dead center in the tent and minus her heels was able to stand virtually upright. Daniel focused his gaze intently in the silence, the cicadas having reverted to part of the overall ambiance, as she bowed her head like a high diver running through the mechanics of the act one last time before taking the plunge. The scarf came off first, released by a single defiant tug. Her hands dropped to her waist, and the belt quickly followed, and Daniel winced from a sharp sensation that seemed part pleasure and part pain. Ruby's elbows thrust forward as she reached behind her head and up under her hair, her movement slow and fluid, deliberate and graceful. Daniel was unaware that he had begun muttering under his breath, a mechanical, ritualistic sound, like a prayer learned long ago and now recited with no regard to its content, a blanket expression of appreciation for the bounty to follow. Having undone whatever it was at the base of her neck, Ruby reached around to her back with both arms, self-inflicting a sort of half nelson while projecting her breasts forward in the same manner that her elbows had been thrust mere seconds ago. The one hand, lower than the other, seemed to pinch and tug at the fabric of the back of her dress allowing the other to grip and, if Daniel's prayer was answered, initiate the slow and steady separation of the parallel rows of metal teeth that were freed like so many dominos falling one after the other.

It's getting serious now, Daniel thought to himself as he tried to maintain his composure, his eyes still glued to the tent. As her hands slid down her back, two triangles collapsed to either side, and as they fell, Ruby quickly moved her arms into such a position that gravity allowed them to slide free. She reached around to her waist, pushed gently with both hands and her dress cascaded to her feet, landing softly in a hunter-green heap.

Daniel found that he had been rubbing his hands together so fiercely that with just a little more friction, they likely would have burst into flames. He grabbed a cigarette as a deterrent so he could keep his attention where it clearly belonged. He tried lighting up with his palm but the heat had already abated.

Ruby stepped up and out of the heap and turned squarely in Daniel's direction. She leaned forward, placing her hands on her right thigh, and rolled one and then the other stocking down to her ankles. She splayed her right leg outward, bent back at the waist, pulled the stocking free of her foot and deposited it in the pile, repeating the action on the other side. She was naked but for her bra and panties and in a move that took Daniel by surprise, she turned to face him squarely, put her hands on her hips and appeared to stare directly at him. Her motionless outline looked as lifeless as a cardboard cutout, but he could feel her eyes and half expected a wisp of flame to appear followed by two holes spanning a distance the width of the bridge of her nose.

He rose up on his fingertips, poised to charge the tent but checked the impulse when he saw movement again. To his great dismay he watched as Ruby bent down and retrieved a garment from the bag she'd carried in earlier. "No, no, no, no, NO! That's backwards. Things come off now, they do *not* go back on," he cried to himself as she shimmied into a pair of shorts. She turned to the side and showed a profile as she crooked her head back toward Daniel and appeared again to be staring in his direction. With no idea where this was heading, Daniel fell back, landing with a thud, ran a hand across his brow and waited.

Ruby's right hand crept up her abdomen, disappeared between her breasts, cut loose the winch and let them tumble. They did not fall far but the effect was mesmerizing. Daniel was back up on his fingertips but this time with no thought of charging the tent, in fact with no thoughts whatsoever. Ruby paused for a long moment and reached down to her bag again and within seconds was pushing her arms through the t-shirt and pulling it over her head. Daniel sighed deeply and concluded it best that he simply recline and try to calm down, mostly because he didn't have the faintest idea what would happen next. Ruby stepped through the tent flap and her form, hued and highlighted by the twilight of the moon and the ember's glow, took on a surreal quality. Daniel watched, transfixed, as the lovely apparition sauntered his way.

Chapter 47

"**N**o problem, mon" the shirt announced with her arrival, though Daniel was not altogether comforted by the Rastafarian assurance. Ruby loomed large in front of Daniel. Her form, partially eclipsing the other celestial body in his constellation, added to the perception and as he eyed her upon her dominant perch, he sensed she had yet to decide exactly which course of action she would pursue. He had been provoked to a heightened state of sexual yearning, but the passion had ebbed somewhat when she stopped disrobing and worse yet donned the shorts and t-shirt. She stood silent and intense, and Daniel fumbled for words, but they were nowhere to be found. As his mind raced, the simple truth shoved aside the chaos and confusion and bullied its way out of his mouth. "You're killing me, Ruby."

He saw a pained looked come over her face as if his words had strung deeply. He started to add that he meant no harm but was struck dumb by the imposition of her lips on his. The kiss, passionate bordering on violent, lasted only seconds, and her arms like tentacles engulfed his neck and enveloped his back and as she straddled his lap. She further secured her stranglehold by clutching his thighs with her knees. She planted soft sensual kisses all the way across his cheek, stopping finally when his earlobe was resting comfortably between her teeth.

Daniel's blood was up, and he wanted his lips hard on hers. He wanted to taste her tongue and revel in its touch, and as he considered wrestling her for position, Ruby probed his inner ear with a moist-tipped spear and subdued the impulse. She sensed his pleasure and wanted to do better. She nibbled, licked, caressed and tugged every part of his ear, inside and out and at least momentarily, tamed the dragon beneath her.

"Daniel," she said tenderly, the proximity of her mouth to his ear making it seem as if she were actually inside his head.

"Yeah," he whispered almost inaudibly.

"I have to ask you a question."

"Okay," he replied, feeling again like he was groping for a light switch in a pitch black room.

"In the parking lot earlier today, when you were tending to the wound, you kind of stopped all of a sudden like…"

"Yeah," he answered in the same dreamlike manner as he looked back over the day in his mind.

"What happened?"

Daniel, normally reluctant to articulate his naked desire, considered what had transpired since the incident, and realized there really wasn't a whole lot at risk. "You are right, Ruby. It's exactly what you're thinking."

"And how, pray tell, do you know what I'm thinking?" she said softly, releasing her vice grip for a second and pinching his back playfully.

Daniel winced slightly through muffled laughter. "The simple truth, Ruby, is that you knocked my socks off! Your calves, the silky smoothness of your thighs and—how do I put this? — and well, that delicate, private area to the north. It felt like I was having a seizure, and there was nothing I could do but let it run its course, and given the circumstances I thought it was wrong or at the very least incredibly inappropriate, and I felt like a complete idiot. I hoped you hadn't noticed, but I guess it was pretty obvious."

Ruby fell silent and Daniel could feel her grip loosening just a bit. She pulled her head back, looked deep into his eyes, cupped his face in her hands and kissed him deeply, warmly, lovingly. The passion had morphed into a profound tenderness, and as she tried to disengage, Daniel turned the tables and laid his lips on hers. "I'm sorry if I offended you," he said softly, his forehead pressing on hers.

She put her finger to his lips as if she would not allow such blasphemy. "Don't, Daniel. Please, don't talk like that," she insisted, dropping her gaze as she spoke. "Initially I wasn't sure what to do. I was actually kind of scared by it all. I didn't want to be too presumptuous, but I felt every bit of it, and I was thrilled. And when I finally felt pretty certain that that's what was happening, I felt flushed like — well you know what I mean — and I just went limp, and all the while I was feeling foolish and guilty for reacting the way I did." She looked up and met his eyes but dropped them quickly before continuing. "Christ, Daniel, I'm a married woman with a family, I can't be getting all hot and bothered in parking lots with strange men that give me a little attention. What does that say about *me* anyway? Boy, talk about feeling like a complete idiot." She looked to be on the verge of tears, and Daniel, naturally empathetic soul that he is, disregarded the "strange men in the parking lot" comment and struggled to find some comforting words.

"Ruby, do you remember what you said after I had slashed your leg and I was feeling inconsolable?"

She didn't answer, and in spite of her best efforts an errant tear snuck through and slid slowly down her cheek.

"You said, 'Things happen, I know you didn't mean any harm.' Well as trite as it sounds it's the absolute truth. This thing happened. It could not have been foreseen, and for whomever you think you may have harmed, your intent was not malicious nor in the grand scheme of things, did it really have anything to do with anyone else."

Ruby threw her arms around Daniel again, but it seemed this time more to hold her up than to pin him down. Her mouth at his ear again broke his rhythm, and he struggled to get back on track.

"I can't do this, Daniel," she whispered hoarsely in his ear before he could resume.

"Can't do what?"

"I can't have sex with you."

"Ruby, you don't have to have sex with me. I mean, well forget that. If you can't, you can't and that's' all there is to it," Daniel averred having discarded any thoughts of supplications or contingencies before speaking.

"Jesus, Daniel, you're so sweet. Couldn't you be a prick for a few minutes so I could storm out of here and try to figure out how I ended up here in the first place and put this thing behind me?" she asked sarcastically finally managing to muster a laugh.

"No can do, darlin'," he replied with a southern drawl that surprised him as much as her and provoked a brief reprieve of shared laughter.

"I almost feel like I owe it to you after the way I've behaved. I mean, I knew you were watching me in the tent when I did my little strip tease. If I'm completely honest, I have to confess that I wanted your eyes on me. I imagined that you were excited, that you might even have had an erection, and it thrilled me all over again. The truth is Daniel, that I meant to step out of that tent stark naked, walk directly to you and let you look, make you look and hopefully get the same reaction I got this afternoon. I imagined you lunging forward and and ...."

"And what???" Daniel exclaimed pleadingly.

"Geez, I can't believe I'm saying this! Okay, um, hugging my thigh and kissing hard, almost biting in that area, and well, you can guess where it went from there. That was the fantasy anyway, but the more clothes I took off, the more afraid I became, and the more I realized that I was half out of my mind and that I could not go through with it."

Daniel mulled that over for a moment, and the vision of the scenario she described jolted him all over again. "I don't suppose you want to go back in there and try it again," he said with a laugh, half serious even though he knew the answer.

Ruby laughed and tugged at his hair affectionately. "I can't, Daniel, I just can't."

"I know—dammit but just so you know, I *will* have my way with you. Maybe not tonight but soon—if only in my dreams" he declared with a comically chivalrous air, and furthermore, he meant it.

Ruby was suddenly seized with a strong pang of desire again, although she didn't let on, and reconsideration was out of the question. "Stop talking now, Daniel, cause you're breaking me down, and I told you I can't let that happen," she said and so as not to take any chances she leaned forward and planted her lips on his.

Chapter 48

The nonsex had been exhausting, and the two of them lay still, a tangled network of limbs in repose. The waning fire, unattended, darkened their surroundings by degrees. "I should be going soon," Ruby commented with little conviction and Daniel didn't discourage her. For reasons unknown, the cicadas cranked up the volume a couple of notches and they looked at one another as if one of them would know why.

"Weird, huh," Daniel said pressing his forehead against hers.

"This is good," Ruby said quietly and matter of factly.

"Yes, it is," he answered.

"Daniel."

"Yeah." "Do you think it's strange that I'm married and yet I'm lying here with you under the stars?"

Daniel rose up on his elbow and seemed to give the matter serious consideration before responding. "Ruby, I think, honestly, that it's a very private matter and one that you have to work out for yourself." His answer, though true, sounded trite and detached as if it were a mere hypothesis. But she *was* here in this place with him, and it was no doubt an issue of some import to her. He felt that he'd cheated her and took another more nuanced stab at the question. "I'm not insensitive to the fact of your marriage. In fact, I've thought all along that it would ensure that this situation wouldn't go beyond an undeclared attraction, but we kept inching forward, and I had to figure that by showing up here, you had your reasons or maybe you had questions that you needed to try to answer."

Daniel considered that he'd improved upon his original answer but sensed that there was still something missing. "Look, Ruby, I'm not going to judge you to be a bad person if that's what you're getting at, and I don't assume that it means you have a terrible marriage."

Daniel stopped suddenly and seemed to hold his tongue a moment before continuing. "I mean, in fairness, what about my role here. Has it occurred to you that maybe I should have taken the high road and retreated once I knew you were married?" he added, his culpability, he imagined, kind of leveling the playing field.

"And don't forget, *you* stopped this thing," he proceeded with a righteous fervor. Maybe you feel that you should have done it sooner or, better yet, that you'd never come here at all, but in the end you made a decision that you couldn't go any further and whatever else you're feeling, you've got to give yourself some credit for that," he concluded his dissertation satisfied that it was the best he could do.

Ruby looked to the stars as she digested Daniel's comments and after a couple of false starts, she spoke. "I've felt invisible to him for longer than I care to remember. He looks past me like it's somehow beneath him to be aroused by me. Do you know what it's like to stand naked and vulnerable in front of the man you love and who supposedly loves you, presenting yourself for his pleasure and approval and getting no response? I mean, nothing, not even disgust or contempt. I almost feel like it's some kind of bizarre test of willpower for him. "

Ruby reacted to her own words as if they were a revelation even to her and Daniel sensed it. "Jesus, Daniel, no wonder I came apart at the seams when you reacted the way you did. I have to wonder now if I chickened out because deep down I was afraid that you'd look past me too," she said her anger mitigated by her dismay.

"Well, dear, if I were a betting man…"

Ruby chuckled lightly as she rolled over on her stomach. She propped her chin on her hands and Daniel instinctively began to scratch her back lightly. She let out a low guttural sound as if the pleasure was unbearable and dropped her head further so that her forehead was resting on her hands. "This is what I'm talking about, Daniel."

"What?"

"What you're doing now. My husband hasn't touched me like that in years. It's a little thing but stuff like that goes a long way with me." She paused for a moment as if she wasn't sure she should finish her thought. "You want to know how long, Daniel, I'll tell you how long! It makes me horny; it makes me want to take you all over again. How ridiculous is that?"

Daniel considered any number of responses but said nothing. Instead, he began scratching furiously with both hands, and the two of them burst into laughter.

Chapter 49

The night air had become cooler, not unpleasantly so but enough to warrant a little stoking of the fire, and Daniel arose and proceeded to do just that. The two of them needed and took this time to step back a bit from the precipice and get a better look at the yawning chasm from a safer distance. Daniel tossed on some sticks and circled the fire, poking and prodding as he went, his stuttered movement suggesting some kind of primitive ritual. He revisited his earlier contemplations regarding Elisabeth Kubler-Ross, and he had to conclude that while a romp in the proverbial hay would have been nifty, this intimate evening with Ruby had become far more than he'd bargained for, and that he should savor it while it lasted.

Ruby, for her part, held court with the apparitions perched on either shoulder. Her allegiance was clearly supposed to be with the winged one in white, but the little fellow clad in red was no slouch either, and with a combination of dastardly reason and a dash of "carrot on stick," he won the day, though not without some substantial concessions.

The hungry fire devoured the tender morsels and was quickly roused to life. Daniel figured it could digest something with substantially more fiber and plunked a much thicker branch into its whirling vortex. He sat back down next to Ruby and grabbed a smoke.

"I should be going soon. What time is it anyway?"

"It's around 11:00," Daniel replied solemnly. When Ruby had raised the idea earlier, he had sensed that she needed to float that option so as to give the appearance of a balanced negotiation, that it wasn't a foregone conclusion that she would stay on indefinitely. He knew without doubt that it was her call and that he had little or no grasp of the equation she was weighing in her mind and what impulse might tip the scales in favor of calling a halt to the proceedings before it became a greater burden than she could bear to impose on herself.

"Is it? Wow, I really should be going." There was a little more oomph in the statement but no more conviction than the first time she introduced the notion. It seemed as if she was trying to get a running start.

Daniel was silent, and as the moments passed, the lack of movement in any direction cried out for action. He harnessed his dismay and reluctantly uttered the *right* words. "Ruby, I'm not going to ask you to stay," he said detecting a hint of disappointment in her demeanor. "On the other hand, I'm certainly not going to encourage you to go," he added, noting that her face brightened a bit even in the semi-darkness. "Actually, I would love for you to stay but for a whole bunch of reasons, I just don't feel that it's my place to ask you to do that." That seemed to be what Ruby wanted or maybe needed to hear, and Daniel sensed that the savoring might just go on for a little while longer anyway, though he maintained his poker face just in case.

"Jesus, Daniel, I'm sorry to have put you through that," Ruby said, a pained expression on her face.

"I'm not sure I know what you mean," he replied, the 'little white lie' born of deep but unspoken gratitude.

"I wasn't going anywhere. I want to be right here with you, right now, and I guess I just wanted some reassurance that you felt kind of the same way."

Daniel's spirits soared though he may as well have been holding a pair of deuces. "Ruby," he started without having fully formulated his response, "I can't or rather I won't—well, forget that. Let me just say that I am awfully glad you're sticking around. Awfully glad!" He paused for a brief moment before jumping. "Look let's stop the dance now. Let's stipulate what I think is obvious to both of us and that is that we've got a thing going on. A limited thing by choice but a thing nevertheless and we should savor it because it's a pretty rare thing, and the dawn will come soon enough." Even Daniel knew that his words had a poetic ring to them, and Ruby's gaze confirmed it. He moved closer and draped an arm over her shoulder.

"Daniel."

"Yeah."

"What exactly does *stipulate* mean?"

Daniel chuckled lightly. "Just that whatever else might have to be negotiated, the parties to the agreement have all accepted certain premises to be solid or settled. It's kind of a contractual term."

"Now I have to ask you another question."

"Yeah, what's that?"

"Did you steal that "thing going on" phrase from that old song about "Me and Mrs. Jones?"

Daniel caught on after a moment and laughed heartily. "Actually, no I never thought of that, at least not consciously, but hey, you never know."

"Daniel, you know my husband's out of town."

"Yes, you said that in the hospital."

"Well, my son is staying at a friend's place. Believe it or not, it was arranged weeks ago. I mean how ironic is that?"

Daniel was thinking that the old "fate intervening card" was about to be played but she stopped well short of that. "I didn't tell you before because I knew if things got *uncomfortable*, I could gracefully say that I had to be home for his sake."

"Imagine that, an exit strategy," Daniel commented with a hint of his own irony.

"Just good timing, I guess. I only hope I can say that a week from now." The unburdening had served its purpose, and Ruby felt relieved if not wholly settled.

"Daniel, I have a bottle of wine in the car. Would you like some?"

"Sure, that sounds good. I'm kind of coffeed out."

"My boss, Mario gave it to me a couple of months ago because he heard it was my wedding anniversary and the bottle has been in the trunk of my car ever since." She paused to acknowledge the implication of the comment but refused to dawdle. "He says the Italians make the best 'vino' in the universe. Of course, he also says that about food and concrete," she said as a look of bemused puzzlement crossed her face. "I never did get the concrete thing but we'll find out about the wine anyway."

Daniel laughed lightly and was grateful that she'd spared him the "cantilever" inflections.

"You want me to go," he offered.

"No, I'll go but give me the flashlight so I don't break anything on the way." "I've already been through one physical trauma today," she said with a playful smile and Daniel covered his eyes in mock shame.

She followed the beam four or five feet before turning around. "It *is* so stipulated that we've got a thing going on," she said with a serious tone. "But I want to stipulate one more matter before I go for the wine."

"And what would that be, Ruby?" he asked, fully expecting a continuation of the levity.

"That whatever communication we have will be the truth, the whole truth and nothing but the truth."

"Okay," Daniel replied after a slight hesitation.

"When the dawn does come and it's looking more and more like I'll be here at least that long, I don't want you to be a stranger anymore," Ruby stated, matter of factly, as she turned away.

Chapter 50

As Ruby made her way to the car, she questioned her motives for codifying honesty and decided that she wanted some assurance that if there was going to be some soul baring going on she wouldn't be flying solo. She wondered for a moment if the 'stipulation' was really necessary and if he might have taken offense at the suggestion but quickly concluded that it probably wasn't, and that he probably didn't, but if he did then it probably was. And with that last twist of logic, she decided she'd had enough and that it was done in any case, a circuitous route back to where she started that Daniel was more than a little familiar with.

The brief spell of panic he'd experienced at the second stipulation had already begun to subside. The prospect of being exposed was a consistent theme in his life, and although vulnerability had its perils, he managed to convince himself that given the reservoir of good will he appeared to have established, he would fare reasonably well under scrutiny. Besides, he recalled his earlier decision not to "try to cover it up." That coupled with his belief that virtually everyone had a dark underbelly and that she too would be bound by the stipulation reduced the anxiety to a mild uneasiness.

As Daniel watched the light bounce toward her car, he took advantage of the time to check on Golda. As expected, she was all tuckered out from what had been a very long day, and he sensed that she was just a tad peeved at having been relegated to third wheel status. "Goodnight, sweet Golda and don't you worry, we'll have more than enough time together. Heck, you'll probably get tired of seeing this face," he said with the false self-deprecation that accompanies willful disappointment.

Ruby arrived with the wine and a couple "plastic" glasses dangling from her right pinky. "Have you got something we can open this with, Daniel?"

He studied the cork and suddenly his eyes lit up. "I've got just the thing," he replied as if he relished the challenge. He practically ran to the tent and emerged with one of those contraptions with which a man stranded on a desert island could cobble together an ark. "It's called a 'Leather Man' which it just so happens was the moniker given to my man Jules," he proclaimed excitedly, instantly feeling a little foolish after his sudden burst of enthusiasm and regretting having further revealed the degree of intimacy he shared with Jules. "Anyway, it's nice to find a practical use for something that I tried to convince myself would come in handy when a little voice in my head was chiding me for buying it just because of its name," he said a little sheepishly.

"Let's go down by the lake," she said disregarding his eureka moment.

"Yeah, that sounds good," Daniel replied, relieved at not having to revisit the marvels of utilitarianism. He draped a blanket over his shoulder, took the flashlight and Ruby's free hand and led the way down the hazardous trail.

They managed to locate a nice level spot and made like a couple picnicking on a Sunday afternoon. This time as they set up shop, distance was a non-issue. They wanted contact, and if there were any lingering doubts to be dispelled, Ruby snuggled up to Daniel as she offered the bottle for his expert attention. She smiled warmly as he worked to unscrew the cork and held out both glasses for Daniel to fill when he completed the task. They both sipped delicately, and Ruby, her lips moist with wine, leaned forward and nuzzled a bit before planting a gentle kiss on Daniel's chin. They raised their glasses in unison and exchanged toasts. "To mysterious strangers in parking lots," Ruby started.

"To tonight," Daniel followed with a chortle.

Chapter 51

The "vino" was as good as advertised and although neither could be considered a connoisseur, Ruby didn't let that stop her from declaring it to be so, though she stopped short of proclaiming it "a very good year". Daniel had a sneaking suspicion that under the circumstances, a four-dollar bottle of Thunderbird would have been just as pleasing to the palate but figured if she liked it that much, that was all the proof he needed. "It is good, isn't it?" Daniel concurred, and furthermore, he meant it.

Ruby reached over and killed the flashlight that had shone to a distant point toward the middle of the lake, leaving only the light of the silvery moon to define their features. She laid her head on his shoulder, and he reached over and gently caressed her arm. Daniel was a quick study but his motives were pure as it didn't occur to him until after the fact that this kind of touching would at the very least win him some points.

The wine seemed to take a little crackle out of the charge, and a sweet languor overcame the both of them, slowing the pace of the proceedings subtly, almost imperceptibly and neither of them felt compelled to speak.

As Daniel wondered about Ruby's domestic situation, Ruby marveled at the fact that Daniel had been so quick to respect her wishes. She knew the drill, "no means no, regardless of when it's said," but she'd also fought off enough rabid suitors to know that much more often than not, it's not so simple a matter. It had been true of "decent guys" she had dated as a teen and young adult as well as the serial philanderers that most girls knew to expect it from. It had even happened with a supposed good friend of her husband's that exploited a confidence and was aware that they were going through a "dry spell." He just knew that she must be dying for it and he was cocksure that he was just the man for the job.

And then there was Daniel. The fact that she had provoked him would have served as conclusive proof to the dogs with the foamy mouths that deep down "she really did want it" and in spite of that, he seemed to see beyond his own needs and desires all the way across the bow to the generally uncharted territory of *her* concerns. It occurred to her that she always seemed to feel a little guilty when she denied all but the most aggressive and repugnant and that had always left her mystified and angry with herself, but with Daniel, it was a struggle not to want to do it for him because deep down in this most unusual instance "she really did want it!" Her train of thought continued along those lines and regrettably Daniel was not privy to the accolades flowing his way.

"I think I know why I like you so much, Daniel."

Daniel was startled by the bolt from the blue but considering the content, he managed to get his bearings pretty quickly. "Is this the inaugural post stipulation statement?" he asked with a grin.

"Well no, I hadn't thought of that, but yes, it does qualify now that I think about it."

"I'd like to hear it, I think," he followed up with an anxious smile.

"I guess the best way that I can describe it is that from the very beginning, I didn't feel like I had to defend or protect myself from you. Does that make sense? I think what I'm trying to say is that I just felt safe for some reason that's hard to explain. It's more what I didn't sense, a missing barrier or something, which is why it's hard to describe, and that somehow created a clear path of some sort, and I was immediately drawn to you. I keep saying "from the start" but the truth is that I may have felt it from the beginning, but I didn't catch on until we were on the way to the hospital. I suddenly found myself wanting to kiss you then. I tried to dismiss the feeling, to push it away but the more I tried, the stronger it became. When I finally stopped denying it, I was left with trying to figure out why. I suspected that the earlier rush had something to do with it, but I knew it was more than the vanity or the sexual feeling. This is going to sound dumb, but it felt like you were a powerful magnet and I was a piece of steel and it seemed at times during the ride that I was actually physically moving toward you without intending to." She paused for a moment before concluding. "It's complicated stuff, Daniel and I honestly don't fully grasp what's going on here, but there you have it. I gave it my best shot."

Daniel was at a loss for words but felt he had to do something to acknowledge her effort. "I can't explain it either, Ruby but I'm glad you feel that way," he finally managed to respond. It was true, he couldn't explain it but whatever it was constituted the foundation that the rest of the evening was built upon. And since he never could resist an architectural challenge, some lobe somewhere deep in his mind set to work trying to unravel the mystery. Daniel was often quick of mind even if he wasn't fully attuned to the ongoing machinations but just as often slow of tongue, and as had been the case a number of times during their brief tenure, Ruby was talking again before Daniel's thoughts had crystallized.

"For instance, I knew, I just knew that you'd be okay with my 'cold feet' I guess I could say."

This time, his mind and mouth were one, and Daniel was quick to respond. "You know, Ruby, if you think about it, there wasn't much else I could do. I'm just not the forcing type, and I don't know that it means I'm good or kind or decent; it just means that I heard you and I had to respect your wishes. Maybe I was afraid that if I forced the issue, I'd scare you away or that you wouldn't like me or whatever, and then where would I be? Anyway, it seems strange that I get points for simply not being a cad but hey, I'll certainly take it," he said as he gave her an affectionate squeeze.

"What do you like about me?" Ruby quickly followed up as if *her* divulgence warranted reciprocity.

"Wow," Daniel commented wryly as if he were surprised to realize that there was actual parity in their relationship and that for once, he got to be the jury of his female peer. He considered starting with the tried and true and telling her she "looked wonderful tonight," but he nixed that idea as conveying primarily a physical attraction.

"Remember the stipulation," Ruby chimed in, seemingly concerned that it was taking so long to answer.

"I like everything about you, Ruby," he said finally, all too aware of the fact that he hadn't said anything at all and feeling pressured to elaborate. "Let's see," he started again as Ruby tapped her watch with a comically impatient expression on her face.

"That, for instance," he continued. "You seem to be an incredibly good-natured person. When you were cut, I half expected a tongue lashing for being such a clumsy bastard, and yet, you could not have been better about the whole thing."

"What else," she demanded with a whimsical tone.

"Hmmm, well, you don't seem pretentious at all. You seem solid and decent and to top it all off, you have the most beautiful legs I've ever seen. There, I filled my quota. Any more, you have to pay for," he finished with a smile and another squeeze.

Ruby gave Daniel a playful shove and immediately donned a pensive demeanor. "Solid, huh?" she said distractedly, her tone suggesting that she had her doubts. "I guess, I fooled you," she added with an ironic chuckle.

Daniel, sensing he had hit a nerve, mounted his white horse. "I take it you don't agree with my characterization," he said as he mulled over his counter offensive.

"I wouldn't exactly say I'm hanging on by a thread but *solid*, I'm not so sure that fits, especially lately."

"You're managing, it seems."

"Barely, I mean, yes, but things aren't right and haven't been for some time."

"You mean with your husband?"

"That's a big part of it but it's more than that. I kind of feel disconnected from everything that mattered in my life, and I'm not sure how to go about fixing it."

Daniel had been prepared to deliver a pep talk about the honor of remaining upright in the face of difficult circumstances. He had intended to argue that adjectives are often really verbs because they're transitory and may characterize a response to one situation but fail to show up at all in another and that it's all part of being human, but he filed his prepared speech as it took on a specious ring in light of her real world anguish.

"You know, Ruby, I could argue with you but honestly, what the hell do I know about your day-to-day struggles." It was hardly a motivational speech, but it was the truth and it seemed to strike a chord in Ruby. "Would it make you feel any better if I told you that I often times feel like a suit of armor that's held together by a single bolt, and that bolt is only a few threads from popping out altogether." Daniel opted for the "same boat" approach and even though it did only expose the tip of the iceberg, he remained true to the rules of engagement.

"Yes, as a matter of fact, it would," she replied with a distant laugh.

Daniel sensed that she wanted to elaborate, to flesh out the details of the alienation she had hinted at, and he sat quietly, patiently, but no words were forthcoming. He glanced over and saw that she seemed to be staring at a fixed point in the lake, a wind blown ripple, crested by a shimmer of moonlight perhaps. She had the same vacant look on her face that he had noticed when he caught her studying his face. It was as if the object of her focus was beamed directly into her consciousness, and nothing could sever the signal. Daniel watched and waited. He considered asking what was on her mind, but she sighed suddenly, and he swallowed the question. It seemed as if the exercise had exhausted her, and to Daniel's surprise, her hand went immediately to the nape of his neck. She tugged a lock of hair, suggesting that a nonverbal assurance that she was still with him was all she could muster.

"I'm tired of the weight I carry around all the time," she said finally. Tired of feeling lousy and smiling through it. Truthfully, Daniel, I'm worn out, and I don't want to spoil this little time we have together droning on about my problems," she said, the words thick with burden.

Daniel thought about protesting that this was by no means a futile exercise, encouraging her even to let it out, but the acknowledgement of the finiteness of their time gave him pause, and again he held his tongue.

Ruby, acting on maybe the same impulse, began to run her fingers through his hair. She tilted him forward and kissed around the area her hand had just abandoned. "Can I kiss you, Daniel?" she asked softly.

"No, Ruby, I'm afraid I can't allow that," he answered in his most authoritative voice. "Jesus Christ, don't you know any harder questions than that?" His hearty laughter pierced the air and tumbled down unanswered with a thud.

"I'm going to take that as a yes," she replied, with a tone bordering on solemn. "I'd forgotten how much I like kissing, how good it feels to be close to a man," she whispered, her voice sensual as she punctuated each sentence with a kiss. "It's funny, but it all feels so natural and easy, and yet these feelings have been locked away for so long, it's like they've become dormant."

Daniel basked in the warmth of her attentions, more than happy to offer himself up for Ruby to shake the rust and get reacquainted with her amorous side.

"What do you like?" Ruby asked suddenly. "Above the shoulders, I mean," she added quickly with a mischievous chuckle. "I read in one of those women's magazines that a good attentive lover makes it her business to know what her partner likes." She got quiet for a moment. "How sad is it that I've been reduced to reading those stupid magazines to pick up pointers that for all I know I may never get to use?"

"If it's any consolation, Ruby, I'm happy to be your— your..." The term "guinea pig" would not pass his lips and he finally settled on 'practice dummy.' "And since you asked, that ear thing you were doing earlier was really working for me."

She smiled broadly with an obvious air of satisfaction and began to work her magic again. After a moment's ecstasy she stopped abruptly, patted Daniel on the chest and draped her arms around him. "Thank you, Daniel," she said with a heavy sigh. It seemed an odd thing to do and say at first but Daniel figured it out pretty quickly and let it go at that.

Chapter 52

"How's the wine holding up?" Ruby asked shyly, cognizant of the fact that in revisiting her sensual side, she had likely provoked him again and wondering if even Daniel didn't have a tipping point.

"I think we can each get a glass out of what's left," he answered with no indication that he had had any such reaction.

Ruby tried to conceal the sudden fatigue that had come over her as she held out her glass, but a yawn that would not be suppressed betrayed her and she pulled it back just as Daniel was about to pour.

"Let's go back by the fire; it's getting a little cool down here. Is there any kindling left?" she asked in a tired voice that wanted to morph into a second yawn before she got the best of it.

"Yeah, a little bit, and I'll get more if need be."

The two made their way back up to the campsite hand in hand as much for safety as anything else. Daniel kind of eased her down into the makeshift seat and sensed her weariness in the process. He set down the wine and realized the glasses had failed to make the trip with them. "We don't need them,"

Daniel said softly. "We'll make like the Bowery boys. It'll be an adventure," he added with a laugh.

Ruby smiled weakly as Daniel moved away to tend to the fire, wondering if she'd still be awake by the time he was done and if she had any idea just what the hell a "Bowery boy" was.

Daniel managed to get a mild reaction by poking the feeble fire. What was left of the larger branch he'd tossed on a while ago was the only discernible shape in the undulating heap, and he quickly exhausted the remaining kindling hoping to have a little more to work with when he'd gathered the next batch. After collecting and depositing a modest amount of kindling and a couple of pretty hefty branches for efficiency, he foraged the tent for a bag of marshmallows to surprise Ruby with. He checked on Golda who looked as vigilant as ever and was satisfied that she was fine. The fire had been reborn and was throwing off just enough illumination for Daniel to see that Ruby was at best inert. He began to tread lightly, recalling as he always did in these situations the stories about how the Native Americans could move stealthily through the woods without making so much as a peep and how that impossibly high standard made his every step sound like his feet had been miked-up.

He found a couple of small branches well suited to the task and pierced the spongy skin of two marshmallows just in case Ruby was sentient, but as soon as he got within ten feet of her he knew the sweet confections were likely to be breakfast if anything. He jammed the branches between the stones that ringed the fire and sat down gently within a few feet of his new found friend.

Daniel reached for a cigarette, and rather than risking the noise of a striking match, he quietly pulled a burning twig from the fire and made do. "Oh, she may be weary," Otis Redding crooned in his mind as he looked upon the sleeping beauty through the smoke curling and rising past his eyes, and a deep tenderness came over him. He felt his own sand-man hovering but he sent him on his way. There would be plenty of time later for sleep.

"A suit of armor that's held together by a single bolt." Daniel knew as soon as the phrase passed his lips that it had been appropriated from something he'd seen or read along the way. He rummaged through the archives of his memory for the source of the unintentional plagiarism and finally heard the voice of Rod Serling describing the main character in an episode of the *Twilight Zone* he seemed to recall was titled "Willoughby" or something to that effect. A harried ad executive on the brink of a nervous breakdown that just wanted out, the storyline went, but a wife whose material ambitions could only be achieved through his due diligence kept him in shackles. And on the train ride home he dreamt of an idyllic place where "everybody knows your name and they're always glad you came" — to borrow from another television offering — the age-old greener pastures syndrome but with a twist.

He'll forgive me, he thought to himself as he turned his gaze back to Ruby. It felt a little bit odd to watch someone sleep, an unauthorized intrusion of sorts. That she could, suggested to Daniel that she did indeed feel safe, that she could reliably trust that no harm would come to her. The very act inadvertently cast Daniel in the role of protectorate and in a fit of chivalry, Daniel imagined that he would slay a dragon if necessary to prove worthy of that sentiment.

He revisited his contemplations regarding R.D. Laing and was acutely aware of the fact that they hadn't even begun to scratch the surface of the depth and complexity of each other's lives and that in any case, there was hardly time for that. No, this was a random encounter that just happened to be a very good fit. What were the odds? Daniel imagined that it was rather like two multi-pronged pieces of a jigsaw puzzle that happened to go "bump in the day" only to discover that their unique configurations constituted sort of an emotional yin and yang. The notion of a tankless water heater popped into his head and he thought the analogy apt. He'd read about them recently and was intrigued by the concept; enough juice to heat water as it moves through the pipe once the tap is opened as opposed to a slow inexorable slow burn that heats the contents of the tank over an extended period of time.

There was conflict in her life; her own words and actions had established that fact and Daniel's curiosity became more acute as the night wore on. Was her husband just your run-of-the-mill-cad, a self-styled lothario who chased skirts and spent his libido everywhere but the one place he was supposed to? Had he met another woman? Was he depressed, crazy or gay maybe? Whatever the case, Daniel assumed that Ruby was getting short-changed and he felt a little surge of anger toward the dragon she'd married. It was, of course, completely unfair to her husband, seeing that he was not available to testify on his own behalf, and Daniel conceded that but still felt pretty strongly that Ruby had likely held up her end. Daniel mechanically looked to the moon and felt the tides shifting inside of him. He reached for the wine and tried unscrewing rather than pulling the cork, hoping to prevent the pop of compressed air. It didn't work. Daniel instinctively covered the opening with his palm to capture any latent belch as he looked quickly toward Ruby to see if he'd disturbed her.

"Jesus Christ, you startled me," he exclaimed upon seeing Ruby sitting silently, eyes wide open.

"I'm sorry," she replied with a laugh.

"Did that noise wake you up?"

"No, I've been up for a few minutes."

"You should have told me."

"You looked to be lost in thought and I kind of followed suit, I guess."

"What were you thinking about?" he asked before she could.

"It will sound strange but I was thinking about some high school friends and a slumber party and a game of Truth or Dare. Daniel imagined stories about boyfriends and goals and school and teenage tribulations and maybe virginity or the loss of it and moved over next to her in anticipation of some of the juicy details. Let it out, girlfriend, he thought to himself with a chuckle.

"So who are you, Daniel and whatever brings you to this part of Indiana?"

It was the oddly worded question verbatim that she had sprung on him on the way to the hospital earlier that day. He hadn't expected it then, and it caught him off guard now, but a good deal of water had seeped under the bridge since the first time she posed the question, and he knew that this time the bar had been set a whole lot higher and then, of course, there was the small matter of the *stipulation*.

Daniel having grudgingly accepted that the titillating account of private conversations was going to remain just that, private, sat back, took a deep breath and began to gather his thoughts. "I assume you're expecting the truth, right?" he asked sheepishly and she just nodded. "Thought so."

The pregnant pause that followed was punctured by Ruby's follow-up question. "Daniel, do you have some deep dark terrible secret?" The question was fraught with so much empathy that Daniel felt a sense of relief and his tongue loosened.

"Well, let me start by saying that no, I don't have some deep dark terrible secret but then maybe that depends on how you define deep, dark and terrible. I mean, sure there are aspects of my life that I don't tend to broadcast but I don't think there's anything terribly unusual about that."

"How about you share a few of those with me?" Her tone was not harsh or stern but Daniel sensed a pending impatience.

"Look, Ruby, what I said before was true. I did work in the furniture industry and I am on kind of a sabbatical. What I didn't tell you was that I was basically a delivery boy, and that the only reason that I can afford to be flitting around the country is because an uncle died and left me a relatively large sum of money, at least by my meager standards."

"Were you particularly close with this man?" Ruby asked in a voice barely above a whisper.

Rather than an answer, an odd deportment overcame Daniel, a tight-lipped smile and a sort of rocking motion as if he were cradling the corpse of his beloved Uncle Howard. "I don't know that I can tell you how important he was to me," he said finally. After another short silence, he continued. "A long time ago, I heard or read somewhere that if there's one person that actually gives a damn where you are and how you're doing, it is enough to sustain you, to keep you going no matter how bad things get. Well, Howard was that person for me." Daniel's voice cracked a bit and his eyes glistened but he did his best to conceal it and Ruby didn't call attention to it.

"I'm sorry, Daniel." "Yeah, thanks," he said with a laugh that acknowledged both the sincerity and the futility of the sentiment.

The beginnings of disclosure had raised another thousand questions in Ruby's mind, but she was hesitant to probe after the first revelation.

Daniel soon bailed her out. "This guy was everything to me from the time I was a little kid until he died recently, and even though he lived a thousand miles away, and I didn't get to see him but every couple of years, it didn't matter. I knew as long as he lived and breathed, there was a safe haven, a place with love and warmth and open arms that I could crawl to if I had nowhere else to turn."

"How long ago did he die?"

"About a month ago, he had been battling congestive heart failure and eventually..." Daniel suddenly stopped talking and a donned pained look.

"And eventually what?" Ruby queried him sensing that Daniel was holding out on her.

"AIDS, he died of AIDS, Ruby," he blurted out, a tone of defiance in his voice. Ruby said nothing, but he knew as he felt he should have before he'd spoken that she would not be shocked or mortified by the manner of his death. "Jesus, I'm sorry, Ruby. I feel tremendously protective of him even in death. I'm so used to the callous, insensitive, even hateful attitude people often have toward gay people that I'm afraid that that's the first and last thing they'll think about him so I tend to avoid revealing that little morsel of information."

"I don't think hate comes as easily to women," Ruby said simply and Daniel was stopped in his tracks. An old image of a beefy, scraggly red-haired woman with tiny eyes and a cavernous mouth, disgorging the most bilious venom at a Ku Klux Klan gathering leapt to the forefront to challenge the veracity of the statement and it was duly noted, but Daniel got what Ruby meant in a general sense and vowed to himself to give the premise a thorough examination at some future time.

"Anyway, he was a beautiful, decent and loving man, and it's not a stretch to say that he saved my life many times over." The moisture in Daniel's eyed had been dried by the fire of his anger, and he took a deep breath to try to get back on an even keel.

The obvious question of "parents" lurched forward in Ruby's mind, but she figured that would come in time. "Tell me about him, Daniel, I really want to hear about this man that meant so much to you."

Daniel was rocked with affection for Ruby. He had wanted to laud the man he loved, to sing his praises to share the news of his profound good fortune at having had this man grace his existence, but there had been no one that he felt he could tell — until now. He took her hands in his and squeezed, his eyes shut tight as if he couldn't quite fathom his good fortune. "And I want to tell you about him," he said softly, releasing her hands and settling back against the log.

Daniel paused momentarily, took a deep breath and proceeded with the narrative.

"He had a partner for many years, a man named Mark, a kind and funny guy, sort of your absent-minded professor type, brilliant but completely disorganized. He taught language studies at a small college in Alabama. He was always full of nervous energy and even though I never saw it, my Uncle Howard told me that he suffered occasional bouts of depression that I guess got pretty bad. Anyway, the point of all this is that Mark died about two and a half years ago, and my Uncle Howard was never the same. After a year or so of being a shut-in, he finally forced himself to get out a little more and apparently he got careless or maybe he just didn't care anymore but whatever the case, he contracted AIDS in what he referred to as a "foolish encounter" and it was all downhill from there."

"Did you get to spend any time with him before he died?"

"Yes and no. I was scheduled to go down the week that he died but I had been with him about three months prior to that." Daniel looked straight ahead as he spoke, the images of Howard floating across his mind's eye. "You know—and this didn't surprise me a bit—he was as remarkable in dying as he had been in living. He counseled me when I lost it with him, can you imagine that? He took my arm and said in a soothing voice, "It's okay, Daniel. I had my shot and I don't have any regrets. I don't have it in me to fight this thing."

The remembrance of the simple eloquence of the statement forced Daniel to pitch forward slightly and kind of paw at his midsection with one hand and reach out like a blindfolded child playing "pin the tail on the donkey" with the other. He forced a misshapen smile to indicate that he was okay, really he was, and after a moment, gathered himself and continued. "And of course, the better he handled it the worse I did until I was such a blubbering idiot that I couldn't see straight." Daniel's voice cracked again as he recounted the scene but he forged ahead.

"There was only one time during the visit that he slipped a little bit and that was when he talked about how much he loved Mark, and in spite of being largely bedridden and looking like a skeleton, Howard practically jumped out of the bed with anger as he recounted the them trying to stop him from visiting Mark in the hospital. It was an indignity so great that this man that was usually as gentle as a lamb had just about "engaged in fisticuffs" as he put it. And he said he probably would have if this Atticus Finch-like character hadn't popped up out of nowhere and somehow resolved the matter." Daniel squeezed at his forehead and fell silent as if in prayer.

"What the fuck is the matter with people, Ruby? Why can't they live and let live? Where does the vitriol come from and now this lunatic wants to change the Constitution, and you know what..." All of a sudden, the screed born of a festering wound came to a grinding halt and Daniel fell silent.

The thinker had gone visceral, and it caught Ruby by surprise. Naked anger usually made Ruby cringe, but this entreaty to the wind was so riddled with anguish that it took the sting out of it, and she wished that there was something she could do to help.

"I'm sorry, Ruby, I didn't mean to get carried away, it's just that—"

"No need, Daniel. The pain of his passing will take some time, I'm sure."

Daniel looked gratefully at Ruby, nodded his head with a crooked smile and continued the stream of consciousness as if there had been no interlude at all. "He taught me about books, not in any formal way but in conversation and by example. He loved them, and he had a boundless enthusiasm for the written word that you couldn't help but have rub off on you. He even tried his own hand at writing and was always coming up with ideas for stories, but I don't think he ever finished much, and I don't think he ever got anything published.

Daniel smiled in Ruby's general direction. "You know, Ruby, he once told me that the coolest thing about writing was that you could finally use all the junk in your mental attic because even the seemingly inane and disparate parts of your life that are stored there are part of the big picture and might actually come in handy." Daniel seemed to think of something and patted his hip pocket, suggesting that whatever had diverted his attention might reside there. "Actually, Ruby, I have a short story he wrote a while back," he said excitedly as he retrieved his wallet and began unfolding a piece of paper. "It's just a short piece and particularly poignant considering that I just lost him. Would you like to see it?"

"Yes, Daniel, let's have a look."

He wrote it a long time ago after my Grandmother—which of course, would have been his mother—died and well, you'll see. It's pretty self explanatory," he said as he handed over the document in such a way that one imagined an exchange of scrolls in some solemn religious ritual.

Ruby flicked on the flashlight and aimed. Daniel sat silently, feeling oddly nervous as if it had been *his* assignment and the teacher was perusing it with a critical eye. He dismissed the notion and allowed himself to believe that Ruby would appreciate its quality in much the same way he had. He tried to read her face and was satisfied that at the very least the narrative had managed to hold her interest.

Having shed Catholicism at the tender age of twelve, I could only wonder about the eventual fate of my beloved mother as she lay dying. Gone were the comforting assurances of a glorious and eternal life so long as you played by their rules. All that was left was the void and of course the guilt, the primary bonding agent of Catholic dogma.

The surgery, expected to take five or six hours, was over as soon as they got a look inside. The only thing left for her to do was to go home and die. As word filtered back to me, I found myself crying softly and uttering the words "look mama" over and over again as my mind ran through the archives of instances where her smile and enthusiasm for whatever I approached her with validated my very being.

After a couple of weeks at home, she would take to her bed for the last time and henceforth all manner of daily activity would be conducted from there. I made the three hour trek once, sometimes twice a week over the course of the next two and one half months. It was a pilgrimage of sorts, back to the source of sustaining love and nourishment.

She always lay motionless as I entered her room, my heart racing a bit as I looked for evidence of respiration. If she was sleeping, I simply sat and waited. The bargaining was done; there would be no eleventh hour reprieve. My acceptance of her fate was coerced by circumstance, which made for an uneasy truce. I knew I was helpless in the face of the agents of death storming relentlessly through her ever more frail body. God how I love her!

We talked when she was able, as we often had. Refraining from my existentialist rhetoric was an easy concession to make in this setting as she reaped the ultimate benefit of her faith. In the end, it would transport her to the "fields of ambrosia", leaving behind the earthly vessel that she had inhabited for seventy-two years.

The movement of her eyelids becoming heavy would tell me that she needed a respite, and again I would sit, my movement as abbreviated as hers. As the hours passed I noticed that the only movement in the room was the slowly shifting shadow. It then occurred to me that in fact everything was moving, that the earth was spinning in its prescribed orbit in an undulating universe. I was suddenly awestruck as I pondered the magnificence of the machinery that almost as an afterthought recast my mother's shadow as we shared the seeming stillness.

She is gone now and still I wonder. Could all this be orchestrated or is it simply chaos that we struggle mightily to give meaning to? I still talk to her of course; my dialogue often instigated by my own shifting shadow during an early morning walk. I have to assume she's listening but I sure would love to hear from her just one more time. Maybe that would be too easy. I don't know.

Ruby finished the piece and began folding the document back to its original configuration without so much as a word. She seemed distracted as she handed it back to Daniel and still no comment was forthcoming.

"You okay, Ruby?" Daniel finally asked, masking his disappointment at the lack of expected enthusiasm.

"Yes, yes, it's just that, well, it's very well written and — Did he really "shed Catholicism" or was that just part of the story?" she asked with a tone of incredulity that such an act might be possible.

"He did and at a young age too. He never talked at length about it other than to say it just wasn't a very good fit."

"So it's that simple, huh," she added wryly and the usually astute Daniel finally got that her reaction had a whole lot more to do with her life somehow than his beloved Uncle Howard's.

"So long as you played by their rules. That is how it works isn't it" she stated cryptically, her expressionless face offering no further clue to her state of mind.

"Ruby, what's the matter? Did the story upset or offend you somehow?" an increasingly perplexed Daniel asked.

"I am Catholic," she replied with a knowing smile, and Daniel assumed he had at least a part of the answer.

"Ruby, don't take offense, it was his choice based on his experiences.

You can't — "

"I don't," she replied flatly. "I really don't at all. If anything I applaud him for having the courage to do what I have been unable to bring myself to do." Ruby forced herself to turn her gaze to Daniel even though her vision was sidetracked by the rush of mental activity that had been unleashed. "I'm sorry,

Daniel. It was a lovely story, very moving. It just really hit home in a lot of ways and it was hard for me to concentrate."

"Well, that's good in and of itself, I guess," he replied, feeling a little silly for wanting her to match his enthusiasm. "What in particular about the Catholic part got to you?"

"Jesus, Daniel, don't get me started," she answered with a snort that was tinged with disgust.

"Start, Ruby, start!" Daniel cajoled, exposing his keen interest.

"Well, for starters, I grew up a Presbyterian so I wasn't born into the faith. My conversion was a concession to my husband's family." There was a pungent mix of anger and regret in her voice, and there were frequent pauses during which a scowl seemed to flash across her face. "My family is not over-the-top religious, but they have always tried to be consistent and to live by the golden rule so I was surprised at how strongly my mother reacted when I raised it with her. It took a lot of negotiating, but I finally worked out a compromise with her. I agreed to attend church with her a couple of times a month and to continue to be involved in some of the community programs they sponsored." Ruby seemed to continue the conversation internally as if there were an ongoing discussion regarding just what was and wasn't appropriate for public consumption.

"My husband's really not a horrible person," Ruby offered out of the blue. "But he has changed, and I haven't felt any kind of connection with him for quite some time. We're either courteous and mechanical, or we're at each other's throats. That's a bit strong actually. It's more like we would be, if we let it get that far and I think that's part of the problem. Things get stirred up and we never finish the fight."

"Why not?" Daniel asked quietly, the question jolting Ruby into the realization that this had become a three-way conversation and that Daniel had not been privy to a number of intervening chapters.

"Sorry, Daniel, I guess I got off the track a bit." Without a word, she leaned forward and kissed him tenderly. The anger that seeped out of her train of thought fostered the impulse, and she was surprised to find it abating somewhat as she pulled her lips from his.

"Anyway, to get back to the religion thing, I went through with it as you probably figured, and I tried very hard to keep everyone happy. It didn't take me long to figure out that neither my husband nor his parents were particularly concerned with their faith. I tried to rationalize it and to excuse them but eventually the resentment just boiled over. I mean, there I was trying to please two masters and they didn't even make the effort to seem like they gave a damn about the church."

"Did you raise the issue with your husband?"

"Yes, I waited longer than I should have, but hey, isn't that the way! He tried to say that I was overreacting and that I was making a lot of unfair assumptions and how did I know what was in his heart or that they didn't go to mass on days other than Sunday. I finally said that if it's such a personal matter, why was it so terribly important that I become one of them, and he didn't really have an answer. Still, I tried to give them the benefit of the doubt and tried even harder to be a good Catholic, but deep down I had serious reservations about all of it and looking back I have to admit that I never really forgave him for it and I never felt—well, I don't know exactly, but it did something to the relationship." Ruby fell silent and Daniel took the intermission as an opportunity to heft one of the larger branches on the fire. He lit a cigarette and waited a moment to see if she'd restart the narrative without prodding.

"So you kind of worked something out on your own and it was never really satisfactory," he said finally.

"Yes, that about sums it up."

"And your husband, did he ever take the religion thing any more seriously?" Daniel asked, confident that the cad had done little if anything to allay her concerns.

"Honestly, Daniel, I wish he hadn't but the truth is that something scared him terribly, and it changed him, unfortunately not for the better. It's his whole life now," she answered, stoking Daniel's curiosity.

"How did that happen?" he asked, more than a little surprised by this latest development.

"I should tell you first that he was a pretty normal kind of a guy. I mean, you know, I don't want to offend you, Daniel but..."

"Hey, Ruby, don't pull any punches for me," he interjected coolly, eager to get back to the story.

"Well, you know, most of them seem to still be little boys deep down. You know how boys are always into something. There's a sense of adventure about everything. Like they wolf down dinner so they can run back outside and continue to do what ever they do, play sports or whatever. He was like that. I mean, he did take care of his responsibilities; he went to work and was an involved dad and all that. And our relationship was important to him, but I often felt like a mother trying to make sure he got his homework done and that kind of thing. I just always figured that he'd continue to grow up along the way, and our relationship would get better with age like wine."

Ruby paused for a moment and got kind of a pained look on her face. "I don't mean to be whiney, Daniel. All things considered it was a good marriage, not perfect but good."

"It was worth the trouble in other words," Daniel added harkening back to Kenny and Wanda.

"Yes, that pretty much covers it."

"So what happened?"

Ruby turned suddenly to Daniel with an almost startled look on her face. "I'm so sorry, Daniel. You were telling me about your uncle and all of a sudden the whole thing became about me."

"It's okay, really. I'll get my turn. This is important and frankly, you've really piqued my interest. Please go on and I promise we'll get back to me later."

She looked to him again for reassurance and a slight nod of his head appeased the guilt and loosened her tongue.

"Okay, here goes. A little over a year ago, he and a friend were out riding motorcycles and his buddy raced ahead of him on a windy country road out of his line of sight. My husband slowed to take a sharp curve in the road, and when he came around the bend, he saw his buddy all tangled up in a big old piece of farm equipment, like a plow or discs. The farmer had been moseying along at about fifteen miles per hour tops, and when he flew around the bend there was no possibility of stopping. He was half conscious and a bloody mess and he called to my husband, who raced madly toward him. When he reached him he was barely conscious, but he grabbed my husband's arm weakly, looked him in the face and said "You gotta help me, buddy."

If you think about it, Daniel, you can imagine what a horrible, horrible thing it must have been to be having a grand old time with a friend one minute and the next seeing him cut to shreds and mangled, the life draining out of him."

Daniel did just that and felt a chill at the unimaginable image. "I don't suppose he survived," Daniel commented gingerly.

"No, he didn't but they did manage to get him to a hospital and they worked frantically to save him. My husband rode in the ambulance with his friend and tried to talk him into living, but of course, he was so badly injured that it was hopeless. His friend kept calling for Jesus before he lost consciousness and my husband started praying. He probably prayed more during that long ride than he had in all of his adult life. When they got to the emergency room, everyone converged on him, and my husband could only stand to the side and watch. One of the staff in the ER tried to console my husband, and it was that person that suggested they call a priest to administer the last rites."

The phrase *extreme unction* flitted into Daniel's head. He seemed to recall reading that the ritual she was describing had been called that until sometime in the 70's and thinking at the time that it would make a great name for a sore muscle balm. He chastised himself for being so easily distracted and refocused on Ruby's tale.

"Well, they did and I guess the Priest made a mad dash for the hospital but Johnny died just as he was rushing to his bedside."

"Would it have made a difference, Ruby?" Daniel asked neglecting to share his cynicism regarding such interventions.

"I don't really know, Daniel. My understanding was that it kind of gives you a boost, like a letter of recommendation or something that might help you get into heaven, but it's like a lot of things they do. It's inferred that it helps, but it's not clear what happens without it." She thought for a second and added, "I seem to remember something about God always reading the disposition of the heart." Ruby fell silent for a moment as she pondered whether her doubts constituted some sort of blasphemy.

"And this incident had a pretty profound impact on your husband?" Daniel queried gently, prodding her to continue.

"He was a mess. He blamed himself, not for Johnny's death so much but for not having thought to call for a priest sooner, like it may have made a difference in his friend's station for all of eternity." Ruby paused briefly and continued. "Johnny had always been bolder than my husband and had had some minor scrapes with the law and who knows what else. Well, I guess my husband knew what else, and maybe that's why he figured that the extra push might have been just enough to get him over the top."

"What's his name, your husband that is?" Daniel asked, not sure why he had.

"Ronald, well Ronnie is what everybody calls him" Ruby replied, hesitating as if saying it out loud added yet another layer of culpability to the already substantial mound.

"Go on," Daniel said softly sensing that he had gummed up the works just a bit.

"Really, Daniel, I figured the kinds of things he was thinking and doing were sort of natural reactions, part of the grieving process. I thought that it would pass with time and he would get to be like his old self. I mean, it was a terrible thing and a very real loss, and I guess you would expect that something like that could have a deep and lasting impact on someone but it changed my husband, it changed him in ways that I never could have imagined."

"How so?"

"He started going to church more. In the past, he barely bothered to go more than twice a month, and after the accident it became every week, and after a while it became three or even four times a week." Ruby paused briefly. "Eventually he got himself hooked up with a real extreme group from church. This is a group that he and Johnny used to mock because of their excessive piety, and all of a sudden, he's running around with them. I don't know. It's like maybe without Johnny to kind of give him direction, he was easy prey but he was more than willing." She stopped again, a snarl creeping over her face, and she looked as if she was about to jump up and challenge the world but eased up after a moment, and stayed put. "I secretly hated everything to do with religion," she continued, switching gears. "But I felt terribly guilty about it and figured that the shortcoming had to be mine. That's why I was so intrigued by your uncle. The guilt part, the bonding agent, everything I do that makes me feel terrible stems from when religion gets in the way of what I feel is the right thing to do. I'm wandering here I know, Daniel, so please, bear with me."

Daniel repeated the silent assent and Ruby proceeded.

"Anyway, my son, Kevin and I, we tried to keep up for his sake, again thinking it would pass with healing time but it never really did. If anything, it got worse and as we dropped off, he became very stern, very judgmental, and there was always a certain amount of tension. It tore me up inside to watch a good father-son relationship deteriorate into almost open hostility. Just a few weeks ago, they got into a screaming match. Kevin had been ridden enough, I guess and he informed my husband that he had found a new religion. Ronnie—saying the name to Daniel still felt a little odd and she gave him kind of a "what are you gonna do" look as she continued—looked shocked and when he demanded an explanation, Kevin told him that he had come to believe that the FM radio was God. My husband balked, and Kevin kept at him. "Do you doubt that he's here with us now?" Kevin said in a mocking tone. "How about I get a short wave radio and you'll see. Not only will he talk to us, He'll speak in many tongues. How much more proof do you need?"

"I couldn't believe what I was hearing. Kevin had never spoken to his father like that before, and I think Ronnie had no idea how to react. It seemed suddenly like the anger got shoved aside by the hurt, and my husband just kind of skulked away. I went to my son's room thinking he would be feeling triumphant for finally having gotten his father off his back, but he was a wreck. He felt abandoned, and he didn't understand why everything had been turned upside down. I handled it as best I could, but I had nothing to back me up. I pleaded for patience and hoped that Ronnie would come to his senses before the damage done was so great that it could never be repaired." Ruby looked away, the thought of her son's anguish, a source of sharper pain that the dissolution of her marriage. "My poor baby," she said in a voice so loaded with maternal angst and helpless empathy that it echoed somewhere deep within Daniel. "He's barely home at all since the blow up and I can't say that I blame him."

"And how are things between you two at this point, I mean, you and your husband?" Daniel asked, unconsciously steering the conversation away from the son-pain equation. She got kind of glassy eyed and had the hint of a smirk on her face all of a sudden. "Pretty barren, if you know what I mean," she said with an ironic laugh, elevating the mood from gravely serious to a sort of somber frivolity. "And until tonight, I really couldn't have cared less." She paused for a brief moment before resuming. "You remember when I fell asleep for a few moments, and you looked over and were kind of startled to see me sitting there?"

"Yeah, sure I do."

"Well, the truth is that I had been thinking about my friend Linda. She was the most active of the group, if you know what I mean, and she used to describe things that the rest of us only dreamt about." Ruby paused and kind of smiled inwardly at a private recollection. Anyway, I got to thinking about me and then all that's happened here and I somehow ended up thinking about that movie with Robert DiNero, *Waking Up* or — no, it was called *Awakenings*. He had some kind of brain disease that left him pretty much a vegetable, and Robin Williams came up with a cure, and he got to taste how sweet life was again, but unfortunately, the cure was only temporary and he ended up in the same state he started."

"Yes, Ruby, I saw it."

"Well, I feel kind of like that with the, the..."

"The what?"

"The sexual feelings I've had tonight," she said as if she couldn't get the words out fast enough. "I feel like I've been cured and allowed to taste those lovely sensations again, and I'm afraid that this will end, and I'll end up in the same state *I* started."

Daniel was at a loss for words, in part because he relished the role of "liberator" and in part because of the seeming impossibility of what she longed for, a sustained loving relationship with all the fringe benefits. This night's entrée had been a feast for him as well in spite of its limitations, and he too privately longed for what he imagined few ever really achieved. He wondered too if maybe he was rubbing off on her as the analogy she used was right out of his playbook. He felt a surge of warmth and desire for her and didn't know what to do with either. Fortunately for him, she continued, shifting immediately back to somber.

"What little sex we had when he was finally ready to resume felt like it was intended strictly for procreation. It felt more like a duty or an obligation, like somehow he hated me for the fact that in spite of everything, he still had this urge that he had to satisfy somehow. Being the good wife, I feigned interest, but my heart wasn't in it. Eventually he decided — or maybe his new circle of friends convinced him — that the use of birth control was not part of God's plan, and I had to take the pill on the sly. I think he suspected it but didn't really want to know so he didn't press the issue. Meanwhile, I acted like I was tracking my cycles, you know, the old rhythm method, to make it seem like I was taking "natural" precautions. A little while later, I forgot and left my pills sitting out. He came across them and all hell broke loose. He was full of righteous indignation, and I had had enough. I told him that I did not want to risk getting pregnant while our relationship was on such shaky ground and that there would be no sex until we got *us* back on track, that I felt bad that he lost his friend, but I didn't understand why he would let that result in the loss of his marriage as well. That was ten months ago, and I've been celibate ever since," she said with an air of finality. And with that, Ruby seemed to withdraw into an inner world, a private place of reflection and regret, and Daniel felt it best to wait it out.

"Daniel," she said finally, rejoining the dialogue.

"Yeah."

"I've got to use the bathroom." The pronouncement was an unexpected segue, but it prompted Daniel to acknowledge that his bladder, too, was crying out for relief.

"Well, there's no shortage of trees to choose from, so pick one and do your business. As soon as I see which direction you go in, I'll take the opposite," Daniel said with a little more jocularity than seemed appropriate to the circumstance.

Ruby chose the "long way" and Daniel stepped behind a tree a few yards from the fire. His fatigue registered on some level, but it was mitigated by his curiosity. This intimate glimpse into the inner workings of the every-day life of another human being confirmed his long standing suspicion that he was not so unlike the rest of the mass of muddled humanity, and it infused him with a quiet excitement. He felt a pang of guilt for seeing a silver lining at the expense of Ruby's travails, and he forced himself to focus on concern for his new found friend. "Be kind, for everyone you meet is fighting a hard battle." He recalled the quote from Plato and marveled at the simple truth uttered so many thousands of years ago. "Amen, brother," he whispered to no one.

As Ruby squatted, she reviewed her narrative and was surprised at how clear everything seemed all of a sudden. It was time, she figured, and yeah, she probably should have engineered a more direct attempt of some kind to resolve the matter sooner without having been prodded by the unusual encounter but then she figured the unusual encounter would likely not have occurred if there had been any movement, any effort at reciprocity on the part of her husband. She thought about Daniel, about the stranger with whom she had exposed her innermost secrets, secrets that she only partly understood, secrets that crystallized in the telling. She felt an urge bordering on compulsion to get back out there with him, to resume the conversation, to be physically close to him. She sensed somehow that the drive toward Daniel had an absolute correlation with her resistance to confronting the facts of her life, and that acknowledgement strengthened rather than diminished the urge.

As she rose from her haunches, she felt weak in the knees. The upward thrust took a little more effort than usual, and she fought her creeping weariness. Daniel had taken the opportunity to allay his guilt toward Golda and to add fuel to the fire. He caught a glimpse of Ruby returning to their spot from the corner of his eye and stood up straight. He looked to her eyes in an attempt to read her mood, and as Ruby approached, she caught his gaze and held it. The fellow travelers were expressionless, but there was a palpable intensity crackling between them and an almost horizontal gravity that drew them together. Ruby threw her arms around him and buried her face in his shoulder, and Daniel caressed her hair as her muffled sobs leaked out. They rocked gently for a moment before Ruby broke the silence.

"You probably figured this out already, Daniel but looking back now, it seems pretty obvious that I didn't just happen to *forget*."

"Yeah, that did occur to me," his answer barely above a whisper.

"I've been kind of living in a haze, just getting through each day. You know things aren't the way they should or could be, but you haven't the faintest idea how to fix them so you live with it and hope that he'll come around."

Daniel sensed that the evening had set in motion an inexorable march toward the O.K. Corral but that ultimately she would have to come to that decision on her own.

"So, where do you go from here?" he asked, leading the witness.

"I don't know, Daniel, or maybe I do. It's bad enough when things are just bad, but when they get to the point that you *have* to face it, it's much worse. I'm going to have to deal with this thing sooner or later, and after tonight, I don't really have much say over the timing. I have to get at it."

Daniel considered words of support and encouragement but held that thought and took a more general tact. "For what it's worth, Ruby, I think lots of people, maybe even most, live lives of quiet desperation, and it usually takes a sledge hammer rather than the obvious to get people to act. Hope is a salve, but it can become a narcotic and it can keep you treading water because you fear what lies on the other side of that hope but it's never what you think." Daniel kind of surprised himself with what seemed to have been a flash of eloquence. It came sometimes when it was least expected and on this night he noted that it often happened when fatigue was at its most potent. He began to ruminate about how counterintuitive it all seemed but was stopped cold by the thought that maybe it just seemed eloquent because he was too tired to know the difference.

The air filling up Ruby's lungs as she yawned snapped Daniel back to the moment at hand. "I'm really tired, Daniel," she said, her words garbled as they rode out on the exhale. "I need to lie down."

"Come on, we'll go to the tent." Daniel put his arm over her shoulder and proceeded toward their shelter. "You know, Ruby, I saw a *Twilight Zone* episode once where a guy was in a psychiatrist's office and he was afraid that if he fell asleep his life would end."

"I don't get it, Daniel." Daniel thought for a moment and realized he had molasses in his brain. "You know something, right now, I don't either."

Chapter 53

The towels had been tossed from their respective corners, and they stopped fighting the weariness. Somehow the ensuing armistice allowed the mood to lighten a bit. The unscheduled fifty-minute hour had run its course, and it had borne fruit. The not-so-original sin had been committed, but the provider had been a benevolent stranger rather than a malevolent snake, and rather than banishment, the act offered at least the possibility of atonement. They smiled contortedly through the contagious yawning as they prepped the sleeping bag for occupancy.

"Do you have an alarm clock, Daniel?" Ruby asked softly, the seemingly autonomic yawning having finally subsided.

"There's one in the car somewhere, but I couldn't tell you exactly where." He thought for a moment before continuing. "I do have a little beeper on my watch. Why?"

"I don't want to sleep too long. What time is it now?"

"Getting close to 1:00 a.m."

"Set it for six, would you."

"Okay," Daniel answered obediently, leaving the mystery of her scheduling unquestioned.

The sleeping bag lay open like an expectant sarcophagus, and Daniel's actions slowed a bit as he plumped and smoothed the pillow.

There was something deeply intimate and sensual about the prospect of nestling into the sleeping bag together that was not lost on either of them.

"I've only got the one," he said with a nervous smile. "I really hadn't planned on company."

"I'll take the inside," Ruby said matter-of-factly as if to suggest that there was nothing at all out of the ordinary going on. And as if a suddenly inert Daniel needed further coaxing, she held the upper half of the bag aloft, smiled warmly and patted the area that he was to inhabit.

He lay down beside her, reached low and zipped them in. The forced proximity seemed to cast a sudden shyness over both of them, and they stared up at the peak of the tent.

"Daniel, why don't you turn off the lantern?"

He worked his arm out of the cocoon and switched it off. The initial darkness was stark but a hint of moonlight managed to sift through the nylon tent and after a few moments of adjusting, they could just make out each other's features.

Daniel closed his eyes as he yawned the definitive yawn, and Ruby turned on her side and began gently tweaking Daniel's sideburns.

"I didn't intend for this whole evening to be all about me, Daniel. I really didn't. And when we get up, I want to hear about you. I want to hear more about your uncle," she said suddenly, her voice tinged with consternation.

"Hey don't feel bad about me, huh. It's really not all that interesting. I think I probably make out better with you filling in the blanks," he said, chuckling lightly even though he was dead serious. He looked to her for a response and sensed her distraction and her follow up confirmed it.

"It was your uncle's story that got me going, the part about religion specifically."

"Yes, I remember," he replied, watching the wheels still spinning in her head.

She closed her eyes, pursed her lips and fell silent for a time.

"You with me, Ruby ?" he asked finally.

"Think about it, Daniel. Religion almost resulted in stopping my wedding. It put a serious strain on my relationship with my mother, and in the end, it may have a lot to do with wrecking my marriage," she spoke, with her voice low but her focus intense. "I've always tried to follow my faith, maybe not always to the exact letter but it's always been an important part of my life." Her surging anger trumped her mounting fatigue, and she leaned up on her elbow as if she might spring into action. "And honestly, Daniel, I've just about had it with the 'test of faith' thing. I have always tried, damnit and now to have that bastard look at me like some kind of Jezebel just because he thinks now that—that, well I don't know what him and his holy roller friends think."

She was roiled and rolling and Daniel found himself thinking about something he'd caught on the History channel one recent uneventful evening.

"Thou shalt not suffer a witch to live."

"What's that, Daniel?"

"Thou shalt not suffer a witch to live." "I saw a show recently about the Salem witch trials and the kind of hysteria that resulted in mostly women being accused and burned at the stake or hung, and it just seemed like even well-intended people can get carried away with that kind of thing, and that kind of sounds like what's going on with your husband."

"Let's hope he's not planning on taking it that far," she said with the first hint that the anger was abating. She was still and silent for a time before continuing. "None of it makes any sense. I get the guilt part that your uncle mentioned in the story, but I find myself balking somewhere down deep and wanting to stand up for myself and say to hell with it all but then that little voice kind of suggests that in the end it might be to hell with me!"

Daniel tried to fashion a response but as usual Ruby beat him to the punch.

"Don't you have a religion Daniel?" The innocent question that could only beget a guilty answer was more than Daniel was prepared for and he handled it as deftly as he could.

"It's complicated, Ruby, and better saved for the morning."

The evasive answer piqued her curiosity, but she didn't have the stamina to pursue the matter."

Okay, Daniel."

"I'll tell you anything you want to know, I promise," he replied hoping to allay any more probative inquiries and sadly thinking to himself that this exchange of deeply personal information was ultimately doomed to futility, like mastering a skill that you'll never use again. A heavy silence fell over the both of them as they wondered what the accepted protocol for bedding down in a sleeping bag with a stranger might be.

"Oh and one more thing, Daniel."

"Yeah, what's that, Ruby?"

"Thanks for a wonderful evening."

"Jesus, you're a sweet woman, Ruby," he replied shaking his head in bemused disbelief at his good fortune. "Your husband is such a fool."

She understood the veiled sentiment and accepted it with graceful silence.

They lay silent, their spinning heads having ground to a dull whirr, both grudgingly accepting that sleep was an inevitable, even desirable interlude.

The misty fog of fatigue enveloped the both of them, and they went willingly into that good night. Golda eventually caught on to the silence, figured there probably wasn't much point in eavesdropping any longer, and she succumbed as well.

The cicadas, on the other hand, finally had the whole place to themselves and they didn't waste any time getting the party started.

Chapter 54

They made love in the mountains
They made love by the streams
They made love in the valleys
They made love in their dreams

John Prine had serenaded Daniel into his slumber, and even in his dream state, ever the gentleman; he refrained from going so far as committing the actual act. There was, however, no shortage of intimacy in Daniel's dreams as he strolled the sunlit uplands with Ruby, and when the heavy petting seemed to be spiraling out of control, he lurched to the penumbra of semi-sleep and by force of habit found himself forty-three miles northwest of Cuzco, Peru at the base of Machu Picchu. That Daniel had read that the term translated meant "manly peak" may or may not have played a determining role in his subterranean choice of destinations. In any case, he set about trying to figure out how with fifteenth century technology, they constructed massive stone buildings with such precision that the thinnest knife blade could not be thrust between the joints of the stones.

Ruby, for her part, was suffering no such nocturnal reluctance. Having already had a mouthful of Daniel's Machu

Picchu, she moved quickly to sate her huge backlog of squelched desire and plundered Daniel in ways that she could not have hitherto imagined.

Chapter 55

Suddenly and without warning there was one less voice in the choir. The cicada had served as an appetizer, but the hunger pangs lingered. The forked tongue caught wind of a possible main course, and the Butler's garter snake followed the scent to the outskirts of the triangular object that it didn't recall having seen in this neck of the woods before. It slithered cautiously in the side-winding style that it routinely employed when traversing unvegetated areas or hard surfaces and stopped just outside the flap from which the delectable aroma seemed to emanate. A quick tap of the tongue suggested that breaching the barrier to the potential horn of plenty may require little more than a nudge. The respirations were audible and a cause for concern but it had encountered these Gulliver-like figures before and knew that they were not easily roused. It was, he concluded, a risk worth taking. As expected, a gentle push with his nose, and the flimsy flap fell to one side, but as quickly as he had penetrated the inner sanctum, he found himself scrambling to throw it into reverse, a gear that always seemed to give him trouble. What he had not, in fact could not have anticipated was a baleful glare the likes of which only Sonny Liston and a notable few of history's other menacing figures could don to scare the bejesus out of you.

Golda withdrew the scowl from her face, wiped her brow and breathed a heavy sigh of relief. She had done her job even though in the midst of it, she felt like she was heading for cardiac arrest. It's all in the bluff, she thought, sighing as she revisited the twilight.

Chapter 56

Daniel vaguely felt the arm drape over him and tug, but he was perplexed by the Herculean task he'd taken on and didn't pay it much mind. While he fretted over the capacity of a chisel forged of bronze to fashion limestone or granite into a perfectly sculpted building block, Ruby was still reeling from her second orgasm. She imagined she knew how the very earth felt when it rumbled and shook and finally exploded, spewing ash and lava in every direction. She stretched mightily and gathered the lustrous silk sheets around her naked body and reveled in the sensuality of it all.

Daniel had taken leave of her for reasons unknown, and she called out to him to bring her a glass of water upon his return. She wallowed in a delicious torpor and felt a thrill as she saw the doorknob begin to spin. She released the silk sheets and lay prostrate so that her lover could take full measure of her ripe and ready body. The water would no doubt be iced, and she was already imagining a number of exotic applications involving various parts of Daniel's anatomy. Closing her eyes, she feigned sleep upon hearing the door swinging open, and the anticipation built. She noted that the footsteps seemed unusually loud and numerous, but she paid it no mind as she waited for her prince to rouse her with his touch. Five seconds passed, then ten. She imagined that he must be drinking her in with his eyes, and her desire surged to even greater heights. Fifteen seconds, twenty, twenty-five and finally, she could stand no more.

She squinted open her left eye and was horrified to see not her lover enraptured by her beauty but her husband and a couple of his cronies from the cult. Suddenly, she was no longer nude but exposed and shamefully so. She grabbed frantically for the silk sheets to cover herself and found to her great dismay that she seemed bound by all four appendages like a condemned man set to be drawn and quartered. She pushed past her humiliation and found her rage, but her planned verbal torrent had no voice. The holy ones stared in hard judgment of her in a perverse scene suggesting a police line-up in reverse. They circled her like vultures, and even in their vituperative condemnation, she could feel their eyes all over her naked body. She yanked and twisted to no avail and in her anguish could muster no more than a silent scream. She slammed her eyes shut and heard footsteps as they moved herd-like, congregating at the foot of the bed, and then the chanting in unison began.

The power of Christ compels you.
The power of Christ compels you.
The power of Christ compels you.

Chapter 57

The lever groaned and creaked and finally snapped, and the corner of the massive stone fell all of three inches back to earth when Daniel felt the vise-like grip on his shoulder. As he shook the cobwebs from his mind, Ruby pulled herself on top of him and squeezed with all her might. "Bad dream, bad dream, bad dream" she kept repeating, her face buried in his neck.

Daniel got his bearings and a pretty good sense of what was going on. "Hey, it's alright. It's over, you're awake now."

Ruby squeezed even harder and then went limp. "I know this is wrong, Daniel," she said in a voice that suggested the voided possibility of redemption.

"What were you dreaming about?" he asked, certain that what she'd envisioned was the culprit in her rude awakening.

Her face remained riveted to his neck even as she reached up and clumsily patted him about the face like a young Helen Keller hoping to *hear* some answer to her darkness. She wasn't talking, and Daniel didn't press the matter. Rather he reached for a cigarette and braced himself for what lay ahead.

"Ruby, I'm going to smoke if you don't mind," he said eager for the rush of nicotine to clear the haze.

"No, you go ahead" she replied as she let go and kind of slid off him.

He flicked on the lantern before unzipping the sleeping bag, and as he climbed out, Ruby rolled over on her back.

Daniel plumped the pillow under her head and zipped the bag back up. "You'll be warmer that way," he said as he threw open the flap with the ease of a Garter snake. The scalloped pattern in the dirt led him to suspect that they'd had an uninvited guest but he dismissed the possibility that it would have been bold enough to break and enter. Besides, he had no idea how Ruby might react to even the suggestion that there might be more than just the three of them in the tent. He drew his knees up to his chest, straddling the vastness and the inner sanctum, and sat mostly in the tent while exhaling into the night air. Daniel puffed in silence, watching the plumes of smoke waft up and out into the wild black yonder. He figured Ruby would reply when she'd sorted through the images and given form to the troubling chaos.

"I want to go with you!" she said finally, and Daniel froze. His heart stopped and his breathing ceased. The last drag got caught in a bottle neck, and the spasm resulted in a coughing fit that he just knew would be taken the wrong way. He wanted to explain his startled reaction, but he couldn't stop coughing long enough to do it. After a few fits and starts during which time his mind raced madly to settle on a response; Was she serious? What about her husband — her son? Was she ready? Was he ready? Was he serious? It didn't make sense in any kind of way. Then, of course, there was the other hand; gauzy dreamlike scenes of the two of them on a lazy riverbank, in the wondermobile, laughing as they exited a matinee, making passionate love on a brilliantly sunny day on the picnic blanket; he managed to get it largely under control.

"You can't" he answered dolefully, his words trailed by a hiccup of a cough for good measure. As confused and conflicted as he was, it was the right answer and he knew it. As he waited eagerly for a reply, she turned toward the small of the tent, dashing any hope of reading her face for some hint of a preview.

"I thought you were going to say that," she answered finally. "Were you serious, Ruby? If I had said yes, it's crazy, but what the hell, would you really have come along?"

She turned and rose up on her elbows. "I don't know, Daniel, maybe. But probably, I just liked the idea of running."

Truth be told, Daniel was thrilled to have been asked, feeling just a tinge of disappointment that she hadn't entertained the notion more seriously even though he knew better.

They smiled at each other and sat in silence for a time. Daniel extinguished his cigarette, closed the flap and crawled back in the tent. "Mind if I join you?"

This time, Ruby unzipped the bag and held it open for him. The naturalness of her motion stopped Daniel in his tracks. It was a simple gesture, warm and inviting, and it made this unnatural pairing seem right and good, and he found himself thinking that it might not be such a bad idea after all. He settled back in, zipped up and thrust an arm underneath Ruby's shoulders, drawing her closer. Ruby had surprised even herself with the initial query and knew as soon as she had asked that whatever she might be feeling, it was not in her to consider something so rash, so wantonly impulsive and she had largely discarded the idea before Daniel had even opened his mouth. Still, a little voice somewhere deep in the recesses of her mind insisted on toying with the idea of an abbreviated adventure, a week, maybe two to sort things out, kind of like what Daniel's doing, she thought, and in spite of repeated attempts, she couldn't quite shake the notion. Ruby reared up on her elbows, raised her knees, glanced sidelong at Daniel and popped the question.

"How about just a week or so?" she said, setting Daniel to thinking that it had come down to kind of a mock bargaining. The matter settled in his mind as he assumed hers as well, he saw no harm in playing along. In fact he rather liked the idea.

"Okay, what the hell" Daniel replied finally, calling her bluff.

"Good, it's settled then. I'll slip home and leave a note. The last thing I need is a nation-wide search for the *missing wife*. And I'll draft a long letter to Kevin to let him know I haven't abandoned him and that I just needed a little time alone. I should stock up on food supplies so nobody starves ..."

Daniel chuckled lightly and shook his head in agreement as she hatched the scheme, but as she continued to recite her game plan, he began to wonder if she weren't serious. "Ruby, it sounds great, but you know as well as I that it's not gonna happen," he interjected with an uncertain laugh, intentionally making her complicit in accepting the "only rational course of action."

"Shit, Daniel, why not?" she shot back, her voice trembling with emotion, startling Daniel.

"Christ, Ruby, I thought we settled this a few minutes ago."

"You said no, but you never said why. Just tell me why, Daniel."

He could feel her anguish and it left him speechless. Daniel was rarely in the position of having to disappoint anyone, and it pained him greatly to even contemplate it. He told himself there were a million and one reasons that the whole idea was completely loco, but at the moment he was hard-pressed to come up with one. He watched the fireworks explode in his mind, the multitude of colors going every which way chasing that elusive answer that was swirling around in there somewhere.

"Because it's all a mirage," he finally blurted out.

"And what does that mean?" she asked pointedly.

And again there was no answer at the ready. "It means we'd be tempting fate. It means that whatever magic was employed to put us in this place together..." he stopped suddenly all too aware of the fact that the gibberish he'd been spouting included terms better suited to a tarot card reading than a heated discussion about the direction their immediate future might take. He took a deep breath, backed up a bit and attempted to recast his reasoning in a somewhat more rational light.

"Ruby, it's been real good tonight, real good, but it's not altogether real. What I mean to say is that it's only partly real. Dammit!" he exclaimed, frustrated that he didn't sound any more sane or logical than he had at the outset of his beleaguered attempt to explain himself. "What I think I'm trying to say is that we've only gotten the smallest glimpse of each other, and even those images have been somewhat tinted by the attraction we have and the sexual tension that we've somehow managed to keep in check."

"Are you trying to explain why it's a good idea or a bad idea, Daniel?" she interjected and he got her point.

He had to concede that he was failing miserably and a subtle desperation started to creep in. He seized on the idea of playing the family card on her, the impact on the husband and the son, but he knew that ultimately that was her decision and besides who knows, maybe it *would* get the cad to come to his senses. Daniel had investigated all the other characters in the realm and found to his dismay that he was the only one without an airtight alibi and grudgingly turned his attention to where it should have been in the first place, on the man behind the curtain.

Chapter 58

"It's me," came the belated reply. The truth imbues the voice with a certain timbre, and Daniel's resounded with perfect pitch, and Ruby felt a release that she couldn't quite put a finger on. A solemn silence followed, but the warm feeling and the gravitational pull toward Daniel surged. Ruby pirouetted, took Daniel's face in her hands and kissed him tenderly. He stopped trying to decide if the little bit of friction between them could by any standard constitute a spat and figured that even if it did, her action signaled a truce at the very least. The kiss grew longer and more intense, and she seemed to want to relish him like a condemned woman chewing slowly on her last meal, the meal where *she* finally got to personally select each item, the first time in many years that she had any real control over anything and perhaps, regrettably, the last time as well.

She withdrew her lips and let his face slide slowly from her hands. "That's all I wanted to hear," she whispered.

Daniel sat motionless, eyes still closed and dumbstruck as a chemical-induced torpor left him in a deliciously flaccid state. He felt something leaking within him, flowing to places that needed nourishment but rarely got it. A sort of extreme unction that targeted the implacable ache of the heart that had become so habitual as to seem a natural part of his person. So foreign was the sensation that he had the odd feeling that maybe he'd dropped something. As the haze lifted, he had a single thought, not that the world should work this way but rather that it could, and implicit in the notion was the understanding that in this place here and now there was nothing to hide and no need to pretend.

His eyes popped open, and he smiled gratefully at Ruby. "I guess we're good, huh!" he said finally, sporting a contented smile.

She smiled back beatifically, and the two of them fell back on the pillow like two ardent lovers that had just consummated the act. A soothing silence followed, which Ruby finally broke. "Just to let you know, Daniel, I did get the "tempting fate" thing and I could have and should have stopped you right then, but I guess deep down, I was just looking for a way to delay the inevitable. I mean, up until this point, everything that's happened has—well it's just happened. There was no planning or anything and that was the beauty of it."

Daniel paused for a brief moment to digest her comment. "You know, Ruby, I was kind of winging it at that point but I do think it's true. It's risky to fuck around with serendipity."

Daniel heard Golda scurrying around in her milieu and instinctively exited the sleeping bag to look in on her. "How's my girl?" he asked in a barely audible voice, but she was too busy with her snack to answer. As Ruby yawned, Daniel repositioned himself and grabbed a cigarette.

Don't think for a second that I wouldn't want you to go," he said earnestly, surprised to find a lump swelling up in his throat. "Hell, I was flattered that you even thought about it," he

372

added, allowing himself a little laugh. "I think, honestly, that I panicked a bit, and I was desperately trying to figure out why."

"Was the idea that scary?" Ruby asked with a playful poke from her sleeping bag sheathed toe.

"No, no, not at all. It had more to do with my own self-doubt than anything else."

"How so?"

"Well, it's like you said a minute ago. Up to now, this whole encounter has just kind of happened and that *has been* the beauty of it." Daniel drew deeply on his Camel Light, looking for the best way to phrase his answer. "I'm just not very good with people, or maybe I should say that there are few circumstances that I'm really very comfortable in, and the prospect of extending our tour of duty kind of made me have to look again at the problems I've had sustaining relationships."

Ruby perked up with the unsolicited disclosure and realized with some regret that with all they'd been through, she'd managed to learn precious little about Daniel. She chided herself for this fact and vowed to make up for it.

He fell silent for a moment while he fidgeted with the wrapper on his cigarette pack, taking note of the fact that he'd piqued her interest as she rose up on her elbows keenly awaiting the next revelation. Daniel smiled to himself at the thought of exposing the "secrets" about his life that he'd managed to finesse away up to that point, but he had come to trust Ruby implicitly, and even as he felt the tightness in his gut, he managed to neutralize it by thinking back on the sensation he'd had a few minutes prior.

"Truthfully, Ruby, I was afraid, I suppose, that given enough time, I'd manage somehow to fuck it up."

"Do you really believe that, Daniel?" she asked but he didn't answer.

"This whole thing has been kind of surreal," he continued. "but it's been very special and before that idea of you 'running away and joining my circus' came up, I was already kind of excited about the prospect of rehashing this experience whenever I needed a boost. Daniel looked to Ruby to gauge her reaction but learned no more than that she was paying very close attention. "That's kind of what I used to do with Uncle Howard," he added.

Ruby seemed about to interject but she held her tongue.

A pensive look came over Daniel as he adjusted to the mild distress he still felt anytime Howard appeared on stage, and he looked to the darkness for a time before proceeding. "In my darkest moments, I would remember the special times I shared with him, and I could always remind myself that this wonderful man held me in high esteem, so really, how bad could I be? Then it occurred to me in a flash that I don't have an Uncle Howard anymore and even though that doesn't negate all the positive stuff, the fact that he's gone somehow changes things. So I guess I was looking to replenish the sustenance catalogue, and I didn't want to do anything to jeopardize that," he finished. Daniel suspected, or was it projected, that his comments bespoke an isolated and anguished existence, and he made a conscious effort not to allow the tinge of *tragedy* to affect his speech or demeanor. It didn't work. Ruby had that look, the look that Daniel couldn't stomach, a mixture of pain, distress and anger that a protective parent feels for an aggrieved child.

"Don't do that, Ruby! Jesus Christ, please don't do that!" His words were soft but powerful, and they stopped her movement toward him cold. "I can imagine what you must be thinking but it really isn't like that, not all the time anyway."

"I didn't mean anything by it, Daniel, I didn't mean to imply...," Ruby stopped mid-sentence not wanting to make matters worse.

Daniel, seeing the anguish and confusion on Ruby's face, kicked himself repeatedly. "I know you didn't Ruby. Dammit, I know you didn't mean any harm and I'm really sorry," he said in his most consoling voice while still scolding himself inside. He took a deep breath and tried to regroup.

"You can tell me what's wrong, Daniel, really." Ruby's voice was calm now and Daniel was the beneficiary by osmosis. He drew another deep breath and exhaled heavily, dislodging some of the venom that had been stirred up in him.

"Ironic, isn't it," he said with a light laugh that signaled that the storm inside had abated somewhat. "That's the kind of thing I was afraid of."

"What's that, Daniel?"

He looked solemn and perplexed, but a hint of a smile was forming at the corner of his mouth. Daniel's dark side was his constant companion, an opportunistic beast lurking close by, looking for an opening, a moment of weakness to pounce and sink its prodigious teeth into soft tissue and drag him down to hell. But Daniel was no longer a willing victim, having discovered to his amazement some number of years ago that to offer some measure of resistance wasn't necessarily fatal. Over time, an occasional victory emboldened him, and there were times such as this that he managed by an act of sheer will to turn the tide and if not send the brute scampering, at least keep it at bay.

After a moment, he spun suddenly to face Ruby head on. "Are you with me, Ruby?"

"Of course I'm with you Daniel," she answered, not sure exactly what he was getting at.

"Do you feel any differently toward me now than you did an hour ago?"

"No, I don't Daniel but why do you ask?"

Daniel grabbed a cigarette, fired it up and went about selecting his words.

"There's nothing extraordinary or even terribly unusual about my life, but the problem is that I don't always believe that. Sometimes, in what I guess you could call my lesser times, I see myself as a tragic figure so disfigured that other less affected human beings would shudder in horror at the site of me."

"Kind of like Jules," Ruby interjected softly.

"Well, yes, a lot like Jules," he replied allowing a bit of a *touché* smile to flash briefly. "John Lennon wrote a song that had as its hook line, "The one thing you can't hide is when you're crippled inside," and every time I hear it I think to myself, you're wrong Johnny. You've got it backwards. That's the one thing you can hide, and the reason I know it is because I've been hiding it for fifteen years."

Ruby listened intently but found herself wondering as she had earlier in the evening why there was never any mention of parents.

"Now, Ruby, there is a part of me that knows better, that understands that we've all got our burdens to bear but there are times when my body betrays me, and I go into a tailspin, and no matter how hard I try, I can't convince myself that it's as simple as that and that I'm not some grotesque abomination that ..."

"That's crazy, Daniel!" Ruby's visceral reaction to the unjustness of it all cut him off midsentence. "How could you possibly think something like that?"

"It *is* crazy and I guess that's the point. I know better—most of the time anyway." Daniel moved his hand and cupped it over his mouth, cigarette in tow and held it in that odd position while he dragged deeply a few times before continuing.

"Let me just say this on my behalf. All I ask when things go awry is space and enough private time to get through whatever it is that's bogging me down. I'd rather I didn't have to go through periods like that, but I do, so I kind of look at it like emotional dialysis. The toxins build up. I get in a funk, and I need to be cleansed. I don't harp on it, and if it's all possible, I don't burden anyone else with it."

As he uttered those words they had a strange familiarity. The dialectic of his fluctuating emotional states and his reaction to them was recognizable, but the inclusion of words suggesting a point of honor for his restraint seemed a new addition to the spiel whose origin he couldn't quite place.

"All that stuff you just said about yourself, I knew all that, maybe not the gory details but I knew that at some point in your life, you had been wounded and seriously but you never let on, you never moped or complained and I respected—I should say, respect you so much for it." It may have been at that exact moment, the mystical and highly charged moment that Chelsea spoke those words, that what had been Daniel's standard operating procedure was elevated to the lofty status of a virtue and he would be forever grateful to her for it, though at the moment, he was unaware of the source.

"I'm not a martyr," Daniel continued, and to ask or expect anything for it would turn the whole thing on its head, but Jesus, Ruby, I can't take the flip side. I can't stand being looked at as if I were some wounded animal. That cuts me much worse than an outright assault on my person." Daniel's impassioned defense against the malevolent windmill had got his mojo stirred up and he felt a welcome clarity. "So yeah, it was certainly in the realm of possibility that I'd screw it up and I think I've proven that with my subsequent behavior, but I've been out of the loop for a time and operating on old assumptions about my emotional capabilities, and with no reality to bang up against, it's easy to go on assuming that nothing has changed. But with you I'm kind of back in a loop, and it's been nothing but good so now I can recalibrate my thinking somewhat." He paused, took a drag, exhaled and continued. "Ruby, I'm like a radio that gets better reception the further away I am from people. Unfortunately, the opposite is usually true as well. The closer I get, the more static I encounter, so my natural inclination is to take my reality in bite-sized chunks, and as great as it's been, being in control of when I dip a toe in the water is something I'm not willing to give up right now. And besides all that, I think we both agree that it's best that you not do anything to further complicate your situation."

"I do know that," she said quietly and Daniel breathed a grateful sigh of relief.

Daniel extinguished the red-orange laser dot that his cigarette had become in the dirt outside the tent, and turned and fully committed to the inner sanctum. He settled next to Ruby, leaned on his left arm draped his right over his knee and locked eyes with Ruby.

"Now, I'm going to ask you again. Do you feel any differently toward me now than you did ten minutes ago?"

"Yes!" she replied without hesitation.

Daniel was momentarily startled. He had fully anticipated a resounding confirmation that none of it mattered, that he was a human being and thus subject to a standard somewhat shy of perfection, but Ruby quickly clarified her response.

"Actually, Daniel, I feel much closer to you than I did ten minutes ago," she said with just that certain timbre. Daniel felt a fresh dose of the stuff that had leaked before coursing through him and found himself gazing at Ruby in much the same way he'd caught her eying him earlier in the evening. He sensed his mind pondering the mystery of this woman and this life, but he was not privy to the process as it was happening in some clandestine way, the way a wound heals, perhaps.

Chapter 59

The mood had lightened considerably. The knowledge that their tenure as an anomaly would conclude sometime after dawn had reestablished their equilibrium and their focus. Ruby had a thousand questions she still wanted answers to, but the one she led with was perhaps the most pressing.

"What time is it, Daniel?"

"Time for me to head for the bushes again," he answered. "Besides that, it's getting close to 2:30."

"You don't need to go far. I won't watch," she said with that impish smile that he'd been struck by earlier in the evening.

"Damn!" he replied, laughing as he exited the tent, his foray to the edge of the bush sending a certain Garter snake scurrying deeper into the woods.

Ruby closed her eyes, yawned lustily and while playing back as best she could the conversation they had just engaged in, realized that she did in fact take issue with something Daniel had said. His claim notwithstanding, to her there was indeed plenty that was "extraordinary or even terribly unusual" about his life. He was, in fact, very different from anyone she'd ever encountered. It did occur to her that maybe he was *crazy*, but she quickly rejected the notion. If he was crazy, she reasoned, what of her husband. Ronnie's certitude regarding bizarre ideas and his seeming willingness to bulldoze into oblivion the life they'd built together at their behest seemed far less sane than Daniel with his apparent doubts and fears. The train of thought made her determined to redouble her efforts to learn more about Daniel before their time together expired. That pungent reminder inspired a momentary sadness, and she was anxious for him to return.

His back to the tent, Daniel's eyes gravitated naturally to the celestial expanse, save for a few recalcitrant embers, the only other available source of illumination. A good ten seconds had gone by before he realized that nothing was happening. It wasn't the usual "shy bladder," rather it was a phenomenon he experienced occasionally when every bit of his focus was elsewhere and a notion or a solution or just a particularly pertinent thought was just out of his mind's eye's field of vision. Orwell's 1984 protagonist, Winston Smith, suddenly emerged from the shadows, and the dam burst.

Once siphoned and flowing, Daniel could turn his attention back to the matter under consideration. Winston and Julia had found a sanctuary above an antique shop on a side street in the prole quarter, a universe unto themselves, away from the prying eyes of the telescreens and the thought police. It was not unlike this situation here and now with Ruby. The world was still a place fraught with peril, and the safety accorded them in their place of refuge was real but there was no escaping the fact that this "carriage" was going to turn into a pumpkin and soon. It was, of course, an extreme illustration of their predicament; they were not likely to be vaporized or even arrested and subjected to unimaginable horrors to force their minds right, but it was a place out of time, a place that was not subject to any rules or penalties save for the ones they imposed on each other.

Daniel was kind of smitten with the analogy and as he shook free the last droplets of urine, he imagined he would share his thoughts with Ruby. He zipped, turned and on his way back he began to have second thoughts about the analogy. He imagined that it was unlikely that she would be familiar with the bleak dystopia, and it wouldn't make a whole lot of sense without a lengthy explanation or worse that she would be and the composite picture of Jules Bourglay and Winston Smith constituting the kind catastrophically alienated gang that Daniel mentally cavorted with, might just put to rest any notion that he had at least a foothold in a reality that she might be reasonably familiar with.

Chapter 60

Daniel closed the door on the idea just as he closed the flap on the tent. A glimpse of the scalloped pattern in the dirt upon entering prompted him to zip it shut. The hermetically sealed refuge gave it whole different feel, one that more closely resembled Winston and Julia's enclave, he imagined but he didn't take the bait. He crawled on all fours toward the sleeping bag and apparently being in an Orwell state of mind found himself thinking. "Four legs good, two legs bad" and chastised himself for being incorrigible. On cue Ruby prepped the bag for his reentry but demanded the password in the form of a question before he could take up residence.

"Daniel, is there some reason you never mention your parents?"

He flinched slightly and came to a screeching halt at the edge of the bag. "Yes, there is a reason, Ruby," he answered solemnly.

Her ears perked up and she looked to his mouth to get a head start on the answer as it passed over his lips. He leaned forward, but she pressed down on the unzipped bag making entry impossible.

"So that's how it's gonna be," he said with a laugh. "I don't talk about my parents because I never knew them," he said as he casually began to tug on the corner of the bag, but Ruby pressed harder and looked him defiantly in the eye, sporting a comically imperious grin. "Okay, you win. The truth is that I don't talk about parents because I was raised by a group of wild, Jewish, homosexual wolves but nobody ever believes me."

Ruby looked startled for a second, and then she burst out laughing. Daniel seized the opportunity to dive into the bag, deciding at the last second to enter head first, and provoking more laughter from Ruby. His discovery of stocking feet was too much to pass up, and in a matter of seconds she was laughing uncontrollably. She plunged her hand into the mystery bag and came up with a handful of Daniel's shirt. She gave a mighty tug and managed only to dislodge it from his pants. Her stomach in spasms, she thrust her hand up under his shirt and grabbed the taut flesh of his lower back and squeezed with all her might. Daniel gave a comic book scream and stopped instantly. She released and he was right back at it. She tightened the screws and Daniel cried uncle.

"You gonna stay stopped? she asked.

"Yes, yes, yes."

She squeezed again and tighter for good measure. "You promise?"

"I swear, I'll stop." Daniel backed out of the bag, did a one eighty 180 and smiled sheepishly at Ruby, who had a mock stern look on her face, which he promptly wiped off with a kiss.

Chapter 61

Daniel felt that stirring below and withdrew his lips to spare himself further aggravation. He laid his head on her chest and listened as her respirations settled back to normal. He liked to think that the kiss had roused her desire as well, but he had to admit that the tickling was the more likely culprit in her labored breathing.

"You gonna answer my question now, Daniel?" the voice from above said softly.

Daniel breathed a sigh of the inevitable and started paging through that catalogue with his usual trepidation.

"When you get home, grab a dictionary and look up the word "sullen" and next to it, there should be a picture of my father," he said as he felt a yawn welling up in him. He wasn't sure whether the fatigue or the subject matter was at fault.

"Not a real happy guy?" Ruby chimed in.

"No, sullen and angry were the two states that he resided in the most and the older I got the worse he became." He paused for a second and propped himself up on an elbow. Ruby could see the wheels turning in his head. "When I was real young, to the best of my recollection, he wasn't always so bad. I mean, I knew he was capable of being a son of a bitch because of the occasional explosions, but there were periods in between that sometimes seemed to last for quite a while where things just kind of went along," he added grudgingly.

Ruby detected the obvious lack of enthusiasm for the exercise but her curiosity trumped her concern and she pushed forward. "How about your mom?"

"Hmmm, my mom, well, she held up okay for a time but eventually he wore her down too." He paused momentarily and Ruby gently prodded him forward

"Go on, Daniel."

"She was always kind of a nervous person, quiet and nervous, but she was generally pretty upbeat so much so that she served as kind of a counterbalance to my father in spite of the fact that there was kind of a growling tension that permeated the atmosphere most of the time. But we adapted and there was actually a time when we would joke about it being "that time of the month" for him when he'd be in a particularly foul mood. Eventually, though, there was no making light of what came to be a very volatile situation." Daniel was wary of where this was headed, and he thought about giving her the abridged version, but he had promised, and of course, there was the stipulation.

"Anyway", he continued after a time, "my dad was very mechanically inclined. Motors of any kind, big or small, he loved to tinker with them, to tear them down and put them back together again. He would clean them and give them the vital fluids they needed to work properly, and he would adjust them continually until he made them hum. It wasn't good enough that they just ran well, they had to hum in a very particular way, and he was very precise about just when that had been achieved. They always sounded fine to me but he would keep adjusting until he heard exactly what he wanted to hear."

"He would try to get me interested, but I really had no interest, and I certainly had no aptitude. But it seemed so important to him that I would hang around just because it seemed to please him. Later in life it seemed to me that it was one of the few things that gave him any real satisfaction. It was like with enough effort and elbow grease he could bend the world to his will, unlike the rest of his life in which he seemed to feel like that ship in the *Perfect Storm*." Daniel was a little surprised at the warmth he suddenly felt for his father. It did happen from time to time, and it lasted until some of the uglier episodes would overwrite it, and those episodes were never far behind.

Ruby was focused intensely on Daniel even as she tried to appear the casual observer. She found herself imagining that she had just those vital fluids that could make Daniel hum, and she smiled to herself and managed again to offer her undivided attention.

"Are you bored yet, Ruby?" he asked with a nervous laugh, half hoping to be let off the hook.

"No, not at all, Daniel. Please continue," she replied in an oddly formal manner.

Daniel sat up and reached for a cigarette. By now it was part of the routine, and hence, there was no need for discussion. He unzipped the flap to the tent and assumed the position. "When I was five or six, that was the first time I really remember Uncle Howard visiting."

Ruby watched with fascination as Daniel's demeanor began a subtle shift. He had begun to sound weary, and she had considered asking if he wanted to catch some sleep and pick up the story after a while. But suddenly, he seemed reinvigorated, as fresh and animated as you could be in the sleep-deprived state they were operating in, and she nixed the idea.

"You know, Ruby, some kids grow up in hellacious circumstances and they don't know any different. I've even seen shows on TV where young girls were raped repeatedly by their fathers, and it took them a long time to realize that that was not the natural order of things. Well, I don't want to suggest that anything quite so horrible happened to me, but still in all, it was—how shall I put this?—not a very healthy environment. What I'm getting at is that my Uncle Howard gave me the first real inkling that life could be very different from what I was accustomed to. So much so that it took me a while to adapt to the separate reality." Daniel smiled inwardly as he watched the two of them whooping it up as they floated swiftly down the mighty Mississippi, caught himself and continued.

"Howard was interested in *me*! It's hard to explain actually. I mean, it wasn't that I was abused or neglected, at least not yet, it was more like my parents were burdened and distracted and so preoccupied with the trauma of their own lives that there just wasn't a whole lot left over for me." Daniel got to looking a little glassy-eyed and Ruby couldn't tell whether he was overcome with emotion or fatigue. Daniel's yawn confirmed her suspicion. "Wow, I guess I am getting a little tired," he said as he extinguished the cigarette that he'd only managed to steal a few drags from. Ruby had been right on both counts. Daniel *was* tired but it was exacerbated by the fact that many of the memories he was dredging up were saturated with a toxic mixture of anger and remorse that added considerable heft to the freight.

"You want to sleep for a while?" she asked, feeling suddenly like a brutal taskmaster.

"No!" he answered emphatically. "Sorry," he added with a weak smile. "I promised, and I want to finish. It all kind of ties in together, and I want to avoid being one big old causal inference error."

"A big what?"

"It's just a manner of speaking," he answered quickly, too tired to elaborate and scolding himself for the unnecessary arcana. "Hey, what do you say we take a walk? Maybe scare up a little pep," he added quickly as if wanting to get the ball snapped before the red flag was thrown.

Ruby didn't budge, and as Daniel looked at her snugly ensconced in the bag, he didn't detect much enthusiasm. He made a move to the flap and stuck his head out to check the temperature when he got his answer in the form of a sharp slap on the butt.

They emerged one after the other from the tent like two confused spelunkers more than a little surprised to discover that the hole they crawled out of was not the one they'd crawled into.

Chapter 62

The waning heat had bleached all the color from the embers, and with the moon playing peek-a-boo from behind a tangle of leaves, the darkness was more severe than it had been prior in the evening. They huddled together as they walked, infused with a small dose of vigor, courtesy of the brisk night air. The casual intimacy had kind of an after school stroll feeling to it, and the familiar strangers fell silent for a time. They moved in the direction of the path that led out to the automobiles, but once they'd gotten beyond the predictable clearing of the campsite, the going got bumpy. The terrain was uncertain, and there was no shortage of shrubs and branches determined to foil their progress. Daniel kept a hold of Ruby's hand, moved ahead to run interference and managed to get them to the open area by Ruby's car.

"This is good," Ruby said, settling the matter of whether the hike would continue, and Daniel had no argument. He hopped up on the trunk of Ruby's car and pulled two shiny cylinders out of the tunnel between his sweatshirt pockets, brandishing them like a couple of Colt 45s.

"The night air helps, but this stuff will kick it up a notch or two," he exclaimed as he handed her a Mountain Dew.

"Where'd you get these?" she asked as if he'd pulled them out from behind her ears.

"I grabbed them on the way out if the tent as insurance because I thought we were both getting kind of droopy. They're warm but hey, you can't have everything."

Ruby raised the can in acknowledgement and took a hearty gulp. "Did you know as a kid that Howard was a homosexual? Ruby asked. The word, rarely a part of her parlance and usually pronounced in such a way that a certain stigma was automatically associated with it, sounded strange as it rolled off her tongue, but she was eager to get back to the story and so didn't give it further thought.

It had occurred to Daniel as they navigated the darkness that she'd really only asked about his parents, but in his mind, you could not separate the two—or three, he thought if you want to get technical about it—and her question seemed to suggest that she understood that as well. He took it as a given that Ruby was genuinely interested, and that thought alone moved him in some small way, giving the task a higher purpose.

"I had no idea that he was gay, none. In fact, I didn't really fully understand what that meant until I was I was almost in high school. What I did know was that there was a lightness about him, an ease and a joy that I had never been exposed to, and it was a revelation. We would go for rides and hikes, and we would talk. We would talk about anything and everything, and he seemed to have answers for whatever questions I could come up with. But it wasn't the content so much that mattered as the fact that he listened to me and encouraged me. I would tell him about books I was reading for school or whatever, and he would deftly lead me to the deeper meanings in them and let me think I had made the discovery myself. It got so I loved to read. In fact, when I learned that he was particularly fond of Oscar Wilde, Mark Twain and John Steinbeck, I read whatever I could get my hands on by them so we could dissect them on his next visit."

"He sounds like a pretty special person," Ruby interjected, and Daniel could only shrug his shoulders.

"What can I say?" he replied as if no words could possibly do Howard justice.

Ruby stood facing him, put a hand on each of his knees and began kneading as if consoling him in advance of what she suspected was coming. Daniel lit a cigarette and proceeded to prove her prescient.

"At first, my father seemed almost relieved to have Howard visit because it meant I would be out of his hair for a while, but before long he came to resent it. It never occurred to me as a kid that there would be any reason that I shouldn't prattle on about all the wonderful things I did with Howard, but I quickly learned that my father wasn't quite as impressed with him as I was. In time, more often than not, when Howard came to spend a few days with us, my father would manage not to be around and truthfully, I could not have been happier."

"How about your father, did he know about Howard," Ruby interjected, consciously avoiding the use of the *word*.

"Eventually, yes but it's hard to say what he thought early on. I'm sure he had his suspicions, but he didn't share that kind of thing with me although I've never had any doubt that my mother knew. There was a family gathering when I was around eleven that Howard's partner Mark—well, we thought, or at least, I thought they were just very good friends at the time—anyway, they attended and even though they weren't demonstrative if you know what I mean, looking back I guess it was pretty obvious but I'm getting ahead of myself here." Daniel took the equivalent of three drags on the Camel Light, knowing that his narrative would afford few possibilities to partake, exhaled a steady stream into the night air, calculated the time-lines of the story and continued.

"My Father started drinking more and he became increasingly hostile to my mother and me. Still, it wasn't all the time. There were still some "family" moments on occasion, vacations and outings and the like, but the ratio was tilting more heavily toward the angry periods. He would get surly, and there would be ugly confrontations with my mother, and sometimes I'd see evidence that he'd hit her, but she always tried to hide it. The only break in the pattern came with the periodic visits from Howard, and I lived for them, but I learned to be very discreet about any "Howard" influence."

Daniel stopped cold and looked hard at Ruby. "You know, Ruby, I can condense this more than I am. I mean, are you sure that this is what you want to hear about?"

"Keep going, Daniel" was all the direction she gave him. It was a bit understated for his taste, but he took her at her word and did just that.

"I kind of had to be discreet because it had gotten to the point that my father would mock me whenever he'd catch me with a book. He acted as if he was joking, but I could sense the contempt, and it sort of drove me underground. I remember actually imagining that I was kind of like Anne Frank in the ways that I would search for ever more creative places to hide to indulge my passion. I even hid books under floor boards, among other places." Daniel kept an eye out for "the look" but was pleased to see only rapt attention.

"Things took a serious turn for the worse when the foundry he had worked in for years shut down, and he was reduced to picking up odd jobs whenever and wherever he could. It got to the point where he was surly most of the time, and as you might have figured he dove deeper into the bottle." Daniel seemed to be cringing unconsciously as he spoke about his father and the words started coming faster, taking on a staccato-like cadence but Ruby thought it best just to listen.

"He would go on drunken rampages and at about that time, whatever the thing was that shamed him when he would turn on us was killed. My mother took some secretarial jobs to bring in some extra money, but he would manage to screw that up with bizarre accusations and ugly scenes that so humiliated her that she couldn't face the people she'd been working with. There are a lot of gory details regarding his behavior generally, but suffice it to say that he became violent pretty regularly, and the generally nasty behavior became downright vicious. The "joking" about the books or anything that hinted at intellectual activity, for instance, evolved into naked rage and he would openly berate and ridicule me.

"How was your mother holding up through all that? Ruby asked in a voice barely above a whisper.

"Well, the way I remember it, she was cowering all the time. She probably wasn't really, but everything about her demeanor suggested a woman expecting the worst at every moment, and still she tried on occasion to set things straight.

She spent a lot of time apologizing for him or covering for him and trying to explain away his behavior, but every now and then she would get her dander up, and she would try to defend her honor and mine, and sometimes she would actually seem to get through to him. And then sometimes, she was in such profound denial that she seemed completely insane. There had been a balance, a sort of equilibrium when I was younger like I said, but with time, he broke her down. She tried to keep me safe, and in an odd way I think the maternal instinct to shield her young from danger was a source of strength for a while, but eventually I think she pretty much tapped that out too."

"After a while, glossing things over and putting on that he was just going through a rough spell and things would settle down soon became such a transparent charade that she stopped trying to sell me on it, and at some point, she mustered the nerve to give him an ultimatum, and it actually seemed to sober him up for a time."

Daniel sucked the life out what was left of the Camel Light, carefully crushed the butt to oblivion and continued. "The biggest reason it was so memorable is that she insisted on sending me down to spend a few days with Howard while they tried to reconcile." As if on cue, Daniels rhythm settled down to a much more leisurely pace and Ruby felt the tension dissipate from her own body as she sensed it ebbing from his.

"I was almost twelve at the time, and even though I couldn't show it, I was thrilled to be getting the hell out of there, even if only for a short while." Daniel paused for a moment as if this were a natural break point in the story, and everyone in the lecture hall could take five to stretch their legs, take a smoke or a bathroom break and reconvene, but Ruby was having none of it.

"Go on, Daniel," she urged forcefully.

"Hey, what do you say we head back to the tent?" he asked instead.

She didn't ask for a reason and seemed to accept that *he* had decided this move, and she didn't waste any time executing it. She took his hand, tugged at him so he slid off the back of the car and proceeded in the direction of the tent. She noticed for the first time that it really had gotten kind of cold out as they navigated by moonlight, but sensed that this wasn't the reason for the move. In short order, they were stooping though the flap and nestled back in the sleeping bag, and without further delay, Ruby commanded that he continue the story. Daniel found her insistence humorous but took it to mean that she had gotten hooked into the soap opera that was his life and was more than happy to oblige, especially considering where he was headed.

Chapter 63

Daniel had a vision from *Midnight Cowboy* of Joe Buck Miami bound, *loping carefree towards the orange dawn* with his dying friend Rico Rizzo by his side, inconsolable for just having just wet his pants. The derelict romantics were headed for the promised land, and Joe Buck would take the opportunity at the next stop to buy them each new outfits and to unceremoniously discard his cowboy garb and with it his delusions of being the gigolo stud that would earn fame and fortune servicing the leisured ladies of the Big Apple who had too much discretionary income and too little passion in their lives. Daniel liked to think that maybe, just maybe, Joe had gone on to modest success as a landscape gardener in the place where *"the sun keeps shining through the pouring rain"* as the film's theme song proclaimed, but then he reminded himself that it was just a movie.

To Daniel bus stations have an ambiance all their own, and he had been enamored with their sights, their sounds and especially their smells ever since he'd boarded a Greyhound headed for Alabama and out of the line of fire to spend a week or so with his beloved Uncle Howard. It wasn't quite a raft on the mighty Mississippi but it would move his person and besides, it was kind of nice to leave the driving to them.

It suddenly occurred to Daniel that this narrative had never really ventured beyond the confines of his mind. He nixed the idea of sharing this fact with Ruby and proceeded with the story.

"It was the first time I'd ever really been away from home on my own and in spite of the reasons for it, it was exhilarating. I assumed Howard knew a good deal about what was happening at home, but he didn't bring it up other than to say that he knew my parents were going through a rough spell and that he hoped they could work it out. His tone led me to suspect that he'd gotten the sugar coated version from my mother, and I was torn as to whether or not I should spell out for him just how gruesome it had all become. But I soon got caught up in the excitement of the adventure, and with him playing host to his "honored guest" as he put it, once I set foot in that parallel universe, dredging up the trauma of my beleaguered life was the last thing I wanted to do."

Daniel paused briefly, kind of smiling inwardly as he drew a deep breath and resumed. "I'm telling you Ruby, I was fascinated by everything, and I soaked it up like a sponge. It was a very different world from the one that I was accustomed to, a world where things matched and there was a certain logic and order to the way things were done. It wasn't that they were right or wrong, rather, it was that there was clearly some thought put into whatever Howard and Mark decided to do. This probably isn't making a whole lot of sense..."

"No, I think I get it, Daniel. Honestly," Ruby chimed in reassuringly and although he had his doubts, he took her at her word. "Did you know then that they were a couple?" she asked before he could continue.

"Yea, I think I did but not in any formal sense. It was a concept I was familiar with in the way that kids are, but I had the advantage of learning about it first hand, and what I saw didn't jibe with the juvenile notions that the other kids used mainly in a mean-spirited teasing way. It seemed a little odd at first when I walked past their bedroom on the way to the bathroom the first morning I was there and saw them snoozing away in a big old bed together, but it was what it was, and I didn't give it much thought after that. I mean, they clearly loved each other, and it all seemed very natural. They didn't hang all over each other, but there were little signs of affection, a quick kiss, Mark rubbing Howard's shoulders briefly while he was cooking breakfast and just the way they interacted in general. And, of course, that stood in stark contrast to the catastrophe of my parents. I mean, shit, how smart do you have to be to know who had the better idea?" Daniel's face lit up and a smile spread across his face.

"What, Daniel? What are you thinking about?" Ruby demanded.

"They had kind of a running gag that had to do with ribbing each other about who was smarter. Howard ran to the closet one day and came out... Daniel paused. That didn't sound quite right, did it," he added with a laugh. "Anyway, he really did do that and he came out with what looked like a child's hat perched on top of his head. Mark rolled his eyes and exclaimed melodramatically "Oh boy, here we go again. Mr. Paleontologist will now expound on the correlation between cranium size and intelligence." Daniel laughed lightly as he spoke. "I didn't have the slightest idea what a paleontologist might be, but I got the gist of what was going on. Howard sauntered over with a snooty look on his face and proceeded to place the hat on Mark's head. It was a perfect fit, but Mark pulled it down past his ears, scrunched his face up and started talking in a goofy voice."

Daniel's joy in recalling the incident was pure and infectious, and Ruby caught the bug. "I remember watching Howard watching Mark and trying to contain his laughter, and you could tell from Howard's expression that there was more to come, and sure enough Mark broke into a routine that I imagine he had performed a thousand times before. 'I ask you, Ladies and gentleman," he said with great animation; "Who shaped the world as we know it?" Jesus Christ, Karl Marx, Albert Einstein, Sigmund Freud and we'll even throw in Groucho Marx and Bob Dylan for good measure. And what pray tell does this august body have in common? That's riiiiight, they're all Jews, just like yours truly and with a heritage like that, don't you think the odds are pretty good that I'm just a wee bit smarter than old melon head here?'" He doffed his cap to the imaginary audience, curtsied and wrapped it up with a booming declaration: 'I rest my case.'

"By that time, Howard was in stitches and I was completely taken in by the whole scene." Daniel stopped talking to relish the memory, a smile spread across his face and Ruby eyed him curiously as she absorbed the contents of the scene he had described. The smile slowly waned, and Daniel's demeanor became stolid until finally a look of consternation came over him. "People don't quite know how to consider Jews," Daniel said flatly.

"What do you mean?" Ruby asked somewhat defensively as if the admonition had been directed at her.

"It just so happened that Rosh Hashanah had started a few days before I got down there and the subject came up a couple of times inadvertently. When Howard and Mark would have a disagreement about something or other, Howard would say something to the effect of "Well, that's another thing you might want to review on Yom Kippur." It was done in a teasing and playful manner, and Mark always laughed when it was said. Anyway, it piqued my interest so I began asking Mark a lot of questions about Judaism. As usual, he was very patient and gracious, and he answered all my questions, and I really didn't get it at the time, but he clearly soft pedaled the strong feelings he had about the ways his people have been persecuted throughout history.

At one point, he dragged an old scratched up basketball out of the same closet Howard had gotten the hat from, then he took a single pea from the refrigerator, and he pointed to the ball and said, 'This is the Middle East' then he rolled the pea next to it and said, 'This is Israel and they even begrudge us this.' I could feel a subtle agitation building up inside him, and Howard kind of stepped in to steer the conversation away from what I assume he thought was a little too heavy for a kid my age, and Mark took the hint. He looked at me for a long moment and finally said simply, 'People don't quite know how to consider Jews. All we want is a fair shake, Daniel, just to be held to the same standards as everyone else.' I didn't really understand, and I kind of got the sense that Howard wanted to move on."

Daniel was suddenly overcome by a gnawing feeling that it had become a one-way conversation, and his narrative came to a grinding halt. He conceded that although these matters held great significance for him, they were not subjects visited without peril and he'd seen enough squeamishness and worse over the years as to make the question of projection a fifty/fifty proposition at best, and he was beginning to sense that maybe Ruby was ready to move on as well. "So what do you make of all that?" he asked awkwardly, fumbling for some sort of reassurance.

Ruby seemed surprised at the break in the action and scrambled to summarize some kind of reaction to the body of information that had been imparted to her.

"It's all very interesting, and it's obvious that these two men were very good people, but I'm anxious to hear what happened when you got home — with your parents, I mean."

"You don't think any of it's strange?" Daniel interjected not ready to move on just yet.

"No, not really. I mean, it's kind of unconventional but goodness is goodness regardless of the source."

"You're absolutely right," he replied almost giddily, marveling at the conciseness of her statement and feeling somehow validated by it at the same time. There had in actuality been no litmus test, yet Daniel felt somehow unburdened. He yawned and draped his arm over his forehead. Ruby promptly removed it and pressed her nose against his.

"Tell me what happened with your parents and then we can sleep."

"You've got a deal," he replied as he leaned up on an elbow and started in with a version that he had already begun to abridge.

"When I got home, there was a different feeling around the house. Some sort of truce had been declared in my absence, and my parents seemed to be at least trying to coexist with some civility. It didn't exactly have a Norman Rockwell feel to it, but it was a start. I was wary, but I felt I had to try, although I was pretty gun shy around my father." Daniel adopted a pensive demeanor for a moment before continuing. "You know how when you've done somebody wrong, and *you* get angry at them because if you don't somehow make it their fault, the blame reverts back to you?" It wasn't really a question so much as a statement, and Daniel looked to Ruby for a reply.

"I'm listening, Daniel, really. Go on, please."

The non-answer answer prompted him to lean down and look a little more closely at Ruby. "Yea, okay. So I went out in the back yard and with nothing more than the junk laying around the property, I built a spaceship and flew to the moon. That sounds completely feasible, wouldn't you agree, Ruby?"

"Yes, Daniel, sure. Go on." Daniel gently proceeded to draw the sleeping bag up to Ruby's chin, and without a word, she squeezed it tight and tucked it up around her neck.

"Goodnight, sweet friend," Daniel whispered and he thought he saw the smallest hint of a smile form at the corners of Ruby's mouth.

"Goodnight, Golda girl," he said softly as he reached gingerly over to turn off the lantern. The day was done, and there was no longer any need to muster any energy for any reason whatsoever. And this time I mean it! he thought to himself with a chuckle. He yawned big and released his body to its natural rhythms. Tackling a major architectural project was not on the agenda for this go-round as the darkness seeped into his psyche without him so much as counting sheep, or calculating how much weight a partition could carry.

Random thoughts flitted in and out without invitation or eviction. He watched Arthur C. Clarke's *star farmers* rocketing through the far reaches of the universe, looping around planets and stars, diving into black holes and shooting out of them as if atop Old Faithful just for the sheer joy of it and finally settling in the neighborhood of our small planet and finding fertile soil in the mind of Moon-Watcher. They were, as he understood it, ethereal beings, comprised of a sort of pure energy that was beyond the scope even of his imagination, but he saw *something* in his mind's eye as they darted through the cosmos at warp speed, something that he had given shape and form, but if asked, he would be hard-pressed to describe it.

As the few remaining vestiges of available consciousness were fading, Daniel caught a glimpse of Moon-Watcher standing in front of the monolith. He could just make out that he was accompanied by another inductee, and upon closer inspection, he saw himself. The two of them were gazing skyward, presumably while undergoing the "treatment" and just as the shutter was canceling out the last inkling of light, Daniel saw "it" beaming down on his prodigy and floating next to "it" with a knowing smile was Howard.

Chapter 64

The night life performed its rituals as it had the night before and the week before, as it had for millions of years. There were creatures stirring and so too was the silent biology of trees and shrubs and grasses. The skies were perusing the menu, trying to decide whether to contribute to the aquifers, hurl lightning bolts, crackle a thunderclap or two or simply chill and save the fireworks for another day. These phenomena occurred as they always had and as they always would, regardless of whether they were chronicled, analyzed, measured or predicted. On this night for some reason, maybe because of a lingering fatigue born of the energies expended giving birth to a new season, calm and temperate was fancied, and Daniel would be the beneficiary.

Daniel, without knowing or caring why, had always been slightly irritated by the term "spooning," but he didn't know what else to call the position he found himself in. His chest was pressed against Ruby's shoulder blades. His left arm was draped over hers and resting atop her breasts. His groin was pressed up so tight against her that had they been sans clothing, it would indeed have been a very short distance to the garden. His knees were bent in perfect harmony with hers, and with his nose touching the nape of her neck, he awoke to discover his face nestled in her hair, which smelled awful sweet in spite of, or maybe because of, the chemicals employed to keep any errant tresses from going astray.

He lay as still and silent as she, coordinating his respirations with hers so that even their abbreviated movement would be in sync, and save for a waking yawn, he didn't flinch. Rather he luxuriated in the wonder of it all for ten or fifteen minutes before extricating himself from nirvana and heading out to check on the movements of the universe. He brought Golda with him, thinking he could get some quality time in before their guest would be aroused to bump her down the couch, and apparently she was in a forgiving mood because there was nary a word about the prior evening's events. With Golda comfortable and doing her morning stretches, Daniel crept just far enough back inside the tent to grab the cooler full of provisions with a plan to get a head start on breakfast before Ruby rolled out of bed. It suddenly dawned on him that he had never set the alarm on his watch, but since nothing else had been on schedule, he took the liberty of assuming that a little extra shut-eye would do her good, that and the fact that although technically he knew how to set the thing, it apparently liked to sleep in on occasion as well.

The first order of business then was to rekindle the flame so he could get the coffee going, and he quickly foraged enough kindling to get a respectable fire underway. The inhalation of Ruby had tickled his senses, but it would take caffeine to really heat up the oil in the old crankcase. Daniel sat on a log next to Golda, and in spite of the old adage, he watched the pot, feeling a little like Pavlov's dog, a little trickle starting here and there in anticipation of the big push. He finally shifted his gaze to the tent and imagined himself back inside "spooning" for lack of a better term and caught a whiff of her hair that had lodged itself somewhere in his brain. He pondered Ruby in a collage of their activity and concluded that there was just nothing not to like about her. It was more than "smitten" although that could fairly describe one part of the whole. No, it was much deeper than that and, and he decided he'd better get back on track. He summed it all up by acknowledging that the whole thing had been remarkable and then he faux pinched himself to make sure it was all real. Daniel considered sharing an abbreviated version of the sentiment with Golda but decided against it lest it be taken the wrong way. "When this is done, little girl, we'll grab a cup of joe and head down to the lake," he said quietly. "It'll be nice this time of the morning."

His conscience appeased, his mind wandered back to the story he'd been telling Ruby. Not the content per se but the semi-paralysis that overcame him shortly before she slipped away. To Daniel, of course, they were simply Uncle Howard and his partner, Mark, no less than family, the both of them and family in the best sense of the word. It's impossible to quantify but Daniel had always taken it as gospel that without the influence of his uncle, he'd have ended up in a whole lot worse shape than he did. It was far more than what Howard did that made a difference. It was that his life illustrated possibilities that were nowhere to be seen in the parochial prison of Daniel's family milieu: relationships that started with the premise that whatever rights and privileges one party enjoyed automatically applied to the other, a sensitivity to the needs and feelings of others, an appetite for learning and well thought out attitudes that were more than regurgitated bias and dogma and a humility and self-effacing humor that coexisted with and often trumped the standard easily bruised ego. It was the great irony of Daniel's life that in time he would discover that the people that he considered to be role models were demonized and vilified and held in contempt by a large segment of most populations.

"People don't quite know how to consider Jews," Mark had said with a quiet dismay many years ago, and that went for homosexuals as well. The hostile aggressive posturing of his father had left Daniel with a deep distaste for confrontation, in part because he sensed that the issues being contested had nothing to do with any reality he was familiar with. Daniel couldn't fathom what these 'issue' might be, only that his father often seemed a madman swatting at a battalion of angry hornets that only he could see. And so it was that Daniel would encounter no small number of people that imagined an angry battalion of homosexuals trying to molest their children, undermine their marriages and generally corrupt the population at large and no small number of people that exhibited outright enmity or, at the very least, a quiet uneasiness with an undercurrent of hostility toward Jews and a surprisingly large number of the latter group that suspected that Jews "controlled the world through some secret cabal."

Daniel had often found himself in the odd position of being the reluctant advocate for people that he shared no genetic or religious predisposition with in spite of being constitutionally ill-suited to the task. He'd been maligned and assaulted verbally and physically and had grown weary of what had come to seem to be a futile endeavor, learning along the way to keep his feelings to himself most of the time.

It was the thought that Ruby might share those sentiments that stopped him in his tracks. The prospect of negating or at least putting a damper on all the good stuff that had taken place since the ill-fated pickle incident, had struck fear into his heart. He cursed himself for having doubted her, before he reminded himself of all the times that people he'd come to hold in high esteem had saddened or angered or bitterly disappointed him. "You never know with people, Golda. You just never know," he said stolidly and Golda shrugged her shoulders in agreement.

In Daniel's world, certain things were stipulated by default, and for better or for worse, his love and respect for Howard and Mark and by extension all that they were, these things were nonnegotiable.

Chapter 65

The percolator erupted one last time with a gasp of finality, and Daniel sprang into action. He realized that in his stupor, he'd forgotten to get cups and cream and sugar. "The trifecta," he whispered to no one as he set off to rectify the oversight. Often times, when Daniel took that first swig, he heard the song that was triggered when Popeye freebased a can of spinach as the charge traveled to the distant points of his limbs. "Good stuff, Golda. You ought to try it sometime." He rose slowly, stretched mightily and was good and ready to face the day. With a blanket slung over his shoulder, Golda's digs in one hand, and his piping hot cup of coffee in the other, Daniel headed for the path to the lake. It was a little after eight in the morning, and by Daniel's reckoning, he might have gotten a little more than four hours of sleep, but all things considered, he felt pretty good, and the promise of an inexhaustible supply of caffeine pretty much ensured that he'd hold up fine.

"What'd I tell ya, Golda," he said with an air of smug satisfaction as he cast his gaze over the expansive body of water that constituted the universe for the unseen multitude of inhabitants that called it home. A quick glance her way confirmed that she was indeed duly impressed. Daniel lit a cigarette and wondered why the water at the lake's edge lapped gently against the shore. He hadn't heard a boat or anything else that might have left a ripple effect in its wake, and he wondered if it was just light wind or if there was something lunar going on. It didn't matter, and he didn't invest further in the mini-mystery. He had planned originally, pre-Ruby, to be sitting at sunrise in this very spot with the very same company and the very same vices. He loved the way the rising sun was coy with its assets, doling out the light and the warmth in increments so infinitesimal that it was close to impossible to detect the change. But he wouldn't complain, he thought to himself. It had saved him the trouble of trying, and besides this was a pretty damn nice time of the morning as well.

It was warmer than he'd expected, and with his hand in salute mode to shield his eyes, he gazed in the general direction of the big orange-yellow ball. Golda seemed to spot it first as was evidenced by the sudden widening of her eyes and it was majestic. A hawk, Daniel imagined, a graceful and magnificent animal riding the invisible currents, and in so far as the two of them could tell, never flapping its wings at all. They sat spellbound, Daniel imagining what it must be like to float at any altitude you chose, and Golda nervously recounting a show she'd happened to catch a glimpse of on the Animal Planet channel. She thought it was called something like "A Countdown of the World's Most Efficient Hunters," a title so ominous in its association for her that the very sound of it vaguely brought to mind another chilling phrase she'd caught one afternoon on the tube "Bin Laden Determined to Strike within the United States".

"Amazing, huh , Golda," an awestruck Daniel exclaimed but she had a slightly different take on the scene. The big bird seemed to have a flight pattern worked out in much the same way a fitness buff would map out an ideal route for a morning jog. It would swoop around an oval route for a few laps, arc left and out of sight and finally buzz back into view directly overhead, seemingly having built up an enormous head of steam. It flew at breakneck speed to what appeared to be a fixed point in the middle of the lake before slowing to a canter and embarking on the same path all over again.

Daniel caught on to the timing and direction of the pattern and made kind of a game out of looking straight up to track the breathtaking display as soon as it entered his field of vision overhead. It was little more than a small brown blur when it blew past, but it so excited him that he tried to recruit Golda to join him in the game of anticipation. He gazed skyward for what seemed a longer interval between sightings and finally concluded that the curtain had come down on today's performance. He was about to exit the theatre when he got the strong sense that there might be one more encore, so he stood in the middle of the aisle and craned his neck to look skyward.

He spotted the "small brown blur" as expected but was disoriented by the mass surrounding it. In his frenzied perception, it seemed as if maybe the hunter had bitten off more than it could chew, and the sheer bulk of its prey was propelling the two of them toward the serene waters like a kamikaze on a bee-line toward the deck of a destroyer. What his eyes actually saw defied all logic and thus was initially refused entry into the part of the brain that normally handles that type of traffic. The placid water was slashed open for a millisecond, devouring the visual evidence while Daniel, having dislodged what he'd expected to see, began to allow for the possibility that he really did see what he thought he saw. He figured to know for sure one way or the other in a matter of seconds.

Chapter 66

Ruby's head burst into view, stirring the waters that were just regaining their equilibrium from the previous laceration and gulping air as she flung water in every direction with a sensual flick of the head. Daniel, for his part, finally accepted that he was right; he had in fact seen a "putty tat."

"Good morning, Daniel" she called out, smiling through shivering lips.

He replayed the scene in his mind in search of any evidence that any part of her was clad in anything, and in spite of the gauzy recollection, had himself convinced that the great likelihood was that there was a naked body, her luscious naked body bobbing up and down underwater, and it made his head spin.

"Come on in, Daniel. The water's fine," Ruby proclaimed, her teeth chattering as fast as her lips were quivering.

"You're gonna have to come out at some point, Ruby," Daniel replied, relishing the inevitable. "And I've got all day."

Ruby's smile was big and knowing. "Come on, chicken," she challenged him.

"Ruby, you are naked, aren't you?"

"Why, yes I am," she answered with her mischievous smile, and he was stricken.

Son of a bitch, I knew it! he thought to himself excitedly as he imagined pumping his fist in the air. "I'm sorry, Ruby but I can't just take your word for it. You're going to have to prove it to me!" he said with a big shit eating grin of his own.

"No, no, Daniel. If you want proof, you'll have to come in to get it," she answered with a taunting laugh.

"I don't know if I can, Ruby."

"Why not?" she shot back with a hint of irritation in her voice.

"Cause I don't think I'll be able to get these pants off over my boner."

Ruby burst out laughing as Daniel tore his clothes off. "Watch these for me, Golda," he said as he made a mad dash for the water. He knew that toe dipping was out of the question, and he braced himself for the shock to come. It was as cold as he had expected, but at the same time exhilarating. He swam furiously toward Ruby, and she dodged him playfully, backpedaling toward the shore and shallower waters before ceding the hunt and wrapping her arms and legs around him as he reached her.

Daniel could just manage to keep his head and hers, for that matter, above water if he stood on his toes, and although he couldn't see her face, he could feel her ear to ear smile. Her nakedness, like a tenacious barnacle, was literally all over him, and yet the barrier of the water made it seem almost as if their bodies were in another place. He kneaded her back lightly for confirmation, and she arched back exposing her breasts momentarily before the water swallowed them up again, the unintended *flash* having left all but a certain portion of Daniel's anatomy bordering on anemia.

"I thought cold water usually shrunk a guy if you know what I mean," Ruby remarked, breaking the silence and the tension, and the two of them laughed heartily through shivering lips.

"Let me see you, Ruby," Daniel implored suddenly. His voice conveyed an almost solemn earnestness, the fire down below reaching temperatures that he imagined might turn the whole of the lake to steam.

She kissed her way around to his lips and pressed hard, taking his tongue and holding on tight. Ruby's boldness had been wildly impulsive, and it suddenly struck her that she had ignited this inferno and that ultimately she would have to put it out. She sucked his tongue harder while that realization sunk in. She made a conscious effort to stop thinking, and drew back, her hands on his shoulders and rose up slowly. She fixed her eyes on his, and as he soaked up her loveliness, she planted her feet on his thighs and catapulted herself up and out, the whole of her body exposed by degrees before she disappeared under the water.

"Jesus Christ," Daniel muttered to himself half in shock at what he'd witnessed as he watched for evidence of her whereabouts. She emerged lakeside, mounted the bank and sat smiling nervously out at Daniel, who walked slowly toward her with the same deliberate tempo of a man walking away from his armed combatant in a duel. She was all chattering teeth, goose bumps and desire, and the closer he got, the worse it got. She raised her knees up to her chest in a futile reflexive attempt to shield her nakedness before she remembered that she had set this stage, and she leapt up self-consciously and stood erect, giving her yet another thing in common with her suitor. Her mind shot back to the initial encounter and Daniel's mute admiration of her, but that provocation was accidental. The hundreds of times she'd imagined a moment like this since then never included the panic she was experiencing as he approached her, the shivering and chattering now as much a result of her anxiety as the cool breeze on her soaking wet body.

Daniel stopped a yard or so in front of her, looked at her and then down at his elongated manhood. "It's all your fault, Ruby," he said simply and to her ear, eloquently, and the meaning thrilled and soothed her at the same time, her nervousness morphing into excitement.

An incongruous image emanated from some hidden place in her mind, a place of hurt and shame and she watched her husband, callous and disinterested, passing by a similar scene without so much as a glance. She felt the sting accompanied by a surge of anger and smiling triumphantly to herself, moved her arms from a crossed position under her breasts and placed them on her hips, a graceful move that transformed her demeanor from tentative and uneasy to open and inviting, and the subtle shift was not lost on Daniel.

"If I'm completely honest I have to confess that I wanted your eyes on me—The truth is Daniel, that I meant to step out of that tent stark naked, walk directly to you and let you look, make you look and hopefully get the same reaction I got this afternoon," she had said earlier, and Daniel, accommodating fellow that he is, was happy to oblige.

417

It seemed strange at first, even with her permission and encouragement, to have full license for lascivious inspection, so accustomed was he to practicing the manly art of seeing without seeming to look. His gaze was intense and so obviously welcome that his natural reluctance melted away, and as he thoroughly examined every inch of her, he caressed her ever so lightly on surfaces close to but never on the more provocative areas. He thought back to how rigid she'd become when he had raised the hem of her dress slightly to study the doctor's handiwork and marveled at the transformation. The two of them were humming like tuning forks, creating a barely audible sensual purring as he ran his fingers down each arm, gave her palms a squeeze and pulled her arms up. He looked to her face and saw that her eyes were closed.

"I can't look, Daniel. I can't look at you now," she said softly, preferring to imagine what was actually happening.

"You okay, Ruby?" he asked, suddenly concerned that she might be regretting the situation she'd gotten herself into.

"Yeah, I'm fine," she answered quickly and he took her at her word.

"You *are* a fine specimen of a woman," he said as a simple statement of fact, and she smiled a smile so sweet that it hurt his heart. Daniel moved around behind her and put a hand on each hip as he eyed the gentle curves and lines of her body, and his passion surged. He had no idea how this would end except that it would have to whether it be by his own hand or by the more obvious means. He drew a line with his fingers from her inner thighs up and over her buttocks to her lower back, and he felt her shudder. Kissing her shoulders, he draped his arms around her waist and drew himself tight against her so that his throbbing member was following the trajectory of her spine, and she grabbed his arms and pulled him tighter thus rendering any doubts about his actions moot. It was as if each of them had a tiger by the tail and to release it would unleash a prodigious power over which there was little chance of regaining control.

Ruby sensed her moistness and ached for Daniel to be inside her, and she held his arms even tighter as their breathing became panting, and they gulped for air. He moved from her shoulders to her neck, burying his face in her hair as he lunged for her ear.

Daniel had thus far managed to stifle the impulse to thrust, but he felt his loins recoiling like a top, taut and eager to be set free to whirr in circles until it spent its tension. Ruby moaned and clutched his arms just shy of pain and the guttural vocalization of her desire pushed Daniel over the top.

"Ruby," he breathed hot into her ear. He had no idea what he was about to propose other than that it would further the cause.

"Lay down, Daniel," she cooed the command, and he was prostrate in the blink of an eye.

Golda had seen enough. She wasn't quite sure what it all meant, she just sensed somehow that it was a private affair and she turned her attention back to keeping a wary eye out for one of the "World's Most Efficient Hunters."

Ruby straddled Daniel on her knees, her hands on either side of him and her breasts dangling mere inches below his chin. He moved his mouth hungrily toward them but got waylaid when she smothered his body with hers and began kissing him fiercely. She clasped her hands on his, pinning him firmly to the ground and the more he squirmed and struggled the more passionately she kissed him.

"Don't talk, Daniel," she intoned between heaving breaths, and it struck him as odd as it was the furthest thing from his mind. Ruby shifted seamlessly to the tried and true erogenous zone and began working Daniel's ear with her tongue, and the charge it sent through his loins made further resistance impossible, and he thrust with such force into the sweaty softness of her belly that it lifted their midsections off the ground. Ruby moaned loudly and unabashedly, and Daniel suddenly felt her spongy plume rising and descending rhythmically against his thigh. She released his hands, cradled his head and looked deep into his eyes as if to acknowledge that she was fully aware of the nature of her act before she pressed her mouth back onto his all the while not missing a beat. She writhed and tugged, groaned and bit as areas that had become parched and arid over the many months saw the drought end with a vengeance, and just as Daniel feared his lip might require more stitches than her leg, she exploded with convulsive force.

It was probably no more than ten or twelve seconds but it seemed like days and when the hurricane passed, there was a deathly calm. Daniel, still in the throes of passion, wrapped his arms around her like an offering of warm dry clothing to a woman that had just been fished out of icy waters. There was no movement save for her fingers tenderly tugging and twirling a lock of his hair that at least confirmed that she was not sleeping. In the stillness, Daniel had begun to consider the possibility that his pleasure might indeed be manually induced when Ruby suddenly stirred. She kissed him softly on the cheek and then the chin, and the throat, and the chest and Daniel, fingers crossed, sensed a pattern emerging. She kissed and licked each nipple, then his abdomen, and as she planted a moist one just above his naval, he felt her fingernail lightly scratching his pubic hair as she continued the inexorable journey to the center of the earth. He felt her hand surround his engorged manhood, another kiss just above the hair line and finally he felt her lips, hot and wet, engulf the tip, her tongue darting around the shaft, planting angel kisses along the way, and he was home.

Ruby had always been the kind of person that finished what she started, and having come this far she fully intended to complete this task as well. Besides, she wanted to do it for Daniel; she wanted to reciprocate the pleasure he'd conferred upon her. She felt sublimely sexual for the first time in as long as she could remember, and she easily dismissed the feeble rumblings of conscience trying to crash the party as she relished the mouthful she'd inhaled. She rolled up and down the shaft, taking great care to maintain sufficient moisture to provide just the right amount of friction, and she looked to Daniel and relished his contorted satisfaction. Bolstered and flush with confidence, she imagined she was racing against the clock or cock as the case maybe, hoping to employ the multiple techniques that were popping into her head faster than she could perform them before she achieved her ultimate objective. Slow down, slow down, Ruby, she thought to herself as she threw a change up and went down as far as she could go at a snail's pace before ascending at the same tempo. She removed it from her mouth, pressed it against her cheek and smiled beatifically at Daniel.

Daniel, though stoked and inflamed, suddenly lost his place, and in that nanosecond he marveled at the significance of circumstance. This was a gift, a sacred gift, he thought to himself and that from a woman that he had known for less than twenty-four hours. It was not kismet, fate or destiny nor was it divine providence, intelligent design or anything of the sort. It was a dash of dumb luck combined with a heaping teaspoon of karma. They had somehow managed to run into one another, and their wildly divergent histories had dumped a million variables into a vat, and the resulting broth was recombinant. Hell, he thought, there were snaggle-toothed girls in truck stops with cum-stained teeth that would perform the same act for ten or fifteen dollars, but in that debased and instinctive exchange, it was simply orifice as commodity. No, this act was a conscious choice, an intimate sharing with a fellow traveler that was nothing less than good and right, and the circumstances made it so. Daniel blinked in foggy disbelief, closed his eyes, and let Ruby get back to the matter at hand.

She ran her tongue slowly down the shaft, circled his balls and took them whole into her mouth, all the while cradling his cock with an open hand to get just the angle she wanted. Slipping her tongue gently beneath each testicle, she pushed lightly upward first on one side then the other and imagined that if she only had a little more room she could actually juggle them. "Oh, my God," Daniel yowled and Ruby felt a warmth inside and was pleased that she had chosen to use her powers for good. She released the boys and ascended the shaft as if there were a circular stairway. She knelt between his legs, reached beneath his buttocks and squeezed. "Look, Ma, no hands!" flashed through her mind, and she smiled inwardly as she accentuated the natural thrust that sent him deeper into her mouth.

Daniel couldn't bear to look. He did not want this to end and he knew the slightest glimpse of a lovely Ruby, breasts swaying as she devoured his manhood, rising and falling slowly, gusts of warm breath alternating with heated saliva raining down on him, would finish him for sure. He slammed his lids down tighter as if that would prevent an errant image from slipping through.

Ruby knew the end was near. She imagined the picture frame on the mantel stutter stepping its way toward the edge, the dishes rattling in the cupboard and the dog, with its mysterious sense of impending calamity, baying wolf-like as the Richter scale relished the infrequent opportunity to perform its sole function in life.

There was always a moment just prior to fruition in which Daniel tried to stop the movement of the universe, to seize the second hand and by dint of sheer force wrangle it from its perpetual motion thus freezing the moment in time for all of eternity, but as the old saying goes "you can't fool Mother Nature," and of course, he couldn't. He felt the gathering storm funneling in a single direction and released himself into sweet oblivion.

Ruby braced herself and moved high up the shaft to allow for maximum capacity. She could have redirected it or simply smothered it but for reasons unknown to her she wanted her fill, and she would have it and have it she did, in spades. Such was the volume that she had to swallow after the third burst lest it pour forth from her nostrils. She felt suddenly like she was trying to stay on the back of a bucking bronco as Daniel seemed to change direction with each spewing thrust, but she managed to hang on, and in a long moment the seizure was over save for a few minor aftershocks.

Daniel took a deep breath, sprung open his eyes and as the world came back into focus, saw Ruby on all fours, her smile skewed by the salty viscous liquid that filled her mouth. "Come here," he said softly, the affection he felt bespoken by the tone of his voice, and the contour of his smile.

Ruby leaned forward and disseminated the semen in a circular motion around his naval with the same careful deliberation with which boys write their names in the snow. Unencumbered, she pitched forward and lay across Daniel, her arms and legs splayed in a graceful reenactment of da Vinci's rendering of the Vitruvian man.

Daniel stroked her hair lightly as the two shared the aftermath in a sensual and sated silence. The light breeze caressing the water and rustling the leaves and the occasional scampering critter constituted the only sound or movement besides their modest respirations, and for those precious few moments, all was right with the world. The great conductor's wand cued the birds to start singing, and their warbling dominated the air waves until Ruby finally broke the silence.

"Daniel," she purred in a soft and sensuous voice

"Yeah."

"I can't have sex with you."

"I know, Ruby. I know"

Chapter 67

The breeze picked up and swept nonchalantly over the tangle of flesh that appeared to have been expelled by a violent cough that emanated from deep in the bowels of the lake. Their pores, gaping chasms forced wide by sweat and various other bodily fluids only a few moments prior began to retract to preserve the rapidly dissipating body heat, and Ruby felt a sudden chill. Daniel, still enjoying the blanket protection of Ruby's prostrate body, saw the goose bumps on her arms and deftly ran his fingers down her backside to confirm his suspicion.

"You gettin' cold, Ruby?"

"Yeah, I think I'm gonna go ahead up and get cleaned up." She rose to her knees and hugged herself, rubbing her upper arms briskly, squashing the stubborn goose bumps and at the same time concealing her breasts in a burst of unexpected modesty. She was smiling mysteriously, Daniel noted as he stood and shook out the blanket, and in his quick scan, he imagined he read affection, relief, defiance, self-loathing and just a hint of embarrassment, but he was no more sure of one thing than another and settled on believing that there was more positive than negative in it. He draped the blanket over Ruby's shoulders in classic chivalrous fashion, and as her left hand clasped it securely around her, the right hand slid down and met resistance at the dried semen that was plastered to her abdomen just north of her pubic hair, and she silently explored its texture.

As Daniel leaned over to gather up his clothes, Ruby leaned forward and planted a soft kiss on his right buttock and he jumped as if he'd been goosed. Laughing nervously, she rose quickly behind him, reached around and drew him tight against her, juggling the blanket in the process. Her hand found the dried semen on *his* abdomen, and she felt a secret and sensual kinship with Daniel, and she maneuvered around to face him and smiled a smile that was at least for the moment devoid of the other considerations. They stood facing each other in a formal silence when Ruby raised the blanket high, enveloped Daniel in her cocoon and perched her chin on his shoulder.

She would head up the hill to the tent momentarily to don the outfit that would forever separate their bare flesh, and she wanted one last time to feel her naked body on his. She squeezed him tight against her and rotated her body back and forth, gently brushing at first and then almost scraping her skin on his while offering her lips for Daniel to kiss. The residual passion still smoldered, but there was a sense of finality to the kiss, and she withdrew after a brief moment, turned and began to make her way up the hill, taking Daniel by surprise. He watched after her for a short time and thought to himself that her pace, the purposeful movement and the blanket draped in that peculiar fashion gave the whole thing the appearance of a coronation or some such other royal spectacle.

The move had seemed abrupt and Daniel hoped that she might turn and offer a final thought or something, but she trod on and he kind of shook his head as he knelt down to pick up

426

Golda. He stopped mid-genuflect and peered out over the vast body of water before him. "You know, if you want to take a quick dip, little girl, I can wait a minute or two," he offered, but it seemed that Golda had had plenty of the lake herself, and she politely deferred, still anxiously peering skyward in search of the pterodactyl that had inhabited the air space above them just a short time ago. "We'll just head back then, say Golda," he added, and he got no argument from her.

The din of conflict had begun to elbow its way in to Ruby's psyche and was finally making some headway. Guilt had been designated as spokesman for the group and it was demanding a voice in a discussion that it had heretofore been excluded from when desire and its exigency had held court and stifled all dissenting opinion. Ruby fought valiantly to keep it at bay and managed for a time to limit it to little more than a minor annoyance, but it was a forceful and determined advocate and it believed that the momentum had begun to swing and that in any case, time was on its side. Ruby sensed the beginnings of a subtle shift but managed to retain control of the floor even as her footing became a little less steady.

As Daniel stood and turned, a voice above called out to him, and he looked up to see Ruby standing perilously close to the edge of the cantilever that had served as a spring board to their erotic adventure.

"Hey, Ruby. What's up?" he answered, strangely relieved by the reengagement. She didn't reply immediately. It seemed as if she either didn't know what she wanted to say or she did but couldn't manage to bring herself to say it, and Daniel, unsure of what was going on, chose not to push her for an answer. He had no way of knowing, but it did occur to him that what they had just been through might be working on her in ways that she hadn't factored in, and that kind of thing was no mere architectural challenge, so he chose to forego any attempt at analysis. He started up the hill himself but heard his name again after a step or two.

"You're inside me now Daniel, and you will be always," she proclaimed, surprising herself with the semi-poetic ring of her statement. She had intended to say "you always will be" but anxiously tripped on her tongue and found the errant syntax much more to her liking.

Daniel smiled up at her and chalked one up for the prescient reluctance he'd had seconds ago to think that he could predict what she might be thinking, but he appreciated the sentiment even if he didn't fully comprehend its meaning.

"Thanks, Ruby," he replied awkwardly, and she smiled back at him. She seemed to turn to head for the tent, and he followed suit when his name floated down for the third time in as many minutes. He looked up slowly and saw Ruby framed by swaying treetops, a pale blue sky, and from stage left, a light yellow bath from the shifting sun. She stood silent, swathed in the blanket, a sultry siren no less seductive in her way than her predecessors of yore that beckoned unsuspecting mariners to their doom on rocky shores. As she raised her eyes to the heavens, her arms, like tendrils followed, reaching as high and wide as she could extend them before releasing the tenuous grasp, holding the blanket at bay and offering Daniel one last visual feast before turning and making off, her laughter trailing behind her.

Chapter 68

"You've got the goods, Ruby, no doubt about," he said to no one as she had already headed up the path. In spite of his satiated state, the boldness of the gesture tickled him a bit down there and he thought wistfully of Ernie Banks. Halfway up the hill, Daniel, still buck naked and still carrying the image of Ruby, made like a mariner and managed to land square on a sharp stone, almost tumbling to the ground. He steadied himself enough to set Golda and his clothes and shoes down before doing the ceremonial ooch, ouch, hip-hop dance, which Golda took great pleasure in. He decided he'd had enough of the nature boy thing and figured that if he was going to put his shoes on he might as well just put his jeans on as well. "Okay, Golda, let's try that again," he said flatly as she stifled a giggle as a courtesy to his pride.

"You're inside me now Daniel and you will be always," she had said, and he mulled over the meaning of her cryptic remark as he began to gather a little more wood for a breakfast fire. Was she referring to the fact that she had cradled his very manhood in her mouth or maybe that a physical part of his person, that tadpole-like elixir that always swam as though life itself was at stake, was literally inside of her or was it inside her in the spiritual sense, kind of an *under my skin* metaphorical thing. He didn't know and suspected that she might elaborate later even as he thought it potentially perilous to ask for clarification.

Ruby, rummaging through her bag for her lipstick and compact with one hand as she ran a brush thru the lost cause of her wet and tangled hair with the other was unwilling to yield the remainder of her time to the representative from the down side even as he became more and more unruly. She was still in a state of disbelief regarding her actions of the last half hour. In rewinding the events, she looked first to the "flashing on the rock" and actually blushed in the privacy of the tent at the thought of her sun-drenched naked body going boldly where it had only gone for the first time moments before and would likely never go again. Daniel had done his part and gazed reverently at her exposure, and recalling that gave her that warm and sensual feeling all over again. "The flashing on the rock," why, it has sort of a religious ring to it, she chuckled to herself but just having heard the "R" word seemed to embolden the muted speaker clamoring for attention. She turned it back again as a flood of images from the encounter washed over the mental landscape and basked unfettered in the glory of the scene while she still could.

Daniel was busy preparing the mornings victuals in his makeshift kitchen and marveled at the fact that "victuals" was pronounced "vittles" and thought it unlikely that Jethro or Elle May would have spelled it that way. He missed the "Word of the Day" and put finding a local paper that carried that feature on the top of his "to do" list. She seems to be taking an awful long time, he thought to himself, wondering what she might be doing and feeling mildly concerned. Whatever his life was or wasn't—and it mostly wasn't he pondered grimly—he reminded himself yet again that he was not plagued by the same type of considerations as Ruby. He wanted, in his naïve innocence, this to be "as good for her as it was for him," but there was little or nothing he could do about the potential fallout this clash of civilizations might impose on her.

The lighting horrible and the miniscule mirror forcing her to address her face in fractional sections, Ruby, ever attentive to her makeup, did the best she could with the tools at hand. With some consternation, she finally conceded that no amount of effort was going to change the outcome considerably. She pulled the brush brusquely through her hair a few more times, and brush still in hand, pushed open the flap to the tent, noticing for the first time the squiggly pattern in the dirt.

"Hey, I liked your other outfit better," Daniel opened the dialogue with a little levity, hoping to break the inevitable tension in their brave new world post intimacy. He suspected, and rightly so it turned out, that whatever else she might be feeling, the universal suspicion that having been "serviced," the male of the species would suddenly revert to form, may well be rattling around her psyche. His hyper-attentiveness having served its purpose, could she expect a diminution, a little less sweetness and just a little more distance. To allay her concern, if indeed there was any, he moved immediately toward her.

Ruby seemed to sense his motive and appreciated the gesture. "Well, I only wear that one on *very special* occasions," she replied coyly, and the two of them laughed nervously, glad to be back in the arena and away from the mordant questions that solitude, even at twenty paces, could provoke.

The bacon began to hiss and sputter, beckoning a grateful Daniel back to his duties. "Ruby, you wanna get the paper plates and the plastic silverware from the back of my car? There should be a bag right inside on the right."

"Sure, Daniel, yeah. Be right back!"

He watched after her and kind of chuckled to himself that he no longer had to *imagine* what that sweet round hinee might look like under her shorts, but the thought that he would likely never see it again either clad or up close and personal dampened his flippancy.

Ruby glanced at her watch as she pressed the button to release the hatch on the wondermobile and felt a touch of panic at the thought that this whole affair would simply cease to be in a matter of hours. The fact that it was taking place in a prescribed amount of time didn't sit well with her, and the advocate sensed an opportunity to cast doubt on Daniel's motives. But she had been an active participant, she shot back. As a matter of fact, it could easily be argued that she was the instigator, so don't go blaming Daniel. But of course, the relentless one would make hay of that admission as well until Ruby finally had had enough. "End of discussion," she admonished herself. "Plenty of time to sort things out later. Now is now and there ain't much of that left." She ran the brush through her drier and thus stiffer hair as she gathered herself and the utensils before shutting the hatch.

BOURGLAY

The name on the license plate loomed large and ominous, seeming to speak to her somehow. Daniel's description of the lonely life of the itinerant stranger had been moving, although it seemed little more than a tragic curiosity at the time of the telling, but now faced with the daunting prospect of having to deal with the rift in her own life, a plight such the strange and lonely Bourglay fellow all of a sudden actually made some kind of sense.

Chapter 69

The smell of cooking bacon dispersed, wafting in every direction and reaching Ruby about midway back to the site, momentarily overwhelming her other senses, and she drew a deep breath to maximize her pleasure. Daniel observed the reaction, mimicked it and smiled to himself at the universal appeal of this olfactory delight.

"When was the last time somebody cooked *you* breakfast?" Daniel asked, moving the bacon to the side to make room for the eggs.

"Gee, I really don't know, Daniel," she answered perfunctorily, settling in next to him and waiting to be useful.

"I think the coffee's just about done, Ruby," Daniel said, and Ruby set about gathering the cups and condiments.

She was dutifully making her way toward the log by the tree that was doubling as a pantry when a lifting fog clarified the image in her mind. It was at least ten years ago on Mother's Day, and as she had awoken, groggy and still wiping the sleep from her eyes, she spotted two figures standing at the foot of her bed holding a tray. She sat up yawning and saw her husband and her son beaming with pride at their creation. It was sausage and eggs, orange juice and toast and a quarter-moon slice of melon rounding out the fare, and they carried their bounty with the loving care of ring bearers at a wedding. Now, kneeling at the bag of cups, she pinched her nose hard between her eyes to banish the thought, stood up slowly and determined not to provide a belated answer to Daniel's question.

Daniel noticed the furrowed brow as she rejoined him but said nothing, focusing instead on trying to keep the yolks intact. "You want cheese on your eggs, Ruby?"

"No, thanks, Daniel, gotta watch the figure, you know." She felt kind of foolish for having made the comment, especially in light of the lavish praise he'd heaped on her physical attributes but her fretting spell was cut short.

"Plates," he said in the same manner that a surgeon would call for a scalpel and no sooner than the request passed his lips, they appeared. Daniel deftly moved the victuals from the frying pan to the plates and apologized with a cautious smile for the fact that the bread would not be toasted. "This is as good as it gets," he proclaimed, trying to up the tempo just a bit and she smiled weakly in response. The pair dined in silence for a time until the void became altogether too large.

"You want to talk about it, Ruby," he asked calmly.

"Talk about what?" she replied unconvincingly.

"Oh, I don't know. Whatever's on your mind, I guess."

"It's nothing, Daniel, really."

"You sure?"

"Yeah, I'm sure" she answered quietly and he let it go at that.

Daniel mangled the soft bread with the hard butter and handed Ruby her slices with an "oh well" shrug of the shoulders. He busied himself for a time with the construction of a bacon, egg and cheese sandwich while Ruby stuck to convention.

"There's just something about dining in the great outdoors," he offered with faux enthusiasm, taking a second stab at bridging the chasm with small talk. "I mean, everything tastes better out here. It's like Mother Nature herself adds some special kind of seasoning to show her appreciation for your having dropped in for a visit." Still nothing. With two strikes in the count, he decided to leave the bat on his shoulder and hold off on swinging at that possible third strike and stuffed his sandwich in his mouth lest any more inanities slip out.

"I'll bet he was harder on himself than the people around him and isn't that always the way?" she offered casually, a tinge of fatalism in her voice, and Daniel perked up immediately. The only clue he had to the person in question was that it was a "he" and he wracked his brain trying to discern just who "he" might be. "I mean, it just doesn't add up."

"What doesn't add up, Ruby" Daniel finally asked, conceding that "as the crow flies" was likely the quickest way to an answer.

"That wandering guy, Bourglay. Doesn't it seem a bit over-the- top to wander alone year after year? I mean, even convicts have sentences that expire at some point unless, of course, they've done something particularly horrible." She paused for a second as a perplexed look crossed her face. "Are you sure he didn't kill somebody, Daniel, maybe his fiancé or how about her father?" she asked excitedly as if maybe she'd solved the case that had been cold for well over a hundred years.

"I honestly don't know, Ruby, except to say that in everything I ever read about him, there's no mention of anything like that. Not even any speculation."

"Then why?" she asked with an urgency that seemed ill-suited to a hypothetical conversation.

There was nothing definitive Daniel could add but the tenor of her entreaty compelled him to come up with something. "It was a different time and place. People had different priorities, different points of honor, *if you will.*" Daniel always felt odd saying that phrase but it seemed to pop out on its own and he could only hope that it had been used properly. "You know, Ruby, it's certainly possible that he was a little crazy to begin with, and whatever the incident was just pushed him over the edge. I mean, if that wasn't obsessive compulsive behavior, I don't know what is," Daniel finished with a nervous laugh as he devoured the rest of the sandwich.

Ruby didn't appear to be overly enthusiastic about the fur trapper's cuisine, the bulk of it still on her plate, having been nudged en masse in every direction before finally ending up in a clump in the southwest corner.

"I'm gonna hit the bushes," Daniel announced suddenly and without fanfare before rising and making his way toward the welcome reprieve of the woods. He had strongly suspected from early on in the discussion that Jules was the beard and that Ruby's disproportionate concern for the long-dead hapless figure was misplaced. It had long been his practice, when he held these suspicions, to gently and patiently probe and prod the real subject matter to the surface lest the narrator take offense at being psychoanalyzed, especially since on more than one occasion he had misread the tea leaves. The problem was that he couldn't be 100 percent certain of whether her theatrical distress was the result of a barely concealed bout of self flagellation or if somehow she was astute enough to have divined the true nature of his own emotional impoverishment and concluded that maybe Daniel did in fact have some deep, dark and terrible secret that had driven *him* into lonely exile.

It took an enormous effort for Ruby to maintain the charade that she'd manufactured in an oblique attempt to calculate how much punishment would be sufficient to ameliorate her tormented psyche without the eye witness seated a few feet from her taking notice. The "Mother's Day" saga reappeared like the proverbial elephant, and she immediately cropped her husband from the picture and zoomed in on her boy; his hair a disheveled mess save for a wayward lick standing tall of its own accord ala Alfalfa; the chocolate icing—a preview no doubt, of some sweet confection that she would be awarded later—adorning his cheek and t-shirt, a swath of a smile that bespoke a confidence in a can't-miss proposition and the innocence, the childish belief that life would always honor and reward such beneficence. It was her job to propagate this illusion and to provide the wherewithal to mitigate against the inevitable discovery of this parental deception. "If you bungle raising your children, nothing much else matters." She'd come across the quote in one of the women's magazines she'd taken to reading when the family fractured and she'd held Jackie Onassis in much higher esteem ever since.

She found herself thinking about Daniel and the brutality he'd been exposed to in the supposed sanctuary of hearth and home, and she was seized by an impulse of fierce protectiveness toward her son. The surge was throttled back a bit when she realized that her son, unlike Daniel, had not so much been in the line of fire but rather had suffered collateral damage by a sin of omission, a kind of changing the rules in the middle of the game. A somewhat more vexing a problem, to be sure, but suffering was suffering and she rallied as she vowed to do whatever *was* in her power to do, and she gained a measure of solace from the fact that they had been a much tighter unit during what are normally referred to as the "formative" years and that at least her boy had had a chance to store some emotional fat to tide him over in the leaner times.

It occurred to Ruby that she was much stronger in this role. While she wavered in the face of self defense, her spine stiffened considerably when it came to her offspring. Her paralyzing doubt regarding what she had a right to expect from her husband—was she demanding too much too soon, had she given sufficient weight to what he had been through, had she made an honest effort to hold up her end, would enough love, patience and understanding finally shift the momentum back toward healing and harmony—all this melted away at the thought of the clear and present danger to her son. The low-grade dread, the persistent gnaw of unarticulated guilt and shame—infections she had been unable to shake—had finally run their course. They did not go willingly; they had to be evicted, exorcized but save for the masochists and the unsalvageable, human beings will at some point reach that tipping point wherein they refuse to continue drubbing themselves and at long last Ruby had had enough.

Furthermore, she didn't care where the strength came from. If it took a nudge from a mysterious stranger that by rights she had no business cavorting with or if it took an impulse, eons in the making, of a mother willing to fight to the death to protect her cub, so be it. Daniel's mother may have exhausted her maternal reserves, but Ruby's tank was full and she was bound and determined not to falter.

An unfettered anger, an anger not diluted by hesitation, an anger toward her husband and all that he had subjected them to was welling up in her and she mocked his *conversion* while at the same time excoriating the clergy that had counseled her to fiddle while Rome was ablaze. All is fair in love and war, she reasoned and she would from this day forward insist, nay demand that he either get with the program or get out of the way and allow them to get on with the business of trying to patch together some kind of life without a cancerous anchor further metastasizing and dooming everyone involved. Ruby, sweet Ruby, it seemed, had found her voice.

Chapter 70

Daniel had concluded midstream that regardless of whether Jules was the understudy for him or her, his approach would be the same. He would fess up about his relationship with the "Leatherman" and let the chips fall where they may, thus, if she *had* him pegged as someone that should that should not be allowed to possess sharp objects, he could temper her perception and balance the picture somewhat. Conversely, if, as he considered more likely, she was struggling with a guilty conscience or distraught at her future prospects, he could share in her burden and maybe convince her that all was not lost.

The stipulation had not been rescinded, and honesty is contagious, he reasoned, a tad smitten with the brilliance of his plan. A little bared soul can go a long way toward disarming the security systems, and who knows, it just might trigger a chain reaction and give her the opening he sensed she was looking for to explore her conflict and hopefully achieve a little clarity. With a plan in place, Daniel began to craft his narrative.

He would tell her about the most difficult point in his life, the most isolated and alienated he had ever been and how he had come upon the story of Jules Bourglay and had adopted him as a kind of patron saint of the disaffected and dispossessed and how

Jules enabled him to sustain for a time the notion that contact with his own species wasn't all that important anyway. How in his despair, he had finally to conclude that his books and his poetry could not in fact protect him and that he knew all along that Simon and Garfunkel never really meant to suggest that they could. He would describe how life had come to seem like little more than an endless succession of failure, pain and frustration and how the notion of ending it all had innocuously entered the realm of notions entertained only to gain a pernicious foothold and systematically silence the appeasers until finally only the thought of how his beloved Uncle Howard would take the news could restrain the impulse. Daniel would go on to explain how the pressure had built until the possibility of the final solution became a certainty in spite of Howard and how he began to set his house in order so as to minimize the mess. He would die like Marat in a bathtub full of water dyed a pinkish-rose color by his spilt blood and he would drop a note in the mail to the county coroner so that his body could be removed and cremated without too much disturbance to his landlady or his neighbors. He would tell Ruby how he almost postponed his scheduled date with destiny to finish reading Ian McKewan's *Enduring Love* but flung the book across the room in disgust only to retrieve it and peruse a few more pages before banishing it from his line of sight by heaving it again. He would tell her how he had doubted the tensile strength of a razor blade and procured a utility knife with the macabre knowledge that it had been terribly effective on a certain September morn nearly a couple of years back and how finally he had drawn the steaming bath and arranged to slide gently down the pelican-beak-like end of the ancient claw foot tub and prepared to do the deed.

Daniel shuddered! It was not, as he first suspected, the little post urination shakes he sometimes got but a visceral reaction to the memories he had dredged up. He knew, of course, that the ending was not so catastrophic as the lead-in might suggest but the memory of what had driven him to consider such a drastic measure dominated this point in the exercise, and he wallowed in that despair for a brief moment until he could extricate his boots from the mud. He stood unsteadily, dick in hand well after it had done its duty, and exhorted himself to continue for Ruby's sake, although he watched a little less dispassionately as the action unfolded.

Still he winced slightly as he recalled that he had discovered too late to ascend back up the steeply pitched porcelain plank that the bubbling cauldron he had prepared was in fact a liquid inferno, and how he had caterwauled and cursed to himself that corporal mortification was not at all what he had intended prior to termination. He was after all simply suicidal, not a masochist.

He remembered imagining his skin would begin sloughing off as a result of immersion in the scalding water and how he felt like he was going into shock, the pain and the imagined trauma worse than any physical sensation he gradually could bring to mind. And he remembered how the fire was gradually tempered in increments by small but sufficient degrees to the point of being mildly uncomfortable, bordering on bearable. And how in his sudden relief, the term he had screamed silently moments prior set him to thinking about the *DaVinci Code* and how much he enjoyed the book even if in the end it didn't matter a wit to him whether there was anything to the notion of the "sacred feminine" and a millennia-long quest to deceive the faithful, one myth being no greater than another in his mind. And how, although initially somewhat dismayed by the fact, he felt soothed and relaxed and not at all of a mind to finish the job. He breathed a sigh of relief and actually laughed to himself as he recalled himself gazing lustily at the copy of *Enduring Love* standing like a pyramid across the room, its page opened, he imagined, to exactly where he'd left off.

The crisis had ended with no harm done. He had been pleased to discover that his skin was still attached to his body, and he was amazed by the mental clarity he suddenly enjoyed. "A thing is not necessarily true because a man dies for it," Oscar Wilde had proclaimed, and although Daniel doubted that he could have envisioned this scenario, he understood. Daniel had created a formula, an equation, a *mental construction* as the guy on the Buddhism tape had called it, in which he didn't make the grade and thus was obsolete. Location, location, location! He recalled with great irony getting a big dose of somber when he realized that it was his choice of where he would do the dastardly deed that was instead his salvation, ultimately serving as the vessel for the baptismal waters in which he would be born again.

His emergence from the tub, while not quite the "eureka" moment that sent a naked Archimedes running excitedly through the streets, had left open the possibility for Daniel to explore this crazy universe in his own small way. And as he stood dripping, he had seen his naked image in the mirror and thought it good and right that he leave the 60 pound leather suit, the penitential sackcloth to Jules. He, unlike his mentor, would take this gift and try to find a way back in.

Chapter 71

Daniel made straight for the coffee pot and asked Ruby if she'd like some as he prepared his own. "Sure, Daniel, I could use a boost." He felt a warmth toward her for the confident tone she'd feigned and decided that the tact he'd chosen was just what the doctor ordered. He didn't see or if he did, he didn't take notice of the sea change that had occurred in his absence and thus could see no need to alter or abandon his strategy. He lit a cigarette as he reviewed the narrative he was about to employ and rehearsed the phrasing in his mind and was satisfied that it was sufficiently inspirational.

Ruby, for her part, reflected on his futile attempts a few moments back to shake her out of her doldrums and began to suspect that he had hatched a scheme to improve upon his prior performance and she felt her own wave of warmth toward her temporary cohort.

Daniel handed Ruby a cup, took a careful sip out of his and began reading from his script. "You may have noticed, Ruby that I either tightened up or got a little flip anytime the subject of Jules came up."

"Honestly, I hadn't,' she answered without solicitation.

"Well, I did," he continued "And since Jules continues to pop up in the conversation, I thought I should share with you the real story behind my fascination with such a lonely and pathetic figure." Daniel glanced up to get a read on Ruby's reaction and was surprised to see not a woman in the throes of despair but one with a look of quiet determination.

"Go ahead, I'd love to hear it," she said in a tone that further heightened his suspicion that this was not at all a damsel in distress and prompted him to do a double take. Something was clearly different, so much so in fact that Daniel could not recall having seen this demeanor in Ruby in all the time they'd spent together, and he knew instinctively that whatever it was had rendered his whole presentation moot. He took a deep drag on his cigarette as he scratched his head and tried to regroup.

"What are you waiting for, Daniel?" she asked, the question an unwelcome prod.

"You won't believe it," he said with an ironic laugh.

"What?"

"I changed my mind," he replied, unable to stifle a nervous giggle.

"You changed your mind!" she answered, giggling right along with him without any idea why.

"When I stepped away a few minutes ago, I was convinced that you were—hmm let's see—well that you were agitated at the very least. I mean, you barely said a word, and when you finally did speak, it was with grave concern for a crazy character that you hadn't even heard of before yesterday. I thought for sure you were distraught about something. I just wasn't sure what."

"You're right, Daniel. I was. But I feel much better now," she replied with a coy air of mysteriousness, and the two of them resumed their goofy giggling still clueless as to why.

"No but seriously, Ruby," he started, but the phrase seemed to provoke even greater fits of laughter.

Ruby made matters worse by clumsily parroting Groucho Marx, tapping an imaginary cigar as she fluttered her eyebrows, a comedic ploy she'd picked up from her husband in the "good-old-days." As the levity subsided, Daniel's curiosity didn't and he pressed her for an answer.

"You want to share with me what was going on, Ruby?" he asked solemnly. He paused for a moment and added, "I'd rather not part with a bunch of loose ends strewn around." The comment seemed somewhat farcical even as it passed his lips as deep down Daniel imagined that no one in the history of the world had ever lived and died with anything other than a bunch of loose ends strewn around much less wrapped up a single encounter of this sort with everything in a nice tight bundle.

Ruby for her part considered the comment to be eminently reasonable even as it failed to establish a heightened sense of urgency, and unaccustomed as she was to anyone being particularly concerned with how events impacted *her*, decided Daniel deserved a thorough airing and set to organizing her thoughts.

Daniel, impatiently waiting for her reply, found himself looking to the final phase of his *plan*, the part where he would provide an opening, an avenue that would serve as a lead in as to why *she* needn't be so hard on herself and figured *what the hell?* "You know, Ruby, truth be told, one of the two scenarios I

448

was envisioning was that you were kicking yourself for what's gone on between us, and after a little soul baring about a particularly difficult time in my life to sort of establish a tone of intimate reciprocity, I intended to suggest that you might consider broadening the definition of fidelity, because if anyone needs atonement, it's your husband."

"Believe it or not, Daniel, I kind of came to the same conclusion myself among others," she replied with a subtle nod of the head to acknowledge his acuity.

Daniel was set to go on but had a sense that she was gearing up to offer an explanation of just what had transpired during the time that he was formulating his master plan.

A pensive look came over her as she tapped out what seemed like a code on her thigh, and after a few false starts, she began. "I knew from the outset that there was something that was not quite right about coming here to see you. But I also knew that there was no way I was not going to come." She paused to gather her thoughts before continuing. "I guess I was aware of the sexual feelings, but before I came here I couldn't allow myself to be too clear about them, and besides I had kind of convinced myself that I could manage them. Looking back, I think I even took it a step further and saw it as an opportunity to prove my virtue, sort of like a challenge to my honor that I could triumph over by resisting temptation or something foolish like that," she added letting out a little sardonic laugh. Ruby sipped her coffee and her eyes fell to the dirt before rising and looking squarely at Daniel. "It's the Catholic way, you know."

"How so?" Daniel asked as unobtrusively as possible.

"I don't know, Daniel. I think they rule by shame, kind of like your uncle said in the story about his mother. They encourage it, and they count on you to practice it. Shit. I mean—oh I don't know what I mean exactly. It has its place I guess, but it seems like it only applies to certain things."

Daniel's mind lunged immediately to the sex-abuse scandals bedeviling the church, the shuffling of the deck with a lethal wild card and the dealing to the various diocese with no warning of the predators they had unleashed in their midst, and tried to recall any demonstration of shame or humility but stopped the train abruptly so as to focus on Ruby.

"It's like my husband can fall down on the job in every way imaginable and somehow I'm the sinner. It's all out of proportion. Anyway, enough is enough. What I'm getting at, Daniel, is that if we'd had this encounter four or five or even two years ago, it would never have gotten out of the parking lot." She looked to Daniel to see if maybe the comment stung but his face told her he understood. "I mean you are a charming fellow and all..." she added breaking the spell of the embittered testimony and the two of them shared a light laugh.

"It all makes perfectly good sense, Ruby," Daniel replied, though he doubted that it needed to be said.

"I have been dreading what I'm going home to face, and believe me I wish it wasn't the case, but I'm not afraid anymore, and I want to settle it one way or the other. To tell you the truth, Daniel, something you said got me to thinking about what this is doing to my son and I found an anger like I've never felt before welling up in me. It was like it took me by the shoulders and shook me violently and made me take a good hard look at what this is doing to all of us, and I knew

450

that I could not live in limbo anymore. I need to do this for my son, and I need to do it for myself. It makes me nervous just thinking about it all, but I have to do it, and I will," she finished with a steely resolve.

The anger rising to a boil and the subsequent diatribe had dislodged a big chunk of the bile that had been poisoning her system for so long, and the release left the whole of her body relaxed, her features softened.

"Well, gee, Ruby, I'm really glad I could help," he said with a self-effacing laugh, mocking the impotence of the rescue mission he had coordinated, and Ruby revisited the surge of warm feelings she'd had a few moments back. They shot a quick reticent smile at each other, and a calm silence fell over them as they recalibrated their thinking about themselves, each other and where they would go from here.

Ruby felt a peculiar gratitude toward Daniel, though she couldn't quite put a finger on it. She recalled her maladroit attempt to describe the attraction to Daniel the prior evening: "I just felt safe with you for some reason that's hard to explain. It's more what I didn't sense, a missing barrier or something, which is why it's hard to describe, and that somehow created a clear path of some sort" she had said, and now she keyed in on the phrase "clear path" sensing somehow that this shelter from the storm had allowed her to peer over the precipice of her life in such a way that convinced her that not only would the jump not be fatal but that in some existential way, not to do so might be. She stole a sidelong glance at Daniel and found herself half regretting what she'd said about what would, or more precisely, what would *not* have happened had the chance meeting occurred four or five years ago.

Daniel did feel a little foolish for having hatched the grand scheme to wheedle the truth out of her but refrained from too harsh a judgment by reminding himself that his heart had been in the right place. He smiled inwardly at recalling her reference to his Uncle Howard's story and considered fanning the flames a bit with a couple of his own poignant observations regarding Church practices but decided it was neither the time nor his place. The mild pang barely registered when she commented on how things would have been different some number of years ago, but Daniel detected it, and it was duly noted that there was more than simply his "animal magnetism" at work here. He chuckled to himself at the thought and was crafting the observation into an anecdote to share with Ruby when he felt as much as he heard her outburst.

"I'll have my shame in proportion to my sin, but there has got to be some balance" she declared suddenly in a literal last gasp, still unwilling to discard the basic doctrine but tempering it in its application to her circumstance. She paused momentarily, and her features were taut, her face a mask of defiance for a brief moment before she donned the relaxed demeanor again. She stood slowly, set aside her coffee cup, brushed off the seat of her pants and extended her hands to Daniel. He quickly abandoned his cup, placed his in hers, and she tugged him gently as a cue to rise and meet her face to face. She draped her arms over his shoulders and buried her face in his neck, her lips, as had become her custom, mere inches from his ear.

"Daniel, I'd prefer that I hadn't done it," she started softly, and before that pang could register, the balm, the extreme unction countervailed. "Or should I say, it would have been easier if I hadn't, but chances are better than good that I'll think back on it many times over the course of my life and relish all of it—especially the taste," she added after a short-lived recess as she corkscrewed her index finger into his abdomen with that impish smile.

Daniel was speechless in his gratitude, forgetting all about what he had intended to say. He felt a special affinity for Ruby admitting that she'd likely tuck the memory away in a secure place and pull it out now and then to cherish the moment. It was, after all, a sustenance that he imagined he could scarcely do without, the occasional deposits in his memory banks whose interest he would siphon off careful not to deplete the principal. He imagined Ruby at Thanksgiving dinner or maybe in church as she genuflected or some such other solemn occasion, a hint of a guilty smile sneaking across her face as she revisited the carnal moment, and it struck him suddenly that he only envisioned her in the midst of plenty. Plenty of family and friends, maybe back with a husband who would surely come to his senses or if not another upstanding fellow that would finally give as good as he was bound to get. This, in contrast to his singular existence save for Golda. He would change that, he vowed, and although past performance as an indicator of future success did not bode well for Daniel, he knew that fretting now served no useful purpose and in fact would detract from one of the rare instances that he had meaningful contact with a fellow member of the species.

"What was the other scenario?" she asked, drawing back and looking at him quizzically.

"Scenario?" Daniel replied, confusing his current stream of thought with her query.

"You said a minute ago that you were considering two scenarios. One of them was that you imagined that I was feeling bad about what happened down by the lake. What was the other one?" she asked again as she sat back down.

Daniel hesitated for a brief moment before dispatching any resistance, feeling that by now it was an archaic mechanism that no longer served any useful purpose. "Well, the other was that you were feeling bad for me, that you had concluded somehow that my life wasn't that much different from Jules'."

"No, Daniel, that never really occurred to me."

"I know that now, but just in case, I had a speech prepared."

"A speech?"

"Well, not exactly a speech. More like a reasoned rebuttal." He detected the confusion swirling around in her head and looked away to recast his response before turning back quickly, engaging her eyes and coming clean.

"I was going to tell you about the time I tried to commit suicide by slitting my wrists in a bathtub," he stated matter-of-factly. "It was part of my plan to get you talking about what was bothering you and to illustrate that whatever it was, there was no reason to think you couldn't overcome it," he added in the same tone. "At the same time, if it was about me, it would serve the dual purpose of telling you that yeah, I've had my rough times but I pulled through and that although Jules and I have some connection, I haven't accepted my fate as a way of life."

Ruby felt "the look" reshaping her features and unable to hide it, she covered her face with her hands to spare Daniel.

"Jesus, Ruby, I didn't go through with it," he proclaimed, feeling like a fool the second he spoke the words.

There was a long and unbearable silence emanating from the mystery behind her hands during which time Daniel's imagination ran wild. What the fuck, he thought to himself. She hadn't even considered the Jules/Daniel scenario until now and it began to look like he might employ the final phase of his narrative after all.

"You're sure, aren't you, Daniel," she spoke suddenly, interrupting his troubled reverie

"Sure about what?" "Sure that you didn't go through with it."

Daniel had taken the question to be a serious one, and it was only when her hands parted like the doors of a cuckoo clock in slow motion, and he saw the whites of her teeth, did he comprehend that she was busting on him and burst out laughing.

Ruby looked at his amusement and was pleased, but truth be told, the unexpected news had grabbed her by the gut and drawn the life from her face, and in a panic she had done what was necessary to mask her horror. She knew instinctively that she had felt that very same depth of despair on at least one other occasion in her life, and her mind had flailed wildly in an attempt to locate the spot that such a malignity could be lodged. She did not believe it to have been her own reaction to any torment she'd ever known because to the best of her recollection, even the worst of times had not evoked so great an anguish.

"Jesus, help me, Jesus" The voice, distant and diluted, called to her and she knew. It was Johnny, mangled and bleeding, pleading, through his agony for the divine intervention that was late in coming that provided Ruby a glimpse into Daniel's soul. That Daniel stood before her with a certain future ahead of him was the not-so-subtle distinction that expurgated the bile and allowed Ruby to begin crafting the silk purse to present Daniel that would pay dividends for years to come.

The implication tucked inside her action, at least as far as Daniel chose to read it, was that his solution though extreme, constituted a perfectly logical response to a world that had not done right by him and that rather than subjecting himself to further pain and indignity, he had opted to simply take himself out of the game. That she seemed to have adopted an explanation other than that he was a crazy, loathsome, miserable wretch that couldn't cut the mustard was not a wholly novel approach to Daniel as he had tried that tact on any number of occasions with some measure of success, but the confirmation of a second opinion went a long way toward cementing the deal. The fact would not ever, of course, become a badge of honor but he sensed that going forward, it was much less likely to constitute the kind of scarlet "S" that he had to take special precautions to conceal.

"You know, Ruby, I've never told anyone that before, and if you had answered any other way than the one you did, I'd be kicking myself for telling *you*, but hey, there is that stipulation," he added with a laugh. Daniel's giddy relief was tempered by Ruby's sudden stoicism, and he fumbled for a follow-up comment to rekindle the jocularity of a moment prior, but before he could untie his tongue, Ruby spoke.

"Daniel, why *did* you try to, you know, to do yourself in?" she asked, not quite able to bring herself to use the "S" word in relation to Daniel.

He paused for a moment as he considered her question. "I guess, I kind of did open Pandora's Box," he answered finally, his giddiness irretrievably lost and his demeanor mirroring hers.

"Daniel, every time you begin to tell me about you, something happens and we end up talking about me." Ruby paused for a moment while she rifled through the catalogue of conversations. "Or you finally get going, and I fall asleep on you—well not on you, Daniel. You know what I mean," she allowed a slight smile to penetrate her sudden change in demeanor. "What I mean to say is that I want to know more about you," she finished with an affectionate poke to the chest for emphasis.

"How much time do we have left, Ruby?" he asked trying not to grind the gears as he shifted.

"Well, it's almost a quarter to eleven now," she replied, the unintentional diversion having shifted her immediate concerns elsewhere.

"And what time do you have to go?" he interjected as she did the math.

"I've got to pick my son up at one, and it takes ten or fifteen minutes to get there, but I really should stop home first and—and get organized," she added, consciously avoiding any discussion of her thoughts of eliminating anything incriminating to be discovered by a curious child.

"How long will that take," he asked, as he imagined her destroying any evidence of her detour.

"Not too long, it's on the way so maybe an extra ten minutes or so."

"So that gives us close to two hours."

"Yeah, I guess that's right, Daniel," she replied with a touch of melancholy, the cold calculation clarifying the end of days with a precision that had hereto-fore been missing.

During the whole of the encounter, they had both had a general sense of a finite resource dwindling toward oblivion, but the stark realization of how quickly it was slipping away was driven home with a vengeance. Ruby moved unconsciously toward Daniel, and he took her by the arm in much the same way a proud father would clasp a beloved daughter's arm as he reluctantly abided his duty and walked her slowly down the aisle to release her into the wild. "Let's head down and sit on the ledge and I'll tell you anything you want to know," he said as they started silently in that direction.

Daniel flinched a bit as a bared root that appeared to be making a prodigious effort to rejoin its compatriots below fell under the already tender arch of his foot. By now it was no longer pain in the true sense of the word, just a suggestion of a tolerable ache that one could revisit at will, just to show who's boss. As they continued on their trek, Daniel wondered if there might not be a better way to spend their remaining time, or at least a good portion of it, other than with him rambling on about the vicissitudes of his life and, for that matter, the strange confluence of events that short circuited his premature death, while Ruby couldn't imagine anything more important than unearthing the inner workings of her temporary suitor and replacing her conjectures with facts, at least as Daniel held them to be.

Chapter 72

The view was predictably spectacular but largely unappreciated as their focus had shifted decidedly inward. The cantilevered rock, although a marvel of geology, left a bit to be desired as the place they would spend the precious little time they had left, and after a somewhat uncomfortable moment of trying to make the best of it, Daniel suggested that he run back and procure the blankets to soften their landing.

"I'll only be a minute," he said before he turned quickly, drew her close and kissed her. Finite lips, he reasoned as he hustled toward the hill, mindfully oblivious of the dull throbbing in his foot and proud of it.

The jaunt up the path left him winded, and with a logic known only to Daniel, that was his cue to reach for a cigarette, that impulse in turn reminding him that there was likely a lukewarm cup of coffee to be had. He moved toward the percolator contemplating Ruby's request, and some quick calculations led him to the conclusion that honoring it without compromising his desire to allow enough time for a proper farewell would require a task no less daunting than distilling *War and Peace* into *Cliff's Notes*.

As he truncated what he had come to believe were watershed moments in his life and pondered the vexing question of just how one describes "despair" without sounding too morose, Daniel felt the slight tug of a concept creating a dissonance with a long-held truth. He had always pegged two incidents — the brutality perpetrated on his mother preceded by the unscheduled departure of his Uncle, the related actions constituting the malevolent magnum opus of his father as well as the date with destiny that stood him up while he lay prostrate in a bathtub — as the "turning points" in his life. It was a given, an article of faith, but the reading of a recent passage in Ian McEwan's *Black Dogs* had planted a seed of doubt in Daniel's mind. "They are, he or at least his character, Jeremy, believed, *the inventions of storytellers and dramatists, a necessary mechanism when a life is reduced to, traduced by a plot, when a morality must be distilled from a sequence of actions, when an audience must be sent home with something unforgettable to mark a character's growth.*

"It's a book for Chris sakes," he chided himself as he poured the tepid liquid into his cup, emptied the sugar packet and opted out of the milk lest it cool the coffee further. Grabbing his cigarettes, he shook his head in mock disgust, chugged the pallid brew and lit up in order to smoke the better part of the cigarette before it was time again for his lines. As he sought the provisions, he made a mental note to look up "traduce" in the dictionary before challenging the right honorable Ian McEwan, thinking it just might shed a whole new light on the paragraph.

"Jesus Christ, I'm sorry, Golda girl," he said, fretting guiltily upon spotting Golda sitting quietly, a half sad-half angry look gracing her little face. With the cigarette dangling awkwardly from the side of his mouth and the curling smoke drawing the moisture from his right eye, he grabbed the blankets, carefully balanced Golda's cage on the heap and turned to make his way back to the ledge.

As Daniel stutter stepped back down the hill, drawing hard on what was left of his cigarette, it struck him that this finite distance separated the infinite chasm between the two universes that he inhabited. The one, a solo rendition, safe if not wholly satisfying, contrasted with the other, a mostly awkward engagement with humanity, fraught with peril but containing the prospect of rewards the likes of which he rarely allowed himself to imagine even when confronted with the kind of hard evidence of possibility this inadvertent interlude had thrust into the limelight. The brief dalliance with Ian McEwan's take on "turning points" had served to remind him of those safe and solitary pleasures that sustained him even as he conveniently forgot that sometimes he despaired that it was all he really had, Golda notwithstanding. That he would be banished once again from the garden in the next couple of hours no doubt added somewhat of a sheen to the allure of the life he was familiar with and made the imagining that much less likely.

"We've got company," he said as he set Golda down gently and positioned the blankets for maximum comfort.

"Hello, Golda," Ruby chirped, sounding genuinely glad to see her and the three of them set about resettling themselves.

Chapter 73

"So tell me, Daniel, what happened? What could have been so bad that you felt like you had to end it all?" Ruby asked in a library voice as if to set a conversational tone that would ensure that the sensitive information he was about to impart was safe from prying ears.

Daniel had been primed and ready to run. He'd even heard the starter's gun, but the consolidation of information was still churning in his mind, and he was unable to settle on a particular etiology. He had reviewed the span of his life in reverse, and like H. G. Wells' time traveler, he overshot the mark and blew past his childhood. Daniel landed in an embryonic state and found himself momentarily pondering the unknowable; how much, if any, bearing his genetic predisposition had on the boy that he had been and the man that he had become before shifting his attention back to events that he had some recollection of. Fortunately, Ruby sensed the bottleneck and rode to the rescue.

"You never did tell me what happened when you got back from Howard and Mark's."

"You remember all that," he said, surprised and grateful for her having settled the matter. Daniel had actually been leaning toward the idea of starting the narrative in his early

462

adulthood, at about the time that things began to fall apart, but he couldn't convince himself that the events he was about to describe weren't crucial to what came later.

"I knew you were fading," he said, "and I wasn't sure at what point the story became a bunch of distant muffled sounds."

"No, really, Daniel, I heard everything up to the point where you'd gone back home, and I think you said they were at least trying to get along."

"Yeah, that's right," he said, impressed that she had somehow remembered to bookmark the conversation before fading to black. Well it didn't work out," he said, stopping abruptly with a laugh as he recalled the paucity of information she'd shared when *he* was trying to get at what was eating her and triggering a spell of the giggles. Ruby looked bewildered for a second, and then it seemed to click. She smiled knowingly before laughingly admonishing him to get on with the story.

"Well, within a month of my returning home, my mother was in the hospital, my father was in jail, and my Uncle Howard, who had come to visit, was heading back to Alabama," he said laconically, suddenly reminded just how gruesome the story really was.

"You know that won't do, Daniel," she said as a gentle prod, and Daniel dutifully proceeded to flesh out the details.

"My parents managed to get through the better part of the month before the ceasefire broke down. It turned out that Howard had given my Mother some money to keep the bill collectors at bay, and during an argument about his lack of effort in getting steady work, she threw that in his face."

"Hmmm," Ruby's utterance suggested that she immediately got the inflammatory potential of the comment.

"Yeah," Daniel answered knowingly with a tilt of the head for emphasis. "You know, he didn't much care for Howard to begin with, and to be told that the only reason we hadn't been evicted was because of Howard's generosity, well, that was all it took."

"How much of what was going on were you aware of at the time?" Ruby interjected, trying to get a better sense of a young Daniel's plight.

"Not much, really. I mean, I didn't know anything about the money but it was obvious even to me that everything was unraveling." Daniel fell silent and pressed his fingers to the corners of his lips like a potter molding a smile onto his face as the word "doubleplusgood" passed through his mind. An Orwellian creation, it was the superlative of choice that Daniel employed when nothing else would quite do. Anyway, Howard had to be in the area on business or something like that and took the opportunity to stop in for a few days. Better yet, my Father decided it was a good time for one of his sabbaticals, and I do remember vividly how excited I was to learn about *that*!"

Daniel looked out across the glistening water and seemingly unconsciously laid his hand on hers. "You know, Ruby, I somehow assumed that Howard had come to fix everything, and I really believed he could," he said shaking his head at his childish naiveté. The natural rhythm of the story, his story, had at least temporarily derailed the ruthless efficiency that he had intended, and he knew it, but this *was* a turning point in spite of what Jeremy said, and although abridged, Daniel was determined to present a sufficient airing to do it justice and provide Ruby with what she had asked for.

"We took a hike down by the creek highlighted by a long talk about *Huckleberry Finn*. It was a revelation to learn how much more there was to the book than I'd managed to discern. Did you ever read it, Ruby? Shit, don't answer that," he added, quickly tugging on the reins and reversing the direction the fond recollection was trying to lead him.

Ruby chuckled at Daniel's sudden about face and stayed silent.

The buoyant lift he'd enjoyed at the mere thought of the hike with Howard faded, and his demeanor shifted toward grave as he felt the pinch of the natural reluctance that accompanies painful revelation, but he swallowed hard and lunged ahead. "We got back from the hike, and I'd gone upstairs to wash up for dinner when I heard tires on gravel and then the unmistakable sound of my Father's truck, and I remember it was all I could do to keep from bursting into tears. I was hoping that he needed something quick—money, food, to verbally abuse my mother—anything that would satisfy him so he could make a quick exit and leave us all the hell alone."

"I'm guessing it didn't work out that way," Ruby interjected.

"No, no it didn't" he replied with a sardonic laugh as he recounted the maelstrom that followed in his mind. "By the time he left everything was damaged beyond repair." Daniel fell silent for a moment, but Ruby's eager gaze prompted him back to the narrative.

"I heard all hell break loose downstairs. Angry, feral noises reverberated all over the house and then a door slammed, and everything was quiet. I ran to the window thinking, hoping actually, that my father had caused the ugly scene and stormed out..."

"It was Howard, wasn't it?" Ruby said plaintively.

Daniel, wearing the same look of disappointment he had displayed on the night of the incident, nodded in the affirmative and continued. "The remaining two picked up where they'd left off with even more ferocity than before. There were more angry words, pots and pans clanging off walls and glass breaking, lots of glass breaking." Daniel stopped cold, and a pained look, a look suggesting profound contempt came over his face. The aversion he had to sharing the next revelation was deep and visceral and would not go willingly from his tongue, but as vile as it was he knew that it had to be told.

"This, this odious bastard had the audacity to imply that he was only trying to protect me from her "fag brother," apparently suggesting with righteous indignation to my Mother that he was only concerned for my safety," he said as if he'd regurgitated, the words. Daniel had been unable to contain the vitriol, and at least for the moment, he didn't care. "Sorry, Ruby," he said sincerely with a voice still dripping with disdain. "

"You've got nothing to apologize for, Daniel." she replied in the soothing voice that Daniel had come to expect, the decency and civility permeating it acting as a natural sedative. He took a deep breath in an attempt to shake loose the enmity.

"What happened then?" she asked softly. "I heard the door slam again, and the deathly silence that followed was actually more frightening than the violent chaos that preceded it. I was shaking even as I felt paralyzed, and for the life of me, I could not stand to make my way downstairs to survey the damage. I finally managed to get upright and over to the top of the steps, and all I could hear was this labored breathing that oozed a whistling sound with each respiration."

It occurred to Ruby that she liked the sound of Daniel's voice. He seemed to her to be a natural story teller. The cadence and timbre felt steady and rhythmic to her thinking, especially considering the painful nature of the content.

What she was not privy to was that this was Daniel's forte, a narrative explored in exacting detail for clues as to when, where and how everything fell apart. A storyline that had been honed to a razor's edge over countless hours, hours that in truth he would have much preferred to have spent engaged in life rather than dissecting it to try to discover what went wrong and how he might fix it. Daniel, who did not include *orator* in any assessment of his strengths or talents, nevertheless, could — in spite of himself and under the proper "laboratory conditions" — be a charming even mesmerizing existential phenomenological historian, skilled in the nuances of the language and seemingly in command of a vast store-house of self-knowledge.

She pushed past the distraction of her musing upon realizing that she had managed to miss the previous sentence completely.

Daniel sensed the disturbance of her attention but plowed ahead nevertheless.

"I tiptoed down the steps, and I could see my mother from the back, standing in a little room off the kitchen. The odd breathing noises got louder the closer I got to her, and I knew it was the result of my father's handiwork, and I was terrified of seeing it. I felt weak in the knees, but I wanted to help, to take her pain away and soothe her somehow and I started in her direction. She turned toward me and then on me, and a wave of hate the likes of which I'd never felt, not even from my father at his worst washed over me, and I was done."

Daniel reached mechanically for a cigarette, the painful remembrance of unnatural maternal repudiation triggering a desire for some kind of oral gratification.

"What did she look like, Daniel," Ruby asked, feeling slightly like a gawker at train wreck but unable to hold her tongue.

"Every bit as horrible as I imagined, an image of the "Hunchback of Notre Dame" from an old black-and-white movie I'd seen flashed through my mind and does to this day when I think about the incident."

Ruby had imagined that the story would include some unpleasantness, but this was out of her realm of experience, and as she imagined the anguish a young Daniel must have felt, she decided that a stiff, if slightly trembling, upper lip was in order. Still, a tear breached her eyelid and snaked down her left cheek before she deftly intercepted it with her tongue.

Daniel caught her in the act but took her swift action to mean that it was a private matter and one that she wanted to keep that way and so said nothing. That a tear had been shed at least in part for him was almost too much to acknowledge, and he jammed the transmission and tried to wrench his focus back on the story.

"He really beat her up," she said, almost as if she wanted there to have been another explanation, an errant pan flung in his Mother's general direction in a fit of rage that just happened to hit the bull's eye, a fall, an unintended collision with a door.

"He beat her to a bloody pulp and broke her mentally," Daniel answered immediately in a monotone that suggested that a part of him had been broken as well.

Drawing hard on his cigarette, he felt a gnawing irritation that this thing was spiraling out of control. That his willingness to give Ruby a ringside seat to the trauma that had shaped him was not just informing her but depressing both her and the atmosphere and this in their eleventh hour, got him to wondering how he might change the karma while there was still time to do so.

He leaned toward Ruby and forced a reassuring smile as if to say that that was then and this is now and in spite of it all that "it's okay, really. I'm still standing."

Ruby seemed to get the intent even if she wasn't completely sold on the proposition, and as she tried to shift the image in her mind away from the terrified child and the gargoyle, a last glance revealed the woman with the Picasso features to be herself and the horrified and distraught boy to be her son.

Chapter 74

He would act unilaterally, Daniel thought to himself. He was satisfied that his motives were pure and that he wasn't simply trying to weasel out of confession, as he found it hard to conceive of something he might share that would put a dent in the esteem in which Ruby seemed to hold him, but he didn't want to go out this way, and besides, this retelling was taking a toll on him as well. He had explored it again almost as an afterthought as he emerged from his recent bout of depression, but that was in the "Phoenix" phase when the dark veil was lifting and there was a distance from the scene that allowed for the kind of clarity that can only be achieved when the emotional component has been rendered inoperable. This felt lousy, and the story didn't get any prettier. Hell, it had already brought Ruby to tears, he reminded himself, and that sealed the deal.

He remembered reading as a kid how Superman squeezed a lump of coal with such incredible force as to condense billions of years of nature's wizardry into fractions of a second to produce a glittering diamond. Daniel had no idea if the author had ever bothered to open a book about geology or if he had simply taken excessive scientific literary license, but it didn't matter a whit. The point was that by some force that maybe as mysterious and unfathomable as the Man of Steel's unearthly strength, Daniel and Ruby had somehow managed to accelerate a years-long process of building trust and intimacy into a span of twenty-four hours, and Daniel would simply not allow the twilight to be tainted. Instead he would engineer a happier ending, a quiet and serene sharing like an elderly couple rocking away on the rickety old front porch, solid in their bond and imbued with the comfort of having managed to somehow pull it off.

"I hate your father," Ruby responded finally, feeling somehow exposed and wincing at the childishness of the comment as soon as it came out of her mouth.

"Well, thank you for that, Ruby," Daniel replied laughing lightly, unsure of what if anything else he should say. He felt a deep appreciation for the sentiment, but it only served to bolster the sense that he needed to follow through with his plan. He paused only briefly as he recalled how terribly effective his last plan had been.

"Ruby, I don't want to do this anymore."

"Do what, Daniel?"

"I don't want to keep rehashing the low points of my life. It just seems like—I mean, it seems to be putting a damper on everything."

A moment's reflection forced Ruby to concede that he had a point, but she found herself fighting a kind of morbid curiosity. He had gotten her hooked on the drama to the point where she'd completely lost track of time, and she was loathe to simply let it drop. It was clear that Daniel had lost some of his zeal for the exercise and that consideration factored into her thinking as well.

Daniel watched as the wheels turned in Ruby's head but he refused to lobby further. After an awkward silence that had Daniel stealing glances at his watch, Ruby came up with the great compromise.

"Daniel," she started in her most persuasive cooing voice, "You can't stop now. You just can't," she repeated for effect. "You have to tell me what happened to your parents and your uncle — then tell me about the bathtub, and we'll leave it at that."

"Fair enough!"

Chapter 75

"My mother's jaw was broken and she had some bleeding on the brain but her body healed in time," Daniel continued as if reading from a police report. "Unfortunately her mind didn't, and after a lengthy psychiatric hospitalization, she was discharged to a "Personal Care Home" where she lives to this day. As I said a bit ago, my father ended up in jail."

"And your Uncle Howard, where was *he* all this time?" she asked with a quiet intensity. She had surmised that therein could be found the silver lining in this whole tragic episode. Ruby had calculated the depth of feeling Daniel had for his Uncle Howard and figured for sure that he must have burst onto the scene on a great white stallion, scooped Daniel up and ridden off into the sunset.

"That's the really tragic part, Ruby," Daniel answered with a rueful sigh that signaled his reluctance to reenter this territory.

"Tell me, Daniel!" she said forcefully, her quiet intensity having found a voice.

"My Father, still half-crazy with anger at the whole turn of events, leveled the same accusations against my uncle that he had screamed at my Mother the night of the incident."

"That he sexually molested you?"

"Yeah, or least that he suspected that it was bound to happen if it hadn't already. I think he figured it was his ace in the hole, the one thing he could come up with that could cast him in a positive light and kind of justify or at least mitigate what he had done to my mother. "

"And they listened to that crazy bastard!!!" she said with a burst of outraged incredulity that left her smiling sheepishly at her imagined transgression.

"Yes, unfortunately, they did. I mean I was questioned and all, and I assume so was my uncle, but no action was taken because there was nothing to it, but the demon seed had been planted and it had a huge impact on everything." Daniel paused for a second before continuing. "And my mother, the one person who could have set things straight, well, anything she had to say was discounted because she was *crazy*. Anyway, the caseworker that had been assigned to me seemed sympathetic to my desire to stay with my Uncle, at least for a time, but the judge that had the final say ordered me to live in a foster home until either my mother was stable enough to take care of me or my father was released from jail to which he'd been sentenced for eighteen months after pleading guilty to the lesser charge of assault. They had actually been talking attempted murder, and I guess his court appointed attorney played the 'fag' card too and managed to get the charge reduced." Daniel chose not to pay any mind to Ruby's poorly disguised look of consternation. After all, this *was* a command performance.

"I wrote a number of letters to Uncle Howard," he continued, "but I didn't know the exact address, and I had to guess at it so I could never really be sure that they were getting to him." Daniel stopped for a moment as if contemplating a vexing question. "Anyway, it would be a number of years before I would find out what had really been going on all that time."

"What finally became of you, Daniel?"

"Well, I never lived with either one of my parents again or my Uncle for that matter," he replied with an odd tone of finality.

Ruby looked taken aback by the thought of so complete an estrangement. There were gaps in the story, and she wasn't sure which of the eighty-four questions swirling around in her head was the most linear. This time, Daniel beat *her* to the punch.

"The agency found me a foster home about an hour from where we lived, and in one of life's great ironies, they put me on a Greyhound bus to make the journey. The driver was given hushed instructions lest I tried to bolt or something and a different caseworker was waiting for me at the other end." Daniel cheated a glance at his watch, duly noted eleven thirty-eight and remembering the old adage that "a task takes as long to do as the amount of time you have to do it in," pegged high noon as closing time.

Chapter 76

Daniel sensed that a deluge of questions was queued up and ready to roll off Ruby's tongue like an assembly line and launched a filibuster designed to keep them to a minimum.

"I ended up being shuffled from one place to another until I finally ended up with an older couple that I actually felt pretty comfortable with, and I stayed with them through most of my high school years." He paused momentarily before continuing. "They were very devout Christians," he added finally. As Daniel reflected he couldn't stop the impulse to digress. "You know, Ruby, the beauty of these people was that they never talked about Jesus. I mean there were the usual religious icons around the house, the praying hands, the statue of the Virgin Mary, the crucifix and of course the picture on the wall of the blonde, blue eyed Jesus that you always see but mostly they just practiced their faith." It registered with Daniel that the comment had been an unnecessary detour and further one that was likely to provoke more questions and he quickly got back on the beaten path.

"My Father's prison term was extended for some type of infraction, and he was released about the time I was starting high school, and just knowing he was out terrified me. I did not want to go back to the craziness, and even though he said all the right things, I threatened to run away or worse if the court forced the issue. He didn't put up much of a fight, and that was the last I saw of him," Daniel added with a disdainful smirk. "Anyway," he continued, "that was the upshot of the night of the broken glass," he said flatly, avoiding the phrase he'd come to associate with the incident.

"What about Howard? You never did tell me when you saw Howard again," Ruby exclaimed, half startling Daniel who'd been preoccupied with the story and the time.

"Oh, yeah. Sorry, Ruby. Well for starters, he never got a single one of the letters I sent. I found that out when I went to visit him after I turned eighteen and was freed from the court's restrictions. My Father, the spiteful prick, had continued to beat that drum and agreed not to pursue custody of me so long as he got a guarantee that I would not be allowed any contact with Uncle Howard. But it didn't matter, Howard was the same good and loving man that he had always been and still." A distant incredulous look came over Daniel, but he continued, "still somehow I felt like an interloper."

He and Mark were as warm and gracious as they could be, and I knew that I'd always be welcome but I felt a certain uneasiness and after a couple of days I was anxious to go home. And that's the really crazy thing, Ruby. I was in turmoil with no idea what I was going to do, and I didn't want them to see that. In spite of the fact that there was literally no place in the universe that I would have gotten more love and support, I didn't want to burden those two with my problems, and in some crazy way, I wanted to know absolutely that they would be there if I needed them, and in my foolishness, I thought I might somehow put that in jeopardy," he finished with a final disgusted shake of the head.

"I wasn't even close!"

"What do you mean, Ruby?"

"I thought for sure your Uncle was going to turn up sooner and…"

"And what?"

She searched for the right words in vain. "I don't know," she said, exasperated. "And save the day, I guess," she finally blurted out.

"You mean like Mighty Mouse?" Daniel asked with a chuckle. "He did what he could, Ruby," he added solemnly.

As Ruby contemplated how things might have been different if Daniel had not been torn violently from the bosom of all that he had known, she imagined herself at that age, suddenly cut adrift from her comfortable and secure universe and felt an icy coldness snake down her spine.

Daniel, for his part was all business. He closed that chapter without a hint of maudlin sentimentality, satisfied that he'd given it all a fair airing. He had described the aftermath of the big bang as requested, and if he didn't go into great detail and extend it out over the next several years, well, time constraints just would not allow it, he reasoned, as he set to plotting out the arc from the foster home to the bathtub via the shortest route possible.

"We're gonna fast track it from here on out, Ruby," he said suddenly and authoritatively. He glanced quickly in her direction but gained no clue as to a reaction. "The next five to six years were pretty unremarkable, and there really weren't any momentous events that you'd find that interesting anyway."

Technically, this was true, he thought to himself, and that was good enough for Daniel at this juncture. Of course, there had been any number of significant events during that span of time but none that could easily be characterized as *turning points,* for lack of a better or at least a different term — he didn't want to revisit that debate just now — Quotidian seemed to best describe that span of time, Daniel had thought when he learned that particular "Word of the Day." There were no scenes that included fireworks or great drama, just the day-to-day struggles of a guy sliding slowly and inexorably into despair, the final tragic result of a steady trickle of abasement, like intravenous Chinese water torture introduced years ago, finally eroding his capacity to fight off the infection.

"I mean life wasn't great during that time but I think it's fair to say that in spite of the chaos, I managed okay," he continued. "I guess you could say that there were old wounds that had never been properly treated, festering inside of me and over time they took a toll on me, and I thought it would make sense just to skip ahead to the point at which everything kind of came apart." Daniel paused for a long moment before continuing. "Because there really wasn't anything that extraordinary that happened to me in those years," he stammered the redundancy and wondered why the hell he tacked it on in the first place.

"How you doing, Ruby?" Daniel asked out of the blue, trying to get a quick read on the pulse of the mood, his as well as hers.

"Good, Daniel, good," she answered convincingly, having moved quickly past her own abandonment scenario. Although just having conceded that more questions weren't in the cards—Daniel's tempo making it all but impossible to slide one in—the burning one had been stoked by the surprisingly sympathetic reintroduction of the religious theme and the tantalizing hint that maybe on some level he actually did believe in something. The good name of "religion" in general had taken a pounding of its own over the course of their encounter, and Ruby felt somehow that the fundamental premise itself was in need of redemption. It had always been a significant part of her life, and she hated the thought that it had been given short shrift, that only the more troublesome aspects had been discussed, and she wanted to rectify that before it was all over. For reasons not altogether clear to her, she wanted Daniel's blessing.

Chapter 77

Daniel surveyed the mental landscape before him and recalled a lonely but bearable existence that, on the face of it, probably wasn't all that different than a lot of the kids his age at the time. He watched a subtle shift taking place in the summer after his first year in Community College wherein the world suddenly seemed tinged much more by the fiendish vengefulness of his father than the inspiring beneficence of his Uncle and how rather than feeling a *little* different than everybody else, which he'd always pretty much accepted—in fact had kind of taken pride in—he'd come to see himself as somewhat of an aberration. And how the few tenuous relationships he'd been involved in came to seem empty and pointless and how finally he'd withdrawn to the point that he had little other than incidental contact with humanity—the "Howard Hughes phase" as he'd come to think of it.

He watched with residual dismay how in a panic he'd mustered all his resources and tried to go the Dale Carnegie route, how life was gonna be good, goddammit, and that's all there was to it. He remembered trying desperately to project at least a reasonable facsimile of what he imagined everyone else was like in a misguided attempt to fit in but deep down feeling like a barnacle trying to attach himself to someone and the disastrous results that ensued. He relived the resentment that he felt at the cruelty his social awkwardness engendered and how in his anger and his pain he had come to see most of humanity as a "mass of imbecile enthusiasms" to borrow once again from the sardonic wit of Orwell, the blanket indictment of humanity a ruse that was hard to sustain because on some level he knew better. He peered through the fog and saw an anguished young man capitulating and reverting to the more familiar and comfortable terrain of books and ideas, a time tested maneuver he'd been forced to employ as a boy by his Father whose derision and ridicule had transformed a rich and rewarding pastime into a shame-tinged surreptitious pursuit. "Alone again, naturally" flitted through his mind, once a familiar refrain that had a particular resonance for Daniel.

Daniel lit up, drew hard on the cigarette and felt an odd sense of relief well beyond that of the nicotine rush, like he'd managed to navigate a hazardous terrain and come out largely unscathed. He was buoyed by that surge of energy one gets when the finish line comes into view and felt a certain elation that this last leg was his strength, the part where things turned decidedly in his favor in spite of the Kafkaesque circumstance that preceded his redemption.

Oddly, the image of Randle Patrick McMurphy, flush with wonder at having been offered a piece of *Juicy Fruit gum* by the supposedly catatonic Chief in *One Flew Over the Cuckoo's Nest* popped into his head and he imagined that his and Ruby's incongruous pairing was only slightly less likely than that of the Joker and the Chief.

He took a drag and turned to look at Ruby, their eyes meeting and locking, and the both of them noticed that this simple act that for a thousand reasons is usually quickly and abruptly terminated seemed comfortable and natural.

"How'd a couple of screwballs like us end up in this predicament, anyway," he finally asked rhetorically, shaking his head at the wonder of it all.

Ruby didn't reply, rather she cocked her head like a curious canine and smiled a wistful kind of smile that said "go figure." And now onto the bathtub," he declared as if bugles would sound as he spoke.

Chapter 78

"It's always seemed a strange phenomenon to me that a human being could actually hate themselves," he started. "It's kind of like a flesh-eating bacteria of the mind that's hard to get control of once it's built up a certain amount of momentum," he added from experience but leaving that aside out.

"I imagine that someone would have to be taught to do that," she replied casually.

"Yeah, I suppose you're right, Ruby," he replied in the same vein but he was struck again by her astute observation of something that he had only arrived at after untold hours of caustic contemplation. He imagined it to be the result of the natural clarity someone enjoys when they can simply comment on what they see but was willing to concede that maybe his "vision" had been impaired.

"Anyway," Daniel proceeded, "I reached a point where my life was a mess and it hurt substantially more than it felt okay. I had run out of people or circumstances to blame, and at some point I had to face the fact that it was me, regardless of whether anyone else had it right or wrong. I suppose that I had always been prone to a certain amount of depression, but this was different and no matter what I tried, I couldn't shake it."

Daniel stubbed out his cigarette and checked himself to see that he was still riding the wave of mild euphoria that had overcome him moments prior. Satisfied, he looked deep into the abyss without fear and dredged up the insight that he had reconstructed in order comprehend just how it was that he could have taken that last drastic step.

"Reaching that point where you can't go on is a complicated process," he continued, his tone cautious and measured as if to suggest that the information he was about to impart was reserved for those lucky, or unlucky as it were, few that had been through the trial by fire and lived to tell about it. "Initially, you find yourself in the throes of a 'bad spell' and you piss and moan while you try to ride it out. And when it holds on longer than maybe you had expected, you kind of think to yourself 'okay, this is more serious than I thought but I've been through some rough patches in the past and managed to get through it.'

He paused to decide if the next sentence was necessary and chose to include it. . "It's of little comfort at the time, but it's at least a foothold on hope," he continued stolidly. "But this anguish is especially tenacious, and it becomes like one of those knots that gets tighter and stronger in response to the same type of tug that releases most others, and the worse it gets, the harder it becomes to buy the notion that that this is just another one of those episodes that will pass eventually like all the rest. A quiet desperation sets in, and you have no idea what the hell to do. You try to function in a 'safe mode' like a computer that's bordering on crashing, and you secretly tinker with your inner workings, hoping that the right command might jar something that will shift the equation in your favor while a part of you worries that maybe an errant keystroke will result in a complete collapse."

Daniel drew a deep breath, hesitated for a brief moment and continued.

"All the while, your mind, almost like it's on a rescue mission, searches high and low in an erratic attempt to track down some kind of relief, but in every direction, it encounters even greater despair, every turn it takes leads down another bleak road that dead-ends in anguish. All neural pathways lead to pain, and it seems there's no way out.

Finally you crack and concede that you can't take it any longer, and for the first time you feel the slightest hint of relief because you understand on some level that if you don't play, you can't lose. It's an extreme solution, to be sure, and initially you reject it out of hand, but you find that in doing so, you sense that the magical pathway to a place that doesn't hurt anymore starts closing up, and now that becomes your greatest fear. So you stop the retreat, and you slowly begin to embrace the unthinkable. It seems unnatural and wrong at first, but each time you swerve, the hurt gets ratcheted back up, and the unnatural becomes natural, and you realize that there really aren't two paths, just the one." —'Maaarrin'—the guttural howling of a young girl relishing the mortal combat of an exorcism jolted Daniel as it always did at this juncture, but he knew it to be a Pavlovian response and paid it no mind.

"And no matter how many times you test the theory," he continued, "you get the same result. Suicide is the only path that gives you relief every time you turn your mind to it and it becomes your salvation," he concluded as if he'd just described how a fouled spark plug could set in motion a series of events that would ultimately shut a car down.

Unbeknownst to anyone, Golda, who imagined that she knew just about everything there was to know about Daniel had listened transfixed and shuddered through silent tears at the thought of how close she had come to never having known this good man.

Ruby had listened intently as well and was preoccupied with some thought that had been triggered by the story. But the subject matter made her nervous and therefore uncertain as to whether her two cents would be worth even that. The judgment that discussing it even from a third-party standpoint would somehow put her in good stead with Daniel by demonstrating her broadmindedness and lending an aura of "normalcy' to the macabre conversation, eclipsed her trepidation.

"We had a lesson in church about suicide," she started after a time, and Daniel groaned to himself. "It was about assisted suicide, actually and why it was a sin and against God's will."

Daniel braced himself for the mini-sermon he was sure would follow.

"The odd thing, Daniel, was that the film they showed was supposed to make the case, but it actually had the opposite effect, or should I say that, well—what I mean is that what you said a minute ago about your life hurting more than it felt okay, well that's pretty much what one the people in the film said. It was a very old woman and she had cancer everywhere and everything hurt, physically, I mean."

Daniel nodded his head to acknowledge the distinction.

"She said something like, 'I had a full and rich life and now I'm ready for the judgment day.' What she got for her honesty was a lecture on the marvels of pain management, but you sensed that if she had her way, she'd have ended it all right there." Ruby seemed somewhat uncomfortable having proclaimed herself at least sympathetic to the Devil's camp. "Anyway, I know the church says it's wrong, but I could see her point," she finished, suddenly recalling the time.

"Same deal," Daniel replied laconically, suspicious that the whole production may have been scripted but grateful for the effort. "It's a very personal decision, and I guess what people are afraid of is that when you take it out of God's hands, there's always a chance that someone else will begin to decide when someone becomes expendable," he added, taking a cue from Ruby and validating her comment with a thoughtful reply. They were meandering now and as pleasant as it was, Daniel was anxious to close the curtain on his one-man play.

"So, yeah, I got to that point at which it seemed that there was only course of action left to me."

"Daniel, did you know from the start how you were going to do it," she asked, moving past the why and focusing on the how.

"Not really," he replied surprised that she'd come up with a question that he didn't have a ready answer to. "I guess I considered a number of things, but this was pretty low tech, and I imagined not horribly painful."

"How close did you come to doing it? I mean, what made you change your mind?" she asked in a hushed, almost reverent tone while suddenly realizing that she no longer felt quite so queasy talking about it.

"I didn't change my mind, really."

"You didn't!" she asked incredulously.

"Well not in the sense that you mean it," he replied, getting that his answer was absurd on its face and letting out an ironic snicker. "It was a done deal, Ruby. I mean, I ran the bath, got my instruments ready and slid down into the tub."

"And that's when you decided to call it off?" she said with a comical roll of her eyes.

Daniel, laughing but feeling a pang of guilt for having strung out the suspense, answered immediately. "What happened, Ruby, was that I had run the bath water hot on purpose but I didn't know just how hot it was. The tub was an old claw-foot type, and I entered like it was a sliding board and once I'd started down that slippery slope—" Daniel paused to consider the likelihood that that's where the expression originated but quickly imagined not—"there was no turning back." He turned his gaze back to the lake and continued as if he were describing the action as he watched it happen. "It felt like I had jumped straight into hell, and I guess a certain part of me figured that's where I was headed anyway," he added, flashing a knowing smile that suggested that their worlds weren't so very different after all.

"Some kind of crazy yelping noise emanated from me, and it felt like I was going to pass out, but I think that rather than actually having lost consciousness, my body just kind of seized up. The pain was so great that I thought that the deed was as good as done anyway and that there wouldn't be any need for the blade, but a funny thing happened on the way to Sheol."

"The way to where?"

"I meant hell," he added quickly, amending the word he'd learned from Mark and not wanting to waste time with an explanation. "Well, obviously, it didn't kill or maim me, in fact even though it seemed like hours then; the lava began to cool in a relatively short period of time."

"And *that's* when you changed your mind," Ruby commented with a smile and a sigh of faux exasperation.

"Yes, Ruby, my, you are the astute one," he retorted with an affectionate dig of his own, before resuming the narrative.

"When my body sensed that the crisis was over, and I began to get my wits about me, the first thing that I did after cursing my failure was to panic because everything looked like I was seeing it through a steamed-up window. I remember thinking that the heat must have boiled the water in my body, and my eyeballs were steaming up!" he added laughing lightly. "Anyway, something significant happened, and when I began to take stock of the situation, I realized that not only did I not want to go through with it, but that I felt a peace and a lightness that I couldn't recall ever having felt before."

"Why do you think that was, Daniel?"

"I don't really know exactly, but I think that it may have been because I not only looked into the abyss, I actually jumped, and as strange as it might sound, there was a perverse kind of courage unleashed in the process, or maybe in letting go, I released a lot of other junk as well." He looked away for a moment while he sorted through the multiple scenarios he'd imagined and ultimately discarded though he kind of held onto the notion of it being like London burning and with it the rats that had carried the plague because he thought it a particularly cool analogy. "The other and maybe more likely possibility is

490

that the hot water had the effect of some kind of inadvertent shock therapy, like a hyper whole-body version of the old systematic desensitization technique people use to relax, but whatever the reason, it certainly did the trick, and if it hadn't, well I never would have had the chance to even ask the question."

"That's some pretty potent bath water," Ruby interjected.

"No shit, huh! I don't see any reason to believe that I wouldn't have gone through with it, if it hadn't been for dumb luck." He paused for a moment and looked over to Ruby to watch her reaction. "It did occur to me that maybe my guardian angel intervened and made sure I wouldn't finish the job." The comment seemed transparently provocative, and Ruby wondered for a nanosecond if Daniel hadn't somehow picked up on her thoughts.

"You rat!" she blurted out playfully as she seized the opportunity to get physical with Daniel by half tackling him and ending up with her head on his chest.

Golda was ambivalent about rats and so took no umbrage at a member of her phylum being used as a derogatory term.

In the mini-frenzy she'd stirred up, Ruby further took the opportunity to deftly interpose the question that had been bugging her for the better part of their adventure. "You don't believe in guardian angels. In fact I'm convinced you really don't believe in anything."

"Sure, I do," he replied in the light-hearted spirit that the subject had been broached. "I'll get to that later," he added.

"Daniel, we don't have much *later*," she said in a much more serious tone.

"One thing at a time, Ruby. You wanted my bio, and the least you can do is let me wrap it up properly," he protested sincerely, but grateful for the out.

"You're right, Daniel, you go ahead," she answered, trying to keep the "curses, foiled again" tone from contaminating her words.

Chapter 79

At long last, Daniel had reached his place in the sun. Unconsciously, he'd been harboring a secret excitement at the prospect of describing his liberation, in part because there was no possible way to embellish the downward trajectory that preceded his crash landing, but the aftermath, well that was another matter. But having arrived at this juncture, he felt a bubble pop in his brain, and when he organized the words strewn around, he understood why that would have been and how an intervening variable had altered the equation.

Some years ago, Daniel had constructed though never employed his own little creation story to preempt the disrepute he would surely suffer should his near fatal flaw ever see the light of day. Yes, there was a terminal despair in the run up to the ultimate negation, but he had dodged the bullet and proceeded to embrace life with a newly discovered vigor, or so the story would go. Why, describing his new lease on life would almost certainly be as inspirational as it would be dramatic, no less than a profoundly articulated exclamation point to the triumphant resolution of his personal Armageddon. He would quote Sartre: "Freedom is what you do with what's been done to you," he would proclaim, and he would talk about how Viktor Frankl had inspired him with his story of survival and redemption, and so compelling would be the telling that all that preceded it would be forgotten in a final blaze of *glory*, and then he remembered. He remembered that it was shame that had spawned the fabrication of the epic tale, shame that he would hide in plain sight by adorning it with the trappings of a heroic conquest, shame that had to be banished lest he encounter 'the look.'

He suddenly felt a great clarity and with it a deep appreciation for his new friend, and he imagined he might retire the phantasmagorical tale forever. It seemed, for now at least, that there was no longer a need for it. After all, there was a woman with her head nestled on his chest that seemed to think he was a pretty okay fellow, and who knows, she may find his story to be extraordinary in its own right. Hey, there's nothing I can do about that, he thought to himself with a mock solemnity.

Daniel's mini-epiphany had chewed up some clock, and Ruby was on the verge of breaking the silence when he spoke. "You remember the author I quoted last evening, the line about 'loping carefree toward the orange dawn'?"

"Ian Mc something wasn't it?"

"Yes, Ian McEwan. Well, a couple of weeks after the incident, I was reading another book of his and in it he refers to life as 'the brief privilege of consciousness,'" the phrase, even now so concise and so powerful that it gave him pause. "And I cried for two hours at the thought of how close I had come to throwing it all away, and ever since then, no matter how shitty things are going, I try to remind myself of that," he finished, wrapping it up as a mother would a bed time fairy tale, the soft clap of the closing book formally confirming *The End.*

They had begun this portion of the program eschewing the temporal world and puttering around an old musty attic. Rumor had it that the place was haunted, and as Daniel pushed aside the cobwebs to allow for a better view, Ruby did indeed detect a spectral presence lurking ominously, though silent and invisible. The tour, though not grand was pretty damn good, and although it didn't completely sate Ruby's appetite for information regarding Daniel, it would have to do, she reasoned as she rejoined Daniel in a sweet languor, sensing suddenly that this intimacy was a kind of knowing that words couldn't enhance. "You know that peace and lightness I told you about a minute ago, Ruby?"

"Yeah."

"Well, I'm feeling it again right now."

"Jesus, how am I going to say goodbye to you, Daniel?"

Chapter 80

Daniel stroked Ruby's hair gently and turned his gaze to the vast blue sky, studiously avoiding his watch while Ruby seemed to find an equal expanse in the fabric of Daniel's shirt, and for a time, they managed to disregard the pea beneath the mattress, but reality being the intrusive prick that it can be, would keep agitating until it got the recognition it demanded.

"I could stay here forever, Daniel," Ruby lamented in a voice barely above a whisper.

"I know, Ruby," Daniel replied, and on cue, they grudgingly began a simultaneous disengagement.

While Daniel retrieved Golda, who was frankly baffled by the subtle pall of disappointment, Ruby gathered the linens and by force of habit had them folded and stacked neatly in what seemed like a matter of seconds. They stood in awkward silence for a moment before shuffling their cargo and kissing softly.

"You go first," Daniel commanded chivalrously, and after a few final pecks for good measure, Ruby turned and headed toward the campsite. Daniel stayed an extra step behind and displaced the weight of finality momentarily by admiring that supple round hinee. "You certainly do have the goods, Ruby," he reprised the comment that followed the "flashing on the rock" and Ruby, too, managed to forget briefly that a most unusual era would soon come to an abrupt end.

Their ascension of the hill seemed longer and more arduous than either one of them recalled, and although they both attributed it to fatigue, each knew better, and the two of them hit the level terrain feeling tentative and torn.

Ruby rubbed her abdomen as if she could massage away the pang as she flashed back to family vacations with grandparents and cousins and aunts and uncles and felt the sudden overwhelming sadness that always accompanied their inevitable parting, and it occurred to her that at least then they could look forward to a reunion in the not-too-distant future.

The amount of traffic speeding through Daniels head was an indecipherable blur, and so he began to busy himself with the task of breaking camp. "Ruby, would you mind getting the stuff together in the tent?" he asked having taken note of the efficiency with which she'd handled the linens down on the cantilevered ledge.

"Do I really have to?" she said, willing a smile and bringing one to Daniel's face.

Campsite etiquette may well be written down somewhere, but it simply made sense to leave a gracious Mother Nature's domain in essentially the same condition you found it, Daniel thought to himself mechanically as he gathered the cooler, the percolator and the various and sundry items strewn about the site and stacked them in a tottering heap at the mouth of the path back to the cars. He heard Ruby rummaging around in the tent and wondered if he had time to urinate on the medium rare embers of the faded fire but chose not to risk her popping out prematurely and relocated his business behind the nearest tree. Better that she remember *that* portion of his anatomy as the *wand* on which she'd worked her *magic* rather than a mere pressure relief valve in the service of his bladder.

Noting the lack of movement in the tent, he wondered briefly if all was well and headed over to check on her progress, halted for a moment along the way by the vivid recollection of her "aborted strip tease." Ah, the good old days, he mused with a touch of melancholy, struck by the notion that they actually had a *history* and by the fact that in the future when he would wax nostalgic about the memorable times — of hikes and books, of clandestine moments in the bunker with his mother, of breakfast in the diner with his all-time favorite waitress — any number of events from the last twenty-four hours would be added to that pantheon of bittersweet recollections.

Ruby, too, felt the pull of history, albeit in a very different way. As she navigated the enclosed space and tended to her chores, she had the odd sense of revisiting the old family homestead and more specifically, the room in which she'd done the better part of her growing up. It was unlike any other space in the world precisely because it reeked of all the attendant events that comprised her personal history. And yet, somehow, she had a similar sense in this Lilliputian realm, a sense that numerous events big and small had taken place here. Not just a "day in the life" kind of thing but a kind of geological change, like the warming after an ice age perhaps. Daniel's 'knock' on the flap ruptured her reverie.

"How you making out, Ruby?" he asked, scanning the interior and noting that everything, save for the sleeping bag, which was positioned with engineered precision in the dead center of the tent, was impeccably folded, neatly organized and laded by the flap.

"Sit down with me, Daniel," she instructed him gently, figuring that the answer to his question was self-evident and he obeyed, ensconcing himself next to her on the sleeping bag, careful not to disturb the equidistant placement of the bag. He felt oddly disoriented, at a loss for words and mildly concerned about it.

"Where *will* you go from here, Daniel?" she asked after a time.

"Oh, I suppose I will lope carefree toward the orange dawn and on into the next day. Who knows," he answered with a strained levity that Ruby detected. "Seriously though," he added as he chastised himself for wasting words and thus time on yet another glib response.

"You're as nervous as I am, aren't you Daniel," she interjected with a knowing look.

"Nervous, hmmm, I don't know about nervous," he replied, acknowledging that she was on to something, he just wasn't sure what. "Agitated may be a better word. I don't know. There's definitely something stirring. I mean, you don't find yourself in this kind of situation every day, and there's something unnatural about just walking away from it." He paused for a moment in a futile attempt to interpret his symptom. "What the hell would B. F. Skinner say," he finally blurted out with a wry fatalism.

"I guess that what makes us adults, Daniel," Ruby retorted with a laugh, glad finally for having taken Psychology 101 in her junior year of high school.

"Yeah, dammit, I guess so," he answered with a puerile grin, feeling a little like the Three Stooges, unsure of just whom the butler was referring to when he summoned the "gentlemen." Still, the simple acknowledgement of a fly in the ointment served to center the both of them. "It's all been kind of surreal, and now that it's winding down, it's kind of coming into focus," he said stolidly.

Ruby nodded a ditto. "How *do* you properly end something like this?" she asked rhetorically, and Daniel, his index finger over his lips as if he were requesting silence, shook his head in agreement.

"I guess we'll write the rule book, you and I," he added finally.

"Seriously though, what, Daniel?" It took him a second but he caught her meaning.

"What I started to say was that sometime over the last twenty-four hours, the idea sort of crystallized that I should go to the banks of the Mississippi to say a proper goodbye to my Uncle Howard, and if my calculations are correct, I don't have too far to go to do that." He paused for a second. "After that, I guess, is when I'll start loping," he added slipping Ruby a sly smile., "But as to where, at this point, I don't have the foggiest idea."

"Well, you know where I'm going," she said with an intended lack of enthusiasm.

"I wish you luck with that, Ruby," he said softly, taking the liberty of rubbing her arm.

"Daniel."

"Yeah."

"Please don't take this the wrong way but why is a smart guy like you delivering furniture for a living?" she asked, unable to resist the impulse to fill in just a few more blanks before time expired. Daniel appreciated the way she had phrased the question, the "smart" part taking the sting out of the under-achiever implication.

"Well, it's honorable. I'm not on the commerce end, or the credit end or the hard-sell end. I just deliver the goods." Daniel paused for a moment before continuing, a smiling Buddha extolling the virtues of "right livelihood" flitting through his mind. "At least that's how I've come to spin it so I'm not too bothered by it, but the truth is that I have what you might call rolling blackouts."

"Meaning what exactly?"

"Meaning that I can't trust my brain because under certain conditions, I just go blank, and well, what do you say we just leave it at that?" he finished, knowing that a full answer or the more likely bumbling attempt at one, would gobble up most if not all of their remaining time.

"Okay, Daniel," she replied, having considered and decided against sharing that she *just knew* that someday he would be able to show his wares, fearing it would sound trite or even patronizing.

"You feel ready to tackle what lies ahead?" Daniel asked, wanting to acknowledge her burden without drawing attention to the fact that no less than the salvation of a marriage was at stake.

"I don't have any choice in the matter, Daniel. It's my marriage, my family, and I have to try to set it right," she said with a quiet intensity."

"You have to or you want to?" he asked reluctantly.

"Both," she averred unequivocally. She halted momentarily seeming to hold a thought in abeyance. "Not at any cost, but I made a pact and I have to see it through," she added, a tone of fierce determination in her voice, the kind that always made Daniel feel just a bit weak and squishy somewhere deep inside.

"I understand, Ruby," he replied, suddenly feeling awkward at their still being intertwined physically.

Ruby answered him by clinging harder to him, raising up and kissing him gently. "Daniel, that's an iffy proposition at best. I will do my best to make it happen, but there aren't any guarantees. This, on the other hand, this is real and solid right now, and I'm gonna enjoy every last second of it."

Daniel, no spoil sport he, could find no grounds on which to object, and the two of them tried desperately to forget the manic ticking of the clock. They studied each other in silence, touching, exploring, both lost in thought and both focused intently on the other.

Daniel pondered her dilemma, her dysfunctional marriage, and the failure of her faith to provide solutions, and it occurred to him that in each instance there was something concrete to repair, a logical starting point, a conflict with a flesh and blood human being that could be held to account on the one hand and a faith shaken and in need of bolstering but unchallenged in its core assumptions on the other. This in contrast to his dilemma of dabbling on the periphery, not bound or committed, nothing embraced to tinker with or improve upon, in short, what he had come to think of in his darker moments as his "hypothetical life."

Kenny and Wanda dropped in unannounced, and he pondered their odds long-term and imagined them at 60/40 at worst. It seemed to work for them because as Kenny said, "It was worth the trouble." Only time would tell if that would be the case for Ruby and old whatshisname.

Still, all this speculation about longevity triggered something in Daniel, a severe protectiveness toward his solitude. For all it left to be desired, it was, he thought, his natural state, the state that he was drawn to, the one that he always felt himself longing for when he spent any length of time in the presence of other people. Daniel sometimes likened his need for human contact to be like that of a snake that gobbles down a huge meal and is sustained by it for the next three months. This wasn't by design nor was it a matter of personal preference, it was simply the way it had come to be, and he had gotten comfortable with the arrangement in spite of the gnawing suspicion that there was an element of pathology to it.

Ruby's mind found its way back to the pressing riddle that had been hinted at any number of times but never solved, her inability to pin Daniel down on just what he did believe. The issue had been a matter of burning curiosity a mere nine or ten hours ago, and what struck her now was how little it mattered and how little it seemed to bear on anything to do with her and Daniel.

Ever since he'd managed the subtle evasion when the subject had been touched upon the previous night, Daniel, for his part, had assumed that that wouldn't be the end of it. Somewhat more troubling was the fact that he had knowingly stoked the furnace with oblique references, each passing comment coupled with the question of why he yet again insisted on inciting her further.

The simple fact was that he had no answer. He thought a lot about a great many things, but the parts did not seem to constitute a cohesive whole. Deep down he sensed and hoped that he really wasn't all that different from most people, maybe just a little more honest about it, and he had encountered scant little evidence to dissuade him from that notion. It was tempting to finger Ruby's faith as the main culprit in the havoc that had been wreaked upon her life, but that, he conceded, would likely have been a gross oversimplification. Furthermore, it was not in his nature to kick someone when they were down, and he was loathe to be too presumptuous about how good or bad a thing it had been in her life.

Still old habits die hard, and if pressed, Daniel had decided he would plead confusion when it came to spiritual matters — that part would be the gospel truth — before working up his most earnest expression and engaging in a little personal diplomacy.

"I think maybe it comes down to faith and trust, and I have a serious shortage of both!" he would start before pausing to reflect. "Maybe if I get better at those things, it will make a difference," he would conclude, thus putting the onus on his deficiencies as a human being and off of what might be perceived as a general renunciation of the whole idea. The great irony, he realized, after hatching yet another master plan was that it might just be true!

But the ambassador's services would not be needed during this part of the junket as it occurred to Ruby that in all likelihood, it was her own dented faith that was driving her curiosity. That coupled with her disquieting suspicion that she would not find his reply comforting, no matter how tactfully conveyed, led her to conclude that it was probably best to get the jalopy into the body shop lest it sustain any more damage in transit.

"Not at any cost," she had declared with conviction a few short moments ago, and now the vexing question of "at what cost, then?" had hemorrhaged into her psyche, displacing altogether any and all matters of faith.

"You've ruined everything," Ruby whispered, the flat intonation hinting at an absence of malice and little else, leaving Daniel free to ascribe motive. He toyed briefly with the notion that she blamed him for leaving her forever tainted, for luring her down the road to perdition and despoiling her, but that was mostly from the standpoint of how he would have reacted in lesser times when his self-hatred was more prodigious and indiscriminate.

"What do you mean, Ruby?" Daniel replied, concerned and not at all sure what to expect.

"What I mean, Daniel, is that my marriage is a mess and before this—this engagement, maybe I would have been satisfied with just a little bit of kindness and communication, something that kind of resembled an ordinary relationship, but I want more now. I want it to feel at least a little bit like it's felt with you," she answered, unable to purge the tinge of melancholy from her voice.

Daniel, his vanity tweaked, stumbled momentarily before gathering his thoughts and crafting a response. "I don't know, Ruby. Jesus, I mean, you'd be wise to look at this whole thing with some distance and consider the circumstances."

Ruby drew back and looked Daniel square in the face. "I'm not a dumbbell, Daniel! I understand that this situation has been special for a million reasons that couldn't be replicated in a million years, but that's not really what I'm talking about."

"Then what *are* you talking about, Ruby?"

"I'm talking about a basic respect and consideration. I know that's vague, but well, maybe a little tenderness, the desire to lighten the load for the other party once in a while, the kind of affection that you described between your Uncle and his friend—Mark, wasn't it. I don't know, Daniel. I mean sure, some passion now and then would be great, but I just don't think that's possible without the quiet stuff. You know what I mean?"

"Yeah, I do, Ruby. You make a lot of sense."

"See, there, Daniel!!! A dumb little thing like that. I can't remember the last time anyone said something as simple as that to me."

"You make it easy, Ruby!"

She responded with a bewildered "how so" look.

"I am getting accustomed to the kudos for saying or doing the right thing. I will miss that about you"

"Yeah, well," she said cryptically while she rubbed his cheek as if there was a genie awaiting his cue.

The exchange had silenced the ticking of the clock, and Daniel had managed to duck around the corner and achieve the impossible, forget momentarily about Damocles sword.

"I've really got to go, Daniel," Ruby said quickly as if tearing a Band Aid from a wound." There would, no doubt be a curtain call, but she felt that someone *had* to do something to signal the festivities were nearing their inevitable conclusion.

The speed with which the comment was made allowed it to slip past Daniel's formidable defenses, and it felt as if someone had reached inside him, grabbed him by the entrails and squeezed with all their might, although he tried to appear stolid in spite of the chaos in his gut. This really is it, he thought while he tried to figure out how he could have been caught so completely off guard.

"You okay, Daniel?" she asked, taking the suddenly dazed look to mean that something was amiss.

"Yeah, yes, I'm fine," he answered with a white lie, determined to follow Ruby's lead in forcibly evicting the gremlin that would dare to taint the final cherished moments.

"I hate to, but I do have to go," she repeated as Daniel struggled to find his voice.

"Just five more minutes," he said sounding like a teenage boy, her teenage boy, she thought with a little burst of affection, beseeching his mother to allow for another couple of hundred winks.

"How about ten," she replied with a laugh, cuddling up with him as if to share in his extended slumber.

"Daniel, set that little alarm in your watch for ten minutes from now and let's"—she paused for a moment—"let's stipulate that when it rings or buzzes or whatever it does, we'll both honor it and do what we know we have to do."

"Agreed," he replied as he dutifully raised his arms up above her back, squinting from the perch of her shoulders as he set their destiny for ten minutes hence only half hoping that it was in the mood to cooperate.

"Did you ever read a book that was riveting from the first word to the—well almost to the end and then it just kind of fizzled out, and all you could think of was what a disappointment it was?" Daniel asked.

"Geez, Daniel, I don't know. Why do you ask?"

"Aw, I don't know. I guess because I think it's important to finish strong."

Ruby tugged the hair at the nape of Daniel's neck while she considered the proposition.

"Now don't you go jinxing us, Daniel," she said suddenly with an exaggerated alacrity, and the two laughed easily.

They had at least momentarily retaken the high ground and commandeered that certain lightness in the air in spite of the gravity of the pending alarm, and the two rocked gently in each other's arms as if slow dancing to a sad song in the gym with the lights down low, a pleasure that to Daniel's dismay he had never actually experienced — until now.

"Wanna hear something odd, Daniel"

"Sure, Ruby. What is it? "

"Well it seems like the kind of thing you might say, but it's kind of strange that I'm holding what I can't have, like you're mercury or sand that's just going to slip through my fingers no matter how hard I try to hold on."

"Very interesting, Ruby, and yeah, it does sound like something I would say," he replied, vaguely recalling that the mythological Mercury had been the God of travel, among other things, and sharing that tid-bit with Ruby as it seemed apropos.

She mulled that over for a moment while Daniel marveled at just *how* well she had come to know him and he her in their brief stint.

"I guess, technically that wouldn't be totally correct," she continued, grabbing Daniel's attention.

"What do you mean, Ruby?

"Well, my guess would be that I *could* have you right now if I wanted to," she said with a dastardly smile as she drew her head back and thrust it forward, going forehead to forehead with her confidant.

"I swear, you're a pistol, Ruby," Daniel exclaimed, laughing deeply and unabashedly, tickled by her playful lechery. His pleasure compounded hers, but the intimate frivolity stalled quickly as the both of them realized that the eloquent convergence that had taken place was fading to black, that they had rendezvoused at that rueful intersection of desire and discontentment, and the tent suddenly took on an elegiac air.

Daniel got caught stealing a glance at the ticking time bomb, and Ruby demanded that he share the booty. "A little more than five minutes," he informed her grimly.

Technically it was more than the normal amount of time left when the pronouncements of the doomed burst forth from deep within because there would literally be no more opportunities, but unlike in an airplane screaming headlong toward its ignoble demise, they had selected the moment of their termination.

"I don't know what to say, Ruby, but it's been a wonderful time," he started feeling far less than eloquent. He felt a profound affection, a deep gratitude and a whole host of other sensations that he didn't quite know how to translate it into words. He thought about a simple "thank you!" but he thought it hokey and somehow off the mark.

"You've been remarkable, and I have to tell you that even though I can't say exactly how, I'll take something very good away from this whole thing that will be with me forever," Daniel said finally, concerned that his wording sounded contrived, but he knew it to be the truth and so let it stand.

"I don't think I'll ever look at the world in quite the same way again," Ruby replied, afraid that the timing would suggest simple reciprocity, but she too knew it to be the truth, though Daniel's sudden laughter gave her pause.

"Ruby, I don't deserve it, honestly. I'm just a furniture delivery guy and a part-time vagabond," he said, shaking his head at the remark and all that it implied, feeling humbled and dumbfounded by his good fortune.

"Don't be so hard on yourself, Daniel," she said in a pained voice, pulling back and giving him a stern look. Under normal circumstances, the comment would have constituted little more than a casual throwaway line, well-intended but with virtually no power of enforcement: Take it easy, take care, hang in there; hey, you know, that sounds like a plan! But this mild rebuke actually had teeth because in some mysterious way, he would in truth ease off ever so slightly.

"Okay, I won't," he replied with a "funny you should say that" kind of laugh without even trying to elaborate. He just leaned forward and kissed her gently before drawing her face back to his shoulder and stroking her hair.

Ruby rejoined the embrace wholeheartedly and snuggled up as close as was physically possible, caressing and kneading whatever parts of Daniel she could reach.

"Daniel."

"Yeah, Ruby," he said fearing the worst.

"I'll take over for your Uncle!

Daniel, bracing for the final farewell and ready to point out that the watch had not yet spoken, did not immediately grasp her meaning.

"I'll wonder about where you are and what you're doing... I'll worry for you," she proclaimed solemnly, and Daniel, the self styled literati, the wordsmith even if his primary source was the "Word of the Day," was speechless, his Adams apple, it seemed, swelling to the point that it felt as if it would burst from his neck.

Ruby sensed immediately that her fearing that such a suggestion might constitute a blasphemy of the highest order was unwarranted. She didn't know what he was thinking except that it was good, and she noted with a certain gratitude that his visage bore a striking resemblance to the stunned look he'd had in the parking lot of the Food Lion upon the inadvertent exposure of her most private area.

"Christ, Ruby," he finally managed to mutter as a notion that he'd toyed with off and on over the last twenty-four hours or so picked up almost enough "ayes" to push the legislation over the top.

Whether Ruby had taken Daniel's dictum about finishing strong to heart or the spirit simply moved her, the end result was the same. She began her fervent dash toward the finish line by going directly after Daniel's jugular, the ear, and all matter of discussion regarding pending legislation was tabled. Ruby smothered him with a passion tinged with desperation. She gorged herself, moving from his ear to his lips, finally taking his tongue with such force that it seemed that she might simply devour him.

Daniel for his part was a willing subject, and if it had been humanly possible to merge at that moment, he would have taken the plunge. A barely noticeable tic, a nanoseconds hesitation prompted Daniel to raise an eyelid a fraction only to discover tears streaming down Ruby's face. She knew he knew and proceeded to come clean.

"I cry at funerals and goodbyes, Daniel. I always have and I suppose I always will," she said without so much as a hint of embarrassment.

"It's okay, Ruby. To tell you the truth I'm honored."

She sniffled a laugh while she gathered herself.

"If it wasn't for my son, I'd go with you and I wouldn't take no for an answer," Ruby proclaimed, rallying past her melancholy.

"That may well change everything, Ruby,?" he replied without hesitating or committing for that matter. She patted him on the back as if to say, good answer, and the two shared a doomed smile.

"And then I'd seduce you and hold out on you until you told me everything I want to know about you," she added with a muted version of that devilishly endearing laugh, and the raucous reaction in the chamber signaled that passage was a foregone conclusion. And as if to signal the end of recess while the ball was in mid-flight, the bell tolled.

Chapter 81

There were a million good reasons not to divulge such classified information, some mildly Machiavellian and some magnanimous and born of concern for the common good. By any objective standard, the encounter had been a resounding success, so much so that Daniel had actually begun pre-nocturnal planning of the design of the museum that would house the abundance of cherished memories borne of this inadvertent tryst. To walk away now would leave that legacy wholly intact and still allow him to root from afar for his friend in all her endeavors, never knowing the outcome but confident that she possessed the right stuff to navigate the perilous path she was about to embark on. At the same time, he would be safeguarding her perception because as he well knew, if history was any kind of barometer there would be no shortage of bumps in his road ahead.

Daniel was certain that it would never be quite so dramatic as his brush with his own extinction, but there was no way of knowing how frequently he would encounter that black dog. No, this was a no-brainer, a slam dunk, as a renowned intelligence analyst would proclaim, turning the phrase upside down and shaking the verity from its pockets like so much loose change. So maybe it wasn't a slam dunk after all. Maybe there *was* inherent in the notion, something born of fear and loathing, two of the more influential themes shaping Daniel's cognitions. Daniel had learned *never* to rule that out. But there was a countervailing force at work here, one that had been tugging at EXCALIBUR with greater determination with each passing moment of their union, and somehow the precise wording of Ruby's last comment provided the boost needed to settle the matter once and for all.

"Do you have a computer?" he asked, unable still to wholly squelch the reluctance seeping into his voice.

"Yes, Daniel, I do. Why?"

"Well, I thought maybe I'd give you my email address and I could, you know, well, I could try to answer some of those lingering questions," he said, noting a spike in his blood pressure as soon as the words passed his lips.

"Gee, I don't know, Daniel," Ruby answered dolefully, the inauspicious reply catching Daniel completely off guard and sending him into a tailspin.

"I mean, I really like the idea," she continued, drawing Daniel back from the brink. "But," she paused to sift through her thoughts. "Daniel, I was halfway out the door of your life forever. I hate the thought of closing it, but I'm already gearing up for trying to fix my life." She pressed her fingers against her temples and watched the conflicting impulses ricochet around her brain. "I don't know, I don't know." She took a deep breath and looked hard at Daniel. "Please don't take it the wrong way, Daniel. This whole thing has been—well, I'm not sure that 'extraordinary' begins to describe it and…"

"I understand, Ruby, really," he replied, oddly relieved as the sting abated. "And it probably *is* best considering—"

"Give it to me, Daniel!"

"But I thought—"

"Just give it to me. I don't know if it's a good or bad idea, and I may tuck it in a book and never look at it again, but I don't want to be kicking myself sometime in the future for having refused it."

"I don't expect you to call, if that's what you're worried about, Ruby." He thought for a moment. "You do what's best for you, Ruby and if you ever want to drop a note, feel free but don't ever feel like you have to."

"Let me guess, Daniel. Your e-mail address is, it's Bourglay @ something something," she blurted out, evoking a hearty laugh from Daniel.

"Jesus, have you got me pegged!" But no it's actually jbourglay@hotmail.com."

"I am really and truly going to go now, Daniel," She said, suddenly smiling in spite of her eyes welling up again. "And you're going to stay here."

"You sure you don't want me to walk you to your car?"

"I'm sure, Daniel. I'll be a blubbering mess by then and well it's just better this way."

"Okay, Ruby. If that's the way you want it," he answered as she grabbed his head and kissed him deeply one last time.

"One for the road," she said as she hugged him tight before willing the reluctant extrication, leaving Daniel puckered blindly like the prize catch that didn't get away.

Ruby began her slow retreat still clasping his hand tightly and not relinquishing it until she had reached the flap. She felt a stab pierce her heart upon seeing a solitary tear slide down Daniel's cheek.

Eyes glistening, she straddled the past and the future, smiling at Daniel and forcing herself to proceed.

"You do something special with that noggin of yours, Daniel." she said as she began to exit the tent.

He smiled back, grateful for the final vote of confidence. "Yeah, we'll see. Who knows, I'll probably end up delivering furniture again."

"Well, if you do, you make sure that they deliver to my neighborhood. Goodbye darling."

"Goodbye Ruby."

Chapter 82

The flap snagged a fleeting breeze, delaying its closure just long enough to give Daniel a final glimpse of the sensual contours of Ruby's calf as it strode purposefully if tentatively away from Daniel and toward a chosen destination riddled with uncertainty.

Ruby would be a lot of things in Daniel's mind but her having adopted the crucial role of keeper of Uncle Howard's flame elevated her status to rarified heights. He imagined her suddenly as a queen bee whose safety was paramount because the very perpetuation of the species was at stake. He chuckled to himself at the outlandish simile but he could not repudiate the impulse that spawned it.

Daniel heard the car door open and shut with a thud. He heard the hum of the engine in the distance and in anticipating the sound of tires on pebbles, recalled that it had always somehow reminded him of the noise he heard in his head when he ate a certain breakfast cereal as a kid. "Goodbye, sweet Ruby," Daniel said softly, finishing with a slight huff and a puff as if the extra oomph would carry the sound waves out of the tent, along the path and into her ear. It struck him suddenly that the car was still idling, that the crunching cereal sound hadn't come, and he imagined her pulling down the visor to inspect her makeup as he had often seen women do, or perhaps to see if what stared back at her could be construed as a "mug shot."

Seconds that seemed much longer passed and still no crunch. Could be too, he considered, that she was fiddling with the radio, seeking just the right station to match her mood or possibly to drown it out. Daniel took note of the fact that each assumption included an ominous overtone, and he chastised himself for his lack of faith. He recalled her "blubbering mess" comment and wondered if it had rendered her temporarily unable to operate heavy machinery. Still idling! He began to think that maybe she had some unfinished business or that maybe she *had* changed her mind and the intensity of the desire to see her again that surged in him was matched only by the fear that she might actually return.

Finally, the sound he'd been anticipating arrived as the engine revved stiltedly with the cautious sound of backing up in an arc and positioning oneself to go forward.

The car seemed to crawl at first as if it had to establish enough momentum to get over a hump before it settled into the familiar pattern and disappeared from earshot. It's official, Daniel thought to himself as he looked to Golda whose solemn nod of the head confirmed it. Something about her stoic demeanor, ever steady and ever ready with just the right word or gesture, touched him deeply and the tears began to flow freely. It was the good pain, the "better to have loved" kind, he thought to himself, that you can't help but revisit because it couldn't exist without something pretty special happening.

Ordinarily, this would have been Daniel's time, the aftermath, that portion of the program in which he began to dissect the vast array of impressions that had registered over the course of the encounter. It was his habit to properly identify, label and ultimately catalogue the various and sundry parts into some fashion of recognizable whole. It had always been the distance from the event that enabled him to engage in *pure induction,* a term that had struck his fancy and which he had adopted after reading somewhere about Darwin's mental habits. But Daniel felt leaden, and any and all attempts at focusing his mind on a particular item seemed to further exhaust him. He thought about heading out for a smoke, but his torpor made standing out of the question. Instead he collapsed backwards onto the neatly folded sleeping bag, acquiescing meekly to his implacable fatigue, capable of little more than observing the clouds in his head and seeing what happened to float by.

Everything was a blur, even the vague sense of sadness and exhilaration coursing through him. "The fucking bard," he whispered to no one as the phrase "such sweet sorrow" managed to bubble to the surface to describe what Daniel couldn't, and he gave an imaginary tip of the hat to the ultimate wordsmith. It's okay, the clarity will come in time, he thought to himself as if he had any choice in the matter, and he lapsed into that languid hypnagogic state that always reminded him of the movies from the old sixteen-millimeter camera his father had insisted on continuing to use well after video tape recorders had made them obsolete. He even imagined the bubbles dotting the screen that seemed to introduce the gauzy, grainy, oddly mechanical images that followed only to fade away and reappear later to signal the end of the film.

Golda too, was spent and unable to focus, and taking a cue from Daniel, she worked herself into a comfortable position and was about to wink the first of forty when a honking congested sound emanated from Daniel. She thought it odd as Daniel had never been a snorer, but she was relieved that it had been a singular event and she uncocked her ear and was tumbling into the twilight abyss as soon as her little lids landed.

"Darling," came the 'Rosebud'- like utterance from Daniel as he followed Golda into Neverland. His last waking thought had been of the subtle thrill evoked by Ruby's gilded farewell, and the smile it brought to his lips remained steadfast even as a couple of snorts and grunts burst forth before his respirations found their rhythm.

The sound of the not-so-distant fog horn jolted Golda, but she had already been prodded wide-eyed by the astonishing proclamation. "Darling," he had called her as he drifted off to sleep. "Darling," she repeated in her mind as she clutched her tiny little heart and sighed. She had never doubted that Daniel cared, but what might have provoked this deepening affection was a mystery to her. She took comfort in the fact that there were a great many things she didn't understand. "Ours is not to reason why," she thought with a smile as warm and contented as the cockles in her heart. As she tucked her head in tight and closed her eyes, her fellow started to snore again, and almost as if a sympathetic response, Golda joined the duet, and the two of them honked a pneumatic symphony, a vision of sugarplums dancing in their heads.

From the Author's Wife

It is with sadness and loss that I find myself in the position of writing this last page. The author, my husband Dennis Cassidy, passed away on January 17, 2017. He was working very hard to get his work to final publishing, right up until the end. It is my honor to help fulfill that last wish, to pick it up and carry to the finish for him.

"Sitting Shiva in the Land of Nod" - the final title of what has been called along the way "The Kindness of Strangers " and "Vagabond " but in our house was always just "The Book." It was a labor of love for Dennis, he worked hours upon hours and for many years, telling this story. He loved words, the turn of a phrase, irony, and obscure references. Little bits of paper with notes, thoughts, and ideas were always floating around the house. He tinkered and refined and rewrote whole chapters, always searching for the perfect words to best reflect his story.

In the beginning he denied that it was autobiographical in any way. He was NOT Daniel. Those of us who knew and loved him knew he WAS Daniel. Eventually even he admitted this. The story is fictional, but the heart and soul are real. The character of Daniel was mirroring the journey to knowledge and self discovery that Dennis was always seeking, they were one in the same. If you come to know Daniel through reading this book, then you have come to know Dennis as well.

I know if he could, Den would dedicate this book to the family and friends that he loved so much. Nick, Sam, Jamie, Jake, Dylan, Pat, Sue, Kevin, Ute, Don, Marv. A special thank you to Magdalene Pagratis, the book designer, who had everything needed and was ready to go when I found her among his files. I hope the readers enjoy this book even a fraction as much as Den enjoyed writing it. Keep your dictionary handy, he threw in some doozies!

Judy Cassidy

Look for the Sequel to *Sitting Shiva in the Land of Nod*:

The Book of Daniel

Dennis Cassidy
1952-2017

www.ingramcontent.com/pod-product-compliance
Lightning Source LLC
Chambersburg PA
CBHW020245030726
47499CB00001B/64